Rosie's WAR

Kay Brellend, the third of six children, was born in North London but now lives in a Victorian farmhouse in Suffolk. This is her seventh novel set in the twentieth century and all of Kay's novels are inspired by her grandmother's reminiscences about her life in Campbell Road, Islington.

Cardiff Libraries
www.cardiff.gov.uk/libraries

Llyfrgelloedd Caerdydd
www.caerdydd.gov.uk/llyfrgelloedd

Also by Kay Brellend

The Street
The Family
Coronation Day
The Campbell Road Girls
East End Angel
The Windmill Girls

Kay Brellend

Rosie's WAR

HARPER

Harper
An imprint of HarperCollins*Publishers*
The News Building
1 London Bridge Street
London SE1 9GF

www.harpercollins.co.uk

This paperback edition 2016

1

Set in Meridien by Palimpsest Book Production Ltd, Falkirk, Stirlingshire

Printed and bound in Great Britain by
Clays Ltd, St Ives plc

MIX
Paper from
responsible sources
FSC™ C007454

ACKNOWLEDGEMENTS

Angela Raby for her absorbing book
The Forgotten Service, detailing the wartime work
of the London Auxiliary Ambulance Service,
1939–1945.

This book is dedicated to all the unsung heroes who served in the London Auxiliary Ambulance Service (LAAS) during the Second World War.

Equally for the volunteers who served in other cities during the conflict.

Not forgotten.

Also, for Mum and Dad.

PROLOGUE

Doctor's Surgery, Shoreditch, October 1941

'My mum died young so I'm a bit worried . . . in case I've got the same disease.' The young woman sat down on the edge of the hard-backed chair. 'Mum was only thirty-three when she passed away.'

'You look a lot younger than that and as fit as a fiddle, my dear.' The doctor raised his wiry grey eyebrows, peering over his spectacles at the exceptionally pretty young woman settling a handbag on her lap. Her platinum hair was in crisp waves and her sea-blue eyes were bright with nervousness. She was nicely dressed and he guessed she had a good job keeping her in such style. He was more used to seeing women with careworn faces, and toddlers on their scruffy skirts, perching nervously at the other side of his desk.

Rosie Gardiner wasn't sure whether Dr Vernon's casual dismissal of her concerns had cheered her or left her feeling more anxious. She'd not yet turned twenty and had a healthy glow from a brisk walk on a blustery

1

autumn day. Or the flush could be a fever. In Rosie's opinion the least he could do was stick a thermometer in her mouth to check her temperature instead of just sitting there tapping his pen on a blotter. Feeling exasperated by his silence she added, 'It's hard dragging myself out of bed some mornings. Then I spend an hour bending over the privy out back being sick. It's not like me to feel too rough to go to work 'cos I like my job at the Windmill Theatre.'

'Mmm . . .' Dr Vernon cast a glance at the young woman's bare fingers. In wartime women sometimes pawned their jewellery to buy essentials. An absence of an engagement ring didn't necessarily mean that the lass hadn't given her fiancé a passionate send-off to the front line, getting herself into trouble in the process.

'Putting on weight?' Dr Vernon asked.

'Not really . . . no appetite . . . so I don't eat much.'

'Monthlies on time?'

Rosie blushed, wondering why he was asking personal questions like that when she was frantically worried she had the cancer that had put her mother in an early grave. Prudence Gardiner had seemed to be recovering from an operation to remove a tumour but then pleurisy had finished her off. But Rosie had only spotted a little bit of blood instead of proper monthlies.

'You look to be blooming, my dear . . . might you be pregnant?'

'No . . . I might not!' Rosie spluttered. 'I'm not married or even got a sweetheart. I've never even wanted to . . .'

'Right . . . I'd better examine you then if there have been no intimate relations to cause trouble.' Dr Vernon got up from his chair, gesturing for Rosie to stand also. 'Abdominal fullness, you say, with sickness . . .' The muttered comment emerged as he got into position to prod at her with his fingers.

Rosie stayed in her chair, the colour in her complexion fading away. *Intimate relations* . . . The phrase hammered in her head and she felt stupid for not having made the connection herself about why her body seemed horribly different. But there had been nothing intimate about that one brutal encounter with a man she'd despised. Rosie's mind wanted to flinch from the memory but she forced herself to concentrate on the man who'd attacked her all those months ago. Lenny and his father had been her dad's associates. They'd worked together churning out bottles of rotgut, much to Rosie's disgust. But what had disgusted her even more was Lenny's attention. She'd made it plain she'd no intention of going out with him but he wouldn't take no for an answer. They'd attended the same school, their fathers were friends and Lenny thought that gave him the right to pester her for dates and then call her names when she turned him down. Rosie had hated her father getting involved in crime and had nagged him to break up his illegal booze racket but she hadn't let on that his association with Lenny was a prime reason for her wanting him to go straight. At that time, she'd been a proud independent woman: a Windmill Girl, and Windmill Girls were able to look after themselves, whether fending off catty theatre colleagues, or randy servicemen lying in wait at the stage door. With youthful arrogance she'd believed she could deal with Lenny herself.

Then one night Rosie had met him by chance in the East End when she was feeling a bit the worse for wear. She'd discovered in just a few vicious minutes that she wasn't as sassy as she'd thought; she certainly hadn't been as strong as Lenny, though she'd fought like a maniac to try and stop him.

'Ah . . .' Dr Vernon had seen her stricken look and turned back towards his desk. 'You've remembered an incident, have you, and think there might be reason to count the months after all?'

'Yes . . .' she whispered. 'But I'm praying you're wrong, Doctor.'

He smiled kindly. 'I understand. But better to incubate a life than an illness, my dear.'

Rosie thought about that one. The odd weight she'd sensed in her belly was not a nasty growth in the way she'd thought; but it could destroy her life. 'If you're right – and I pray to God you're not – I think I'd sooner be dead than have his baby,' she whispered.

CHAPTER ONE

February 1942

'Well done, dear . . . good girl . . . just one more big push. Come on, you can do it . . .'

Rosie knew that the midwife was being kind and helpful but she just wanted to bawl at her to go away and leave her alone. She had no energy left to whisper a word let alone shout a torrent of abuse. She didn't want to push, she didn't want the horrible creature fighting for life in her hips but she knew the agony wouldn't stop unless she did something . . . She raised her forehead from the sweat-soaked pillow, dragging her shoulders off the rubber sheeting to grip Nurse Johnson's outstretched hands. Rosie clung on to the two sturdy palms as tightly as she might have to a piece of driftwood in a raging sea, and gritting her teeth she bore down.

'What're you planning on calling her?'

The whispered question emerged tentatively as though the man anticipated a tongue-lashing. And he got it.

'Calling her?' Rosie dredged up a weak laugh from her aching abdomen. 'How about bastard . . . that should suit. Now go away and leave me alone.' Rosie turned her pale face to the wall and groaned, drawing up her knees beneath a thin blood-streaked sheet.

The fellow hesitated, then tiptoed about the bed. He knew the poor cow had been driven mad with pain because he'd heard her shrieking even above the din of the wireless. When things had quietened down overhead he'd guessed the worst was over. Then he'd spied the dragon barging down the hall, uniform crackling. As soon as she had disappeared into the front room with a bucket of stuff to burn he'd crept upstairs while the coast was clear.

'What do you think you're doing?' Trudy Johnson burst into the back bedroom and glared at the intruder; childbirth was nothing to do with men, in her opinion. They might put the bun in the oven but should stay well out of the way at the business end of things. The midwife had been disposing of soiled wadding in the parlour fire while waiting for her patient to enter the final stage of labour. But she'd heard voices and speeded up the stairs to see what was going on.

'I've every right to be here.' John Gardiner sounded huffy. 'She's me daughter and that there's me granddaughter.' He pointed at the swaddled bundle at the foot of the bed. The infant was emitting mewling squeaks while punching feet and fists into her straitjacket. He almost smiled. The poor little mite was unwanted but she was a fighter. John moved to pick up the newborn but the midwife advanced on him threateningly, fists on starched hips. He backed away, muttering, his hands plunged into his pockets.

6

'I think your daughter deserves some privacy, Mr Gardiner. I'll let you know when she's ready for a visit.'

Chastened, John trudged meekly onto the landing, then peeped around the bedroom door. 'Put the kettle on, shall I? Bet you'd like a cuppa, now it's all over, wouldn't you, dear?' He addressed the remark to his exhausted daughter but gave Nurse Johnson a wink when she raised an eyebrow at him.

'I'd be obliged if you'd make yourself scarce till it is over. But you can put the kettle on. I need some more hot water. Leave a full pot outside the door for me, please.'

Trudy looked at her patient as the door closed. The girl was fidgeting on the protective rubber sheet, making it squeak. The afterbirth was about to be expelled. After that it would be time to set about tidying up the new mum; Trudy hoped having a wash and a brush through her hair might give the poor thing a boost.

Rosie Deane didn't look more than nineteen and was as slender as a reed. She had battled to get the baby through her narrow hips and finally succeeded after a lengthy labour.

'Here . . . have a cuddle . . . she's fair like you . . .' The midwife placed the baby against Rosie's shoulder, hoping to distract the young woman from dwelling on her sore nether regions.

'Take her away from me. I don't want her.' Rosie's hands remained clenched beneath the sheets and she turned her face away from her firstborn.

''Course you do; just got a bit of the blues, haven't you, love? Only natural after what you've been through. All new mums say never no more, then quickly forget about the rough side of it.' Trudy knew that to be true, but not from personal experience. She had no children, but she'd delivered hundreds of babies over more than a decade in midwifery. Some of the women on her rounds in Shoreditch seemed to knock out a kid a year, even into their forties. Mrs Riley, Irish and no stranger to her old man's fists, had borne fifteen children, twelve of them still alive, and eight of them still at home with her.

Trudy was about to say that the pelvis opened up more easily after a good stretching in a first labour in the hope of cheering up this new mum. Then she realised the remark would be insensitive. The girl's father had told her that Rosie's husband had been killed fighting overseas only months ago, so Trudy kept her lip buttoned. In time Rosie would probably remarry and go on to have a brood round her ankles. She was plainly an attractive girl, despite now looking limp and bedraggled after her ordeal.

'You've got a wonderful part of your husband here to cherish.' Trudy glanced at the child her patient was ignoring. She pushed lank fair hair from Rosie's eyes so she could get a better view of her baby. 'See, she's got her eyes open and is looking at you. She knows you're her mum all right . . .'

'I said take her away from me.' Rosie levered herself up on an elbow, grabbing at the child as though she might hurl her daughter to the newspaper-strewn floorboards. Instead she held the bundle out on rigidly extended arms. 'Take her . . . give her away . . . do what you like with her . . .' she sobbed, sinking down and turning her face into the pillow to dry her cheeks on the cotton.

'Come on, love; don't get tearful.' Trudy placed the

baby back by the bed's wooden footboard then gave her hiccuping patient a brisk, soothing rub on the back. 'Just a few minutes more and we can give you a nice hot wash down. You're almost done now, you know.'

'Almost done?' Rosie echoed bitterly. 'I wish I was. It's all just starting for me, Nurse Johnson . . .'

CHAPTER TWO

'You don't mean that!'

'If the girl says that's what she wants to do, then that's what she wants to do,' Doris Bellamy stated bluntly. 'A mother knows what's best for her own child . . .'

'I'll deal with this,' John Gardiner rudely interrupted. Doris was his fiancée, and a decent woman. But she wasn't his daughter's mother, or his grandkid's nan, so he reckoned she could mind her own business and leave him to argue with Rosie over the nipper's future.

'You won't change my mind, Dad. I've already spoken to Nurse Johnson and she says there are plenty of people ready to give a baby a good home.'

'Does she now!' John exploded. 'Well, I know where that particular baby'll get a good home 'n' all. And it's right here!' He punched a forefinger at the ceiling. 'The little mite won't have to go nowhere. She's our own flesh and blood and I ain't treating her like she's rubbish to be dumped!'

'She's not just *our* flesh and blood, though, is she, Dad?' Rosie's voice quavered but she cleared her throat and soldiered determinedly on. 'She's tainted by *him*. I can't even bear to look at her in case I see his likeness in her.'

'Forget about him; he's long gone and can't hurt you no more.' John flicked some contemptuous fingers.

'It's all right for you!' Rosie was incensed at her father's attitude. 'You just want a pretty toy to show off for a few years till you're bored of teething and tantrums. You certainly won't want her around if she turns out anything like that swine.' Rosie forked agitated fingers into her blonde hair.

'I think you'd better take that remark back, miss!' John had leaped up, flinging off Doris's restraining hand as she tried to drag him back down beside her on the sofa. 'How dare you accuse me of play-acting? It's you keeps chopping 'n' changing yer ideas, my gel.' John advanced on his daughter, finger wagging in emphasis. 'I offered at the time to put things right. Soon as we found out about your condition I said I'd stump up to sort it out. Wouldn't have it, though, would yer? Insisted you was having the baby and was prepared for all the gossip and hardship facing you as an unmarried mother.' He barked a laugh. 'Now you want to duck out without even giving it a try.'

'I said I'd have the kid, not that I'd give it a permanent home,' Rosie shouted. 'I've got to act before it's too late: once she gets to know us as her family it wouldn't be fair to send her away.'

'It ain't fair *anytime*, that's the point!' John roared.

'But . . . I might never love her. I might even grow to hate her,' Rosie choked. 'That'd be wicked because she could have somebody doting on her. She's not got a clue who we are!' Rosie surged to her feet at the parlour table, knocking over her mug of tea in the process.

11

Automatically she set about mopping up the spillage with her apron.

She couldn't deny that some of what her father had said was true. She'd not wanted an abortion; the talk of having something dug out of her had made her retch. The idea of enduring horrible pain and mess had been intolerable; now she knew that the natural way of things was pretty awful too.

Yet Nurse Johnson had been right when she'd said the memory of the ordeal would fade; her daughter was only four weeks old yet already Rosie felt too harassed to dwell on the birth. She guessed every other new mum must feel the same way. But she doubted many of those women were as bitter as she was, and her father, much as he wanted to help, was just making things worse.

'Cat got yer tongue, has it?' John was prowling to and fro in front of the unlit fireplace. 'You should be ashamed. And I ain't talking about what happened with Lenny. I know that weren't your fault.' After a dramatic pause he pointed at the pram. 'But if you abandon the little 'un you should hang your head, 'cos it should never have come to this.'

'I'm not a murderer,' Rosie muttered. 'I'm not a hypocrite either. Don't expect me to play happy families.' Attuned to her daughter's tiny snickers and snuffles Rosie glanced at the pram. It was an ancient Silver Cross model that her father had got off the rag-and-bone man for a couple of shillings.

He'd brought it home a month before the date of her confinement. The sight of it had shocked and frightened Rosie because up until then she'd shoved to the back of her mind how close she was to having Lenny's child. John had ignored his daughter's announcement that he'd wasted his time and money on the pram because the Welfare was getting the kid.

The creaking contraption had been bumped down the cellar stairs and John had toiled on it in his little workshop, as he called the underground room that doubled as their air-raid shelter. Screws had been tightened and springs oiled, then he'd buffed the scratched coachwork and pitted chrome until they gleamed. At present John's labour of love was wedged behind the settee, with the hood up to give the baby a bit more protection from the chilly March air in the fireless room.

'She's gonna be as pretty as you, y'know.' Taking his daughter's silence as an encouraging sign, John tried a bit of flattery.

'Good looks don't make you happy,' Rosie stated bluntly. 'If you force me to keep her, none of us'll be content.' She didn't hate the child: the poor little thing was an innocent caught up in a vile web of violence and deceit.

'We'll make sure this is a happy place, dear.' John sensed his daughter was softening. 'No point in suffering like you did, then having nothing good to show for it in the end, is there?'

With a sigh, Rosie gathered up their tea things, loading them onto the tray ready to be carried into the kitchenette. She knew it was pointless trying to win over her father. It was always his way or nothing at all. But not this time. She had one final duty to perform before she slipped free of the yoke the poor little nameless mite had fastened around her neck.

She avoided her future stepmother's eye. Rosie knew that Doris had been watching her, pursed lipped, throughout the shouting match between father and daughter. The woman had resented being told to shut up and had sat in stony silence ever since.

'Nurse Johnson's due soon. She said after today it's time to sign us off home visits.' Rosie was halfway to the door with the tea tray before adding, 'I'm going to tell her to start things moving on the adoption.'

'If you ain't got the guts to look after her, I'll do it meself,' John sounded adamant. 'No granddaughter of mine's ending up with strangers, and that's the end of it.'

Doris leaped to her feet. 'Now just you hang on a minute there. Reckon I might have something to say about getting landed with kids at my age.' They'd recently spoken about getting married in the summer so Doris thought she'd every right to have a say.

'If you don't like it, you know where the door is.' John snapped his head at the exit.

Doris gawped at him, her expression indignant. 'Right then. Couldn't have made that plainer, could yer?' She snatched up her handbag, then marched over the threshold and into the hallway.

'Well, that was bloody daft.' A moment after the front door was slammed shut, Rosie sighed loudly. 'If Doris never speaks to you again it'll be your own fault, Dad.'

'Don't care.' John shrugged. 'There's only one person I'm interested in right now.' He kneeled on the sofa and peered over its threadbare back into the pram. The little girl was sleeping soundly, long fawn lashes curled against translucent pearl-spotted skin. A soft fringe of fluffy fair hair framed her forehead and her tiny upturned nose and rosebud mouth looked as perfectly delicate as painted porcelain.

John stretched out a finger to stroke a silky pink cheek before pulling the blanket up to the infant's pointed chin. 'Don't know you're born, do you, little angel? But I won't let you down,' he promised his granddaughter in a voice wobbling with emotion.

'You're just feeling guilty,' Rosie accused, although she felt quite moved by her father's melodramatic performance. But what she'd said about him feeling guilty had hit the spot. And they both knew it. A moment later John flung himself past her and the cellar door was crashed shut as he sought sanctuary in his underground den.

Rosie placed the tea tray back on the table. For a moment she stood there, leaning against the wood, the knuckles of her gripping fingers turning white. The baby started to whimper and she automatically went to her. Seated on the sofa she reached a hand backwards to the handle, rocking the pram and avoiding looking at the infant, her chin cupped in a palm. Within a few minutes the room was again quiet. Rosie stood up, drawing her cardigan sleeves down her goose-pimpled arms. She took off her pinafore and folded it, then looked in the coal scuttle, unnecessarily as she knew it would be empty.

It was a cold unwelcoming house for a visitor but it didn't matter that her father was too thrifty to light the fire till the evening. When Nurse Johnson turned up Rosie intended to say quickly what she had to, then get rid of her so she might start planning her future.

She wandered to the window, peering through the nets for a sighting of the midwife pedalling down the road. It had been many months since she'd hurried from Dr Vernon's surgery to huddle, crying, in a nearby alleyway. She'd been terrified that day of going home and telling her father the dreadful news that she was almost certainly pregnant, yet he'd taken it better than she had herself.

But now, at last, Rosie felt almost content because the prospect of returning to something akin to her old life seemed within her grasp.

Under a year ago she'd been working as a showgirl at the Windmill Theatre. Virtually every waking hour had been crammed with glamour and excitement. She'd enjoyed her job and the companionship of her colleagues, despite the rivalry, but she couldn't go back there. Her body was different now. Her breasts had lost their pert youthfulness and her belly and hips were flabby. Besides, Rosie felt that chapter of her life had closed and a new one was opening up. Whether she'd wanted to or not, she'd grown up. The teenage vamp who'd revelled in having lavish compliments while flirting with the servicemen who flocked to the shows, no longer existed. Wistfully Rosie acknowledged that she'd not had a chance to kiss goodbye to that sunny side of her character. That choice, and her virginity, had been brutally stolen from her by Lenny, damn the bastard to hell . . .

But once her daughter was adopted Rosie knew she'd find work again, and she wanted her own place. Her father's future wife resented her being around and Rosie knew she'd probably feel the same if she were in Doris's shoes.

Suddenly she snapped out of her daydream, having spotted Nurse Johnson's dark cap at the end of the street. Rosie let the curtain fall and pulled the pram out from behind the sofa so the midwife could examine the baby. Although she was expecting it, the ratatat startled her. Rosie brushed herself down then quickly went to open the door, praying that her father wouldn't reappear to embarrass her by making snide comments.

Half an hour later the examinations were over and

Rosie was sitting comfortably in the front parlour with the midwife.

'She's a beautiful child but would benefit from breast milk rather than a bottle, Mrs Deane. She might put on a bit more weight.'

Rosie smiled weakly; she hated people calling her by the wrong name. Her father and Doris had persuaded her to pass herself off as a war widow to stop tongues wagging. But that hadn't worked: the old biddies were still having a field day at her expense. Rosie had chosen to use her mother's maiden name as her pretend married name. She cleared her throat. 'What we spoke about last time, Nurse Johnson . . .'

Trudy Johnson put down her pen on the chart she'd been filling in. 'You still want to have her adopted?' she prompted when Rosie seemed stuck for words.

'I do . . . yes . . .'

'Why? You seem to be coping well, and you have your father's support.'

'I'm not married,' Rosie blurted, although she was sure the midwife had already guessed the truth. 'That is . . . I'm not widowed either . . . I've never had a husband.'

Trudy sat back in the chair. It wasn't surprising news, but Rosie's honesty had taken her aback. Families who were frightened of ostracism often came up with non-existent husbands to prevent a daughter's shame tainting them all. And now it was clearer why the baby still hadn't been named. Much of the falsehood surrounding illegitimate births unravelled when awkward questions were asked at the registry office.

'I guessed perhaps that might be the case.'

'You don't know the ins and outs of it all.' Rosie

bristled at the older woman's tone. 'Nobody does except me and Dad.'

Trudy Johnson could have barked a laugh at that. Instead she put away her notes in the satchel at her feet. At least this young woman had had the guts to go through with it, whereas lots of desperate girls allowed a backstreet butcher to rip at their insides. She had been approached herself over the years by more than one distraught family to terminate a 'problem' for them. Trudy had always refused to abort a woman's baby but it didn't stop them going elsewhere. And, to Trudy's knowledge, at least two of those youngsters had ended up in the cemetery because of it.

'Your situation's more common than you think.' Again Trudy's tone was brisk. 'Unlike you, though, I've seen some poor souls turfed out onto the streets with their babies. Your father is keeping a roof over your heads.'

'It's the least he can do, considering . . .' Rosie bit her lip; she'd said enough. Besides, she didn't want to get sidetracked from the important task of finding her daughter a new home.

Trudy stood up, buckling her mac, and gazed into the pram. The baby was awake. She'd been just five pounds at birth and was struggling to put on weight. Arms and legs barely bigger than Trudy's thumbs were quivering and jerking, and just a hint of a smile was lifting a corner of the little girl's mouth. It was probably wind but Trudy tickled the adorable infant under the chin.

'I want her adopted,' Rosie stated firmly. 'And I want it done soon, before she gets attached to us.'

'If you're sure that's what you want to do, then I'll have her. I've never been married but I've always wanted

18

a child.' Trudy sent Rosie a sideways smile. 'I almost got married when I was seventeen but . . .' She shrugged. Her memories of Tony were too precious to share. She even avoided talking about her dead lover with her elderly parents. They'd liked him, and had mourned his passing almost as much as she had herself.

'I see . . . sorry . . .' Rosie finally murmured, recovering from her shock. On reflection she realised that the child would probably get no better care than from someone with Nurse Johnson's skills. 'Will having a baby interfere with your work?' Rosie didn't think that the midwife would leave a tiny baby for long periods of time, yet neither did she expect the woman would pack in her vocation just like that.

'I share shifts with other nurses and know a good nursery,' Nurse Johnson explained.

'I'm not sure . . .' Rosie felt awkward. She didn't want to upset Nurse Johnson but her intention had always been that her baby be taken into a family where she could be mothered properly. Then in the evenings the woman's doting husband would come home from work to coo over his new daughter. 'I'll think about it and I'd better let Dad know, too,' Rosie said slowly, avoiding the older woman's eye.

'Of course . . .' Trudy withdrew her hand from the pram. It wasn't the first time that she'd attempted to foster a child only to be shunned because of her age and spinster status.

'Did your sweetheart ever get married?' Rosie blurted, keen to change the subject.

'He lost his life in the Great War. He was too young to join up, but he went anyway. Lots did. He was killed at Ypres, still eighteen. I've grown old without him.'

'You met nobody else?' Rosie asked, saddened but still inquisitive.

'I'd have liked to find somebody, but so many young fellows of my generation are still in Flanders, aren't they?' Nurse Johnson's expression turned rather severe, as though she regretted betraying her feelings. 'Does your father agree with your plan for adoption?'

'It's up to me to decide what's best for her,' Rosie blurted. 'He doesn't like the gossip going round, in any case.'

'Neighbours chinwagging?' Nurse Johnson asked with a slight smile.

'They've been told I'm Mrs Deane, too, but they're not green. I did go away and live with my aunt in Walthamstow for a few months, so I could say I'd had a whirlwind wedding before he bought it overseas.' She smiled. 'I've already had a run-in with Mrs Price; I don't suppose it'll be the last time.' She frowned. 'I'm going to find work that takes me away somewhere. Then I can start afresh and Dad'll marry his fiancée . . .' Rosie glanced at the midwife. She was not a bad sort. She'd not turned sniffy on knowing the baby was illegitimate. Neither had she gone off in a huff when her offer to take the baby hadn't been snapped up. 'I think you'd make a good mum,' Rosie said kindly. 'Good enough for me, anyhow,' she added on impulse.

'You mean . . . shall I start to make arrangements for myself then?' Trudy's eyes had lit up, her voice shrill with emotion.

'I'm glad it's you.' Rosie sounded more enthusiastic than she felt. 'I only want the best for her, you know.'

'I know you do, dear.' Nurse Johnson stood up and Rosie did too. They took a step towards one another as though they might embrace but instead shook hands just as the baby started to cry.

'She takes her bottle without any trouble,' Rosie informed the midwife quickly. She'd never wanted to feel a soft pink cheek against her naked breast and the baby gazing up at her with steady, inquisitive eyes.

Rosie glanced down and noticed that her clothing was wet.

'You'll need to bind yourself up, dear.' Trudy nodded at the damp patches on Rosie's bodice.

'I know . . . it's a right nuisance.' Rosie frowned, grabbed the pinafore and put it on again, hiding the stains on her blouse. 'How long will it all take . . . the adoption?'

'You're sure you don't want to think about it for longer?' Trudy felt conscience-bound to ask although she prayed Rosie wouldn't back out now when she was considering Angela as a lovely name for such a blonde cherub.

Rosie nodded vigorously. 'I'd offer you tea, but I've a pile of ironing to do.' There were only two of her father's shirts and one of her blouses in the basket, but Rosie wanted the woman gone. She felt a strange raging emotion within that was making her want to sink to her knees and scream. She guessed her conscience was troubling her but she mustn't let it. Her father might accuse her of being selfish and heartless, but she truly wanted the best for her daughter.

'It's all right . . . I've got to get on too.' Trudy realised that the young woman wanted to be on her own now. With a surreptitious look of longing at the baby, she gathered up her things and followed Rosie towards the front door.

21

CHAPTER THREE

'Gone has she, the interfering old bag?'

Her father must have been waiting for the midwife to leave. He'd emerged from the cellar almost before Rosie had shut the front door, having seen the woman out.

'Yes, she has . . . but you've no need to speak about her like that. She's all right, is Nurse Johnson.' Rosie knew that crossed-armed, jaw-jutting stance of her father's meant another row was in the offing. He was likely to hit the roof when he found out what arrangements she'd made, and spit out a few more choice names for the nice nurse.

'Go and see if little 'un's all right, shall I?'

'She's fast asleep; I've only just come out of the bloody front room and you know it,' Rosie retorted in response to his cantankerous sarcasm.

'How long are we going to keep calling the poor little mite "she"? Getting a name, is she, before her first birthday?' John continued sourly.

His barbs were starting to get on Rosie's nerves but

she reined in her temper. They had a serious conversation in front of them and she'd as soon get it over with. 'Come and sit down in the kitchen, Dad. There's something I've got to tell you.'

Rosie took her father's elbow and, surprisingly, he allowed her to steer him along the passage.

'Let's wet our whistles.' Rosie began filling the kettle, hoping to keep things calm if not harmonious between them.

John pulled out a stick-back chair at the kitchen table and was about to sit down when he hesitated and glanced up at the ceiling. Rosie had heard it too: the unmistakable sound of aeroplane engines moving closer.

'Must be some of ours,' Rosie said, putting the kettle on the gas stove and sticking a lit match beneath it.

There'd been no warning siren and the afternoon was late but still light. The Luftwaffe mostly came over under cover of darkness. Since the Blitz petered out last May, German bombing had thankfully become sporadic and Londoners – especially East Enders who'd borne the brunt of the pounding – had been able to relax a bit.

John peered out of the window, then, frowning, he opened the back door and stepped out, head tipped up as he sauntered along the garden path. His mouth suddenly fell agape in a mixture of shock and fear and he pelted back towards the house, shouting.

But the sirens had belatedly begun to wail, cutting off his warning of an air raid.

Rosie let the crockery crash back to the draining board on hearing the eerie sound and sprang to the back door to hurry her father inside. Before John could reach the house a short whistle preceded an explosion in a neighbour's garden, sending him to the ground, crucified on the concrete at the side of the privy.

Crouching on the threshold, arms covering her head in instinctive protection, Rosie could hear her father groaning just yards away. She'd begun to unfold to rush to him when debilitating terror hit her. She sank back, shaking and whimpering, biting down ferociously on her lower lip to try to still her chattering teeth. Tasting and smelling the metallic coppery blood on her tongue increased the horrific images spinning inside her head. She rammed her fists against her eyes but she couldn't shut out the carnage she'd witnessed in the Café de Paris a year ago. Her nostrils were again filled with the sickly stench of blood, and her mind seemed to echo with the sounds of wretched people battling for their final moments of life. Some had called in vain for loved ones . . . or the release of death. Limbless bodies and staring sightless eyes had been everywhere, tripping her up as she'd fled to the street, smothered in choking dust. For months afterwards she'd felt dreadfully ashamed that she'd instinctively charged to safety rather than staying to comfort some of those poor souls.

'Rosie . . . can you hear me . . . ?'

Her father's croaking finally penetrated Rosie's torment and she scrambled forward, uncaring of glass and wood splinters tearing into her hands and knees. She raked her eyes over him for injuries, noting his bloodied shin, although something else was nagging at her that refused to be dragged to the forefront of her mind.

'Think me leg's had it,' John cried as his daughter bent over him.

Rosie was darting fearful looks at the sky in case a second attack was imminent. The bomber had disappeared from view, but another could follow at any moment and drop its lethal load. Obliquely Rosie was aware of neighbours shouting hysterically in the street as they ran for the shelters, but she had to focus on her father and how she could get him to safety in their cellar.

'Take my arm, Dad . . . you must!' she cried as he tried to curl into a protective ball on hearing another engine. Thank goodness this aeroplane, now overhead, was a British Spitfire on the tail of the Dornier. 'Come on . . . we can make it . . . one of ours is after that damned Kraut.' Rosie felt boosted by the fighter avenging them and murmured a little prayer for the pilot's safety as well as their own. But then her attention was fully occupied in getting her father to cooperate in standing up. He was slowly conquering his fear and squirming to a seated position with her assistance.

Regaining her strength, she half-lifted him, her arm and leg muscles in agony and feeling as though they were tearing from their anchoring bones. Gritting her teeth, she managed to get both herself and her father upright. With her arm about his waist she dragged him, limping, into the kitchen. John Gardiner wasn't a big man; he was short and wiry but heavy for a girl weighing under eight stone to manhandle.

Slowly and awkwardly they descended the stairs to the cellar, crashing onto the musky floor two steps from the bottom when Rosie's strength gave out. John gave a shriek of pain as he landed awkwardly, attempting to break his daughter's fall while protecting his injured limb.

Rosie scrambled up in the dark, dank space and lit the lamp, then crouched down in front of her father to inspect him. The explosion had left his clothes in rags.

Gingerly she lifted the ribbons of his trouser leg to expose the damage beneath. His shin was grazed and bloody and without a doubt broken. The bump beneath the flesh showed the bone was close to penetrating the skin's surface.

Her father's ashen features were screwed up in agony and Rosie noticed tears squeezing between his stubby lashes. She soothed him as he suddenly bellowed in pain.

'Soon as it's over I'll go and get you help,' she vowed. 'We'll be all right, Dad, we always are, aren't we?' She desperately wanted to believe what she was saying.

Rosie thumped the heel of her hand on her forehead to beat out the tormenting memories of the Café de Paris bombing. It seemed a very long while ago that she'd gone out with two of her friends from the Windmill Theatre for a jolly time drinking and dancing to 'Snakehip' Johnson's band, and the night had ended in a tragedy. Three of them had entered the Café de Paris in high spirits but only two of them had got out alive.

Rosie forced the memories out of her mind. She sprang up and dragged one of the mattresses, kept there for use in the night-time air raids, closer to her father, then helped him roll off the floor and on to it to make him more comfortable. There was some bedding, too, and she unfolded a blanket and settled it over him, then placed a pillow beneath his head.

Sinking down beside her father, Rosie pressed her quaking torso against her knees, her arms over her head as the house rocked on its foundations. Another bomber must have evaded the Spitfire to shed its deadly cargo.

'We've taken a belting . . . that's this place finished . . . we'll need a new place to live,' John wheezed out

26

between gasps of pain, his voice almost drowned out by the crashing of collapsing timbers and shattering glass. 'Come here, Rosie.' He held out his arms. 'If we're gonners I want to give you a last cuddle. Be brave, dear . . . I love you, y'know.'

They clung together, terrified, the smell of John's blood and sweaty fear mingling in Rosie's nostrils. After what seemed like an hour but was probably no more than a few minutes the dreadful sounds of destruction faded and the tension went out of John. Pulling free of his daughter's embrace he flopped back on the mattress, breathing hard.

'That's it over then, if we're lucky. Everything seemed all right while we still had this place.'

Rosie knew what her father meant. This had been the house her parents had lived in from when they were married, and it was Rosie's childhood home. Wincing as she picked a shard of glass from her knee, Rosie mentally reviewed their options. Doris lived in Hackney and she might let them stay with her until the housing department found them something. Then Rosie remembered the woman had stomped out, making it clear she wasn't getting landed with kids . . .

As though the memory drifted back through a fog in her mind Rosie realised that it wasn't just her and Dad any more. Her baby was upstairs. She'd saved her own skin and her father's, oblivious to the fact that there were three of them now. Her little girl was all alone and defenceless in the front room and she'd not even remembered her, let alone made an effort to protect her from the bombing.

Rosie pushed herself to her feet. She stood for less than a second garnering energy and breath, then launched herself up the cellar steps, her hands and knees bloodied in the steep scramble as she lost her footing on the bricks in her insane haste. The door was open a few inches and she flew into it to run out but something had fallen at the other side, jamming it ajar. With a feral cry of fury Rosie barged her arm again and again into the door until it moved slightly and she could squeeze through the aperture. Frenziedly she kicked at the obstacles blocking her way.

Masonry from the shattered kitchen wall was piled in the hallway but she bounded over it, falling to her knees as the debris underfoot shifted, then jumping back up immediately. She'd no need to fight her way into the front room. The door had fallen flat and taken the surround and some of the plaster with it.

Rosie burst in, her chest heaving. The top of the pram was covered in rubble and a part of the window frame, jagged with glass, lay on the hood.

Flinging off the broken timbers, she swept away debris with hands and forearms, uncaring of the glass fragments ripping into her flesh. Oozing blood became caked with dust, forming thick calluses on her palms.

Hot tears streamed wide tracks down her mucky face as finally she gazed into the pram. Very carefully she put down the hood, and removed the rain cover. She was alive! Rosie picked up her daughter, wrapped in her white shawl, and breathed in the baby's milky scent, burying her stained face against soft warm skin until the infant whimpered in protest at the vice-like embrace.

'Thank you, God . . . oh, thank you . . .' Rosie keened over and over again as the white shawl turned pink in her cut hands. She bent over the tiny baby as though she would again absorb her daughter into herself to keep her safe. Her quaking fingers raced up and down the little limbs, checking for damage, but the infant's gurgling didn't seem to be prompted by pain.

'Let's go and find Granddad, shall we?' Rosie softly hiccuped against her daughter's downy head. 'Come on then, my darling. I'm so sorry; I swear I'll never ever leave you again.'

When she pushed open the cellar door Rosie found her father had crawled to the bottom step and was in the process of pulling himself up it. He choked on a sob as he saw them, flopping back down against the wall.

'I forgot about her, too,' he gasped through his tears. 'What sort of people are we to do something like that?' He shook his head in despair, wailing louder. 'It's my fault. I was too concerned about meself to even think about saving me granddaughter.'

'It's all right, Dad. She's fine, look . . .' Rosie anchored the baby against her shoulder in a firm grip, then descended as quickly as she could, hanging onto the handrail. 'Look, Dad!' she comforted her howling father. Gently she unwrapped the child to show her father that the baby was unharmed. 'We're not used to having her around yet . . . that's all it is. No harm done. She's in better shape than us,' Rosie croaked. She felt a fraud for trying to make light of it when her heart was still thudding crazily with guilt and shame.

John blew his nose. For a long moment he simply stared at his granddaughter, then he turned his head. 'Can see now that you're right, Rosie,' he started gruffly. 'She'd be better off elsewhere. Let somebody else care for her, 'cos we ain't up to it, that's for sure.'

Somewhere in the distance was a muffled explosion, but neither John nor Rosie heeded it, both lost in their own thoughts. Rosie settled down on the mattress. Her lips traced her daughter's hairline, soothing the baby as she became restless. She placed the tiny bundle down beside her and covered her in a blanket, tucking the sides in carefully.

John studied his wristwatch. 'Time for her bottle. I'll watch her if you want to go and get it.' Muffling moans of pain, he wriggled closer to peer at the baby's dust-smudged face. He took out from a pocket his screwed-up hanky.

'No! Don't use that, Dad. It's filthy; I'll wash her properly later . . . when we go upstairs.' Rosie smiled to show her father she appreciated his concern. But she wasn't having him wiping her precious daughter's face with his snot rag.

'She's hungry,' John said, affronted by his daughter's telling off.

Rosie made to get up, then sank back down to the mattress again. 'Kitchen's blown to smithereens. Won't find the bottles or the milk powder; won't be able to wash her either, if the water's off.' She began unbuttoning her bodice. 'I'll feed her,' she said. Turning a shoulder to her father so as not to embarrass him, she helped the child to latch onto a nipple. Her breasts were rock hard with milk, hot and swollen, but she put up with the discomfort, biting her lip against the pain. She encouraged the baby to feed with tiny caresses until finally she stopped suckling and seemed to fall asleep with a sated sigh.

'What you gonna call her?' John whispered. He had rolled over onto his side, away from mother and child to give them some privacy. His voice sounded different: high-pitched with pain still, but there was an underlying satisfaction in his tone.

Rosie smiled to herself, wondering how her father knew she'd been thinking about names for her daughter. 'Hope . . .' she said on a hysterical giggle. 'Seems right . . . so that's what I'm choosing. Hope this bloody war ends soon . . . hope we get a place to live . . . hope . . . hope . . . hope . . .'

'Hope the doctors sort me bloody leg out for us, I know that.' John joined in gruffly with the joke.

'You'll be right as rain with a peg leg . . . Long John Silver,' Rosie teased.

They both chuckled although John's laughter ended in a groan and he shifted position to ease his damaged limb.

In her mind Rosie knew she'd chosen her daughter's name for a different reason entirely from those she'd given. Her greatest hope was that her daughter would forgive her if she ever discovered that she'd abandoned her like that. The poor little mite could have suffocated to death if she'd not been uncovered in time. Or the weight of the shattered window frame on top of the pram might eventually have crushed the hood and her daughter's delicate skull. The idea that Hope might have suffered a painful death made bile rise in Rosie's throat. She closed her eyes and forced her thoughts to her other hope.

She hoped that Nurse Johnson would forgive her. The woman desperately wanted to be a mother, and Rosie had promised her that her dream would be real. Rosie sank back on the mattress beside Hope and curved a protective arm over her daughter as she slept, a trace of milk circling her mouth.

But Rosie had no intention of allowing anybody to take her Hope away now. She'd do anything to keep her.

'Hear that Dad?'

'What . . . love?' John's voice was barely audible.

'Bells . . . ambulance or fire engine is on its way. You'll be in hospital soon,' she promised him. While she'd been cuddling her little girl she'd heard her father's groans although he'd been attempting to muffle the distressing sounds.

'Ain't going to hospital; they can patch me up here,' he wheezed.

'Don't be daft!' Rosie said but there was a levity in her tone that had been absent before. She couldn't be sure which of the services was racing to their aid and she didn't care. She was simply glad that somebody might turn up and know what to do if her father passed out from the pain that was making him gasp, because she hadn't got a clue.

'Anybody home?'

The shouted greeting sounded cheery and Rosie jumped up, clutching Hope to her chest. This time she emerged carefully into their wrecked hallway rather than plunging out as she had when in a mad scramble to rescue her daughter. A uniformed woman of about Doris's age was picking her way over the rubble in Rosie's direction.

'Well, you look right as ninepence,' the auxiliary said with a grin. 'So does the little 'un.' The woman nodded at Hope, now asleep in Rosie's arms. 'Can't say the same for the house though, looks like a bomb's hit it.' She snorted a chuckle.

Rosie found herself joining in, quite hysterically for a few seconds. 'Dad's in the cellar . . . broken leg. He caught the blast in the back garden.'

'Righto . . . let's take a shufti.' The woman's attitude had changed to one of brisk efficiency and she quickened her pace over the rubble.

Even when she heard her father protesting about being manhandled, Rosie left them to it downstairs. She had instinctively liked the ambulance auxiliary and she trusted the woman to know what she was doing. A moment later when she heard her father grunt an approximation of one of his chuckles Rosie relaxed, knowing the auxiliary had managed to find a joke to amuse him too. Stepping carefully over debris towards the splintered doorway she stopped short, not wanting to abandon her father completely by going outside even though the all clear was droning. She found a sound piece of wall and leaned back on it, rocking side to side, eyes closed and crooning a lullaby to Hope, who slept contentedly on, undisturbed by the pandemonium in the street.

CHAPTER FOUR

'My, oh my, look how she's grown. Only seems like yesterday little Hope was born.' Peg Price stepped away from the knot of women congregated by the kerb. They were all wearing a uniform of crossover apron in floral print with their hair bundled inside scarves knotted atop their heads. Peg ruffled the child's flaxen curls. 'She'll be on her feet soon, won't she, love?'

To a casual observer the meeting might have seemed friendly, but Rosie knew differently and wasn't having any of it. She attempted to barge past the weedy-looking woman blocking her way. But Peg Price was no pushover and stood her ground.

'Some of 'em are late starters,' another woman chipped in, eyeing the toddler sitting in her pram. 'Don't you worry, gel, kids do everything in their own sweet time.'

'I'm not worried about a thing, thanks.' Rosie gave a grim smile, attempting to manoeuvre around the trio of neighbours stationed in front of her. They were all aware that her daughter was walking because they spied over the fences and watched Hope playing in the back garden.

Even after two years the local gossips hadn't given up on probing for a bit of muck to rake over. Rosie knew what really irked them was that she had so far managed to remain unbowed by their malice. She'd never crept about, embarrassed. She'd brazened out their snide remarks about her daughter's birth. And her father and Doris had done likewise.

After the Gardiners' home had been destroyed at the bottom end of the street the council had rehoused them in the same road, so they were still neighbours with the Price family.

'Coming up to her second birthday, by my reckoning.' Peg stepped into the road to foil Rosie's next attempt to evade her.

'She's turned two.' Rosie glared into a pair of spiteful eyes.

'Shame about yer 'usband, ain't it? Proud as punch, he'd be, of that little gel.' May Reed chucked the child under her rosy chin. ''Course, she'll ask about her daddy, so you'll be ready with some answers for the kid, eh, love?'

'Yeah, I've already thought of that, thanks all the same for your concern.' Rosie's sarcasm breezed over her shoulder as she moved on, ignoring May's yelp as the pram clouted her hip.

'Looks like you, don't she, Rosie? Just as well, ain't it?'

It wasn't the sly comment but Peg Price's tittering that brought Rosie swinging about. 'Yeah, she's just like me: blonde and pretty. Lucky, aren't I, to have a daughter like that? Jealous?' Rosie's jaunty taunt floated in her wake as she marched on.

It wasn't in Rosie's nature to be vindictive, but she was happy to give as good as she got where those three

35

old cows were concerned. Over two years Peg and her cronies had done their best to browbeat her into admitting her baby was a bastard and she was ashamed of Hope. But she'd never been ashamed of Hope, even in those early days when she'd considered giving her away.

Everybody knew how to shut Peg Price up: rub the woman's nose in the fact that her only child was an ugly brat. If anybody was ashamed of their own flesh and blood it was Peg. Not only was Irene a spotty, sullen teenager, she had a reputation for chasing after boys.

'Conceited bleedin' madam, ain't yer?' Peg had caught up with Rosie and grabbed her arm. All pretence at geniality had vanished.

'Well, that's 'cos I've got something to be conceited about.' Rosie wrenched herself free of the woman's chapped fingers. 'Bet you wish your Irene could say the same, don't you?'

'What d'yer mean by that?' Peg snarled, shoving her cardigan sleeves up to her elbows in a threatening way. 'Come on, spit it out, so I can ram it back down yer throat.'

Rosie gave her a quizzical look. Peg's pals were enjoying the idea of a fight starting. May Reed had poked her tongue into the side of her cheek, her eyes alight with amusement as she waited expectantly for the first punch to be thrown.

'You don't want to let the likes of her talk to you like that, Peg.' May prodded her friend's shoulder when a tense silence lengthened and it seemed hostilities might flounder.

'At least your Irene's decent, unlike some I could mention.' Lou Rawlings snorted her two penn'orth. 'Widow, my eye! I reckon that's a bleedin' brass curtain

36

ring.' She pointed a grimy fingernail at Rosie's hand, resting on the pram handle.

'Decent, is she, your Irene?' Rosie echoed, feigning surprise and ostentatiously twisting her late mother's thin gold band on her finger. 'Go ask Bobby West about that then . . . 'cos I heard different, just yesterday.'

Rosie carried on up the road with abuse hurled after her. She already felt bad about opening her mouth and repeating what Doris had told her. Peg's daughter had been spotted behind the hut in the local rec with Bobby West.

Although they'd lived close for many years the gap in their ages meant Rosie and Irene had never been friends. Previously they'd just exchanged a hello or a casual wave; once Irene found out who'd dropped her in it Rosie reckoned she'd get ignored . . . or thumped by Irene. In a way she felt sorry for Peg's daughter. The poor girl had every reason to stomp about with her chops on her boots with that old dragon for a mother.

Lost in thought, Rosie almost walked straight past her house. They'd been rehoused for ages but the Dorniers had kept coming although their street had so far avoided further damage. She still headed automatically to her childhood home, further along. She found it upsetting to see the place in ruins so usually took a detour to avoid the bomb site it now was. She unlatched the wooden gate, fumbling in her handbag for her street door key. Glancing over a shoulder, Rosie noticed that trouble was on its way: Peg was marching in her direction with fat Lou and May flanking her. The unholy trinity, as her father called the local harridans, looked about to attack again before Rosie could make good her escape.

Rosie stuck her bag back under the cover of the pram then wheeled it about and set off along the road again. She was feeling so infuriated that, outnumbered or not, she felt she might just give Peg Price the scrap she was spoiling for. She wasn't running scared of them; but Rosie was keen to avoid upsetting her little girl.

Hope was sensitive to raised voices and a bad atmosphere. Just yesterday her daughter had whimpered when Rosie had given Doris a mouthful. Rosie didn't mind helping out with all the household chores, but she was damned if she was going to act as an unpaid skivvy for her new stepmother.

Since she'd moved in as Mrs Gardiner, Doris had made it clear she thought her husband's daughter had outstayed her welcome and she'd only tolerate Rosie's presence if she gained some benefit from it.

Rosie didn't see herself as a rival for John's affections, but Doris seemed to resent her nevertheless. Naturally, her father's second wife wanted to be the most important person in her husband's life. Unfortunately, John still acted as though his daughter and granddaughter had first claim on him. John and Doris weren't exactly newly-weds, having got married six months ago, but Rosie thought that the couple were entitled to some privacy.

'And so do I want some bloody privacy,' she muttered to herself now. She dearly wished to be able to afford a room for herself and Hope, but the cheapest furnished room she'd found was ten shillings a week, too dear for her pocket. So for now, they'd all have to try to muddle along as best they could. On fine days like today Rosie often walked for miles because the balmy June air was far nicer than the icy atmosphere she was likely to encounter indoors.

Now that her daughter was potty-trained Rosie felt ready to find Hope a place at a day nursery so she could get a job. Her father had never fully recovered his fitness after they'd been bombed out and Rosie wasn't sure he was up to the job of caring for a lively toddler, although he'd offered. Rosie didn't want to be beholden to her stepmother. Doris had a job serving in a bakery and was always complaining about feeling tired after being on her feet all day.

Rosie turned the corner towards Holborn, tilting her face up to the sun's golden warmth. It was late afternoon, but at this time of the year the heat and light lingered well into the evening. If John had prepared her tea he'd put the meal on the warming shelf for her to eat on her return.

'Hey . . . is that you, Rosie Gardiner? Is it really you?'

Rosie was idly window-shopping by Gamages department store when she heard her name called. Pivoting about, she frowned at a brunette hurrying towards her bouncing a pram in front of her. She didn't recognise the woman, and assumed she'd been spotted by a forgotten face from schooldays.

'Don't remember me, do you? Bleedin' hell, Rosie! It's only been a few years!' The newcomer grinned, wobbling Rosie's arm to jolt an answer from her. 'I can't have changed that much.'

It was the young woman's rough dialect and unforgettably infectious smile that provided a clue. The poor soul *had* changed; in a short space of time her acquaintance from the Windmill Theatre looked as though she'd aged ten years. If Rosie had relied on looks alone to jog her memory, she'd never have identified her. 'Oh . . . of course I remember you. It's Gertie . . . Gertie Grimes, isn't it?'

Gertie nodded, still smiling. Then she gave a grimace. 'It's all right, nobody from the old days recognises me. Look a state, don't I?' She sighed in resignation.

'No . . .' Rosie blurted, then bit her lip. There was no point in lying. Gertie Grimes was nobody's fool, Rosie remembered, and wouldn't appreciate being treated as one. 'Been a bloody long war, Gertie, hasn't it?' she said sympathetically.

'Oh, yeah . . .' Gertie drawled wearily. 'And it ain't done yet.'

'There's an end in sight, though, now the troops have landed in Normandy.' Rosie gave the woman's arm a rub, sensing much had happened in Gertie's life since they'd last spoken to make her sound so bitter.

'Perhaps we'll be having a victory knees-up soon.' Gertie brightened. 'Come on, tell me all about it.' She nodded at the little girl spinning the beads threaded on elastic strung between the pram hood fixings. 'Beauty, she is; what's her name?' Gertie lifted Rosie's hand and saw the wedding ring. 'I suppose you married an army general to make me really jealous. I remember the top brass were always fighting over you at the Windmill. Could've had yer pick, couldn't you; all the girls envied you.'

'I was a bit of a show-off, wasn't I?' Rosie replied with a rueful smile. 'Her name's Hope; but you go first. I remember you had boys, but this isn't a boy.' Rosie tickled the cheek of the little girl with dark brown hair and her mother's eyes. The child looked to be a few months older than Hope and the two little girls were now leaning towards each other sideways, giggling, to clasp hands.

'Never got a chance to tell you I was pregnant, did I,

'cos I left soon as I found out?' It was a fib; Gertie had concealed her pregnancy for quite some time from everyone at work, and from her cuckolded husband. 'She's called Victoria and she's gone two and a half now.'

'Crikey, you've got your hands full, Gertie. I know you've got four sons, so a girl must've been a lovely surprise for you and your husband.'

Gertie frowned into the distance. None of what Rosie assumed was true. Gertie now had just two children alive and, far from being delighted about another baby, her husband had knocked her out cold when he found out he'd not fathered the child she was carrying. 'Got just the one boy now. Three of them was lost in a raid during the Blitz. Direct hit . . . happened before Vicky was born.'

'Oh . . . I'm so sorry,' Rosie gasped. The memory of almost losing Hope when their house was destroyed still tormented her. Her remorse over that day was a constant companion and she could see in Gertie's eyes that the woman was battling similar demons.

'Don't blame yourself,' Rosie said softly. 'I can't know how you feel, not really, so I won't say I do. But I nearly lost Hope so I know what it is to feel guilty.' She paused. 'She was nearly crushed to death in her pram on the day we got bombed out in Shoreditch. It was my fault, no getting away from it.' Rosie cleared the huskiness from her voice with a small cough. 'My dad had been injured in the back garden, you see, and I was so concerned about getting him indoors that I forgot all about my baby in the front room.' It was the first time Rosie had admitted to anybody what she'd done. Not even Doris knew what had occurred that terrible afternoon.

41

'I still wake up at nights howling about the night my boys were killed. I feel so ashamed,' Gertie croaked. 'Least you was close enough to put things right before it was too late.' She sunk her chin to her chest. 'I wasn't there for them . . . nor was me husband . . . or me eldest boy. All out, we was, and Simon and Adam and Harry perished all alone in the house. Harry was just about the age Vicky is now. But it's the other two that I ache most for. Being older, they might've understood and been so frightened, the poor little loves.' Gertie swiped the heel of a hand over her cheeks. 'Please God they didn't suffer too much.'

Rosie put an arm about Gertie's shoulders and hugged her tight. 'They're at peace now, Gertie,' she soothed. 'You've done it so far, you can carry on a bit longer . . . then a bit longer after that. That's what I told myself, when I felt like beating my head against the wall to punish myself.'

'The ambulance girls . . . they fought like demons to keep my Harry alive. He was protected a bit by being in his pram, you see.' Gertie gulped back the lump in her throat. 'But they couldn't save him. One of the poor lasses was bawling almost as loud as me when they put the three bodies in the back of the ambulance.'

'Oh, Gertie, I'm so sorry . . .'

Gertie sniffed and blew her nose. 'Wanted to join the ambulance auxiliaries after that. Rufus wouldn't hear of it. But I went along for the interview anyhow.' Gertie looked crestfallen. 'Didn't pass the test, though. Best if you've got no young kids, they said, 'cos of the dangerous nature of the job.' Gertie grimaced. 'I told 'em about the dangerous nature of living in the East End. Didn't go down too well with the snooty cows.'

Rosie was impressed that Gertie had tried to join the auxiliaries. It seemed such a fitting thing to do in the circumstances. She remembered how efficiently the ambulance teams had got on with things when they'd been bombed out at home. At the time Rosie had been wrapped up in caring for her daughter and had happily allowed the auxiliaries to take over tending to her father. The middle-aged woman who'd patched him up, along with a younger female colleague, had almost carried him up the cellar stairs. Though the two of them looked like butter wouldn't melt, they'd come out with a few risqué jokes to distract John while loading him into the back of a makeshift ambulance.

With bad grace Doris had offered Rosie and Hope a roof over their heads with her in Hackney until John came out of hospital and the Council re-housed them. None of the trouble they'd suffered though could compare with Gertie's suffering.

'What's your oldest lad's name?' Rosie asked 'Bet he's quite the young man now, isn't he?'

'Oh, Joey's cock of the walk, all right. Thirteen, he is, and giving me plenty of lip.' Gertie managed a tiny smile. 'Mind you, that one always did have too much to say for himself. Gets that off his dad.'

'I bet your husband dotes on his princess.' Rosie nodded at Victoria. 'My dad calls Hope his princess.' She gave her friend a smile. 'Best be getting off, I suppose . . . be late for tea. Dad'll wonder where we are.' Rosie regretted drawing attention to her own circumstances; Gertie would wonder why she was referring to her father so much rather than to a husband.

'Fine reunion this has turned out to be,' Gertie's mumble held a hint of wry humour.

43

'Glad I bumped into you, Gertie,' Rosie said, glancing at her daughter, clapping hands with Victoria.

'Shall we meet up again?' Gertie looked at Rosie quite shyly as though anticipating a rebuff. 'The little 'uns seem to be getting along. We could take them for a stroll round a park another day. Perhaps have a picnic . . . if you like.'

'I'd like that very much,' Rosie said enthusiastically. 'We can reminisce about old times. What a to-do that was about Olive Roberts. Who'd have thought it?'

'Never liked that woman,' Gertie's eyes narrowed as she reflected on the kiosk attendant at the Windmill Theatre who'd been unmasked as a dangerous Nazi sympathiser.

'Quite hair-raising, wasn't it?' A gleam of nostalgia lit Rosie's eyes. 'We saw some times there, didn't we? Good and bad.'

Gertie grunted agreement. 'I miss the old place,' she said. 'Funny thing is, when I was at work, I couldn't wait to finish a shift and get home to me boys, though they drove me up the wall. Now I'm home all the time I wish I'd got a job.'

'Now Hope's turned two I'm after a nursery place for her so I can get back to work.' Rosie tidied her daughter's fair hair with her fingers. 'I want to help bring this damned war to an end.'

'Not going back on stage?' Gertie asked.

'No fear.'

'Before you disappear, you must tell me about your other half.' Gertie teasingly prodded Rosie's arm.

'Tell you more when I see you next week,' Rosie replied, turning the pram about, ready to head back towards Shoreditch. 'How about Thursday afternoon at about three o'clock? We could meet right here outside Gamages . . .'

'Suits me; Rufus goes to a neighbour's to play cards on Thursdays.'

'Your husband back on leave, is he?' Rosie asked.

'Oh . . . 'course, you wouldn't know that either. He's been invalided home from the army,' Gertie said briskly to conceal the wobble in her voice.

Rosie read from Gertie's fierce expression that the woman felt she'd suffered enough condolences for one day. 'See you Thursday then.' Rosie let off the brake on the pram.

The two women headed off in opposite directions, then both turned at the same time to wave before settling into their strides.

Rosie walked quickly, aware her dad would be wondering where she'd got to, but at the back of her mind was the conversation she'd had with Gertie about the ambulance auxiliaries. Rosie wanted to do a job that was vital to the war effort and in her book there was nothing more important than saving lives. So she reckoned she knew what employment she'd apply for. All she had to do was break it to her dad that she was going to volunteer for a position with the ambulance auxiliaries.

CHAPTER FIVE

'Long time no see, mate.'

John Gardiner almost dropped the mug of tea he'd been cradling in his palm. He'd opened the front door while carrying it, expecting to see his daughter on the step. He'd been about to say, 'What, forgot your key again, dear?' because Rosie had earlier in the week knocked him up when he'd been snoozing on the settee.

Instead his welcoming smile vanished and he half closed the door in the wonky-eyed fellow's face. It'd been a year since he'd caught sight of Frank Purves, and then they'd only nodded at one another from opposite pavements. On that occasion John had been tempted to hare across the road to throttle the man for having spawned a fiend. But, of course, he hadn't because that would have given the game away. And John would sooner die than cause his daughter any more trouble. He kept his welcome to a snarled, 'What the hell d'you want?'

'Well, that ain't a very nice greeting, is it?' Frank stuck his boot over the threshold to prevent John shutting him out. He stared at his old business partner although just one of his eyes was on the man's face and the other appeared to be studying the doorjamb. Popeye, as Frank was nicknamed, had never let his severe squint hold him back. 'Just come to see how you're doing, and tell you about a bit of easy money heading your way, John.'

'I told you years back that I ain't in that game no more, and I haven't changed me mind,' John craned his neck to spit, 'I've got a wife and family, and I don't want no trouble.'

'Yeah, heard you got married to Doris Bellamy. Remember her. All used to hang about together as kids, didn't we?' Frank cocked his head. 'Gonna ask me in fer a cuppa, then?' He nodded at the tea in John's unsteady hand. 'Any left in the pot, is there, mate? I'm spitting feathers 'ere . . .'

'No, there ain't.' John glanced to left and right as though fearing somebody might have spotted his visitor. 'Look . . . I'm straight now and all settled down. Don't need no work.' As a last resort he waggled his bad leg at Frank. 'See . . . got a gammy leg since we got bombed out up the other end of the road.'

'Yeah, heard about that, too.' Frank gave the injury a cursory glance. 'Thing is, John, that bad leg ain't gonna hold you back in your line of work, is it?' He shifted his weight forward. 'You owe me, as I recall, and I'm here to collect that favour.'

'Owe you?' John frowned, the colour fleeing from his complexion. Even so, he was confident that what he was thinking wasn't what Frank Purves was hinting at. John reckoned that Popeye couldn't know anything about that, 'cos if he did the vengeful bastard wouldn't be talking to him, he'd be sticking a knife in his guts.

47

Lenny's actions had started a feud between the Gardiners and the Purveses that Popeye knew nothing about. But one day he would and when that day came John wanted to get in first.

'When you chucked it all in you left me high 'n' dry with a pile of labels I'd run off. Never paid me for 'em, did yer? Plus I had a fair few irate customers waiting on that batch of gin.'

John's sigh of relief whistled through his teeth. He ferreted in a pocket and drew out some banknotes, thrusting them at Frank. 'There! Go on, piss off!'

Frank looked contemptuously at the two pounds before pocketing them. 'I'm in with some different people now. They're interested in you, John. I been singing your praises and telling 'em you're the best distiller in London. They ain't gonna like your attitude when they've stumped up handsomely to sample your wares.'

John's jaw dropped and he suddenly reddened in fury. 'You had no right to tell a fucking soul about me. I don't go blabbing me mouth off about you doing a bit of counterfeiting.'

'Yeah, well, needs must when the devil drives, eh?' Frank leaned in again. 'Lost me son, lost me little bomb lark business 'cos me employees crippled themselves. A one-armed short-arse and a fat bloke wot got nobbled in France. Ain't saying they aren't keen but, bleedin' hell, they're a fuckin' liability.' Frank finished his complaint on a tobacco-stained smile. 'Got nuthin' but me printing press to fall back on.' He glanced over a shoulder. 'Need a few extra clothing coupons, do you, mate?' He gave John a friendly dig in the ribs. 'That'll put you in the missus's good books. Get herself a new frock, can't she? Get herself two if she likes.'

'You forging coupons now?' John whispered, aghast.

'I'm forging all right, just like I was when I run off all them dodgy spirit labels for your hooch.' Frank's lips thinned over his brown teeth. 'We need to talk, mate . . . seriously . . .'

John knew he'd never get rid of Popeye until he'd let him have his say. And he didn't want the neighbours seeing too much. Popeye lived the other side of Shoreditch but he had a certain notoriety due to his ducking and diving. Not that you'd think it to look at him: Popeye had the appearance, and the aroma, of a tramp. 'Just a couple of minutes; they'll all be in soon fer tea. Don't want no awkward questions being asked,' John snarled in frustration.

'Right y'are . . .' Frank said brightly and stepped into the hall.

John pointed at a chair under the parlour table by way of an invitation. He limped into the kitchen and quickly poured a cup of lukewarm tea with a shaking hand. 'There, get that down yer and say what you've got to.' John glanced nervously at the clock, dreading hearing his wife's or his daughter's key in the lock.

'Look at us,' Frank chirped, watching John fidgeting to ease his position. He pointed at his left eye. 'There's me with me squint and you with yer gammy leg.' He guffawed. 'Don't hold yer back, though, John, do it, if you don't let it?' He grinned wolfishly. 'Bet you still manage to show Doris yer love her, don't you? Bit of a knee trembler, is it, balancing on one leg on the mattress?' He winked. 'Gotta get yer weight on yer elbows.' Popeye leaned onto the tabletop to demonstrate, rocking back and forth on his seat. 'I've got meself a nice young lady works in the King and Tinker, name of

Shirley.' He paused. 'Your daughter's called Rosemary, if I remember right. Heard you'd got a grandkid; so young Rosie's given up the stage, has she, and got married now?' Popeye paused to slurp tea.

'Fuck's sake, you got something to say, or not?' Agitatedly, John snatched Popeye's cup of tea off him. He'd been about to throw it down the sink but knew if he disappeared into another room, Popeye might decide to follow him. And he was desperate to get him out of the house, not further into it.

'So what's the nipper's name? Rosie call her after her mum, did she? Prudence, God rest her, would have liked that, wouldn't she, John?'

'Me granddaughter's name's Hope,' John ejected through his teeth. 'She's a lovely little darlin' and I don't want her coming back home and having you scare the bleedin' life out of her with yer ugly mug.' John grimaced at Popeye's dirty clothes and the greying stubble on his face.

Frank ran a hand around his chin, understanding John's look of disgust. 'My Shirley's always telling me to smarten up. Perhaps I should.'

'Sling yer hook before they all come in!' John had almost jumped out of his skin at the sound of next door's dustbin lid clattering home.

'Right, here's the deal.' Suddenly Popeye was deadly serious, mean eyes narrowed to slits. 'I know this outfit what's deep in with anything you like: dog tracks, bootlegging; pimps 'n' spivs, they are. Based over the docks—'

'I get the picture,' John interrupted, having heard enough. 'You're out of your league and you've promised 'em stuff you can't deliver. Ain't nuthin' to do with me, Popeye. I've paid you up. That's us quits.'

'It ain't me who's got to deliver on this occasion, it's you, mate. I've run 'em off a nice line of girly mags in the past and I've been doing their booze labels. Trouble is they've got no bottles of Scotch to stick 'em on. Their distiller got his still broken up by the revenue men a while back.'

'Well, let yer big mates buy him another one.' John hobbled to the door and held it open.

Popeye ignored the invitation to leave and sat back comfortably in his chair. ''Spect they would do that, but trouble is the fellow what knows how to use it's doing a five stretch. So I told 'em I knew how to help them out.'

'Right . . . thanks for the offer of the work. But I ain't interested. Ain't even got me still now.'

'Now, I know you ain't destroyed it, John.' Popeye pulled an old-fashioned face, crooning, 'Don't you tell me no lies, now. Might not be down in the cellar . . . where is it?' He jerked his head back, gazing at the ceiling. 'Attic? I reckon since you moved here you've stashed it away all neat and tidy, ain't yer?'

'I got rid of it when we was bombed out of the other place.'

'Don't believe you for one minute. It's here all right . . . somewhere . . .' Popeye glanced around thoughtfully as though he might set off in search of it.

'Get going; we're done here.' John yanked at Popeye's sleeve to shift him.

'Don't think so, mate.' Frank ripped his arm out of John's grasp. 'If you don't sing along they're gonna want their cash back, ain't they?'

'What?' John tottered back a step, apprehension stabbing at his guts. 'What fucking cash?'

'The cash they give me, to give to you.' Popeye shrugged. 'I told them you'd need an advance to buy stuff to get going so they give us a monkey up front.'

John licked his lips. Five hundred! That was a serious sum of money. 'Well, you'll just have to give it back, won't yer?'

'Can't . . . do . . . that . . .' Popeye warbled. 'Make me look like a right prat. Anyhow, I ain't got it.' He sniffed. 'Needed some readies meself so I had to use it to keep someone sweet. You know the old saying: rob Peter to pay Paul, but John's getting it in the end.' He gave a wink. 'You know I'm always good for my word. Never once not paid you up, have I?'

John swallowed noisily. 'Sounds like you've got some explaining to do then when they come looking for you.'

'Not me . . . you.' Popeye nodded slowly. 'This is where they'll head. You don't cross people like that, John. You should know that.'

'They come here looking fer me I'll call the Old Bill and tell 'em everything, especially that you've just tried to blackmail me to get involved in counterfeiting.'

Popeye came to his feet in quite a sprightly fashion considering he was over sixty and overweight. 'Now, that ain't wise, talking like that, John. I'll pretend I never heard it.' Popeye walked up to the smaller man and eyeballed him as best he could, before strolling out into the hallway. 'Right . . . be seeing you then. You come to me next time; only fair . . . my turn to make the tea. Say, end of the week and we can make arrangements to put the still up in my basement if it's likely to cause ructions with your Doris. Give the missus my regards now, won't you?'

'Fuck off.' John slammed the door after Popeye and

ground his teeth when he heard the faint laughter coming from the other side of the panels. He paced to and fro then went upstairs as quickly as his limp allowed. He found the steps in the airing cupboard and positioned them beneath the loft hatch. A few minutes later he poked his head into the cool, dark roof void, his heart thumping so hard he thought it might burst from his chest.

He'd promised Rosie on his life that he'd never make another drop of moonshine. Doris had no idea that he ever had run an illegal still. Nobody had known, other than his daughter and his business associates. Now Popeye had blabbed his business about, God only knew how many people were aware he'd once risked a spot of hard labour.

John hauled himself into the loft, wincing from the effort, and approached the dismantled still covered in tarpaulin. He crouched down and peered at the tubes and funnels and receptacles. Suddenly he smiled wryly. The contraption had survived the bombing, having been wedged in the corner of the cellar with a cover over it. Now he was wishing that the bloody thing had been in the loft of his old house, and been smashed to smithereens with the roof. But the hundred pounds in his Post Office book had come courtesy of this little beauty. And that money was being saved up for another little beauty, and one day she'd thank her granddad for buying her presents. John felt his eyes fill with tears as he put the hatch back in place. He'd do anything for his little Hope, and protect her with his life, if need be.

CHAPTER SIX

'Insult my Irene again, you bitch, and I'll wipe the floor with yer.'

Rosie spun about to see that Peg Price had sprinted down her front path to yell and jab a finger at her. The woman must have been loitering behind the curtains, waiting for her to return, Rosie realised. On the walk home her surprise meeting with Gertie, and everything they'd talked about, had been occupying her mind and she'd not given her run-in with her rotten neighbours another thought.

Rosie contemptuously flicked two fingers at the woman's pinched expression before pushing the pram over the threshold and closing the door behind her.

A savoury aroma was wafting down the hall from the kitchen, making Rosie's stomach grumble.

'That you, Rosie?'

'Yeah. Sorry I'm late.' Rosie carried on unfastening Hope's reins, thinking her father had sounded odd. But she gave his mood little thought; she was too wrapped up in counting her blessings. And she was determined to work for the London Auxiliary Ambulance Service. If she got turned down, as Gertie had, she'd try again and again until she was accepted.

Rosie cast her mind back to the time when the female ambulance auxiliary had entered their bombed-out house and with a simple joke made her laugh, then tended to her father with brisk professionalism. Rosie had been impressed by the service, and the people in it. But her baby daughter had taken up all her time and energy then. Now Hope was older, toddling and talking, and Rosie had the time to be useful. She wanted her daughter to grow up in peacetime with plentiful food to eat and a bright future in front of her. Wishing for victory wasn't enough; she needed to pitch in and help bring it about, as other mothers had throughout the long years of the conflict.

From the moment Gertie had recounted how the ambulance crew had battled to save her baby's life, Rosie knew that's what she wanted to do . . . just in case at some time the baby dug from beneath bomb rubble was her own.

John appeared in the parlour doorway wiping his floury hands on a tea towel.

Lifting her daughter out of the pram, Rosie set Hope on her feet. The child toddled a few steps to be swept up into her granddad's arms.

'How's my princess?' John planted a kiss on the infant's soft warm cheek.

In answer Hope thrust her lower lip and nodded her fair head.

'See what Granddad's got in the biscuit tin, shall we, darlin'?'

Again Hope nodded solemnly.

'Don't feed her up or she won't eat her tea,' Rosie mildly protested, straightening the pram cover. She watched her father slowly hobbling away from her with Hope in his arms. Lots of times she'd been tempted to tell him not to carry her daughter in case he overbalanced and dropped her. But she never did. Hope was her father's pride and joy, and his salvation.

In the aftermath of the bombing raid, it had seemed that John's badly injured leg might have to be amputated. Sunk in self-pity, he'd talked of wanting to end it all, until his little granddaughter had been taken to see him in hospital and had given him a gummy smile. At the time, Rosie had felt pity and exasperation for her father. In one breath she'd comforted him and in the next she'd reminded him he was luckier than those young servicemen who would never return home.

John carefully set Hope down by her toy box and started stacking washing-up in the bowl.

'You stewing on something, Dad?' Rosie asked. Her father was frowning into the sink and he would usually have made more of a fuss of Hope than that.

'Nah, just me leg giving me gyp, love.' John turned round, smiling. 'Talking of stew, that's what we've got. Not a lot in it other than some boiled bacon scraps and veg from the garden but I've made a few dumplings to fill us up.'

'Smells good, Dad,' Rosie praised. 'Sorry I didn't get home in time to give you a hand. We had a nice walk, though.'

"S'all right, love. Enjoy yerself?' John enquired, running a spoon, sticky with suet, under the tap. 'Anyhow, you can help now you're back. There's a few spuds in the colander under the sink. Peel 'em, will you?'

Having filled a pot with water, Rosie sat down at the scrubbed parlour table and began preparing potatoes while filling her dad in on where she'd been. 'First I went to the chemist and got your Beecham's Powders.' She pulled a small box from the pocket of her cardigan and put it on the table. Her dad relied on them for every ailment. 'Then I took a walk to Cheapside and bumped into an old friend from the Windmill Theatre—'

'You're not going back there to work!' John interrupted. 'If you want a job you can get yourself a respectable one now you're a mother.' He had spun round at the sink and cantankerously crossed his wet forearms over his chest.

'I don't even want to go back there to work, Dad,' Rosie protested. 'Gertie doesn't work there now either. She's got a little girl a bit older than Hope. The two kids had a go at having a chat.' Rosie smiled fondly at her daughter. 'Made a friend, didn't you, darling?'

'Gertie? Don't recall that name,' John muttered, and turned back to the washing-up.

Rosie frowned at his back, wondering what had got his goat while she'd been out. But she decided not to ask because she'd yet to break the news to him about the employment she was after and she wasn't sure how he'd take it.

'Gertie was one of the theatre's cleaners. She left the Windmill months before me.'

'Mmm . . . well, that's all right then,' John mumbled, flicking suds from his hands. He felt rather ashamed that Popeye's visit had left him on edge, making him snappy.

'I am getting a job, though, Dad.'

'Ain't the work I'm objecting to, just the nature of it,' John muttered.

'You didn't mind the money I earned at the Windmill Theatre, though, did you?' Rosie reminded him drily, dropping potatoes in the pot.

'If you'd not been working at that place you'd never

have got in with a bad crowd and got yourself in trouble,' John bawled. He pursed his lips in regret; the last thing he wanted to do was overreact and arouse his daughter's suspicions that something was wrong.

'I got into trouble because of the company *you* kept, not the company *I* kept,' Rosie stormed before she could stop herself. It was infuriating that her father still tried to ease his conscience by finding scapegoats. In Rosie's opinion it was time to leave the horrible episode behind now. They both adored Hope so something good *had* come out of bad in the end.

The slamming of the front door had John turning, tight-lipped, back to the sink and Rosie lighting the gas under the potatoes.

'What's going on?' Sensing an atmosphere, Doris looked suspiciously from father to daughter.

'I was just telling Dad that I saw an old friend from the Windmill Theatre. The poor woman has had dreadful bad luck. A couple of years ago their house got hit and she lost three of her young sons.'

Doris crossed herself, muttering a prayer beneath her breath. 'She was lucky to get out herself then.'

'She was very lucky, and so was her husband and eldest boy,' Rosie said after a pause. She knew Doris could act pious, so she wasn't going to mention that the three children had died alone. Her stepmother would have something to say about neglect despite the fact that her own daughter-in-law and grandson rarely came to visit her because they were never invited.

'Didn't realise it was bad news you got from your friend,' John said gruffly by way of apology. That terrible tale had momentarily edged his own worries from his mind.

Doris's sympathy was short-lived, however, and she was

quick to change the subject. 'Just got caught outside by Peg Price; sounding off about you, she was.' Doris wagged an accusing finger.

Rosie shrugged, refusing to take the bait. Doris would always make it plain she felt burdened by the duty of sticking up for her.

'Saw somebody else with a long face.' Doris gazed at her reflection in the mantel mirror and started pushing the waves back in place in her faded brown hair. 'Nurse Johnson was in civvies down Petticoat Lane.' Doris looked at the little girl crouching on the floor. 'You'd think she'd pop in once in a while to see how Hope's getting on.'

'I expect she's too busy,' Rosie said succinctly. Doris enjoyed bringing to her attention that she'd caused enmity on several fronts.

Rosie hadn't spoken to her midwife since the day she'd broken the news about withdrawing from the adoption. At the time Rosie had thought that the woman seemed to take it quite well. Trudy had listened to her explanation, then said the sort of things that Rosie had been expecting to hear about being surprised and disappointed. Ever since, if they met out walking a brief nod was the most Rosie got from the woman. Rosie couldn't blame Trudy Johnson if she had felt bitter about what had happened.

'Going upstairs to put a brush through me hair before we have tea.'

Once his wife had gone out of the room John said, 'Didn't mean to snap earlier, Rosie; just that I worry about you, y'know, grown up though you are.' He pulled out a chair at the table and sank onto the seat. 'God knows we've had to cope with some troubles these past few years.'

'Not as much as some people, Dad,' Rosie said pointedly, to remind him of Gertie's catastrophe.

'I know . . . I know . . . but you're still my little girl, however old you are. And I won't never stop worrying about you and Hope s'long as I'm drawing breath.'

'You've no need to worry, Dad, I'm able to look after myself and Hope now.' After a short silence Rosie saw her father seemed to have gone into a trance, staring into space. 'What is it, Dad?' She sat down opposite him and rested her elbows on the tabletop. 'You seem odd . . . thoughtful. Something up?'

'Nah, just this leg getting me down,' John lied. He forced a smile. 'Wish you could meet a nice young man, dear.' He took Rosie's hands in his. 'You need somebody to care for you, 'cos I ain't always going to be around. Robbie likes you, y'know, and he's not short of a bob or two . . . or a couple of pork chops.'

Rosie tutted in mock exasperation at her father's quip. Robbie Raynham was the local butcher, and at least fifteen years her senior. He was pleasant enough and not bad-looking but Rosie didn't like him in that way. She didn't like any man in that way. Rosie knew Doris often sent her to get their meat ration in the hope the smitten butcher might slip a little bit extra in for them in return for the promise of a date.

But Rosie didn't have any interest in marriage or men. Since she'd been dragged into an alleyway then thrown to the ground and raped, a cold dread had replaced any longing she'd once had for an exciting romance and a husband. Love and affection were saved for her daughter; all she wanted to do was keep Hope safe and make plans for her future.

Rosie took a deep breath and blurted, 'I'm going to apply to join the London Auxiliary Ambulance Service.'

John gawped at his daughter as though she were mad. 'Why?' he eventually asked.

'Because it's an important job needs doing.'

'Being a mother to that little girl's an important job needs doing,' John replied pithily. 'Ambulance work's too dangerous. You'll be covered in blood and muck.'

'I was covered in blood and muck when the Café de Paris got bombed and again on the afternoon our house was wrecked. I'm used to it now.'

John had the grace to blush as he recalled how she'd nursed him and dressed his wounds till they could get help on that dreadful afternoon.

'Dad, d'you remember how that auxiliary helped you that day?'

''Course . . .' John muttered. 'And I was grateful to her, but that don't mean I want you taking them sort of risks.' He pointed a finger. 'She were a lot older than you, for a start . . .'

'Her colleague who helped you up the stairs wasn't. And she was driving the ambulance, if you remember. She looked to be in her twenties, like me . . .'

'Don't want you doing it, Rosie . . .' John began shirtily.

'I'm going to apply,' Rosie said firmly. 'Hope'll be fine in a nursery. I'm going to the WVS tomorrow to see if they can sort out a place for her.'

'If you're determined, me 'n' Doris can see to the little 'un between us.' John sounded affronted.

'I'd like her to make some more friends,' Rosie answered diplomatically. 'She had a lovely time playing with Gertie's little girl.'

'Time enough fer that when she's older. I'll mind her.' John sounded stubborn. He'd always been very protective of his granddaughter but suddenly after Popeye's visit it seemed more important than ever to keep a close watch on Hope.

'It's time for me to get my own place, too, Dad. Now you and Doris are married you deserve some privacy. Besides, I need to learn to stand on my own two feet. So as soon as I'm earning I'll be able to pay rent.' Rosie had been planning on saving that blow for another day. But as her father had seemed to accept her work, albeit reluctantly, she had decided that 'in for a penny, in for a pound' might be the best approach.

'Leaving home and standing on your own two feet backfired on you once before.' John pressed his lips into a thin line. He'd not wanted to hark back to that episode. 'Anyhow, people my age don't need a lot of fuss. Ain't as if me and Doris are starry-eyed. Known each other too long for any of that.' John coughed, recalling Popeye's dirty talk.

'Still, it'd be nice for you both to have some peace and quiet.' Rosie understood her father's unease about discussing intimate things.

'I know kids have tantrums, so that don't bother me one bit. I brought you up, remember,' he added darkly.

Rosie smiled faintly. Her stepmother wasn't happy about losing her sleep. The woman had let Rosie know she'd been kept awake by Hope crying as she'd barged out of the bathroom that morning.

Suddenly Rosie was missing her mum with such strong sadness that she felt momentarily unable to speak. Prudence Gardiner had passed away when she was in junior school but Rosie could recall her vividly. She could also remember that her mother's affair hadn't lasted, but the bitterness between John and Prudence had. He'd taken her back . . . *for the girl's sake* . . . the words stuck in Rosie's mind as the reason he'd bawled at his wife when she'd shown up again, suitcase in hand. Rosie knew that Prudence would have adored her beautiful granddaughter. Had her mother still been alive perhaps Hope might have succeeded in doing what Rosie had yearned to do but had failed at: bring her parents some shared happiness.

She glanced at her father's lined face, feeling a rush of pity that his second wife was unlikely to bring him any more contentment than his first had. 'I'm grateful that you've taken care of me and Hope till now. But I'll cope on my own, Dad.'

'You won't!' John's anxiety had manifested itself in anger. 'You're staying right here where I can keep an eye on you both.'

'Might be that yer daughter's got a point about being independent and paying her own way,' Doris said, entering the kitchen. 'And as your wife, you might like to ask me my opinion on things that concern me.'

Rosie knew that Doris was thoroughly in favour of her moving out, and the sooner the better.

'Stew's done.' John turned his back on his wife, stooping to open the oven door. With a teacloth protecting his hands he drew out a sizzling-hot clay pot.

'That's yer answer, is it?' Doris snorted in disgust. 'Dinner's ready!'

'Let's eat, then talk about it later.' Rosie gave her stepmother a smile, signalling a truce. It seemed there was something eating away at her father and she'd no idea what it might be. But she was quite sure it had little to do with her wanting a job and some independence.

CHAPTER SEVEN

'So you can hear it 'n' all, can you, Rosie love? I thought me ears were playing tricks on me.'

John was crunching along the cinder path in the back garden dressed in his pyjamas and bedroom slippers. His palms batted against his ears at intervals as though to unblock them.

At the sound of her father's voice Rosie turned and gave him a quick nod before fixing her eyes again on the moonless sky.

It was a humid June night and Rosie had been restlessly dozing, when the wail of an air-raid siren had brought her swiftly to her feet. She'd glanced at Hope, sound asleep, then padded to the window to stare out. It was just a week away from midsummer and, though not yet dawn, the sky hadn't fully darkened. She'd been able to see for some distance. She'd heard the ack-ack guns start up and seen bullets tracing the heavens, but a weird noise had made her snatch up her dressing gown and investigate further.

A few months ago the first warning wail would have

had Rosie grabbing her daughter and flying downstairs to the safety of the cellar, but there had been a lot of false alarms recently; German reconnaissance planes had skimmed over the capital but there hadn't been a bombardment since the winter. The Normandy landings had been such a success that nobody was expecting one while the Luftwaffe had their hands full elsewhere. But something was surely closing on London, or why were the defence batteries blasting away?

The drone of approaching bombers was terrifyingly familiar to East Enders, whereas whatever was up there tonight was making an odd roaring noise as though a mechanic's giant blowtorch had taken flight. The searchlights were in full swing yet Rosie hadn't had a glimpse of a plane's silhouette. She rubbed the back of her stretched neck, wondering if the eerie throb was coming not from above but from some new-fangled machinery down on the Pool of London, where supply ships heading for Normandy were being loaded up.

Suddenly the sky directly overhead was striped by a searchlight, making Rosie anxiously blurt out, 'Not taking any chances, Dad. I'm getting Hope and going to the cellar. Come on . . . don't care if it is another false alarm. Never heard anything like that before and it can't be one of ours or the guns would have stopped.'

'What the bloody hell is that?' John yelled, pointing towards the south. ''S'all right, love. Look, it's not a bomber. It's much smaller . . . a fighter plane, I reckon, and the Jerry bugger's taken a hit. Look!' He wagged his finger at the sky.

Rosie halted by the back door, again gazing heavenwards.

There, caught in a crosshair of searchlights, was the

outline of a plane; and it did, indeed, have a plume of brilliant fire spurting from its tail.

'It'll crash, Dad,' Rosie shouted. 'Get inside.'

'It's gonna crash all right,' John said in awe, watching the fast-moving object. 'Blimey! Wonder if the pilot's ejected. Keep an eye out for a parachute, love. Don't want no Kraut landing on me roof.' Suddenly he went quiet, as did the V1 rocket, but the weapon glided on silently before its nose dipped . . .

'Come on, Dad!' Rosie was already inside the back door, holding it ajar for him. 'Quick! Let's get in the cellar!'

'What in God's name's going on?' Doris had shuffled into view, belting her dressing gown. 'We got a proper raid?'

'Is that Jerry? Taken a hit, has he?' a fellow bawled across fences. 'Bailed out, has he? See anything, did yer, John?'

'Dunno what the hell it is, mate,' John yelled back at Dick Price. Peg's husband was yawning and scratching his pot-belly beneath a grimy vest. John had noticed that the trail of flames had disappeared at about the same time that the aircraft's engine cut out. He didn't reckon that the pilot would've managed to extinguish that fire. As the thing had got closer he'd also noticed that it had the Luftwaffe cross on it but it wasn't even big enough to be a Messerschmitt.

'Reckon it might be wise to get under cover.' Finally John's fear overtook his amazement. He waved his arms in warning at his neighbour before limping into the house and following Doris down the cellar stairs. Rosie joined them seconds later with Hope clinging sleepily around her neck.

When the explosion came a few minutes later Rosie instinctively curled her body protectively over her small daughter until the mortar that had been loosened from the bare brick walls had finished coating them in fine dust.

'Reckon that was over Bethnal Green,' John said after a short silence. 'Bet Jerry sent over some sort of Kamikaze pilot in a toy plane. 'I ain't never seen the like of that before.'

'If you're right, I hope there's just the one of them.' Rosie cradled Hope, soothing her whimpering daughter with gentle murmurs.

'Don't reckon Hitler'll get many volunteers. Jerry ain't like the Nips when it comes to that sort of thing.' Doris picked up the knitting she kept in the cellar to while away the time during air raids. 'If this is a sign the Blitz is starting all over again then I'm getting out of London. I was living on me nerves last time, never knowing which way to run to the nearest shelter.' Doris threw down the needles, unable to concentrate on counting stitches. 'D'you reckon there'll be more of those blighters tonight?' She gazed at her husband for a response but John was still shaking his head to himself in disbelief at what he'd seen and heard out in the garden. 'Well, I ain't having it,' Doris said shrilly. 'I'm off to me son's place in Kent for some peace and quiet. Already been invited to stay so I'm taking me daughter-in-law up on it.' Still John sat rubbing his bad leg and gazing at the ceiling. With an agitated tut, Doris picked up the cardigan sleeve and started knitting a row of pearl.

As soon as Rosie's father had shouted out that there was a letter for her it had been a relief to give up the pretence of rest and hurry downstairs. They'd all trooped up to bed when the all clear sounded but Rosie had found it impossible to get back to sleep. The sinister chugging that had first woken her had continued to pound through her brain. She'd buried her head in the pillow to try to block it out but by then the sun had been filtering through the curtains.

Her father was obviously not in the mood to share any news about her forthcoming job interview so with a sigh Rosie returned to her bedroom with her letter. Within half an hour she had got dressed, neatly filled in the Form of Application for National Service, and put on her mac as it was drizzling outside.

'Just off to the post box. Will you mind Hope for a few minutes?' Rosie poked her head round the kitchen door to ask her dad. 'She's still asleep so shouldn't be any trouble.'

'What name you going under then?' John asked, pointing at the envelope in his daughter's hand.

'My real name. I'm Rosemary Gardiner, aged twenty-two, spinster, born and bred in Shoreditch.'

'So your daughter doesn't exist then?'

'Oh, she does!' Rosie vehemently declared. 'But Hope's my private business and there's no reason to bring her into it.'

'Well I say there is!' John retorted. 'Round here you're Mrs Deane now and that's the way it should be. Using two different names'll brew up trouble.'

'Answering questions about my poor dead "husband" will brew up trouble,' Rosie replied flatly. 'I don't want to start off in a new job telling a pack of lies about myself; they always trip you up in the end.'

John muttered beneath his breath but he couldn't

deny the truth in what his daughter had said. He wished in a way that he'd agreed to brazen out Rosie's pregnancy. It had been what his daughter had wanted rather than stooping to deceit. At the time he'd sided with Doris and insisted his daughter protect the family name by inventing a story. It hadn't stopped the gossip; in fact he could see now that it had just provided more grist for the mill. But they couldn't backpedal on it now or it would make matters worse.

Rosie felt frustrated with her father's attitude but she didn't want an argument with him so tried a different tack: 'Look, I've been shirking conscription for years, pretending I'm a married woman.'

'Ain't shirking. Women with kids – legitimate or not – ain't breaking the rules in staying home and caring for them,' John returned. 'Anyhow, you've been fire watching plenty of times.'

Rosie gave up trying to put her point across and headed for the front door.

'It'll come out you're an unmarried mother,' John called out after her. 'Then when they're all talking about you behind yer back you'll wish you'd done things differently.'

The deputy station officer of Robley Road Auxiliary Ambulance Station in Hackney – or Station 97 as it was better known – was seated behind a battered wooden desk. Having studied the notes in front of her she inspected the young woman perched on a chair opposite.

Rosie neatly crossed her ankles, nervously clasping her hands in her lap. She was wearing a smart blue two-piece suit purchased years ago when she was flush

69

from working at the Windmill Theatre. It was a bit loose because she'd lost a few pounds running round after her toddling daughter, but was still in pristine condition. And the colour suited her. Her pale blonde hair had been styled into a sleek chin-length bob rather than jazzy waves, and she'd applied her make-up sparingly: just a slick of coral lipstick and some powder to cool the colour of her peachy complexion.

'Your references are very good.'

Since leaving her job at the Windmill Theatre Rosie hadn't had much to deposit in her bank account but the elderly manager of the Barclays Bank in the High Street had agreed to give her a character. And so had the retired draper who'd employed Rosie as a youngster, winding wool for pocket money on Saturdays. Rosie had carefully chosen her referees from people who were unaware she was a mother and had always known her as Miss Gardiner. She might be withholding personal information, but it wasn't the same as lying in Rosie's opinion.

'Do you consider yourself to be strong and healthy?'

'Oh, yes, I'm fit as a fiddle,' Rosie immediately returned.

'You'll need to be,' Stella Phipps emphasised. 'It's surprising what a severed limb weighs. Then there are the stretchers to lug about. Lifting those to the upper position in an ambulance can put a person's back out.' Stella cocked her head, examining Rosie's figure dubiously. She looked soft and petite, whereas most of the female recruits were strapping individuals.

'Oh, I'm used to lifting . . .' Rosie's voice tailed off. She'd been on the point of adding that she'd got a chubby two-year-old who liked to be carried about but stopped herself in time. She was Rosemary Gardiner, spinster, no dependants. 'My dad's got a bad leg injury so I've lugged him up and down the cellar steps in the past, amongst other things.'

'That's the sort of stuff that comes in useful, but you do seem a bit weedy, dear, if you don't mind me saying so.' Stella took off her glasses to polish them. 'Of course, you're very attractive so no offence meant.'

'I'm very capable,' Rosie returned stoutly. 'And I'll prove it.'

'I'm sure you'll do your best, Miss Gardiner. It's just that I feel obliged to impress on you that the work is arduous . . . and gruelling.' Stella sighed. 'Apart from physical sturdiness you need to be prepared for some harrowing sights. Have you had any medical training?'

'No, but I'd quickly learn,' Rosie said eagerly. 'And the sight of a bit of blood doesn't bother me. I tended to my dad when he got badly injured.'

'The sight of "a bit of blood" is what you might encounter here when the sanitary bin in the ladies' convenience overflows.' Stella replaced her spectacles and gazed grimly at her interviewee, ignoring the girl's blushing. If Miss Gardiner were serious about getting a job with the London Auxiliary Ambulance Service she'd better be prepared for some plain speaking. 'If you're accepted and your experience follows mine you'll encounter rat-eaten bodies and scraps of terry towelling nappies containing burned flesh . . . all that remains of what was once a human baby.' In the silence that followed Stella stabbed her pen nib repeatedly on the blotter, eyes lowered. 'I'd been in the job just a fortnight when I observed a parachute descending and in the dark I thought it might be a German who'd bailed out. It was something far deadlier . . . a landmine. It exploded in Brick Lane about a hundred yards from where we'd just

71

been called to another incident. That was during the winter of 1940 at the height of the Blitz.' Stella paused. 'We lost two of our ambulance crew that night.'

Rosie swallowed, hoping she didn't look too green about the gills. She knew the deputy station officer wasn't being deliberately cruel. In fact, she was being very kind. 'I understand . . . I'm prepared for the worst,' Rosie vowed in a quavering yet resolute tone.

'You're a better person than I then, Miss Gardiner,' Stella replied. 'I wasn't up to it at all; I brought my heart up the first time I had to deliver a man's leg to the fridge at Billingsgate Market.' She saw Rosie shoot her a horrified glance from beneath her thick lashes. 'Oh, that's sometimes the first stop for odds and ends before they make it to the mortuary, you see. We're not cannibals in England . . . not yet, anyhow, despite the paltry rations.'

Rosie smothered a giggle. Stella Phipps might be a fierce-looking dragon but she had a sense of humour. Rosie realised that it was probably an essential requirement for working in the LAAS, the London Auxiliary Ambulance Service. Having heard those stomach-churning anecdotes, she relaxed and decided she liked the woman who might soon be her boss.

'I can book you on a first-aid course with the St John Ambulance if you pass the interview.' Stella closed the manila folder in front of her. 'Any driving experience? We could do with drivers.' She sighed. 'Most of the men we had in the service have gone off on active duty, you see.'

'I used to drive my dad's car,' Rosie burst out. She was determined to be taken on; and if that meant embellishing the truth a little, she'd do it. The only driving she'd ever done had been at the age of fifteen when her father had taken her for a day trip to Clacton and after much badgering had allowed her to get behind the wheel in a country lane. It was the first and last time, though; Rosie had scraped the paintwork of John's pride and joy after swerving into a hawthorn hedge while fighting with the stiff gears.

'Do you still drive a car?' Stella asked optimistically.

'Um . . . no,' Rosie owned up. 'Since Dad got injured he's sold the Austin. And I never actually passed a test.'

'At least you've a head start, dear. An RAC course might be all that's required to bring you up to scratch.'

Rosie nodded, feeling a fraud. None the less she added stoutly, 'I'm sure I'll do fine so long as I can remember where the brake is.'

Stella chuckled, then looked thoughtfully at the new recruit. The volunteers were usually keen, eager to be of service. Some lasted just a few weeks before they took fright. Others, like herself and her friend Thora Norris, had been serving since the start of the Blitz. In those days they'd turned up for work dressed in their civilian clothes without even a pair of sensible shoes between them. As the war dragged on the service had become a lot more organised and efficient.

'Following the landings in Normandy it seemed as though we might wind down when victory seemed finally within reach,' Stella said. 'The routine here had become quite mundane. Oh, we still got called out, but on the whole we were dealing with domestic incidents or road accidents.' She shook her head in despair. 'You'd be surprised at how many dreadful injuries have been caused by the blackout. It's as lethal as any Jerry bomb.'

'But if the damage done by that bloody rocket coming

over and causing havoc is anything to go by, you might need more volunteers . . .' Rosie had anticipated what Stella Phipps was about to say and blurted it out, rather bluntly. She blushed, mumbled, 'Sorry . . . language . . .'

Stella smiled. 'You'll hear worse . . . say worse . . . than that, dear, if you join our little team at Station 97. Letting off steam is essential in this line of work. So no apology required.'

Rosie smiled sheepishly.

The recent explosion in Bethnal Green had everybody talking fearfully about a fiendish new weapon, although Whitehall was doing its best to keep the details under wraps to avoid a panic. But rumours were already spreading that the blazing plane Rosie and her father had watched speeding across the sky was a bomb shaped like a rocket and there had been whispers of others falling across London.

'I saw that first one come over; the noise it made was deafening and very eerie,' Rosie said. When she noted Stella's interest she rushed on, 'Dad and I watched it from the garden. Dad thought it was a miniature Messerschmitt and wondered whether the pilot might bale out and land on our roof because it seemed to be on fire.'

'Let's hope the rumours are just that,' Stella said. 'We don't want a return to the Blitz.'

Stella's concern reminded Rosie of her stepmother fretting about London being heavily bombarded again. Doris had moaned constantly whilst they'd waited for the all clear to sound that night.

'I'll get one of my colleagues to show you around our station, though you might be posted to another one. Have you any preference where you'd like to be sent?'

'As close to home as possible,' Rosie answered quickly, following the older woman out into the corridor. 'Here at Station 97 would be just fine.'

'Righto . . .' Stella said, striding along at quite a pace. 'Of course when we get called out it's not always to local incidents. If a Deptford crew for example are engaged on a major incident we might be required to cover for them on their patch.'

'I understand,' Rosie said, trotting to keep up with the older woman.

'Have you seen Thora Norris?'

Stella's question was directed at a brunette who was propped on an elbow against the wall, smoking. She turned about, flicking her dog end out through an open door into the courtyard. 'I think she's gone shopping with the new mess manager, ma'am. We're low in the cupboards, by all accounts.'

'I'm hoping there are no petrol cans stored out there, Scott.' Stella Phipps angrily eyed the stub smouldering on concrete.

'Sorry . . . didn't think.' The young woman trotted outside to grind the butt out with a toe, looking apologetic.

'Mmm . . . and not the first time, is it?'

The young auxiliary was dressed in a uniform of navy-blue safari-style jacket and matching trousers. The letters 'LAAS' were picked out in gold embroidery at the top of a sleeve. She turned to look Rosie up and down. 'How do? You mad enough to want to join us, then?' She stuck out a hand and gave Rosie's small fingers a thorough pump.

'Nice to meet you, and yes, hope I've got the job.' Rosie sent a peeking glance at the deputy station manager.

'I think you'll fit in,' Stella said with a severe smile. 'I'll leave you in Hazel Scott's capable hands.' Her eyebrows hiked dubiously. 'She'll show you round the place and even if you're not posted here, you'll get a feel for things, Miss Gardiner. The auxiliary ambulance stations are all much of a muchness.'

'Only ours is best.' Hazel said sweetly, earning a smile from her superior.

'Don't mind her,' Hazel hissed as Stella's rigid back disappeared round a corner. 'Bark's worse than her bite and all that. I've worked in three different stations now and some of the DSOs – that's deputy station officers to the uninitiated – well, they're worse than the top dog.' Hazel stuck her hands in her jacket pockets and chuckled. 'Got something to prove, I suppose.'

'She seemed very nice, I thought.' Rosie managed to get a word in edgeways. She was glad to have any information about ambulance station life. She realised that there had been no need to turn up looking so demure: Hazel's eyelashes were laden with mascara and crimson lipstick outlined her wide mouth.

'Nice? Really?' Hazel rolled her eyes in a show of surprise. She drew out her pack of Players and offered it to Rosie. 'Don't smoke?' she snorted when Rosie declined with a shake of the head.

'Used to . . . gave it up.'

'Not for long in this place, you won't. Couldn't get by without a fag an hour, me.' Hazel's cockney accent seemed to have become more pronounced. She took a long drag on the cigarette then pointed with it. 'Fancy a cuppa? Canteen's just down this way.'

'I'm Rosemary Gardiner, by the way. Rosie, friends call me.'

Hazel slanted a smile over a shoulder. 'I'll call you Rosie then, and I'm Hazel to my friends. Most of the others here address us by our surnames. But I don't go for being formal with people I like.'

It was a typical canteen set with uncomfortable-looking chairs pushed under Spartan rectangular tables. Hazel led the way into the kitchen at the back and filled the kettle at a deep china sink. Having rummaged in a cupboard for some cups and saucers she turned to give Rosie a searching stare.

'Got a man in your life?'

Rosie shook her head, having noticed that Hazel was glancing at her fingers, probably searching for a ring of some sort. Her mother's wedding ring was wrapped in tissue in her handbag. 'You got a boyfriend?' Rosie always turned a leading question on its head. Her home life wasn't up for discussion.

'Mmm . . . he's a sailor. Chuck's due back on leave soon.'

'Lucky you,' Rosie said with a friendly smile.

'Lucky him . . . if you know what I mean,' Hazel winked a weighty eyelid, lewdly puckering up her scarlet lips. She cocked her head. 'Can't believe you've not got a feller.' She tutted. 'Sorry, that was a bloody stupid thing to say, all things considered. There've been so many casualties in this damned war.'

'No, it's all right; I've not lost anybody over there or here. Just not got anybody special in my life . . . a man that is . . .'

Rosie's private smile as she thought of Hope went unnoticed by Hazel.

Hazel spooned tea into a small enamel pot. 'Best get this down us before the hordes descend. Teatime at four

77

thirty.' She glanced at her watch. 'Oh, got half an hour to spare.' She poured boiling water onto the leaves and stirred. 'Come on, while that brews I'll show you a bit more of the set-up.'

Hazel was tall and solidly built. From the young woman's forthrightness Rosie reckoned Hazel was no shrinking violet when it came to cleaning up the human wreckage left behind after Hitler had dropped his calling cards.

'This is the common room.' Hazel waved at a young fellow who was filling some hurricane lamps ranged in front of him on a table. In response he called out a cheery hello.

'New recruit, Tom,' Hazel informed. 'Tell Miss Rosie Gardiner she's barmy; go on, she won't believe me.'

'Listen to Hazel,' Tom called with a rather effeminate wave. 'Scarper while you still can.' He then turned his attention to the funnel he was using to drip oil into the lamps.

'Tom Anderson is a conchie,' Hazel said quietly. On seeing Rosie's bemusement she explained, 'Conscientious objector. We've had a few of those sent here. He might not want to fight but he's a bloody godsend with the ambulances. He's a driver and knows a thing or two about mechanics. He used to drive a tractor on his dad's farm.'

Rosie hoped Tom was unaware that Hazel had been gossiping about him. His boiler-suit-style uniform made him look more like a plumber than an ambulance driver.

'Table tennis . . .' Rosie had spotted the net shoved into a corner, bats and balls scattered on the top. 'I used to be pretty good at table tennis.'

'I'll give you a game if we end up on the same shifts,'

Hazel offered. 'What did you do before this damned war buggered us all up?'

'Worked in a theatre a few years back.'

'Me, too!' Hazel burst out, delighted. 'Which theatre?'

'The Windmill . . .' Rosie started examining the table tennis bats. She never volunteered the information that she'd worked as one of the theatre's famous nudes. But neither did she deny what she'd done, if asked directly.

The Windmill Theatre had stayed open throughout the war. But Rosie had never felt any inclination to go back for old times' sake and see a show, or look for the few old colleagues who might remain working there.

'I worked as a magician's assistant,' Hazel informed her. 'He was always trying to have a fiddle down the front of me costume so I dropped him and went out on my own. I could do a bit of singing and dancing but never made much of a name for myself.' Hazel click-clacked a few steps with toes and heels, hands jigging up and down at her sides. 'I was in the chorus at the Palladium once when one of the girls went sick at the last minute.' She sniffed. 'Never got asked back, though. They said I was too tall for the chorus line.' She gazed at Rosie admiringly. 'The Windmill! Now why didn't I try there!' She grinned. 'What's the place like? Bit racy, ain't it, by all accounts? All the servicemen flocked there. Chuck and his navy pals used to race to get a seat at the front. Bet you had a few followers, being as you're so pretty.'

'Take a look at an ambulance, can I?' Rosie asked brightly. 'I'd better see what it's all about just in case I'm lucky enough to get to drive one.'

'You think that's lucky? Oh, come on, the tea'll be stewed.' Hazel led the way back towards the canteen.

'Getting behind the wheel of a meat wagon is no picnic, I can tell you. Gilly Crump had held a motor licence for years yet she drove an ambulance straight into a wall in the blackout. Knocked herself sparko and ended up in the back of the blighter on a stretcher.' Hazel chuckled. 'Gave in her notice shortly after when she got out of hospital. You'll need to do a few practice runs under instruction before they'll let you loose on your tod with an assistant.'

'You won't put me off, you know.'

Hazel poured the tea then held out a cup, grinning. 'You look like the sort of girl that does all right whatever she turns her hand to. Some people just have that sort of luck. Whereas me . . . I bugger up everything.'

'I bet you don't!' Rosie returned, thinking ruefully that if Hazel knew her better she'd be revising her opinion.

Rosie rather liked her new colleague's droll manner. She knew already that she'd chosen well in applying to the service; it didn't feel like home yet, but it did feel right being here with Stella Phipps and Tom Anderson and Hazel Scott. In fact, she was itching to get started.

CHAPTER EIGHT

'Didn't know if you'd still come over for a picnic after what's gone on,' Gertie called out as soon as she saw Rosie rounding the corner.

''Course I'd come for a picnic. Been looking forward to it. Take more than a load of flying bombs to keep me away from our day out.' Rosie grinned although she wasn't feeling quite as chipper as she sounded. While heading to their rendezvous spot Rosie had also wondered if she was making a fruitless journey. She wouldn't blame Gertie for wanting to stay day and night right by an underground shelter after losing three children in the Blitz.

'Head off towards the park, shall we?'

Gertie nodded. 'We had a couple of close shaves in our street. Get any blasts your way from those damned rockets?'

'Where I live they're always coming too close for comfort,' Rosie replied with feeling. 'Thankfully, no hits in the street. I saw the first one come over, though.' She shook her head as she recalled that night. 'Couldn't believe my ears . . . or eyes.'

That first doodlebug had come down in Bethnal Green, blowing to smithereens the railway line and several houses. Unfortunately, Stella Phipps' hopes that the rumours weren't true had been dashed. Hundreds more of the missiles had whizzed overhead since in a relentless German onslaught. The sight of a fiery tail approaching, coupled with a sinister roaring, was dreadful enough, yet when the rocket's engine died and it carried on silently for several seconds, the uncertainty of where it might drop was even more terrifying.

They turned in through the iron gates of a small square recreation area. A couple of urchins in plimsolls and short trousers raced past, almost colliding with them. Having mumbled an apology they hared off again. The local school had turned out and the park was crowded with mothers and children making the most of the afternoon sun. But Rosie noticed that a lot of women looked anxious and were keeping an eye on the open skies. The missiles hadn't only been arriving after dark and there was a tension in the air despite the children's joyful voices.

'Here'll do.' Gertie swiped away a crust of bird droppings on a bench's slats. Having sat down she delved into her shopping bag, pegged on the pram handle. 'Brought a flask.' Gertie held out the Thermos. 'Not much in the way of a picnic, though. Sorry, me rations are low.'

'I've got some Spam sandwiches.' Rosie dug into her bag and found a small packet. She unwrapped it and offered the sandwiches to Gertie. 'Would have been corned beef but Dad wanted to keep that to fry up for our teas tonight.'

'Blimey! They're fit for a queen!' Gertie looked admiringly at the tiny neatly cut triangles, unlike the doorsteps of bread and jam encased in greaseproof paper that she'd brought along. 'Thanks.' She took a bite before unscrewing the Thermos and pouring two weak brews into plastic cups.

'Bread's a bit dry; only had a scraping of Stork left in the pack,' Rosie apologised.

'Tastes fine to me,' Gertie said truthfully, taking another hungry bite. At home she never had sandwiches with butter or marge. Those rations were saved for her husband and kids.

'Your little 'un's good.' Gertie nodded at Hope, sitting quietly in her pram. Victoria, on the other hand, was rocking herself on her bottom and banging her heels against the thin mattress to get her mother's attention.

'She's too big for the pram now,' Gertie said, giving her daughter's nose a wipe. 'Like to get out and walk, don't you, Vicky?' Gertie lifted her daughter out of the pram and let her sit beside her on the seat. 'Behave yourself,' she warned. 'Be a good girl like Hope.'

'You wouldn't have said that if you'd heard the little madam last night,' Rosie responded ruefully. 'Thought Doris was going to have a fit . . .'

'Doris?' Gertie asked, holding out Rosie's tea to her. She noticed Rosie's expression change. ''S'all right . . . not prying, honest.' Gertie rummaged for a jam sandwich. She broke off a piece for her daughter and Victoria stopped fidgeting and tucked in. 'Can Hope have a bit?'

'Yeah . . . I've got her bib somewhere.' As Rosie fastened the terry towelling about her daughter's neck she said, 'Doris is my stepmother. Dad got married again recently.'

'Take it things ain't always easy between you two.' Gertie followed up with a knowing laugh. 'I had some of that with me mother-in-law. Mustn't speak ill of the dead, though, so enough said.' She handed a morsel of bread oozing thick dark jam to Hope who promptly took a bite then threw the remainder overboard.

'She's not very hungry,' Rosie apologised. 'Dad gave her a few biscuits about an hour ago. He spoils her.' She glanced at Gertie. 'You've probably guessed that I've not got a home of my own and live with Dad.'

'Me 'n' Rufus started off married life at my mum's,' Gertie replied flatly. 'Couldn't wait to get out and into me own place.'

'Drive you mad, did they?' Rosie asked.

'Wasn't them; they did what they could for us. But couldn't take living with me younger brother.' Gertie clammed up. She never spoke about Michael. She didn't want to see or hear from him ever again. In fact she hoped that the nasty bastard was six feet under. He'd been a thorn in her side for decades; even as kids they'd not got on. Then he'd plunged a dagger in her heart when her little boys died; she blamed him for the children having been left alone in the house that night.

In Gertie's experience most of life's troubles revolved around the men in her life. And she reckoned that Rosie was reluctant to talk about Hope's father because she held the same opinion.

'Army, is he, your husband?' Gertie asked sympathetically. 'Rufus ain't the easiest man to live with yet when he was in France I fretted no end about him. Almost came as a relief when he got invalided home; I know that's a wicked thing to say.' She wiped her jammy fingers on a hanky. 'Sometimes I'd not have the wireless on in case of any bad news about the Middlesex

84

Regiment. Didn't want Joey to hear it; it didn't seem fair landing that on him as well after he'd lost his brothers. 'Course, now his dad's back we don't have that bother.' Gertie gave a bashful smile. 'Sorry, going on a bit, ain't I?'

'I like to hear about your family, Gertie. You must miss your sons so much,' Rosie said quietly.

Gertie nodded. 'Joey took it badly. Thought at one point he'd need a dose of something from the doctor to calm him down. But we got through it . . . the two of us. After Rufus enlisted it was just me and him for a while, before Vicky was born.' She sniffed, glanced at Rosie. 'I understand if you don't want to talk about your husband, though . . .'

'I said I'd tell you more about myself today, didn't I?'

''S'all right; you don't have to say a thing if you don't want to. Plenty of stuff in my past I never talk about.' Gertie grinned. 'Bet that's come as a surprise to you after listening to me rabbiting nineteen to the dozen.'

Rosie sat back sipping her tea. 'I don't have a husband,' she suddenly blurted. 'My name's still Rosie Gardiner and never been any different although some people think I'm a widow called Mrs Deane.'

'Stops 'em yakking, don't it, if they see a ring on your finger?' There had been a long silence before Gertie's reply, but when it came it sounded matter-of-fact. 'Wrong 'un who ran off, was he, the father?'

'He was a wrong 'un all right,' Rosie said bitterly. 'But he didn't run off. He never knew, thank God.'

'Didn't want no help off him?' Gertie asked, surprised.

Rosie shook her head vigorously. 'Never wanted to see him again. And I got my way. I never did. He died before I even found out I was expecting.'

'Killed in action?'

'He got discharged as unfit before he'd ever held a rifle. Didn't do him much good, though; he perished in a nightclub fire. The day I found out I could have jumped for joy. Some people might think that wicked.'

'Not me. He raped you.' Gertie's quiet statement was husky with sorrow.

'I didn't say so,' Rosie rattled off. Suddenly she regretted revealing too much about her past. Her dearest wish was to protect Hope, and hearing gossip that your father had raped your mother was a dreadful thing for any child to deal with. Having a chat and a picnic couldn't alter the fact that she and Gertie still didn't know one another well enough to share secrets.

'You don't need to worry,' Gertie reassured. 'Like I said, there's plenty of stuff in my past I don't talk about. So I'd never talk about your'n, promise.'

'Thanks,' Rosie mumbled. 'Hark at us! Right pair of miserable cows, aren't we? Thought I was getting out of the house to cheer myself up.' She got to her feet, brushing sandwich crumbs from her skirt. 'Let's have a quick stroll round the grass before the heavens open.' A cliff of dark cloud was menacing the horizon. People were gathering up their belongings and hurrying towards the park gates as they noticed the air changing.

'Don't fancy getting drenched.' Gertie put the flask back in her bag and they headed off side by side, pulling the hoods up on the prams in preparation for a downpour.

'I volunteered to work as an ambulance auxiliary. I've been talking about making myself useful for ages, so I finally did something about it.'

Gertie looked surprised, then smiled. 'Glad to hear it!

They'll take you on, no trouble, especially if a fellow interviews you.' She glanced sideways at Rosie's stylish skirt and blouse, so much prettier than the faded cotton frock she was wearing herself.

'A woman interviewed me. And I got a letter this morning offering me a job.'

'Good for you!' Gertie glanced at Hope. 'Yer stepmother going to mind the little 'un for you?'

'Dad'll help out as Doris is working.'

'I'll give a hand babysitting, if you like,' Gertie volunteered. She's such a cutie it'd be a pleasure to have her round to play with Vicky.'

'Dad got moody when I spoke about getting Hope a nursery place. He's determined to mind her,' Rosie quickly rattled off. She liked Gertie but the woman was a rough-and-ready sort and she didn't know enough about the Grimes family to let Hope stay there.

Rosie felt bad for thinking she was a better mother than Gertie. Considering what life had thrown at the poor woman she deserved praise for coping so well.

At the park gates Rosie turned to give Gertie a spontaneous hug. 'Thanks . . . for everything.'

'Ain't done nothing,' Gertie replied bashfully.

'Yeah you have, and I'm so glad we bumped into each other that day. Don't know what my shifts are going to be yet but I hope we can keep on meeting up.'

Gertie took a scrap of paper from her bag. 'Shopping list,' she explained the spidery scrawl filling half of one side. Turning it over she printed her address on it with a stub of pencil found in a pocket. 'There. When you get a day off, come and see me, if you like. I'm usually about.'

With a wave the two women quickly set off in opposite

directions as fat raindrops were spotting the hoods of the children's prams.

It had been clear skies when Rosie had set out for a picnic so she hadn't bothered to stuff a scarf in her pocket, fearing the weather might turn. By the time she trotted up to her front door her stylish fair locks were glued to her cheeks in sleek rat's-tails.

'Crikey, you did get caught in it, didn't you?' John clucked his tongue while inspecting his daughter's bedraggled figure.

Rosie gave her head a shake and quickly unbuttoned her cardigan and took it off, hanging the sodden wool over a chair back.

'How's yer friend? Have a nice time, did you, dear, despite getting a soaking?' John seemed in jovial mood, fetching her a towel from the kitchen and draping it over her scalp. Doris followed him out and between them they managed to get Hope out of the pram without tipping on the floor the water that had pooled on the gabardine cover.

Rosie was surprised to see her stepmother. She stopped drying her hair to remark, 'Thought you were on shift this afternoon, Doris.'

'Got some time off. Anyhow, I'm handing me notice in tomorrow as we're moving to Kent,' Doris called over a shoulder as she set off, gingerly holding the cover, to tip the rainwater down the sink. Rosie thought she must have misheard but when Doris reappeared she added, 'It's time to start packing things up.'

Rosie suddenly glanced at a box in the corner of the room that she'd not paid much attention to before. 'Moving to Kent?' she echoed.

'Now don't make out you didn't hear us talking the other night.' Doris sounded prickly as she hooked the cover over the fireguard to drip dry on the hearth.

'I heard you say your daughter-in-law offered to put you up for a break if there's no let-up with the doodlebugs. I didn't think it was a permanent arrangement.'

'I'm going for as long as she'll have me. Can't stand this a moment longer.' Doris whirled an agitated hand over her head. 'This war ain't coming to an end! Hitler's got his second wind and I'm done with living on me nerves! I saw me old neighbour in Commercial Road earlier. She said three bodies got dug out of my old house. One of 'em could've been mine. Always the Londoners what suffer.' Doris ceased ranting to draw breath. 'I'm off where it's safer and yer father's coming with me.' Doris gave her husband a glare, daring him to defy her. 'You can too, if you want, Rosie.'

Rosie knew her stepmother wasn't exaggerating the effect the V1s were having on her. And Doris wasn't alone in feeling wretchedly despondent. Rosie had been queuing in the butcher's the other day when a woman behind had gone into hysterics because she'd thought she could hear a rocket on its way. The alarming noise had turned out to be a steamroller lumbering towards the rail yard. But nobody had made a joke of it in the way they might have done a couple of years back. During the Blitz a natural belligerence and optimism had seen people through. But now the mood had changed; the euphoria following the D-Day landings was fast evaporating and Doris was by no means alone in wanting to throw in the towel and flee to a safer place.

'All settled then, is it? You're definitely going to Gravesend?' Rosie looked at her father. He avoided her eye when she added drily, 'Thanks for keeping me in on it.'

'While Charlie's away on his frigate . . .' Doris referred to her son's active service. 'Me daughter-in-law says there's room for all of us. Her boy, Toby, can kip in with her. We'll have the spare bedroom, and you and Hope can have Toby's small bedroom, if you want. But ain't forcing you to do nothing you don't want to do.'

''Course Rosie wants to come,' John snapped. 'She ain't daft enough to want to stay here with the little 'un now we all know what's in store for us. It's far too dangerous.' He glared at his wife. 'I told you to let me bring this subject up. Shouldn't have flung it at her like that. Look, she's not even had a chance to dry herself off yet.'

'Sorry, I'm sure,' Doris said sarcastically. She went into the kitchen and returned with crockery to stack in the box, ignoring the tense silence between father and daughter.

'And you can give that a rest for a while; it ain't urgent,' John testily addressed his wife. 'Time for Hope to have her tea. It's gone five o'clock.'

'It's all right, Dad.' Seeing Doris's boiling expression, Rosie tried to smooth things over. She didn't want the couple to row on her account. She felt a fool for not having realised her stepmother had been dropping serious hints when mentioning staying with her family in Kent. 'Hope's not hungry anyhow; we had a picnic in the park.' Rosie's conciliatory smile for Doris wasn't returned.

'Sorry about that, love,' John mumbled after his wife had clattered the crockery into the box and stomped off upstairs. 'She means well and she ain't exaggerating how it's affecting her. She hardly gets a wink of sleep for fretting we'll be next to get our roof blown off.' John hung his head. 'Think I'm in danger of losing me marbles too, way things are going.'

John wasn't just thinking of Gravesend being a safe haven from the bombardment; he wanted to get away from Popeye. He'd had another visit from the man but had managed to avoid any discussion. John had been outside on the pavement, talking to Dick Price at the time. Popeye had loitered by the lamppost on the opposite pavement trying to catch John's eye, but John had walked off up the pub with Dick. By the time he got back Popeye had disappeared.

'I'm sorry I snapped, Dad, but it came as a shock about you going to Gravesend.'

'You're not thinking of staying behind?'

'I am,' Rosie replied quietly. She'd not had time to give the upheaval much thought but realised her spontaneous answer was the right one.

'That's bloody selfish!' John erupted. He peered suspiciously at Rosie. 'What is it? Found a boyfriend? Thinking of him rather than Hope, are you?'

Rosie limited her exasperation to a long weary sigh and a pithy, 'Thought you realised I've got no time for men in my life.'

Hope was becoming upset by the hostility between her mum and granddad. The child trotted from the kitchen into the parlour, lower lip thrust out, and threw to the floor the muddy potato she'd been playing with. Rosie sat down at the table with her daughter on her lap, her chin resting on a small crown of silky fair hair. 'A week on Monday I'm starting work at Station 97 in Robley Road. I know you're worried about me staying behind, but I'll do all right and I'll take good care of myself when on duty.'

'I reckon you should take good care of the little 'un first by getting her out of harm's way.'

Rosie used an edge of the tablecloth to rub potato mould from her daughter's fingers. 'Hope's going to have a future; I want to do whatever I can to make sure of it.' She gazed at her father with fierce eyes. 'She'll go to school and get a good job and meet a nice man when her time comes. And live in peace.' She smiled ruefully. 'Until she has kids of her own to drive her up the wall. But by then I'll have done my bit.'

'Give her here!' John tried to wrestle his granddaughter from Rosie, making the child whimper. 'Someone's got to look after her properly.'

'Leave her alone, Dad. You're frightening her.' Rosie took a deep breath before blurting, 'When you go to Kent I want you to take her with you.'

That took the wind out of John's sails. He sank down into the chair opposite Rosie at the table.

Rosie stroked the side of her daughter's face. The idea of being separated from Hope had put a thick wedge of emotion in her throat. But she quashed it. Thousands of Londoners had known the heartache of sending their children away to be cared for by strangers. At least she had the comfort of knowing that Hope had her doting granddad watching over her during her evacuation.

''Course I'll take her with me,' John finally croaked out. He glanced at his wife who'd just entered the room. 'Love to have her, won't we?'

Doris chewed her lower lip. 'Yeah,' she muttered before going into the kitchen. 'As nobody else's made a start I'll get a pot of potatoes on the go, shall I?'

Rosie went to help her stony-faced stepmother prepare their teas. Her eyes were so teary that she misjudged what she was doing and cracked the enamel pan on the side of the sink when she tried to fill it with water. She gritted her teeth against an urge to blurt out that she'd changed her mind and Hope must stay with her. Rosie became aware that her daughter had appeared at her side and was gazing at her with huge blue eyes.

Swiftly Rosie crouched down and gently removed the thumb from Hope's mouth. 'Guess what? Granddad's going to take you on a lovely holiday in the countryside soon. Like that, won't you, sweetheart?'

Hope nodded solemnly. 'You come?' she whispered.

'When I can,' Rosie replied softly. 'And I'll speak to you on the telephone now you're getting a big girl, promise I will.'

'Reckon we'll see about that, won't we?' Doris sniffed. 'Could be you'll find you're too busy having a good time to remember your little kiddie out in the countryside.'

Rosie stood up slowly, realising how strongly she disliked her stepmother. 'When I had my interview, my station officer told me to prepare myself for some awful sights on a call-out. If you reckon that collecting body parts is having a good time then I'm not sure you're the sort of person I want around my daughter.'

'She don't mean nuthin' by it, Rosie.' John had come out into the kitchen and given his wife a glare. 'Doris is talkin' out of her backside because all this bombing's got to her.'

'Charming, I'm sure!' Doris, boiling with anger, barged past and stamped up the stairs.

John swooped on his little granddaughter and lifted her up, making her squeal in delight as he threw her a few inches into the air. 'Going on holiday with Granddad, aren't you, you lucky gel.'

Hope gave his bristly cheek a soft kiss, making her mother's strained expression soften.

'She'll be right as rain with us, Rosie,' John vowed solemnly. 'You just make sure you're all right too.'

CHAPTER NINE

'Just come to say I'm moving away so don't come looking for me 'cos you'll be wasting your time.' John was turning away when he heard the sound of a striking match. He darted his eyes back past his old business associate glimpsing, behind the tobacco smoke snaking his way, a dark silhouette in Popeye's gloomy hallway. If he'd known Frank had company he'd have given him a wide berth this evening. A sunset-streaked black saloon was parked at the kerb and John silently cussed at having ignored an obvious clue that Popeye wasn't indoors alone.

'Can't stop; said what I had to.' John hurried down the path as fast as his limp would allow, his mouth dry. Although he'd not got a clear view of Popeye's visitor, he had a bad feeling about him.

In a few days' time John was taking his wife and granddaughter to Kent. But there'd been something he had felt duty-bound to do before he caught that train. He distrusted and feared Frank Purves but had forced himself to come here. The last thing John wanted after he'd gone was this man turning up on his doorstep looking for him and frightening the life out of Rosie.

'This is a nice surprise, John, and right on cue. Don't rush off now, mate. There's somebody here I know'd like to meet you.' John had reached the gate but, before he managed to unlatch it, Popeye had snatched his elbow. 'You'd best not upset him; he'll have yer guts fer garters,' Popeye snarled, jerking his head at his front door. ''Ere . . . come on inside, don't be shy.' Popeye's voice was now loud and jolly for the benefit of his acquaintance.

Popeye's banter didn't fool John. But he knew if he didn't sort things out between them before he went to Gravesend, his fears for Rosie's safety would eat him alive every day he was away.

'Just a few minutes then; me wife's waiting on me to help her pack.' John's trepidation mounted as Popeye suddenly stuffed some cash into his pocket.

'That's a bit up front to buy goods. Don't go telling him I've tried to stitch you up, 'cos I ain't, see,' Popeye hissed in his ear.

John tried to free his hand to return the money but Popeye propelled him into his house and shut the door, trapping the three of them in a dark narrow corridor.

'So where you off to then, mate? Somewhere nice?' Popeye asked amiably.

John wasn't falling for that one. If Popeye found out where he was heading he wouldn't put it past the bastard to come after him.

'The missus has got family over in Wales,' John lied, hoping to flummox him.

'Doris a Taffy? Well, I never!' Popeye drawled ironically. 'Glad you stopped by, 'cos I was going to pay you a visit tomorrow. Just saying to Mr Flint here that it was time to prod you over that order.' He rolled his wonky eyes and emphasised his warning by baring two rows of brown teeth. 'Told him your missus is cutting up rough over it all and delaying things,' Popeye again muttered close to John's ear.

'Ain't a story!' John spluttered. 'Doris'll go berserk.'

Sweat slipped down his spine as he glanced at the fellow who was standing sideways on to them, hands dug in his pockets and cigarette drooping from his lips. Far from seeming bothered, he looked bored stiff with proceedings.

John's eyes were adjusting to the dimness inside the house and he could see the bloke looked to be fit and strong. And young. He put his age at about thirty and his snug-fitting suit jacket was moulded on biceps any man would envy.

'Now I promised you a cuppa, when you come to see me, didn't I, mate? Sit yerself down and I'll stick the kettle on.' Popeye sounded hospitable but the shove that accompanied the offer of tea sent John stumbling down the corridor.

It seemed the other fellow wasn't having tea. He wasn't having a seat either. He'd stationed himself by the empty hearth in Popeye's back parlour and upended against his lips a silver flask, taken from an inside pocket.

John watched him screwing the top back on the flask then flinched when a steady gaze bored into him.

'Frank's forgotten his manners,' the stranger said. 'Seems he's not making formal introductions.'

At least he wasn't stranded in the company of one of Frank's Brummie associates, John thought hysterically. He had met a few of those when he'd been distilling, and thought them mad as a box of frogs. Of course, the

97

East End had its fair share of dangerous lunatics too, so a London accent wasn't necessarily a relief.

John sidled closer to the door, wondering whether his quaking legs would be up to him making a dash for it. He sensed he was under observation again and flinched beneath Flint's quiet amusement.

'Look, dunno what Frank's told you, but I ain't agreed to do no distilling . . .'

The young man held out a hand, ignoring John's breathless excuse. 'I'm Conor Flint, and you must be John Gardiner. Right?'

John backed away a pace as though fearing those long dark fingers might suddenly leap to squeeze his throat. He quickly shook hands, pulling free as soon as possible.

'You were saying about the distilling?' Conor prompted, levelling a navy-blue stare on John's blanching face.

'Dunno for sure what Pop's game is . . . well, I do 'cos he told me . . .' John cleared his throat. 'But he's wrong, see. I don't get involved in that no more. Got married again . . . got a daughter and a grandkid now . . .' He suddenly clammed up, features frozen in regret. Belatedly he realised that the last thing he should have advertised to this stranger was that he had vulnerable dependants.

'Right . . .' Conor propped a hand on the mantelpiece again. 'That's disappointing, 'cos I was expecting to take a sample of the stuff out of here with me.'

'Ain't been in touch with Popeye fer years,' John stressed. 'Then he turns up outta the blue and starts going on about setting up me still again. I told him straight—'

'Told me straight you was up for it, didn't yer?' Popeye ambled into the room, giving John a poisonous look.

But he thrust a cup of tea at him, slopping some over the rim to wet the solitary Rich Tea biscuit balanced on the saucer.

John dropped the crockery on the table. 'Don't want no fuckin' tea,' he exploded. 'Tell him I said I wasn't getting involved. Go on!' He pulled the wad of cash out of his pocket and threw five ten-pound notes on the table. 'And you can have that back.'

John sensed Flint believed him until the man laughed, soft and chilling, and swung a look between him and Frank.

'Which of you's trying to stiff me? Popeye?' It was a mild query but Conor began drumming his fingers on the mantelshelf in strong, irritated rhythm. 'That's not all I handed over, is it?'

'No, it ain't, Mr Flint.' Popeye turned to John, all indignation. 'If you're trying to weasel out of this deal, you'd better divvy up the rest.'

'What rest? That's all you've given me!'

'I ain't playing games, John. You come up with all the cash now, or you get started on the distilling.'

John licked his lips, reading in Popeye's triumphant expression that he thought he had him backed into a corner. An uncontrollable urge to throttle the deceitful bastard made John lunge forward but his quarry dodged aside.

'Now, now, John. That ain't any way fer a man of your age to behave. We can do this civil—'

John stabbed a finger at Popeye's chest. 'I'm off out of town and you'd better leave me and mine alone, y'hear?'

'Just give us a few days to get started, Mr Flint.' Popeye sounded all concerned now. 'John's daughter, Rosie's,

99

been widowed, see, and her with a little 'un . . . he ain't hisself at the moment.'

'Don't you go spreading my business!' John roared, outraged.

'No harm meant, mate, y'know that.' Popeye sounded sincere. He turned to Flint. 'I bet if you ask nicely, John'll find you a couple of good vintages from way back when. Got some ain't yer, John? Can't save it all fer Christmas.'

Conor suddenly pushed off the mantelpiece and walked to the door. 'Way I see it, between you, you'd better come up with my monkey, plus twenty-five percent interest, plus another hundred for wasting my time.' He glanced between the two middle-aged men. 'Reckon you can do that, 'cos I'm out of patience.'

'Yeah, 'course . . .' Popeye flicked idle fingers but his receding hairline was shiny with sweat. 'Give us a couple of weeks, we'll sort this out.'

'You've got a few days.' Conor glanced at his watch and smiled. 'One of 'em's nearly over.' He walked up to John and gazed down at the man's ashen, lined face before turning to Popeye. 'So just to be clear, that's seven hundred and twenty-five quid.'

'Mental arithmetic,' Popeye chortled nervously. 'My boy used to be a dab hand at adding up, God rest him.' He tapped his forehead.

As Flint strolled out into the hallway Popeye was right behind him, still making promises.

John glanced at the tenners abandoned on the table. On impulse he picked them up, pocketing them. He knew Popeye would come back into the room itching to have a scrap. Now all John wanted to do was get home and get packed. He barged past Popeye and out of the house on the crook's heels, then loitered by the hedge. The moment the Humber drove off he hopped outside the gate, employing it as a barrier between him and Popeye.

Popeye came bursting out of the house, snarling, 'Give us that back, you thieving bastard, or get that still up 'n' running.'

John looked at the Humber turning the corner. Flint had seen him throw that cash on the table. So if the crook believed what he'd said about that being all Popeye had given him, he was in the clear. John knew he should give it back to Popeye but he could do with a bit extra while he was away from home. But that wasn't the main reason for him being unable to pull the notes out of his pocket. Popeye had tried to pin it all on him. He'd made out he'd handed over five hundred quid when in fact John hadn't seen a penny piece before today. He wouldn't have had five tenners slid into his pocket if it hadn't suited Popeye's devious purpose. Popeye deserved getting turned over for fifty quid for trying to turn him over for ten times as much.

'Don't come looking fer me 'cos I ain't coming back to Shoreditch for a while. And you ever pull a stunt like that again and I'll . . .' John let his threat tail off. A couple were strolling across the road.

'You'll do what?' Popeye scoffed.

'You've dropped yerself in shit dealing with the likes of him, and you can pull yerself out.' John saw his chance to get going. He nodded politely at the young couple and hobbled off up the road directly behind them.

He took a quick peek over a shoulder and saw a pair of crossed eyes on him. When Popeye jabbed a finger threateningly John swallowed noisily. He'd let revenge and temper get the better of him and might have just made things worse for Rosie, not better.

'What you doing up?'

'Hope's been a misery; I brought her downstairs for a breath of air. It's so close tonight.'

John limped slowly towards his daughter, who'd been pacing up and down in their small front garden with the child in her arms.

Rosie glanced at Hope, thumb in mouth, drowsing on her shoulder. She guessed it to be about nine o'clock from the faint shine on the horizon. She had on her dressing gown and slippers and she squatted down on the front doorstep with her daughter on her lap. John closed the gate and Rosie could see from his furrowed features that he was fretting on something.

'What's up, Dad?' she asked. 'Where've you been?'

'What is this? Spanish Inquisition?' John barked, before sighing regret. 'Sorry, love.' He stooped to ruffle his grand-daughter's fair hair. 'Sleepy head . . .' he crooned softly.

'I'm not checking up on you . . . just worried,' Rosie explained.

'I know, love. It's just there's a lot of sorting out to do before we go. Had a couple of people to see and bills to pay; posted 'em in the box now, though, so I can tick that off the list.' He sighed wearily. 'Where's Doris?'

'She was packing up stuff in the bedroom. I expect she's turned in now.' Rosie angled her head to read his expression. 'What needs sorting out? Is it something I can help with?' She smiled. 'I know you think I haven't got a clue, but I can write a cheque for the electricity and post a letter. I'll make sure the rent's paid too, while you're away.'

John gazed at his daughter's lovely face turned up to his. 'Sometimes, dear, I know you've got more sense in your little finger than I've got in me whole body.'

Again Rosie sensed something more than household accounts was behind her father's moping. She was about to dig further into it and ask him again where he'd been when the air-raid siren started wailing. She scrambled up, putting her daughter unsteadily on her feet. 'Oh, here we go!' She pointed up to a depressingly familiar object in the sky.

'That blighter's heading west.' John breathed in relief.

'What about those?' Rosie cried, squinting at the horizon. 'Oh good God, there are dozens of them.' She felt her stomach curdling in fear.

The dusky sky was becoming scarred with fire and the humming sound grew louder as a host of V1 rockets, scattered across the heavens, speeded in their direction.

'Come on, Dad, quickly . . . cellar.' Rosie again scooped her daughter into her arms. 'We could be down there for hours before the all clear. I wanted a good night's sleep, too.' Sensing her father wasn't right behind her Rosie glanced over a shoulder. He was by the gate staring at a car, its shaded headlights dying, parked at the opposite kerb. She had been half aware of a vehicle stopping but hadn't taken much notice of it.

Now she did; she couldn't clearly see the driver, but the glowing end of a cigarette was visible in the gloomy space above the steering wheel. 'Who's that? D'you know him, Dad?' The sudden tension in Rosie's chest was caused as much by her father's hunted expression as the imminent danger from the German attack.

'Get inside, Rosie,' John croaked. 'Go now!' he thundered when she hesitated.

She did as she was told, colliding with Doris in the hallway as the woman scurried down the stairs.

'Let's get that front door shut. Is yer father home?' Doris demanded, agitated.

'He's just outside. He won't be a tick.' For some reason Rosie kept to herself her suspicion that John had gone to speak to the car driver. She thrust her daughter into Doris's arms. 'You take Hope to the cellar; I'll help Dad down the stairs.' She knew Doris didn't mind her taking the brunt of the heavy work where John was concerned.

Rosie rushed into the front room. A tremor from a bomb a few days earlier had put a diagonal crack in a windowpane. The glass had been criss-crossed with tape to prevent lethal flying shards in an explosion. She gingerly lifted an edge of blackout curtain to peer into the street. Rosie watched her father steady himself against the vehicle then duck down to speak to the driver. Fascinated, she saw the stranger lower the window and she caught a glimpse of a strong male profile. Rosie certainly didn't recognise him. He appeared younger than any friend of her father's she'd known. A moment later John was hurrying in an uneven gait back towards the house and Rosie rushed to meet him in the hallway.

'Who was that, Dad?' She took her father's arm, supporting his weight as they started to descend to the cellar.

'Nobody important . . . just somebody come to say goodbye.'

'At this time of the night?'

John held back as Rosie tried to shift him down to the next step. He turned, gazing at his daughter's frowning face. 'I want you to come with us on Friday,

Rosie,' he burst out. 'It ain't safe here; you're acting daft staying, and you know it.' He sounded angry and frustrated yet spoke in a voice that was pitched to prevent his wife's hearing.

'We've already spoken about my job. I thought you'd accepted I need to stay in London and do my bit.' When he avoided her eyes Rosie asked quietly, 'Are you worried about that bloke in the car, Dad?' As far as Rosie was aware there was only one sort of dodgy business her father had ever been in: distilling. He'd been lucky not to have ended up in gaol considering the amount of moonshine he'd dispatched from their cellar, but he'd sworn on her life he was finished with all that.

'What did he want with you, Dad?'

'Don't question me. Just listen to me,' John hissed.

Rosie remained quiet, chewing her lower lip, but though her father's mouth worked he seemed to be finding it difficult to spit out what he wanted to say.

'Frank Purves came round here one day when you was out and tried to force me into starting up me still again,' he eventually burst out. 'Told him to go to hell.' He winced at his daughter's appalled expression. 'That's why I want you to come with me. Just want you out of his way, dear, in case he calls by looking for me again. He thinks I'm going to Wales; I told him that to throw him off the scent, but he could turn up to check that I've not spun him a yarn about scarpering.'

'That wasn't Frank Purves outside in the car,' Rosie ventured, finally conquering her shock. 'That fellow looked far younger.'

'Business associate of Frank's, he is, name of Conor Flint. You know the sorts Popeye knocks about with, so 'nuff said on that score.'

'What you two doing up there? Want a hand, Rosie, getting him down the steps?' Doris called out. 'Hang on, I'll put Hope down on the mattress and be with you.'

'No, it's all right,' father and daughter chorused.

'I'm not bothered by either of them, Dad, honestly,' Rosie whispered. 'If anybody comes looking for you I'll soon tell them to sling their hooks. And if they don't get the message, I'll get the Coppers on them—'

'No!' John interrupted, vehemently shaking his head. 'Whatever you do, don't go involving the police. Ain't done, Rosie!' he stressed. 'No, I'll stay with you.' He suddenly swiped a hand about his quivering mouth. 'Ain't leaving you behind on yer own 'cos it's too risky. I'll have a word with Doris about taking the little 'un with her on Friday. 'Least that'll get Hope somewhere safe, then I'll join them later on when this is sorted out.'

'You'll do no such thing!' Rosie shook her father's arm. 'I've said I can look after myself. I'm not a child, you know. I'm a parent myself.' She gave a grim smile. 'I'm no use to Purves or his pals 'cos I don't know the first thing about distilling, and even if I did I'd refuse to give 'em the time of day. They won't waste their time with me. So you're going, and that's that.'

John started to protest but an explosion close by made him quickly resume descending the cellar steps, leaning heavily on his daughter's shoulder. 'I hope you're right, Rosie. But if you're not, don't say I didn't warn you.' He sank his bony fingers into her soft flesh, reinforcing the seriousness of his concern.

John lay down on the mattress, pulling the blanket over himself and his wife. He turned sideways, watching his daughter and granddaughter. Rosie was cuddling Hope, softly singing a nursery rhyme and tickling her under the chin to distract the child from the lethal commotion that ebbed and flowed above their heads.

He closed his eyes, playing over in his mind the one-sided conversation he'd just had with Flint. He'd told him again, truthfully, about Popeye stitching them both up. Flint hadn't commented, he'd just sat, smoking, in that eerily thoughtful way of his, while the rockets roared closer.

John had burbled out everything he could remember about the day Popeye had turned up out of the blue, and at the end of it the fellow had given a nod as though in acceptance. But John couldn't bring himself to pull the fifty pounds out of his pocket and hand it over to its rightful owner. If Flint knew he'd taken back the cash off Popeye's table he'd smell a rat. As it was, Flint seemed to believe Popeye was the culprit.

But as John had limped towards his front door he'd glanced back and seen Flint staring at the house in a way that had made the blood in his veins run cold. But it'd been too late then to run back and beg the fellow to take the fifty pounds and never come back.

CHAPTER TEN

'Tea should be brewed by now. Pour yer dad his cuppa, will you, Joey, while I see to Vicky?'

Joey Grimes raised his chin from his palms. He'd been sitting reading at the table but he folded his *Dandy* comic, then lifted the woolly-clad pot by his elbow. With a private wink for Rufus he snaffled a Bourbon out of the tin and put it on the saucer by the custard cream Gertie had placed there earlier.

'Good lad,' Rufus praised his son, eagerly taking a swig from the deep brown brew. He fidgeted, making himself comfortable and his injured hand, braced on the chair arm, buckled and he upset the tea with a yelp.

'No better'n a bleedin' baby, am I!' he bawled in frustration, hurling his soggy biscuits to the floor. 'Can't even get tea to me mouth without wetting meself.' He gazed forlornly at the dark stain down the front of his trousers. 'Burned me balls 'n' all . . . not that that matters much,' he muttered, throwing his wife a sour look. 'They're out of action . . .'

'Fer Gawd's sake! What now?' Gertie spat, getting up

108

from where she'd been crouching by her daughter. She lifted Victoria off her potty and wiped the child's bottom.

'Pull her knickers up, Joey, while I see to your father,' Gertie called over her shoulder, halfway to the kitchen for a towel to dry off Rufus.

Obediently Joey jumped up again and helped his little sister get dressed before settling her on the couch. He perched beside Victoria, solemnly watching his parents battling their irritation. But Joey knew that things had turned bad for them as a family long before his father had been shipped home on a stretcher. His mum and dad had started arguing before Vicky had been born, worsening after his little brothers had been killed in an air raid. And Joey knew it was his fault that Adam, Simon and Harry had been left alone in the house that night. If he'd stayed at home with them he'd have woken them up and got them to the safety of an air-raid shelter. But instead he'd chased after his mum who'd hared out to stop his dad battering another bloke. Up until then his mum had made sure to keep all her kids close by, especially after dark when an attack was likely, in case they needed to dive into an underground shelter.

'Here, use that while I clear up this bloody mess you've made.' Gertie lobbed a cloth her husband's way.

Rufus dabbed his trousers, glancing sullenly at his wife. 'Need me other pair to put on.'

'Well you can't have 'em, 'cos I only did the washing this morning and none of it's quite dry yet.' Gertie carried on crawling around on her hands and knees by his feet, using a rag on the rug to soak up the spilled tea and mashed biscuits.

'Get chaps, I will, sitting about in wet stuff,' Rufus grumbled.

'You want to try dunking sheets out in that bleedin' washhouse; that'll give you something to complain about,' Gertie came back at him. She snatched the towel he was flicking aimlessly at his lap and took over mopping him with vigour.

As far as Rufus was concerned he was still master in his own home, even if he was a war cripple. He looked in disgust at his withered right arm that terminated in a hand with just three digits. The thumb and index finger were rotting somewhere in France, or more likely had been eaten by rats by now. His right leg had also taken some shrapnel and was weaker than the left, making him slow getting about.

'For heaven's sake!' Gertie exploded as she heard somebody rattling the handle on the kitchen door. 'If that's the milkman, Joey, tell him I ain't in and I'll settle up with him next week.'

'Ain't interruptin' anything, I hope?' a lewd voice asked a moment later. The new arrival had entered the parlour to find Gertie on her knees fiddling with her husband's trousers.

'Fuck's sake, look who's here,' Rufus breathed in shock.

Gertie scrambled up and gawped at her brother. Slowly her eyes filled with loathing. Joey fidgeted by the door, shamefaced; he was very aware of the feud between his parents and their visitor. He had recognised his fugitive uncle straight off although none of them had spoken to him for years.

'Don't blame him,' Michael Williams said, as his sister's reproachful gaze fixed on her son. 'He tried to block me way but I thought it was time we all had a little get-together. Lucky Joey did let me in or I'd've clumped the little bastard.' Michael glowered at the nephew he'd grown to resent, then at the niece he'd never met. 'Oh. hang on . . . wrong one. That's the bastard, ain't it?' He nodded at Victoria, gazing up at him with limpid brown eyes.

It was her daughter's shy smile for the uncle who'd insulted her that made Gertie's control snap. 'You mind your mouth around my kids!' she hollered, slapping out. But even with his disability her brother managed to swipe her aside so she bounced down beside Victoria on the couch.

'What d'you think yer doin' to my wife?' Rufus snarled, manfully struggling up from his chair. His arm and leg wobbled and he fell back, screwing up his face in frustration.

'Ain't so easy, mate, is it, throwing yer weight around when you've got a useless mitt?' Michael sauntered closer, raising the stump that had once been his right arm. He sniggered at Rufus's humiliation, grabbing him and holding their maimed limbs together, comparing them. 'Almost snap. You're still better off 'n me. Got a piece of paw left, ain't yer, Roof?'

'Fer what bleedin' use it is.' Rufus wrenched himself free of his brother-in-law.

Gertie had watched the two men with mounting disbelief as they swapped self-pity. 'You gonna let him speak to me and Vicky like that?' She sprang to her feet, rage shaping her features as she advanced on her husband.

Rufus coloured up, aware of his cowardice but inwardly making excuses for it. He knew he could have another go at staying upright and swinging a left hook. But Midge – as his short-arsed brother-in-law was nicknamed – was no pushover despite his size; the weasel

111

would play dirty and knee him in the nuts before he could nip aside.

A few years back Rufus had been a fine figure of a man: broad and strong. He could have taken Midge on with one hand tied behind his back. But he was fat and unfit now from sitting day in day out in an armchair. He regretted not having heeded his wife when she'd nagged him to stop wallowing and get out of the house for a walk after he'd been discharged from hospital.

Rufus knew he'd never live down his pint-sized brother-in-law flooring him . . . not when over the years he'd often put Midge on his back with no more effort than was needed swatting a fly. To his son he was still a hero, if a bit battered around the edges, but he wouldn't be for long if he acted on the message blazing at him from his wife's despising eyes.

'He's just having a lark, ain't yer, Midge?' Rufus mumbled. 'Not funny, though; tell yer that fer nothing.'

'I see. Lost yer bottle!' Gertie snapped in disgust. 'I'll deal with him then.' She surged at Michael, fists on hips. 'You're not welcome here. On yer way, or I'll call the police.' Gertie pointed at the door. 'Don't think I won't. The law's still after you. Couple of plain clothes come round not so long ago asking after your whereabouts.'

It was a lie; it had been years since the police had bothered her with questions about her brother because he was wanted for murder and desertion from the navy. Gertie had known where he'd been hiding, too, and had later regretted not having grassed him up when she'd had the chance.

'Don't take it to heart, Gert; just a bad joke, like Rufus said,' Midge scoffed, brushing past to sit down next to his niece. 'Beauty, ain't she, like her mum? Looks like you. That's handy, ain't it?' He tickled the little girl under her chin, making Victoria giggle. Slyly his eyes slanted up, tormenting Gertie. 'Any more tea in that pot?' He nodded at the table.

Gertie swung Victoria up in her arms, out of Midge's reach, not deigning to answer him. She darted glances between the room's occupants. She didn't want to create a bad scene in front of her children, but she couldn't trust herself to remain in her hateful brother's company without ending up ripping his eyes out.

'You're taking a risk, ain't yer, showing yer face round here?' Rufus knew his wife was boiling up and tried to defuse things by changing the subject. Besides, he was very curious to know what had brought Midge back to his old stamping ground where he might get recognised and arrested. If he was taken to court on a murder charge, Rufus reckoned that Midge'd swing because he knew his brother-in-law had killed a fellow seaman before deserting. Oddly, Rufus was glad Midge had resurfaced; if the law caught up with him it'd do what he was itching to do, but couldn't: put the swine six foot under.

'Old Adolf's done me a favour sending over them rockets.' Midge grinned. 'Coppers are too busy helping to shovel up bricks and bodies to bother coming after us duckers 'n' divers.' He chuckled then began to sing 'Happy Days Are Here Again' in a tuneless croak.

'Could be you'll be one of them bodies getting shovelled up if you stick around these parts.' Gertie gave a sour laugh. 'If there's any justice in this world, that is.'

'Got the luck o' the devil, me.' Midge sniffed cockily. 'But when me number's up, I'll go quietly. So I'll kip on the couch tonight, shall I?' he tacked innocently onto the end.

'You certainly won't!' Gertie stormed. 'I'll turn you in meself if I have to, to get you outta my house.'

'Don't think you will, sis. I know things . . . remember . . .' Midge eyed Joey, sitting tensely on the couch, listening to every word.

Gertie glanced at her son, too. At thirteen Joey was old enough to pick up on a lot of the hidden meaning in adults' talk. And she didn't ever want him knowing that his little sister had a different dad from him. Her brother was hinting at letting that cat out of the bag if he couldn't get his own way. It would kill Rufus, too, if word got round that his wife had got knocked up with another man's child and was rearing it as his own. All her husband had left was his pride; he spent every day in the same clothes, in the same chair, smiling vacantly into space, sheltering in the memories of the confident active fellow he'd once been.

But they still held the ace in the pack: nobody, other than her and Rufus, knew for sure who had fathered Vicky. So her brother could threaten all he liked but he was spitting in the wind, and she told him so.

Midge ignored his sister's triumphal hiss. 'I got some news about a pal of ours. Want to hear it?' He grinned at Rufus, banking on his brother-in-law not being able to turn down a gossip about old times.

Gertie watched Rufus's features lift and felt her spirits sink. He'd told her once that if he ever crossed paths again with her brother he'd kill Midge after what he'd done to their family. Now it looked like he wasn't going to make good on that promise any time soon.

'You've got ten minutes,' Gertie snapped close to her

brother's ear before she marched towards the door, carrying Victoria in one hand and the sloshing potty in the other. 'Don't make me come back and repeat meself, 'cos I meant what I said about calling the Old Bill if you don't leave.'

'I meant what I said 'n' all,' Midge purred through a set of dirty uneven teeth, giving his nephew a significant nod. He couldn't prove that his niece was a cuckoo in Rufus's nest, but Midge strongly suspected Victoria was the sprog of a fellow that Gertie used to char for a few years back. Midge had caught them at it on one occasion. The repercussions of him spying on his sister and her lover, then recounting what he'd seen to Rufus, had been the reason the couple had been out, arguing and fighting in the street, on the night their home was demolished with three of their sons in it. Before the tragedy they'd barely tolerated him; now he knew they hated him even though in his opinion he'd done nothing wrong. The way Midge saw it, he'd done Rufus a favour telling him his missus was cheating on him, even if he had done it out of spite.

'Joey! Come on, I need a bit of shopping fetched in.' Gertie narrowed her eyes at her husband on quitting the parlour. As soon as her brother had gone, she'd have something to say to Rufus.

Once Joey had been sent up the road for tea and milk, Gertie stopped slamming around in the kitchen and tiptoed to hover outside the closed parlour door, listening to the conversation going on inside.

'Seen Popeye a few times lately,' Midge said. 'He was asking after you.'

'Yeah? What d'you tell him?' Rufus replied. He was well aware that his wife was irate, and the longer Midge stayed put, to rub it in that he'd leave when he was ready and not before, the more inadequate and guilty Rufus felt at not being able to protect his family from this man.

Midge shrugged, fishing out of a pocket his pouch of Old Holborn. With great deliberation he opened it, pulling out papers and tobacco to have a smoke. 'Nothing much *to* tell Popeye, being as I ain't spoken to you in so long.' Midge rolled the cigarette one-handed on his knee. 'He knew you'd been invalided home, so that weren't news to him.'

'How d'you find out what happened to me?'

Midge's tongue swiped an edge of a Rizla, then he stuck the limp cylinder in his mouth and struck a match against the box wedged between his knees. 'Make it me business to know about me family, don't I?' he said from behind the wagging cigarette. 'I ain't been far away, never fear.'

Rufus could believe that. If anybody could slither out of sight when required, it was this man. He wouldn't be surprised to discover that Midge had been spying on them for some time, picking the right moment to make his presence known.

At one time they'd been partners in crime, and done pretty well at it, too, hoisting goods in Popeye's gang, until Midge injured his hand on a job and the wound turned gangrenous, resulting in an amputation. Then, like a row of dominoes, they'd all slowly toppled. Even Popeye had suffered. Rufus blamed his brother-in-law for his little sons' deaths. In the aftermath of that terrible night, crazy with grief and fired up with revenge, Rufus had sworn he'd get even. He'd gone looking for Midge to batter him, but his brother-in-law had already disappeared, something he was a dab hand at doing.

116

Midge winked, as though reading his brother-in-law's thoughts about their past antics. 'We had some larks in the old days. Remember that time we nearly got caught with a barrow-load of army boots, right outside Popeye's warehouse?' Midge snorted back a guffaw. 'You told those two rozzers that we was taking 'em down to the docks to get shipped out to the artillery. *And* they believed you.' Midge dragged on his wonky roll-up and started coughing. 'Hand it to you, mate, you had the gift of the gab that night,' he croaked. 'If they'd've opened up that warehouse and taken a gander inside, we'd all have been for it.' Midge merrily shook his head. 'Popeye owes you a good drink 'cos he'd still be serving time over that one.'

'So would we be,' Rufus pointed out sourly. A moment later he was reflecting that he'd sooner have done a bit of hard labour than volunteered: at least he'd still have his health and his little sons. If he'd been in prison, then Midge wouldn't have been able to wind him up over Gertie's affair. Left alone, he and his wife would've worked things out between themselves, but Midge hadn't wanted that. Midge was only happy when he was making everybody else as miserable as he was.

Midge struck another match and relit his dying cigarette. He puffed away on it while thinking along similar lines to Rufus that he'd've been better off doing a stretch inside. If he'd got arrested, instead of returning to his ship, he'd not have heard Jack Chivers calling him a little runt. Midge was sensitive about his size and the rating had always delighted in belittling him. So Midge knifed him, but he'd not expected the stupid bastard to die . . . just lick his wounds a bit and keep his gob shut in future.

Rufus stared into space, torn between pride and regret as he recalled how after his road-sweeping shifts for the council he'd go bomb chasing at night in Popeye's gang. When an explosion took out a shop front, he and his cronies would be waiting to dive in and pinch everything they could reach. Domestic houses had also yielded rich pickings. People would return home from the underground shelters to find they'd been cleaned out during a raid. When he thought about it now, Rufus felt guilty about having thieved from ordinary folk. The affluent shopkeepers he couldn't give a toss about. He might have damaged his arm but the chip on his shoulder was still in place.

After the spoils were divided Rufus would have his pockets full of cash to spend. He'd have a different tart every night when Gertie gave him the cold shoulder and he'd live it up in Soho dives till the early hours. But after his sons had perished Rufus had put all his bad ways behind him, sure he was being punished for his sins. He'd gone to fight the Boche and avenge his dead boys to make amends. And look where that had landed him: back at home, no use to anybody.

'Popeye's got some stuff needs doing; asked me to find out if you was interested in coming out of retirement.' Midge sat back comfortably on the couch, crossing what was left of his arms over his chest.

'Sod me!' Rufus chortled. 'He's hit rock bottom if two cripples are all he can afford.' He was starting to enjoy his chat with his brother-in-law and that made him feel guilty. Midge had caused bad trouble for him and Gertie and Rufus knew the last thing he should be doing was having a laugh and a joke with him. He grimaced to show his lack of interest in the work, adopting a bored expression and staring out of the window.

Midge sensed that Rufus was going cold on him so decided a bit of flannel wouldn't go amiss to bring him round. Midge had always been able to manipulate his brother-in-law. It was one of the reasons why his sister hated him. But this time he'd need to tread carefully or Gertie would burst in on them. He knew the nosey cow was just outside the door with her ear pressed to the keyhole. 'You 'n' Gertie done well to hold it all together after what the Germans did to yer.' Midge eyed his brother-in-law from under his brows, nodding solemnly, 'Them little boys didn't deserve to go like that.'

'Seem to recall you had a hand in it,' Rufus snarled.

'Weren't my fault, mate, you know that. We might've had our fallings out over the years but Jerry bombed yer house, not me.'

Rufus flicked a hand as though he couldn't be bothered arguing with Midge. In fact he would've loved to be able to jump up and smack the smug smile off his brother-in-law's chops.

'You might have taken a few knocks in France, getting back at 'em for what they done to yer, but I bet you took a few of them Krauts down first, didn't you?'

Rufus gave a sulky nod, his mouth tilting in the start of a smile.

Midge tapped his skull, 'Can see you've stayed strong up here, where it counts, ain't yer Roof?'

'Had to . . . family relying on me, ain't they?' Rufus sat straighter in the chair, chest puffing out. He turned to face his brother-in-law. 'So, what sort of pony work has Popeye got that suits a couple of cripples like us, then?'

'Might be that cripples are just what he needs.' Midge squinted craftily through a haze of tobacco smoke.

'Ain't going out begging, and that's final,' Rufus stated. 'If I wanted to use a crutch and rattle a tin, could do it on me own. Don't need him.'

'Ain't begging,' Midge replied scornfully.

Rufus frowned. 'Gonna explain then?'

'Popeye's still doing his printing . . .' Midge offered up the titbit then got up with a comfortable stretch and placed his open pack of rolling tobacco on Rufus's lap.

Rufus had watched how his brother-in-law made himself a smoke with one hand and fierce concentration. He knew that Midge's lazy gaze was on him, challenging him to match his skill. And Rufus would like a fag. He'd felt jittery having this man turn up on him out of the blue, and he hadn't yet fully calmed down.

Midge and Popeye were ghosts from Rufus's past and just hours ago he'd have said he didn't want memories of them haunting him. But Midge was hinting some cash might be in the offing, and Rufus definitely liked the sound of that. He pushed his good hand into the tobacco. 'Well, spit it out, if you've got something to say.'

'Pop's counterfeiting ration books and wants our help with it 'cos he knows he can trust us. That's what he said.'

Rufus slowly withdrew his empty fingers from the tobacco pouch. 'Eh?' He screwed up his features as his hopes died. He knew nothing about working a printing press but guessed he'd never manage it one-handed.

'Pop's sidekick's had his collar felt delivering ration books to clients. The bloke didn't grass Pop up, though. Bad news for Pop was that he had to shell out to keep the geezer's missus sweet. She went berserk when her husband went inside and started threatening calling the police unless she got a payout.' Midge sat down again on the couch as he got further into his tale. 'Pop's lost a lot of stock, 'cos the ration books the bloke had on him when he was nicked got confiscated. Pop needs to get going again quick 'cos he borrowed the hush money off a docker, name of Flint. And Flint's not happy 'cos he was expecting a nice big consignment of rotgut off Popeye's contact in return for his cash. Now he wants his money back and Popeye ain't got it.'

'Sounds like a right mess to me,' Rufus said.

'And me,' Midge chirruped. 'Thing is, s'long as I get paid I don't give a toss how Popeye sorts the rest out.'

Rufus grimaced agreement to that. 'So . . . we're supposed to take over from Popeye's pal who's in prison?'

Midge gave a nod.

Rufus threw back his head and chuckled softly. 'I like old Pop's sense of humour. He wants two blokes who ain't got a full set of hands between 'em to do deliveries.'

'We'd be inconspicuous . . . left alone, Pop said. Nobody's gonna suspect two poor old soldiers are up to no good now, are they?'

Rufus was listening intently. 'How we supposed to be getting about delivering these here fake ration books? Takes me ten minutes to get to the corner shop.'

'He's got a car we can use.'

This time Rufus exploded in laughter, his fat belly wobbling and tears of mirth running down his cheeks.

Midge chuckled too but he carried on explaining: 'Left-hand drive, it is; Pop got it shipped in cheap, just before the war started 'cos he fancied a French coupé to show off to the tart he likes down the pub.'

Midge got up from the sofa, settled his backside on the chair arm next to his brother-in-law and demonstrated steering with his left hand. He nudged Rufus. 'Now you change gear.' He nudged Rufus again, harder, when he refused to play along.

Rufus mimed wrenching on a gear stick and handbrake with his left hand.

'See, easy as pie.' He winked at Rufus. 'Let you drive once in a while, if yer like, and I'll do the gears.'

'Sounds daft to me,' Rufus said, but there was a smile in his tone.

Outside in the hallway, Gertie had almost danced on the spot in rage when she heard her husband laughing with the brother-in-law he was supposed to detest. When she'd heard Midge talking about her dead sons she'd almost burst in to batter him for daring to mention them. But she'd not done so because she'd wanted to learn more. And the rest of what she'd overheard had shocked and worried her.

Of course she'd known Rufus had been a member of Frank Purves' little gang of looters, so hearing the two men reminiscing about that hadn't come as a surprise. Years ago she'd been pleased to share the benefits of her husband's illegal profits. He'd brought her in clothes and household goods that had been filched from top stores, although he always kept for himself the cash he earned from Pop. But that had all occurred during the height of the Blitz, when things had seemed delightfully carefree compared to the dogged unhappiness of their lives since.

Now she'd lost three of her beloved children, and her husband. Oh, Rufus might be a physical presence in her life, but he wasn't the man she'd fallen in love with and married. That strapping attractive fellow no longer existed. When she thought hard about it, she realised Rufus might just as well have been buried along with Adam, Simon and Harry. He'd not withered in France, but on the night he'd unearthed three small bodies from the rubble of their home.

Much as Gertie wished her husband could get himself out of the house to work, becoming involved again with Midge and Popeye seemed like trouble they could all do without. Suddenly her mounting fury and anxiety were no longer controllable. She burst into the room and swung a glare between her husband and brother.

'Time's up . . . get going.' Gertie jerked her head at the door.

Midge got to his feet without comment. He removed his pack of Old Holborn from Rufus's lap and rammed it into a pocket.

'Be seeing you then,' Midge said cheerily.

Rufus mumbled a reply, regretting that he'd not managed to get a smoke out of Midge. A fag was one of the few pleasures left to him and Gertie was always grumbling about the cost of tobacco. But he was thinking about the carrot his brother-in-law had dangled. It sounded a ridiculous scheme, but he'd thought that when Midge had first tempted him with the bomb lark. And how he'd love a return to those days.

'Don't ever show yer face here again.' Gertie followed her brother out into the kitchen to the back door, shoving the bolt home after him the moment he was outside.

She heard his laugh, triumphant and low. Midge was letting her know that he'd got what he came for: Rufus was his for the taking and she, and the kids, didn't matter.

CHAPTER ELEVEN

'Doing Mummy's shopping again, are yer, Grimesie?'

Joey's response to being taunted was to thrust two fingers up at the sniggering boys. They used to be his friends although they were in the year below at school. Joey didn't spend much time with any of his school pals now and couldn't wait to leave at the end of term and find work. Sticking close to his mum for the past few years had made him a joke figure amongst the lads he used to knock about with, but he didn't care. Joey had grown up since tragedy struck his family.

After his brothers' funeral his dad had made him promise to look after his mum when he went off to fight. His mum had been expecting Vicky then, and after she was born, staying at home had stopped being a chore for Joey. From the first peep at his tiny sister, he'd adored Victoria, and had gladly lent a hand with nappies and bottles. Now that she was older, toddling and causing mischief, Vicky still had him wrapped around her little finger. Joey regretted now having made excuses to skive off when his mum had asked him to mind his younger brothers. He'd give anything to have them back, sitting on the hearthrug with him, playing a game of cards. They'd been useless at it, too: too young to understand even a game of Snap. But he'd enjoyed teaching them as they'd gazed up at him with wide, admiring eyes, while their mum worked out in the wash-house.

One of the taunting boys made a lunge for the bag of shopping Joey was swinging in a hand. Instinctively Joey jabbed with a fist in the way his father had taught him, when Rufus had still been capable of giving him boxing lessons.

'I saw that, Joey Grimes,' a lecturing voice said.

A mousy-haired girl had been sitting on her front step, watching the boys while shelling peas into a colander. Wiping her hands on her pinafore, Becky Pugh got up and joined Joey as he carried on down the street, leaving the boys bawling abuse.

'You'll get into trouble,' Becky warned, crossing her thin arms over her middle. 'He'll go crying to his dad.'

'So what?' Joey shrugged. 'He started it.' A few years back no man in the neighbourhood would have come to their house to complain to Rufus Grimes about his son in case he got a thick ear. But things were different now. Much as his dad might want to defend him, Joey knew he couldn't.

He looked up, noticing in the distance somebody else capable of causing trouble for them. His uncle had just left their house and was bowling towards him in that cocky way he had. Deliberately, Joey crossed the road to avoid Michael.

'Who's that?' Becky nodded her head in Midge's direction, trotting after Joey. She'd also seen the short fellow swaggering out of the Grimeses' back gate.

125

'Nobody . . . he ain't nobody.' Joey muttered contemptuously. He slung Becky a frown as though annoyed at her tagging along when he was brooding on important stuff.

His uncle was too far away for Joey to read his expression, but Midge was sure to have a smirk on his ferret-like features. His turning up out of the blue seemed a very bad omen to Joey. He would never forget his brothers, but for all of their sakes he didn't want his uncle's spite breathing new life into a tragedy that had occurred years ago.

Becky huffed, trying to gain Joey's attention as he strode on down the street. She ignored the hint to get lost when she received another irritated look from him.

She liked Joey, and was sure that under his gruff exterior he liked her too. They'd both turned thirteen and Becky was ready for her first proper boyfriend. She glanced at Joey's stocky body and wiry auburn hair as they strolled side by side. His jaw and upper lip had a fuzz of gingery whiskers that made him resemble his father as he'd once been. Now Becky hardly recognised the big, strong neighbour who'd once kept the local men in awe of him.

'Oi, Joey, see you again soon, mate.'

Joey ignored his uncle's cheery shout because he knew Michael was trying to wind him up. Joey wouldn't take his bait in the way his mum and dad did. He stared straight ahead, swallowing the urge to spit in the gutter as they passed on opposite pavements.

Midge hated him, and Joey knew why that was: when his uncle had injured his hand on a looting spree the others hadn't wanted him along any more, slowing them down. Joey had taken Midge's place in the gang before he'd turned ten years old and had been the one nipping in and out of small spaces, gathering up the merchandise, in the way Midge used to do. He'd enjoyed the work, and the tanners he'd earned in wages. But Midge had let him know in snide remarks that he resented losing his job to a kid.

'He been visiting yer dad?' Becky asked. 'Looks like he's been in the wars too,' she remarked sympathetically. 'Old army mates, are they?'

'He ain't done nothing to be proud of, take it from me,' Joey said sourly, and let himself in the back gate.

'You should come to the station to see us off.'

Rosie shook her head, blinking back her tears. 'I can't, Dad.' She forced the words out past an enormous lump in her throat. She knew that if she went with them she might break down on the station platform and refuse to let go of her daughter. 'We'll say our goodbyes now, won't we, sweetheart?' she whispered, swaying her body to and fro with the little girl clasped tightly to her.

'There's no need fer goodbyes.' John gripped Rosie's shoulder. 'You can still come with us. We'll catch a later train,' he urged. 'I can see you're eaten up, love, at the thought of being without her. Get a suitcase packed on the quick and I'll get the taxi to come back in an hour . . .'

'Fer Gawd's sake! How many times does the girl have to say she's staying behind?' Doris interrupted. She was pulling on her white cotton gloves. She'd dressed in her Sunday best for the train trip to Kent, and was ready and raring to go. And nobody would have begrudged Doris her eagerness to get out of London. In the past few days the doodlebugs had hardly let up, and the damage to property and the loss of life was shattering the morale of even the sturdiest folk.

Rosie buried her face into her daughter's sweet-smelling hair. Last night she'd given Hope a bath and let the little girl choose which outfit she wanted to wear the following day for her big adventure. Even as Rosie had folded small clothes and packed them in a trunk it hadn't fully sunk in that Hope was going away from her . . . and, if fate decreed, they might never see one another again. Constantly Rosie impressed on herself that her sacrifice wasn't unique; every day mothers stood weeping on station platforms waving off their children to safety. Then they turned round and went to work, braving the dangers of driving buses or mobile canteens, never knowing if they'd survive another night of the Luftwaffe's bombardment.

Rosie avoided looking at her father; she knew if he begged her again to go with them, her resolve might yet waver despite her good intentions.

'Give her here . . .' Doris firmly removed the child from her mother's possessive clutch. 'Come on, that's the taxi driver getting impatient.'

A car hooter had blasted twice outside in quick succession.

''Bye, Dad.' Rosie hugged her father before cupping his face and brushing away the tears on his cheeks with her thumbs. Picking up his suitcase in one hand and Doris's in the other, she set off down the hallway, knowing that if she kept occupied she'd be less likely to break down as well. The little party filed out into strong summer sunshine. The moment he'd seen them emerge from the house the cabby had jumped out to open the back door of his vehicle.

The practicalities of getting the cases stashed away safely took Rosie away from her daughter. By the time the boot was slammed shut her little girl was sitting between John and Doris on the back seat.

John immediately wound down the window and put his hand out to take Rosie's. She kissed its clasped knuckles but her hand was soon weaving past to stroke her daughter's soft, smiling cheek. With a pang she realised that Hope was excited to be going on holiday without her.

'What did I tell you?' Rosie whispered.

'Be good girl . . .' Hope murmured with a grin for her mum.

'And what else?'

Hope shook her head to indicate she'd forgotten.

'Love you lots and lots.'

Hope repeated the mantra, blinking solemnly.

'She will be good . . . you're always good, aren't you, poppet?' Doris gave Rosie an encouraging smile as her stepdaughter pulled a handkerchief from a sleeve to wipe her eyes. An uneasy truce had formed between the two women following their bad argument on the day Rosie learned about the planned move to Gravesend.

'Take care of yourself, Rosie,' John called as the driver put the cab into gear. 'Remember, we're just a phone call away, any time of the day or night. Where's that number I gave you?' he demanded agitatedly, turning on the seat as the car started to move. 'Have you put it somewhere safe?' He poked his head out of the window to shout out.

Rosie pulled the scrap of paper from her pocket and shook it to reassure him.

As the cab picked up speed she saw that her dad had

helped Hope to her feet so the child could wave to her from the back window. Frantically, with both hands, Rosie waved until her shoulders ached but her daughter's face soon blurred to an indistinct pink oval as Rosie's eyes were awash with tears.

Hazel Scott dropped her crochet and jumped up from her armchair. 'You remember me, don't you?'

Rosie juggled the folded uniform in her arms to shake hands with her new colleague. 'Of course I remember you.' Rosie was pleased to see the young woman again.

'I'll let Scott introduce you to everybody,' Stella Phipps said, hands on her hips, creasing the three stripes on her navy-blue sleeve. There was a proprietary tilt to her chin as she glanced about the room scented with burned toast from the canteen. People were reading or doing handicrafts while waiting to go on duty at nine o'clock. 'Let's hope the peace and quiet continues for your first day, Gardiner. It might look like we're all skiving, but when the tide *does* come in . . . by God, we all know it.' She sighed. 'I'm going to be in my office for an hour or two, writing up the week's timetables with Norris. When Lawson turns up, she'll give you your instructions.' The deputy station officer strode off, wafting lavender water in her wake.

'You've not yet met Thora Norris, have you?' Hazel said. 'She's a shift leader, going off duty soon. Her and Stella are *good friends*, so they shut themselves in the office when they can, if you get my drift.'

Rosie didn't, and she frowned enquiringly.

'Pair of lesies, but nobody here turns a hair at that. A couple of the conchies have a smooch when they think nobody's about. We're very broad-minded at

130

Robley Road.' Hazel's mascaraed lashes drooped in a subtle wink.

Rosie bit her lip, suppressing a smile and hoping she wasn't blushing too obviously. She didn't think Hazel was joking but her candid account of some of her associates' love lives was startling and rather bizarre. It was also quite terrifying to Rosie. She liked Hazel, and hoped they'd become friends, but the brunette obviously enjoyed a gossip and that made Rosie determined to guard her tongue over her personal circumstances.

A woman who appeared to be knitting a length of scarf raised a hand to welcome Rosie.

'That's Clarice. She's all right, is Clarice. Office orderly; answers the phone and dishes out the dockets for incidents and so on. She'll be going on shift with us at nine o'clock. What time is it?' Hazel glanced at the clock on the wall. 'Oh, shame: no time for another cuppa. Have you eaten breakfast?'

'Had a chunk of bread and jam before I left home.' Rosie realised that the people who were due on shift with her were packing away their things. She'd reported for duty in Stella Phipps's office at eight fifteen that morning, but it seemed she wasn't the only one to have arrived early for work.

'Damn! I overslept again!' a newcomer announced, hurrying into the room, clipboard and pencil poised theatrically.

'Should've kicked him out of bed sooner,' Hazel muttered dirtily.

'Oh, really, Scott! You are crude.' The young woman approached them, smiling amiably. 'The DSO said somebody was starting today.'

'I'm Rosie Gardiner. Pleased to meet you.'

131

'I'm Janet Lawson, shift leader.' Two manicured fingers tapped briskly at a pair of stripes on her upper arm. She looked at her watch. 'I'd better go and start the inspection so we don't get lumbered cleaning up the previous lot's shoddy work. I found an upturned bucket of pigswill by the shed yesterday. I know there's a water shortage, but they could've put a bit of elbow grease behind a broom.'

Rosie watched the pretty redhead disappear, admiring her outfit. 'She looks very smart.' Rosie had noticed that Janet's uniform was of far better quality than the safari-style serge jacket and plain navy-blue skirt and trousers that she and Hazel had been issued with. A gabardine cap with earflaps and a tin hat rested on the top of the clothing she was carrying, as did her auxiliary's badge.

'Her father's something big in the city so she's got plenty of money to splash. Janet gets her uniform specially tailored . . . unlike the rest of us, who have to make do with regular kit.' Hazel hitched her thick navy skirt to display that her black stockings had an obvious darn in them. 'All sorts volunteer to be auxiliaries, you know,' she added. 'We've got posh ones and intellectual ones . . .' Hazel nodded at a grey-haired fellow who was stuffing a novel into a pocket of his navy-blue fatigues. 'Jim Warwick's a university professor. He reads poems aloud to us sometimes. He mucks in as a driver in between his lectures. No airs and graces . . . unlike some.'

Having heard his name mentioned, Jim gave a polite nod and Hazel made proper introductions.

'Right, come on then, Rookie,' she said. 'You'd better get dressed for action. I know I've got to clean the inside of our ambulance so no point putting it off. They do get in a right state.' She grimaced revulsion. 'As you can imagine. You can lend a hand, if you like.' Hazel led the way to the door. 'I work as Tom Anderson's assistant. You remember Tom, don't you, from the day of your interview?' Hazel indicated her partner, who was boxing some dominoes. 'Tom's a bloody good driver as well as being our mechanic. Perhaps when you pass your driving test I can pair up in a wagon with you instead.' Hazel giggled. 'It'd be a hoot, the two of us!'

Rosie hoped she didn't look too surprised, or disappointed. She'd imagined that ambulance auxiliaries tended the sick and wounded rather than the equipment. While waiting for an emergency call-out she'd visions of the staff winding bandages and fastening them neatly with safety pins, or making themselves useful in other ladylike ways.

'It's bloody hard work,' Hazel snorted, reading Rosie's mind. 'And not all guts and glory, or doctor-and-nurse romance, as you'll find out.' She nudged Rosie. 'Mind you, there is a particularly nice young GP who pops in and out at the Sparrow Road first-aid post.' She gave Rosie a knowing glance. 'You're in the market for a boyfriend, aren't you? I'll introduce you to Richard Clark!' she declared.

Rosie chuckled, but kept to herself her aversion to a romantic entanglement. It seemed there'd never be a dull moment with Hazel Scott about.

By lunchtime Rosie felt shattered even though she'd not lifted a single heavy stretcher. She could certainly understand why Stella Phipps had asked her if she considered herself to be physically fit. Regular housework was nothing compared to this.

Hazel hadn't been joking when she said the vehicles needed to be gleaming to pass muster. And they weren't even proper ambulances but motors that had been converted by adding a box van body and fittings for four stretchers. Makeshift or not, the inside had to be scrubbed from top to bottom and finished off with furniture wax, especially the stretcher runners to help them slide easily. The blankets had to be inspected and aired or replaced with clean ones. All the internal fittings had to be checked. While she and Hazel had beavered side by side, jostling and bumping in the confined space, Tom had washed and polished the Studebaker's coachwork before opening the bonnet. He'd topped up the tanks, then tinkered about with nuts and bolts. Tom had told Rosie that the basic engine checks would be her responsibility if she were successful in passing through as an ambulance driver, so she'd watched carefully as he dipped the oil and wrote his findings and the mileage in a logbook.

'So, what did you think?' Hazel asked when they sat down in the canteen at one o'clock to have lunch. 'Not what you signed up for?'

Rosie sank her weary spine against the chair back. 'Give me a while to recover and I'll let you know.' She took a hungry bite from a cheese sandwich. Never had anything tasted so good.

'So, what's next on the agenda?' she asked eventually, feeling energised by the two strong cups of tea she'd downed.

'You could tackle a bit of sewing, if you like. The spare set of blackout curtains are on the mending shelf. Any good with a needle and cotton?' Seeing Rosie's expression hovering between disappointment and disbelief, Hazel slapped the table in glee. 'I promise you, in a few weeks' time, when you're out on a call, soaked to the skin from fire hoses, you'll be crying out for a day like this.'

Rosie smiled; Hazel was no doubt right. But the thought of being doused with water was preferable to that of tending to the injured and dying. She'd briskly patched her dad up when the blast had torn open his leg and ever since she'd rescued Hope from her rubble-strewn pram she had managed to quash the debilitating fear that had been with her since the Café de Paris blast. What frightened Rosie now was that she'd be found wanting when her help was essential. Gertie's tale of begging the ambulance auxiliaries to save her sons' lives on the night they'd perished haunted Rosie's mind. Those women hadn't been able to grant Gertie her greatest wish, and Rosie sensed such inadequacy would be hard for her to bear when thoughts of her own daughter were never far from her mind.

CHAPTER TWELVE

'My dad's gone away.'

'Yeah, I know.'

His lazy answer threw Rosie, as did his unexpectedly casual attitude. When she'd first opened the door she'd been stunned into gawping idiotically. Previously she'd only caught a glimpse of his profile in the twilight, yet she'd immediately recognised him.

During their hushed conversation on the cellar steps as doodlebugs roared overhead her father had mentioned his name but now she couldn't bring it to mind. He was Frank Purves' friend, she remembered that, and Popeye was a person Rosie wanted nothing to do with, ever.

Suddenly she realised that her unwanted visitor might try to barge past to check if her dad was home, so she jerkily repositioned in readiness to shut him out. She prickled beneath the assessment of a pair of deep-blue eyes. 'If you know my dad's not here, why d'you bother coming round?'

'To see you.'

'To see me?' Rosie demanded hoarsely, unwittingly pulling the door open again.

'Last time I saw you, you were in your nightie.' He settled back comfortably against the porch wall. 'Can't blame a bloke for coming back for another look.' He cast a jaundiced eye over her navy-blue uniform. 'No such luck . . .' he muttered wryly.

Unable to conjure up a quick riposte, Rosie slammed the door in his face, her cheeks burning.

Nervously she yanked it open again. She didn't want him to know he scared her. He hadn't moved; he was still leaning against the rose trellis, hands in pockets, as though he'd known she'd succumb to curiosity about him. She was glad he hadn't started hammering on the door and brought the likes of Peg Price out to find out what was going on. The nosy old cow would enjoy gossiping about her having gentlemen callers in her father's absence.

'I know you're friends with Frank Purves, my dad told me,' Rosie challenged. 'He said one or other of you might come round asking after him. He's gone to Wales and he's not coming back.'

'Wales, eh?' The comment was heavily ironic. 'Taking the scenic route via Kent, is he?'

Rosie licked her dry lips. So his air of boredom was fake. He'd been checking up on them. 'Don't know what you're talking about. Now get lost or I'll . . .' Her voice tailed away. Her father had impressed on her not to use the police as a threat against him.

'Or you'll do what?' he prompted.

'Just get fucking lost,' Rosie choked and again made to close the door. But this time his hand stayed it, sending her stumbling back into the hall. She saw then that he

137

had a perfect opportunity to come in if he wanted to. He turned on the step, his height and breadth filling the open doorway. He'd only to put a foot over the threshold and close the door behind him.

'Phoning up your dad later, are you?'

Rosie bit her lip.

'Easy question: are you speaking to John later?'

Rosie clamped her lips together and gave a curt nod.

'Tell him I'd like my money back. He can put a cheque in the post.' A corner of his mouth quirked. 'Pick it up from here, shall I?'

'My dad doesn't owe you any money, he told me so. Go and bother Frank Purves about it.'

'Yeah, I would, but he's in hospital.'

Rosie's eyes widened in alarm, her heart drumming beneath her ribs.

'Nothing to do with me, honest.' He put his hands up in mock defence. 'Cross-eyed git got his finger trapped in his printing press and it gave him a nasty turn.'

Rosie frowned, wondering if the man was joking.

'Straight up. Tell you what, Mrs . . .?' He paused. 'What is your name, by the way?'

'What's yours?' Rosie threw back at him.

'Conor Flint. Call you Rosemary then, shall I? Frank Purves said your name was Rosemary although he didn't know your married name.'

Rosie darted to the door to slam it but he had stepped over the threshold and past her without so much as brushing her slender figure with a smartly suited elbow.

'Get out!' she ordered. 'If you don't, I'll call the police.'

Within seconds she regretted letting him panic her into saying that when he sent the open door into its frame by a flick of his fingers, cutting off the mellow

138

evening sun. Then he frowned at the ceiling. 'Not a good start, this, is it?'

Rosie remained silent and still for a few seconds, gathering her courage. Then she pointed at the door. 'Go away. I've got to go on late duty.' It was a lie; she had just finished work at Station 97 and had got home only about fifteen minutes ago. She'd been on the point of going to the phone box on the corner to have a chat with her dad before settling down for the evening. She wondered if Conor Flint knew she was lying and had watched her come in.

'Ambulance Auxiliary, are you?' He glanced at the badge pinned on her lapel.

'Very astute,' Rosie mocked.

'Where's your daughter?'

'Daughter?' Rosie echoed.

'You had a little blonde girl with you last time I saw you. Reasoned it must be the granddaughter your dad spoke about.'

'My dad spoke about her?'

'You going to repeat everything I say?'

'No, I'm going to repeat what I said. Clear off and don't come back.'

'I take it John didn't ask you to give me something?'

'Like what?' Rosie demanded after an uneasy pause.

'An envelope stuffed with cash?'

'The only thing I'll give you is a warning not to harass me or there'll be trouble.' Rosie knew that her empty threat hadn't worried him in the least, but for some reason he allowed her the victory.

'All right, I'm going. But when you speak to your dad tell him I said hello and that I want my five hundred quid.'

'Five hundred quid?' Rosie choked.

'You're doing it again.'

Rosie's fretting was interrupted by a ratatat on the door. Her heart leaped to her throat and she cursed beneath her breath that somebody else had turned up at such an embarrassing moment. She watched Conor Flint raise an enquiring eyebrow then, when she stayed put, he reached out a hand and turned the latch.

'Collecting for the Turners, Mrs Deane.' Peg Price thrust out a cup with a few coins in it. 'Spare something, can yer, for the poor souls?' The woman's sly eyes swung towards Conor. 'You can chip in, too, if yer like, Mr . . . ?'

'Flint,' Conor said, digging in a pocket.

'Ooh, you're a gentleman, Mr Flint; come back again, you can,' Peg simpered as he folded a crisp ten-shilling note and placed it on top of the copper and silver.

Rosie was aware of his smile deepening as she smothered a snort at Peg's praise. Then her neighbour whipped the cup gleefully in her direction.

'Oh . . . right . . . I'll just get my purse,' Rosie said although tempted to tell them both to sling their hooks.

The Turners had lived a few streets away until a rocket destroyed their home and possessions and killed their eldest son. Rosie was pleased that the local community was rallying round for the family. But she wasn't glad that she'd been wrong in thinking Peg might be oblivious to a stranger in the vicinity. The woman made it her business to keep her eyes peeled. The old muck-spreader must have been hovering behind her nets to have arrived so promptly.

'Saw you come in from work, dear, and thought I'd pop along before you went to bed.' Again Peg's crafty eyes veered between the couple. 'Won't keep yer long. Don't mean to interrupt nuthin'.'

'You're not,' Rosie ejected between her teeth.

'Oh, forgotten yer wedding ring, have yer?' Peg nodded at Rosie's bare fingers, her expression amused.

'No, I haven't; I don't wear it to work, 'case it gets lost, if you must know.' It was a lame excuse and Rosie felt blood flood her cheeks. Most married women never took off their gold bands, whatever they were doing. She turned away quickly to go to rummage for a few shillings, then realised it would be best not to leave her unwanted visitors alone together. Flint had already learned more about her because of the woman's big mouth. Peg would take a delight in telling him everything she knew . . . or suspected . . . about the widow *Mrs Deane*.

'I'll come up to yours with some money in a moment.' Rosie nodded at her front gate in a significant way.

''S'all right, I've got to be off.' Conor gave Peg a smile then glanced at Rosie. ''Bye, Mrs Deane. Be in touch . . .'

Rosie was sure he'd used her fictional name sarcastically, as though he also believed she'd never been anybody's wife.

'Don't run off on my account,' Peg called after him cheerily.

He didn't reply as he closed the gate after him.

'Sorry, love, didn't mean to scare him off like that. Charmer, ain't he?' Peg cocked her head at Rosie, challenging her to say what was on her mind. She didn't have to wait long to get a response from the younger woman.

'I bet you put those coppers in yourself, didn't you, just so you could make out you was collecting and come

141

round and spy on me? Well, you're wasting your time thinking you've found something to chew over with your cronies. He knows my dad, that's all there is to it.' Rosie was about to slam the door in Peg's face but she wanted to contribute something to the Turners' whip-round. She didn't like Peg Price but she did trust the woman to hand over what she'd collected. Rosie was halfway down the hall to fetch her money when Peg's remark drifted after her.

'So the mice are at play while the cat's away, eh?'

'Sorry . . . don't get you?' Rosie said, although she knew very well what Peg meant. The old witch still wasn't satisfied that she'd stirred the pot thoroughly enough.

'Good-looking feller . . . generous, too.' Peg shook the cup, smirking. 'Bet you get lonely don't yer, dear, now the family's gone down Kent?' She jerked her head after Conor. 'He asked me if John was in; told him he'd gone to Gravesend. Still come 'n' knocked, though, didn't he?' She leaned to pat Rosie's sleeve. 'Nobody would blame a pretty young widder wanting a bit of company, specially once the kiddie was out of the way.'

'You've got a dirty mind, Mrs Price.' Rosie marched back towards the door. 'And I'll thank you to keep your nose out of my family's business.' She dug in her uniform pocket for a bit of change to get rid of the woman quickly. Dropping a florin and a thrupenny bit in the cup, she shut the door in Peg's livid face. 'I told you he's a friend of my dad's!' she yelled through the panels, unable to stop herself again justifying Flint's presence in her house. Immediately, though, she felt irritated at herself for having done it.

'So now he knows yer dad's not about, he won't be

back, I suppose,' Peg crowed. 'I'd put ten bob on it that he will.'

Rosie heard the woman stomp off and slam the gate. Peg reckoned Flint would be back and, with a feeling that was part dread, part thrill, Rosie feared the old cow might be right.

Rosie unbuttoned her jacket. She was going to telephone her father later from the box on the corner, but she wouldn't mention Flint's visit. Her father would panic and want to come home and protect her. Rosie knew they had all settled in well at Doris's daughter-in-law's because John had told her so when they'd spoken on the phone at the beginning of the week. He'd put Hope on the line that evening. There'd been no tears from her daughter; her little girl had chattered on about cows in a field and her pink eiderdown. But Rosie had sobbed all the way back to her front door. She was missing her daughter dreadfully but it was the knowledge that Hope was content without her that really made her feel melancholy.

CHAPTER THIRTEEN

'What you so happy about?'

Gertie had lugged a bag of shopping into the kitchen to find Rufus whistling while making himself a pot of tea.

'Oh, just feeling in a good mood.' Rufus set another cup and saucer for his wife then hobbled jauntily to the pantry to fetch a bottle of milk. He splashed some into china then spooned in a generous amount of sugar.

''Ere! Steady! That's all we've got left.' Gertie snatched the bowl away, then dumped the shopping bag on the table to unload it. The few pounds of potatoes were stowed under the sink, together with a cabbage; the loaf and bag of broken biscuits she left out, ready for teatime. She wasn't feeling as chirpy as her husband, having just spent over an hour queuing at the bakery so they could have jam sandwiches later.

'There y'are . . . get that down yer, Gert.' Rufus pushed his wife's tea towards her on the wooden draining board. 'I'll put the wireless on, shall I? Just catch the end of *Worker's Playtime*. I know it's your favourite.'

Gertie mumbled thanks and watched Rufus as he disappeared into the parlour. She only half listened to the programme being tuned in because she was brooding on the remarkable change in her husband.

Rufus was brighter and moving about faster than she'd have thought possible after he'd been invalided home. Gertie knew who she had to thank for that, and it wasn't his doctor. It was her detestable brother. Midge was the one who'd got Rufus to buck his ideas up with talk of wages and old times. A couple of weeks had passed since Midge put in a surprise appearance but ever since his visit her husband had been in training for something.

Not so long ago Rufus would lie in bed till noon and not bother bathing till his wife told him he stank. Now he got up before she did and boiled a kettle every morning for a wash and shave. Rufus would never have offered to bring in the groceries; now he made a point of asking Gertie if he could go shopping to stretch his legs. He'd have done the trip today if he'd not been up to his elbows in soil. He was slowly digging them a vegetable patch . . . and that was a first in all their years of marriage. Previously, even cutting the hedge had been too much of a chore and Joey had been given the task as soon as he was old enough to handle the shears. Now Rufus only sat in his armchair during the day to take a breather from his hectic activities.

Midge hadn't been back – leastways, not while Gertie had been home. But she suspected that the swine had been in the house. She knew how her brother's mind worked; he'd loiter out of sight till he was sure that Rufus was on his own, then sneak round to the back door and persuade his brother-in-law to let him in. What annoyed Gertie was that Rufus had been denying any secret meetings had taken place when she confronted him.

Gertie had returned home once to a smell of tobacco smoke in the parlour. Rufus had said he'd rolled himself a smoke, but Gertie knew he was lying. He'd not had any tobacco or any cash to nip out and buy some. Sooner or later she'd catch the two of them cosying up and all hell would break loose.

'Off out later this evening, Gertie,' Rufus blurted in a way that was, at the same time, appealing and assertive.

Gertie put down the slab of margarine she'd been about slide onto the butter dish. 'Oh . . . where you off to then?' she demanded.

'Now don't go getting all narky, but me 'n' Midge got a job on. You're always saying we need proper money coming in, love,' he added persuasively.

'So owning up at last, are you?' Gertie snapped, ramming her fists on her hips. 'He's been in here with you while I was out. I knew it!'

Rufus opened his mouth on a lie, then let the truth roll off his tongue instead. 'Yeah, Midge called in and I'm feeling strong enough to go off to work this evening with him. We're doing some deliveries for Popeye.'

'Are yer now?' Gertie stormed. 'Forgot all about your little boys already, have you, 'cos your brother-in-law's waved a quid in yer face?'

'Ain't just a quid,' Rufus exploded excitedly. 'Got the chance to pull in more'n that, Gertie.' He saw the subtle change in his wife as she considered that information, so pressed home his advantage. 'I've told Midge to piss off a couple of times, love, but I know I'm just cutting me nose off to spite me face.' He shrugged. 'I hate him, he knows that . . .' He hesitated, darted a nervous look

Gertie's way. 'But weren't all his fault, what happened. We left the boys in on their own that night the house got hit.'

'Only 'cos of the trouble he'd started!' Gertie yelled, infuriated that Rufus seemed to be defending Midge. 'I wouldn't never have chased after you in the blackout if it hadn't been for him stirring things up between us in the first place!'

'I know . . . I know . . .' Rufus soothed her with clumsy pats. 'But I can use your brother to get what we need.' He gripped Gertie's shoulder with his good hand. 'Ain't only gonna have wages coming in, but lots more of this 'n' all.' He pointed at the bread and marge on the table. 'Be able to get you all the coupons you want, courtesy of Popeye's printing press. Meat, clothes, sugar . . .' With his three remaining fingers he spun the glass sugar bowl that she'd taken off him earlier. 'You name it, I'll get it for you.' He winked. 'Be able to get Vicky kitted out like a princess, won't we?' Rufus knew which buttons to push where his wife was concerned; her little daughter was the apple of her eye.

'So Popeye's gone into counterfeiting, I take it?' Gertie narrowed her gaze on her husband but she didn't push him away. She'd overheard snippets of that first conversation between Midge and Rufus. As the weeks had passed and nothing changed Gertie'd thought she'd listened to two invalids spouting hot air about rejoining Popeye's gang.

'I'm feeling chipper; don't spoil it for me, love.' Rufus massaged her shoulder. 'I ain't forgiving Midge, ever, just calling a truce. He's a nasty piece of work but he ain't a Kraut, is he? They're the *real* enemy. Don't mean I wouldn't like to see your brother punished. But the law could yet catch up with him.' He chucked his wife under the chin. 'Ain't gonna be asking him round fer tea, if that's what's eating at you.'

Gertie pondered on Rufus's tempting offer of extra rations and realised she'd have to trek further afield for them. If she regularly went to the same places she'd be asking for trouble. But she could certainly use more coupons: Joey was always hungry because Rufus expected the lion's share of every meal she prepared before she or the kids got a look in. But equally important to Gertie was the thought that she might have been handed on a plate a little income of her own: if Rufus gave her the coupons she'd have a chance to sell on any that were surplus to requirements.

'How good are these fake ration books? Ain't turning up at stores and getting me collar felt.'

'Better than the Real McCoy, Midge said.' Rufus gave his wife a spontaneous smacker on the lips and, unusually, Gertie let him.

A moment later, when Rufus tried to get his fingers inside her blouse, she elbowed him away, having heard her daughter whimpering. Vicky had been snoozing on the trip home from the shops and Gertie had parked the pram in the hallway.

'Go upstairs for ten minutes, shall we?' Rufus breathed against his wife's cheek. 'This is feeling stronger 'n' all . . .' he growled, thrusting her hand to a hardening bump at his groin.

'That's Joey back.' Gertie sprang away from her husband as she heard the key, hanging on string on the front door, clattering through the letterbox. Joey never knocked these days: ever since his father had gone away to fight he'd got used to letting himself in.

He was searching for work now he'd finished at school at the end of term.

'Had a good day?' Rufus greeted his son jovially despite his wife's rebuff.

Joey mumbled something indistinct. He had his little sister in his arms. He'd picked Vicky up from the pram where she'd been grizzling and straining against her reins to get out. 'Starving. Tea ready?' He gazed eagerly at the uncut loaf, standing Vicky on her feet.

'I'll do you a sandwich, if you want. You get your sister on the potty for me before she wets herself.' Gertie started sawing at the loaf. 'Any luck with a job?'

'Can start at Higgins, if I want; only seven shillings to begin with, though,' Joey muttered unenthusiastically. The butcher had told him he could have a week's trial as a delivery boy.

Rufus gave his son a playful punch in the shoulder. 'Saw you and young Becky Pugh out walking the other day. Taking her to the flicks Saturday, are you, mate, now you've got a job?'

Before Joey could deny everything his mother jumped to his defence, pointing the bread knife at Rufus. 'No, he ain't; he's got better things to do than spend his money on girls.' She glanced at Joey. 'Mrs Smith wants you to cut her hedge at the weekend. That'll boost your wages and keep you out of trouble.'

'Right . . .' Joey mumbled gruffly. He didn't mind doing odd jobs for neighbours and putting a bit of cash in his pocket. He got nothing off his mum and dad for all the chores he did, though he was willing to help out, especially with Vicky. He'd go to the moon and back for stardust for his little sister if she asked him to.

'Definitely be able to take the girl out if you're flush,

won't yer?' Rufus's teasing sent Joey scuttling out of the room to find the potty.

'Our luck's turning, Gertie, I know it. Things'll be back to how they were for us.'

Gertie gave a wan smile, spreading marge. 'Most of them old days weren't nothing to romanticise about, y'know.' She'd sounded wistful. The times her husband was fondly speaking of had seen her working at the Windmill during the day and charring most evenings as well while he was out either robbing or whoring till the early hours.

Yet when she'd had an affair with one of the clients she cleaned for, Rufus had gone berserk. He would never have found out about it, and would have believed Vicky his own daughter, but for her bastard of a brother telling Rufus from pure spite.

But in those early Windmill days she'd had all her boys. And that alone made Gertie yearn to put back the clock.

'Are you all right, Gardiner? Not about to keel over, dear, are you?'

'I'm cold, that's all.' Rosie had been supporting a hip against the ambulance to keep herself upright when Jim Warwick came over to see how she was bearing up. Briskly Rosie began banging together her rubber-gloved palms to warm her fingers and stir herself into action. Despite it being a summer night she was chilled to the bone.

Hazel Scott had warned her that she'd likely get soaked by fire hoses when on an incident, but it was the sight of the headless corpse that had put ice in her veins, not the mist from water jets. The woman's body had been strung in the remnants of her nightgown. It had been impossible for Rosie to look for more than a few seconds at the mutilated flesh wearing ribbons of cotton. Jim, describing himself as an old hand hardened to such sights, had guessed the deceased was about Rosie's age. The other three dead bodies were, it seemed, a family: husband, wife and teenage daughter had been unearthed sheltering together under what remained of their dining table.

The brigade was still dousing the ruins although the flames were almost extinguished and sizzling steam bathed the black atmosphere. Firemen were sloshing in and out of craters in their gumboots as they shifted position to redirect the hoses. Rivulets eddied and flowed off the toppled masonry, carrying debris that tumbled over Rosie's galoshes.

She stooped, picking up a soggy rag doll that had bumped against her foot.

'You'll get used to it,' Jim said kindly as he removed the toy from her fingers. He put it on top of a pile of rubble. 'If they heeded the siren and got to safety she might come back with her mum looking for it tomorrow,' he explained.

Rosie gazed at the dome of jumbled wreckage off to her right. Once it had been a corner shop and three terraced houses. She wished she'd not spotted the doll because it had brought bile back to her throat.

She'd believed that she'd cope with stomach-churning sights, but now she knew her arrogance had been foolish. Passing her St John Ambulance first-aid test with flying colours had boosted her confidence no end, but hadn't prepared her for what she'd been confronted with that evening. Beneath her rubber gloves, Rosie knew her hands were sticky with blood from the wadding she'd pressed on injuries while working at Jim's side. Like a true gent, he'd taken the brunt of the grisly work, leaving her to fetch and carry, and attempt to soothe the traumatised victims on this, her first major incident.

'Have they brought out any children?'

'Not as far as I know. People round here should've had the sense to evacuate their kids when the doodlebugs started arriving. I'm praying we've no more to load up.'

Rosie gazed up at the benevolent-looking heavens, twinkling with pretty stars, from which a couple of hours ago a V1 rocket had dropped, killing at least four people and maiming others. She thought of her beautiful little daughter, sleeping soundly in Kent, and silently echoed her partner's plea that there'd be no more bodies.

Jim's eyes crinkled at Rosie from beneath the brim of his tin helmet. 'My boy's too old to be evacuated: flies bombers – Wellingtons, to be precise.'

'Just the one boy?' Rosie asked, glad of something – anything – to talk about to distract her eyes and mind from the row of blanketed cadavers yet to be loaded into the ambulance.

Jim nodded. 'The wife wanted more children, but it didn't happen. Now she works as my secretary at the college and goes fire watching three times a week. She grumbles because I spend so much time at Station 97. But Bob's home on leave soon; that'll keep her occupied. She spoils him rotten. Time he got himself wed.' Jim cast an amused eye Rosie's way. 'Like an introduction, Miss Gardiner? He's an accountant by trade and takes after his dad so he's a good sort.'

'Hazel's already got me engaged to her doctor friend down at the first-aid post. Not that I've met him either.'

152

Rosie finally felt able to smile; she was grateful to Jim for creating a normal little interlude amidst the horror. 'If the road was clear the others should've reached the hospital by now,' she said.

Hazel and Tom had sped off ten minutes ago to take the casualties to the infirmary. For Rosie and Jim there was no rush: the mortuary was their destination. And now she was feeling strong and ready to finish the job and she told Jim so. He patted her arm and led the way to the first stretcher.

It seemed unbelievable that just a few hours ago she'd been sitting in the common room with Hazel, knitting scarves for the crew of her boyfriend's ship; Rosie kept her mind whirring although her teeth were gritted and her shoulders protested at the weight they were bearing. Finally the bars of the stretcher were in the runners and with an almighty shove from her and Jim it slid into position on the top rung.

As she jumped down from the back of the vehicle to help Jim with the next body she estimated that the time had been about nine o'clock when a call had come through for crews from Station 97 to assist at an incident at Marylebone. Clarice had shouted through the message hatch that local crews were already out dealing with another blast on their patch. While Tom and Jim had run outside to start up the ambulance engines, Stella had rounded up the attendants. As Jim's usual partner hadn't turned in on her shift, Rosie had been allocated to him although she wasn't yet fully fledged. Now she was glad that her baptism of fire had been with Jim Warwick at her side. His quiet calm manner had been just what she'd needed.

They'd set off, with sinister fire from the rockets

pluming overhead, Rosie feeling light-headed with dread. Now she felt anaesthetised with mental fatigue; even the burn in her muscles as she lifted dead weights didn't trouble her as much as it should. But she'd know about it tomorrow . . . and after that she'd be stronger, in every way, she'd make sure of it.

The last stretcher had been loaded and Jim handed her a towel from the back of their ambulance and took another to mop his brow. 'Once you get the first call over, it's all downhill,' he said wryly, attuned to her thoughts.

Rosie nodded, sniffing. She took off her tin helmet, rubbing vigorously at her perspiring face with the cloth, till her cheeks fizzed with blood. She felt glad of the sensation, glad to be alive. Perhaps next time she might help to save a life rather than transport the corpses.

CHAPTER FOURTEEN

'That blonde bitch is making a play for your Conor.'
Ethel Ford poked her daughter in the arm.

'Ain't my Conor, Mum, he's made that plain enough.'
Patricia took a gulp of port and lemon, then plonked
the glass down on the table.

The two women shifted on their chairs, craning their
necks to get a clear view across the crowded pub. Conor
Flint had an elbow resting on the bar. A woman who
looked to be about the same age as he had draped herself
on his shoulder. As though irritated by his sister-in-law's
unwanted weight he straightened, dislodging her.

'She's got some brass neck with her husband not yet
cold.' Ethel rummaged in her bag for a pack of Capstan.
Having lit up, she pursed her lips and eyed her daughter
through a swirl of smoke. She whipped the cigarette out
of her mouth and pointed it at Patricia. 'You gonna let
him slip through yer fingers just like that, then?' Ethel
banged a length of ash into the ashtray at the centre of
the stained table.

Patricia helped herself to the cigarettes when Ethel

made no move to offer her one, brooding on her mother's comment.

'Ain't no wonder you're still single with that attitude,' Ethel muttered. While her daughter struck a match she gave Patricia the once-over. Ethel had been married at seventeen and as soon as Patricia turned that age she had nagged at the girl to get engaged and out from under her feet. Seven years on, Ethel still had Pat living at home with her. But Patricia was a good looker with hair that was thick and black and eyes of deep hazel. She suited make-up: bright red lips and powdered cheeks enhanced her dusky beauty. Several of the dockers who frequented the Red Lion had been sending her appreciative looks.

But when Conor had arrived a short while ago he had barely acknowledged the girl he'd thrown over a few weeks back. Not that it had been any lengthy romance. They'd started walking out when he came home on leave from the army at Christmas. But Ethel had had hopes of it leading somewhere. The Flints were important people round these parts. Or they had been until Hilda Flint's eldest boy, Saul, got killed in an air raid. Saul had been the guvnor. Now all anyone knew was that Conor was back from France, recuperating from a bullet wound in the shoulder, and running the show.

'If you ain't gonna make an effort to talk to him, I'm off.' Ethel opened her bag, perched on the table, and lobbed her Capstan inside. 'Ain't missing me programme on the wireless for no reason and I ain't shellin' out fer no more drinks fer you, neither.'

Pat eyed her mother from beneath heavy eyelids. 'Righto! I'll go and speak to him.' She almost got to her feet, then the port kicked in and she slid back to the seat. 'And don't blame me if I take a swing at that smug cow.' Pat made out she'd sat down on purpose because she'd thought of something to say.

With an effort she shoved back her chair and successfully stood up. On her way towards the bar she slapped away a calloused hand that fondled her behind, making her stumble.

'On yer own, love? Want some company?' Beery breath fanned Patricia's cheek.

She tossed back her dark wavy hair from her face to snarl, 'Piss off. I'm with him . . .' She nodded at Conor, then slid into position at his side.

'Been waiting for you to come over and buy me 'n' Mum a drink, Conor.' She swayed, putting a hand on the bar to steady herself.

Conor jerked his head, ordering two port and lemons from the barman without losing place in the conversation he was having with his younger brother.

Patricia bit her lip; she was tipsy but not so far gone as not to feel humiliated. She glared a challenge at Angie Flint, but the woman looked to be equally unhappy with the treatment she'd been getting from her brother-in-law. 'Angie . . .' The single word from Patricia was all the greeting Saul's widow got.

The blonde gave a brittle smile, crossing her arms over her ample bosom. 'You can fill that up 'n' all if you're getting a round in.' Angie tapped her empty glass by Conor's elbow. She'd be damned if she'd let him buy the drunken slut a drink without offering her one as well.

'Charmer, ain't he?' Patricia said loudly. 'Can't even be bothered to have a little chat with the women he knocks about with.'

Conor turned his head then, cold blue eyes travelling over her. 'Reckon you've had one too many bevvies, Pat. Why don't you go home and sleep it off?' He picked up the drink he'd just ordered her and knocked it back in one swallow, making Angie snort gleefully.

'Find that funny, do you?' Patricia spat through gritted teeth. She pushed off the bar where she'd propped herself and tottered the few steps needed to yank at Angie's peroxide locks.

Ethel had been waiting for a catfight to erupt. With a gleam of satisfaction in her eyes she surged through the stevedores who were hooting and slow clapping as Angie in turn grabbed at Pat's dark waves.

'You ought to be ashamed of yourself,' Ethel hissed, poking Conor's bicep but making no attempt to free her daughter's hair from Angie's fist.

Finally Conor successfully separated the women. He held them apart at the end of his rigid arms while they kicked savagely at each other and mouthed obscenities. Unable to take the cigarette from his lips he spat it on the floor, growling an angry curse.

'Your brother ain't been gone a few weeks and you're carrying on with the likes of her?' Ethel's pinched features were contemptuous as she pointed at Angie. 'Bet she's throwing herself at him when you're not about.' She jerked her chin at Steven Flint.

Conor glanced at his younger brother. Steven seemed to be having trouble knowing whether to speak up or get going. In the end he chose to do both.

'Fucking hell, I'd shoot meself if she did! I'm off down the Railway fer a drink where the company's better. Coming?' He pushed off the bar and wove through the crowd towards the exit.

Conor grabbed his sister-in-law's elbow, ignoring the twinge in his shoulder at the sudden movement, pushing her in front of him to the door in Steven's wake.

'Come back here and buy me a drink, you bastard!' Patricia yelled after him.

The nearest docker saw his chance. Hitching his trousers up neatly around his spare tyre, he slapped some coins down on the counter. 'Get the lady a drink.'

Billy Morris wearily did as he was told and slid another port and lemon in front of Patricia, wishing that Conor had done him a favour and taken her with him as well. The Ford women were a handful and he reckoned that Ethel's old man preferred kipping at the bottom of the sea to sleeping next to the old dragon every night. Roland Ford had perished at the Battle of the River Plate, soon after the war started, but the loss hadn't tempered Ethel's moods, and Patricia seemed to be following in her mother's footsteps.

Pat looked at her drink, aware of her mother fuming at her side. She was in two minds whether to down it or chuck it in the bloke's ugly mug. She smiled sweetly and upended the glass against her mouth before handing it to the barman. 'You can get me another, if yer like, and one for me mum 'n' all.'

'And what do I get?' the docker whispered in her ear, but not as quietly as he might.

Billy Morris's expression turned yet more cynical as he shuffled off on his slippers to fill two glasses.

'A big thank you, that's what you get,' Patricia said as soon as the drinks had arrived and she'd downed half of hers.

The docker sat down amidst his pals' jeering laughter.

'You'll go too far one of these days, my gel,' Ethel

said. 'You don't tease the likes o' them in front of their mates.' Picking up her port and lemon, she stomped back to the table to sit down.

'Get indoors.'

'Coming in with me then?'

'Get the fuck inside.' Conor spun his sister-in-law away from him as she tried to slide her arms up around his neck and gave her a shove towards her front door.

'You going back to her?' Angie had flounced about and jerked her head at the Red Lion on the corner. 'She's a bleedin' drunk. Don't know what you ever saw in someone like that. She's got no self-respect.'

'And you do?' Conor replied drily. 'Saul deserved better than you as a wife.'

'And I deserved better than him,' Angie returned. She gazed at Conor. 'I *had* better than him . . . I had you.'

'Long, long while ago.'

'Could go back to that now,' Angie whispered. 'We're both free and it was always you I wanted, Con. Only married him 'cos you went off to fight in the bloody war.' She again tried to draw his dark head down to hers so she could kiss him.

He yanked her hands from his lapels and stepped backwards, swearing in irritation. 'You're a right bitch, aren't you? Saul thought the sun shone out of your backside and you can't even make a show of grieving for him.'

Angie shrugged. 'I ain't a hypocrite. Anyhow, you can't pick who you fall in love with; if you could I wouldn't want you, would I, when you treat me like dirt?'

'You can pick who you fucking marry! You should

have left him alone and let him find someone else if that's how you felt.'

Angie started chewing the inside of her cheek, eyeing him from beneath her lashes. 'Don't make out you didn't have feelings for me, 'cos I know you did.'

'My feelings for you were basic and temporary, and I never made out otherwise. Saul saw you differently.'

'I'll take what we had, fer now,' Angie said persuasively, sliding his hand inside her jacket to press against her large round breast. 'Basic enough for you? Just give it another go, Con . . . eh?'

Conor withdrew his fingers, shaking his head in disgust. 'You should've pissed off when we broke up, Angie, and let my brother settle down with somebody decent.'

'He didn't want anyone decent!' she snorted. 'He loved what I did to him, and so did you.' Angie was incensed at being rejected when she'd have let him take her in the alley against the wall. 'Ain't *so* long ago that I was your girl; I can remember what we used to do in the back of your Humber down by the canal . . .'

'Get indoors,' Conor said quietly, unwilling to argue with her. He knew she'd love to provoke a commotion in the street just so she could kid herself she had the upper hand and he was dangling off it. 'Stevie's waiting for me up the road.' Conor started walking towards the corner. 'And don't wake Mum up when you go in.'

Conor heard the door slam and knew the cow had made a noise on purpose, because he'd asked her not to. He searched in a pocket for cigarettes and looked up at the sky, wondering if there'd be a raid. But for the ache at the top of his arm where twenty stitches were holding a bullet wound together he'd still be dug in

161

around Sword Beach and he was beginning to think it'd be preferable to what he was doing now. Separating the two warring women in the Red Lion had set off a slow throb in his shoulder and he gave the sore area a massage as he strolled along smoking and thinking.

His brother Saul had been one of the first victims of the V1 rockets. His mum couldn't get over her eldest son's loss, but Saul's wife had managed to . . . in record time. But then, as Angie readily admitted, she'd never really wanted Saul in the first place. Sometimes she'd made that so embarrassingly apparent that Conor had avoided visiting his family when on leave in case she threw herself at him. He had taken up with Patricia in the hope that Angie would accept he'd moved on to someone else and there was no going back to the summer of 1939. He was a different person now. That lairy chancer had disintegrated in the army, finally dying at Dunkirk, along with half his regiment.

In a way Conor resented Saul for getting himself blown up and forcing him to sort out his mess. He didn't want to deal with people he didn't like . . . such as Frank Purves and his pals. His thoughts transferred to the distiller's daughter, a rueful laugh scratching his throat. He could come to like Rosemary Deane . . . more than he should . . .

'Didn't think you'd be coming,' Steven said as Conor joined him at the bar in the Railway Inn. 'Thought one or other of 'em would dig their claws in.'

Steven had been about thirteen when Conor joined up. He could recall the fight that'd broken out between his brothers when Conor came back on his first home leave and discovered Angie married to Saul. Then things calmed down and Conor returned to his regiment, having made it clear he wished the couple well and no hard feelings. Saul and Angie had moved into the house next door and everything seemed back to normal, except that Conor didn't turn up on leave very much after that.

'Which one you going for then?' Steven was mildly curious as to whether Conor would choose his sister-in-law or the younger and prettier of the two women.

'Neither of 'em,' Conor smiled, and ordered a light and bitter. 'You still thinking of enlisting?'

'Yep, so don't try and stop me.'

Conor struck a match, dipping his head to the flame. 'Mum won't be happy.' He blew smoke out of the side of his mouth, shoving the pack of Weights over the bar in his brother's direction.

'Ain't coming as a surprise to her. I told her I'd go when I was eighteen.'

'You're not eighteen till October.'

'Only a few months to go . . . close enough fer me.' Steven got comfortable on his bar stool. 'Time to get this war won or none of us are gonna have anything left. Poor bastards over there'll have fuck all to come back to. Won't be a London street standing, way them rockets are raining down every night.' He glanced at Conor. 'You going back soon as you get signed off by the army doc?'

Conor gave a brief nod. 'That's why I reckon you should stay fer as long as you can. You'll get your enlistment papers soon enough but right now Mum needs you.'

'She's got her daughter-in-law to look out for her.'

'Yeah . . .' Connor sounded sarcastic. 'Already thought of that . . . so I reckon you should stay and take care of Mum 'cos Angie'll only ever look out for herself.'

'Get that monkey back off the distiller over Shore-ditch?' Steven changed the subject. He didn't want a row but he wasn't about to alter his plans and babysit his old mum. Saul had always taken care of business and family problems.

His eldest brother had got an exemption from call up by blackmailing a quack with a gambling habit into giving him a lung condition. Saul used to say it was more important to keep the home fires burning and the businesses chugging for the family than join the fighting. Steven had reckoned that for a bloke with a lung condition Saul could come out with a lot of hot air. Saul had chosen to stop at home from cowardice rather than a duty to the rest of the Flints. It was ironic that he might have survived a stint overseas in the army whereas ducking and diving at home had proved fatal for him.

'So Popeye's mate's coming up with the booze after all, then, is he?' Steven's thoughts had returned to the Shoreditch deal and he prodded his brother to gain his attention and get an answer about it.

Conor puffed on his cigarette, looking preoccupied. 'Nope . . .' he finally said.

'Not writing off five hundred quid, are yer?' Steven sounded shocked. 'Saul wouldn't have let anybody get away with it. You can't let the bastard make us a bleedin' laughing stock.'

'Didn't say anybody'd got away with it, did I?'

'Saul reckoned that consignment of rotgut would make us thousands. He knew a bloke worked down Harringay dogtrack who could shift it under the bar, no trouble.'

'Perhaps it would've shown a good profit if the bloke with the still had come in on the deal. Five hundred quid's worth of Popeye's whisky labels stuck on empty bottles ain't much to shout about.' Conor took a swallow of beer. 'Saul jumped in with both feet on it without doing his homework.'

'You've been turned over 'cos you ain't got Saul's clout with these geezers.' Steven slammed his tankard on the bar. 'I'll come with you and pay the distiller a visit. He needs a lesson.'

'He's left London.'

'He's done a fuckin' runner? And you've let him? I knew that cross-eyed sod couldn't be trusted to set up the deal. Only met Purves the once when he ran us off some girly mags. Never liked him. Go after him instead, then, shall we, Con?' Steven hopped off his bar stool, spoiling for a fight.

'Calm down,' Conor said. His younger brother was too hot-headed. His older brother had been the reverse. If Saul hadn't been so easily led by a well-spun yarn, he'd never have got hooked up with Angie Rook, and he might still be alive.

The night the first V1 came over Saul had driven to East London to meet Frank Purves and pay for some boxes of stolen silk stockings. Purves had heard the sirens and got himself to safety rather than risk the rendezvous. But Saul, driving on through the blackout in Bethnal Green to buy his wife the luxuries she wanted, had ended up in the wrong place at the wrong time.

Angie had definitely mourned the loss of those stockings, if not the husband who'd lost his life trying to get them for her. And much as Conor disliked Angie's attitude, he hated his dead brother too. He wished Saul were still around just so he could shake the life out of him for getting himself killed and putting a spoke in things.

When they were growing up Conor had given his

brothers plenty of space to do what they wanted, so that he could too. But now he couldn't escape; his mother expected him to be the engine of the family. Her husband and her eldest son had died and her attention had finally turned to him to keep the money rolling in. And he wasn't sure why he felt duty-bound to please her when she'd never bothered with him.

His father had always run a small-time racket alongside his shifts down the docks. All Harry Flint's sons had followed in his footsteps to the Pool of London as stevedores. When Harry died of a heart attack in 1926 Steven had just been born and Saul had just started work. Conor had always been the boy in the middle and he occupied himself while his mother fussed over the son who was now the man of the house, and the baby in her arms.

'We gonna do something about this, then, or not?' Steven was pacing to and fro in agitation. 'If you ain't got the balls to get that monkey back I'll go meself and take Mickey with me.'

Mickey Rook was Angie's brother, a few years older than Steven, and mad as a box of frogs.

'Perhaps you're right,' Conor said coolly. 'You should get yourself joined up. Dodging bullets might knock some sense into that thick head of yours.'

Steven shoved his snarling face close to his brother's. 'Getting yourself promoted to sergeant don't mean a fuck round here.'

'Don't mean a fuck over there either. You're as pissed as Patricia. Go home.'

'When I'm ready.' Steven sounded belligerent but glanced warily about. He was drawing attention to himself and he knew if he carried on his brother would chin him. It wouldn't be the first time Conor had slapped him down. And over in the corner, with her dad, was a girl Steven had liked since he'd sat behind her at school.

'Ain't drunk . . . just bleedin' angry,' Steven muttered, by way of apology. He thumped his elbows on the bar. 'That cash would have paid for Saul's wake a hundred times over.'

Their brother's send-off had gone on for two days and close to a hundred people had attended. Billy Morris had run out of rum to serve their late dad's old navy pals. With a snort of amusement, Steven reminded Conor about that. 'Could've sold the miserable old fucker some rotgut . . . if we'd had it earlier.' Steven started to guffaw and after a moment Conor's smile turned to laughter. So infectious was their hilarity that half the people in the pub started chuckling, though they'd no idea why.

'I'll get more out of this deal with Purves than crates of booze,' Conor finally said, wiping mirthful tears from his eyes. 'What I've got in mind won't require a still, just a printing press.'

Steven sniffed himself into seriousness, then frowned in curiosity.

'Purves has taken to counterfeiting in a big way. He's good, too. While he was out of action with his dodgy ticker I let myself into his warehouse. Stacked high with fake ration books, it is.'

'We gonna nick 'em?' Steven suggested brightly.

'No need to steal what we own. He can't come up with the moonshine, or the money, we'll have the coupons instead. Extra petrol's always handy, I reckon, 'specially since the allowance got cut.'

'So we forget about John Gardiner and concentrate on Popeye to come up with the goods?'

Conor swigged from his glass, eyes half closed. He wasn't thinking about a couple of old timers at all. He still had the image of Rosemary Deane in her nightdress stuck in his head. And the obsession to go back again and see her was driving him mad.

Something about her seemed familiar. He'd racked his brain over what it might be, or where he could have bumped into her before. The silvery shade of her natural blonde hair and the turquoise of her eyes were memorable, and he reasoned he should know why that was. He knew he'd go back and see her if for no other reason than to ease his curiosity about that . . . and this time he'd be the one asking her why she didn't wear a wedding ring although the answer was pretty damned obvious. Rosemary Deane led a double life: one at home and another at work at the LAAS.

The spiteful old biddy up the road might call her Mrs Deane but she'd guessed too that Rosemary hadn't ever had a husband.

The idea that John Gardiner's daughter had got herself in trouble should have boosted Conor's hopes of an easy conquest; instead he felt strangely angry that a bloke might have run out on her. Sorry, too, that the bastard might have turned her off getting involved with other men. She'd certainly not responded to him in the way most women did when he gave them a look and a line. Nevertheless the desire he felt for her was still niggling at him, putting a cramp low in his belly.

He knew he was acting like an idiot wanting to chase after a woman with a kid when he had two willing women wanting to sleep with him.

'You listening to me?'

Steven's words penetrated the fog in Conor's mind.

'Yeah. What?' Conor finished his beer.

'Just forget it . . .' Steven muttered moodily, aware his question didn't need an answer.

'Better get back and check on Mum.' Conor pushed his empty glass away. Hilda Flint had always been a problem but since Saul got killed she'd used his death as an excuse to be an even greater pain in the arse.

'Good luck,' Steven muttered, ordering himself another drink with a whisky chaser.

CHAPTER FIFTEEN

'Slam your foot on the brake!'

'Me foot is on the bleeding brake.'

The Citroën shuddered to a stop, scraping the kerb, and Rufus breathed a sigh of relief. 'This ain't a good idea, Midge. Shanks's pony's safer than us driving this contraption.' Rufus sank back in his seat. He'd thought they'd been about to career into a lamppost at the edge of the pavement. 'You probably can't steer it 'cos it's French.'

'Ain't me, or it! It's you!' Midge exploded. 'You're putting me off, barking in me ear 'ole like a bleedin' old woman. "Right! Left! Brake!"' he mimicked. 'I know what I'm doing, so stop interfering.' He let go of the steering wheel and reached across, slapping Rufus's fingers off the handbrake. Then he jerked his chin repeatedly at the gears. 'That's your job fer now and I'll tell you when I want otherwise. Now shove that stick in first, and away we go.'

With a mutter Rufus did as he was told and they pulled off smoothly, continuing for about a hundred yards in sulky silence.

'Shit! Coppers at two o'clock,' Rufus hissed, making Midge lose concentration and tug the steering wheel to the left though he corrected the swerve quickly.

Midge darted a glance at the Black Maria coming to a halt at the junction ahead. 'Just act natural. They aren't on to us.' Despite his boast Midge again let go of the steering wheel to adjust the brim of his hat so it obscured more of his face. He was still a wanted man, but enough years had elapsed since he first went on the run to make him confident even his mother would have difficulty recognising him. He'd aged ten years in four: his face was haggard and his hair already turning grey although he had only just turned thirty. 'If you stop staring at 'em we'll breeze past,' Midge snarled.

They did; and fifteen minutes later they'd pulled up at a builder's yard in King's Cross and were making their first delivery of petrol coupons in Popeye's foreign motor.

'We collecting payment as well?' Rufus asked when they'd done the deal and were back by the Citroën.

'Pop won't let us handle the cash . . . only these . . .' Midge pulled a few stray vouchers from a pocket. 'He's sorting the rest out himself.'

'So, no chance of a bit of hey diddle then?' Rufus said forlornly. In the past when working for Popeye he'd often use his guvnor's money on a dead cert at the race track and to top up his wages. Then after collecting his winnings he'd go and divvy up with Popeye.

'Well, that depends on how you see it . . .' Midge opened the car door with his good arm, sliding onto the driver's seat.

Rufus got in beside him. 'How do you see it?' he enquired. He knew that his crafty brother-in-law always had an eye to the main chance so was all ears when Midge spouted his pearls of wisdom.

'This *is* as good as money.' Again Midge pulled the coupons in his pocket into sight.

'Pop's got every one of them logged up here,' Rufus scoffed, tapping his forehead. 'You won't get one over on him like that.'

'Pop might do his sums, but those blokes in that yard aren't gonna notice straight off that a number are missing from a batch of hundreds. When they do I'm guessing they'll either think it's one of their own got sticky fingers, or Popeye's short-changed them. So they'll either feel too stupid to bring it up, or they'll swallow it in case the forger gets the hump and won't deliver no more.' Midge looked back at the yard where an open-back truck was being loaded up with ladders and lengths of timber. 'Petrol coupons are manna from heaven where these blokes are concerned. No fuel, no work . . .'

'You reckon they'll swallow it, do you?' Rufus's warning was laced with sarcasm. He jerked his head at a fellow in overalls lumbering towards him with an associate in tow.

'Shit!' Midge moaned. 'I only had six out of all that lot.'

A bang on the car window made him regret that they'd not driven off the moment they'd got in the Citroën.

'All right, mate? What can I do fer you?' Midge said cheerily, winding down the window with an effort.

'Me pal 'n' me would like some clothing coupons,' the bloke whispered. 'Got any spare on yer today so we can keep the missus sweet?'

'Nah, sorry, all allocated. Tell Popeye, shall I, and bring yer some next time?'

''Spose so,' the man answered grumpily, and ambled back to work.

'Like taking candy from a baby,' Midge chortled beneath his breath, putting up the glass.

Rufus stretched out his hand, palm up. 'By my reckoning six nicked coupons divided by two means three's mine. I'll take 'em now 'cos I can walk home from here.'

'Not coming fer a pint?' Midge sounded disappointed.

'Nah, Gertie's a bit under the weather . . . gotta look after the nipper.' It was a lie. Gertie was fine, but she'd bust a gut if she found out that he was supping in a pub with the brother she hated.

'Pick me up tomorrow, same time, top of Commercial Road?' Rufus asked, pocketing the three coupons Midge reluctantly handed over.

They had agreed to have their rendevouz point somewhere busy where nobody would take much notice of another vehicle stopping and picking up a passenger. A meeting under Gertie's nose was out of the question; she tended to spit fire at any sight of her brother. Also Midge didn't want any of the Grimeses' neighbours taking notice of the flash car. Some of them had been around long enough to remember Gertie had a half-pint brother who'd deserted. Midge had stayed away from his sister's place not simply because he knew he'd not be welcome but because he ran the risk of being recognised.

'Dunno what's happening tomorrow. Popeye said he might want the motor to take his girl out now he's feeling better.'

'What?' Rufus frowned. 'Ain't he well?'

'Silly old sod had a bad turn after he trapped his hand in the machinery.'

'This caper's going down the pan before it's properly started, is it?' Rufus huffed in disappointment.

'Nah, far from it.' Midge leered at Rufus. 'If he's had a heart attack it's 'cos he's exerting hisself more than he should. That bird he's knocking around with's built fer speed, just like this jalopy, and poor old Pop can't handle either at his age.' Midge's dirty laugh filled the car. 'But he's feeling good as new, so he said.'

'How you doing, Nurse Johnson? Not seen you in quite a while, gel.'

Trudy swung about to see a fellow propping an elbow on the doorjamb of the pub she'd just passed. She'd not recognised him at first because his appearance had altered in the few years since she'd last clapped eyes on him. She'd heard the rumours that Frank Purves did all right from a thriving printing business, and had some dodgy sidelines going on, too. His squint hadn't improved but she knew his grin was aimed at her so she approached him for a chat, pushing her bike at her side. Other people might think this man a villain but she'd always felt rather sorry for him losing his wife in childbirth.

'I've been nursing at St Thomas's for almost three years,' Trudy said, explaining why she'd not been seen around. 'Can't train the girls up quick enough at the hospitals, what with the war dragging on and casualties on the rise again at home. But I'm back on the beat as a district nurse a few days a week.' She swivelled the handlebars of the ancient pushbike. 'Just hope this old thing holds out so I can get to my new mums quick as I need to when their husbands bash on me door in the middle of the night.'

'Still a midwife as well then, are you?' Popeye sounded impressed.

'Oh, yes. The babies keep coming, no matter what.'

'More than ever since the Yanks arrived with their fags and nylons, I expect . . .' Frank coughed. He'd forgotten for a moment that he wasn't exchanging banter with a bloke at the bar. 'Sorry, love, didn't think . . .'

Trudy shrugged. She was too long in the tooth and too jaded by her job to be offended by a salty quip. 'Been in the wars, have you, Mr Purves?' Frank had removed his hand from his pocket and she'd noticed a bandage wound about it.

'Ah . . . that's nothing!' Frank indolently waggled his fingers. 'Me own fault, that was; got a thumb caught in me printing press fer being careless.'

'Ooh, bet that hurt.'

'Cor, not 'alf!' Frank sucked his teeth, wincing at the memory of it. 'Gave me a nasty turn but I managed to get meself home before I passed out cold. Me neighbour sent for an ambulance 'cos he couldn't wake me. But I'm all right now. Shock set me angina off or something, so the quack said.'

'Want me to take a look at that dressing? I'm off up to number sixty-one to do a leg ulcer but I'll pop in on the way back, if you like.'

'If it ain't no trouble, dear. I was heading home anyhow once I finish this.' He raised the tankard in his healthy hand.

With a wave Trudy continued on her way up the road and Frank finished off his pint of mild. He was looking forward to having the nurse visit. As a young probationer she'd delivered his only child. Trudy Johnson was sure to remember that day because he'd lost his wife giving birth to Lenny. Not that Frank blamed Nurse Johnson for his wife dying. He could remember the poor cow, probably not more than twenty-five at the time, sobbing her heart out while fighting to stanch the haemorrhage. If anybody had been to blame it'd been Lenny, tearing his mother's insides to shreds. But his son was dead now, too, so reluctantly Popeye knew there was nobody left to accuse but himself. He'd got her pregnant, after all, when she'd told him she didn't want kids spoiling her figure.

Just as he was about to set off home, Frank hesitated, thinking he recognised a sailor who'd just ordered a pint at the bar. Keen to jog his memory, he put down his empty tankard and slid onto the stool next to the young fellow.

'On leave, son, are yer?'

'Yeah, just a weekend pass. Gonna make sure I enjoy it 'n' all. Deserve a break from over there.'

'Ain't no picnic over here, neither,' Popeye said drily. 'Feel I should reckernise you; don't know why. From round here, are you?'

'Used to be. Grew up in Shoreditch.'

'Might know your folks, then. What's your name?' Popeye asked.

'Charles Bellamy.'

Popeye slapped his thigh. 'Doris's son! Now I know you. If you've come on a visit, you'll be out of luck. Yer mum 'n' stepdad's gone off out of town. Didn't they write 'n' let yer know?'

'I've just come from Gravesend,' Charles said with a sour smile. 'Can't swing a cat in my place with everybody there. Me missus is run off her feet. I'm stopping in London with a pal for a night or two before heading back to Portsmouth. Some leave this has turned out to be.'

'That's it, Gravesend,' Popeye said with a smile. 'I remember now where John said he was off to. Said

I might pop down and see him sometime, being as we go way back. Got his address, have you, mate?'

Bellamy wrote it down and Popeye pocketed the scrap of paper and plonked down his glass.

'Fancy a drink?' Bellamy said.

'Can't, mate. Got a woman waiting on me,' Popeye winked, thinking about Nurse Johnson.

Bellamy downed his pint. 'Hoping the same,' he muttered, and ordered another.

Twenty minutes later Frank was at home and had set the cups ready to receive his visitor. The moment he heard the knock on the door he put the kettle to boil.

'Want a cuppa, love?' Frank helped Trudy park her bike against his front wall then followed her into the back parlour.

'Best not. Got to get back and write up my notes.'

'Oh . . . right y'are . . .' Frank said, disappointed. He went into the kitchen and turned the gas off under the hissing kettle.

'Remember the day you brought my Lenny into the world, do you, Nurse?' he called out.

Trudy nodded and gave a sigh. Even after more than twenty-four years the memory of that tragedy remained in her mind. Mrs Purves had been the first patient to die on her. Since then many more women had succumbed to the ravages of childbirth during her career spanning more than a quarter of a century. 'Dreadful shame about your wife—'

'All in the past, love,' Popeye interrupted. 'No need to mention it now. I've found meself a young lady, y'know. Shirley works in the pub and we keep each other company since her husband passed on. She's almost young enough to be me daughter, but we rub along all right.'

'And how's Lenny?' Trudy asked. Taking Frank's hand, she began unwinding the bandage.

'Oh, course you wouldn't know,' Frank said. 'Lost Lenny 'n' all, three years back now.'

Trudy stopped what she was doing and sighed sadly. 'Oh, so sorry to hear that, Mr Purves. Was he home or abroad when it happened?'

'Oh, he weren't serving. Bad eyes . . . like me.' Popeye knew there'd been nothing wrong with his son's vision. Lenny had swung the lead to avoid conscription because he was a coward. But Frank couldn't let Nurse Johnson know what a useless specimen his son had turned out to be. His late wife wouldn't have liked him being disloyal to the child that had sent her to her grave.

'Got caught in a fire in a nightclub,' Popeye briefly explained, turning his face away in a pretence of grieving. He didn't want any more questions on the subject.

'There've been some dreadful tragedies.' Trudy patted his arm in comfort. 'Please God we'll see an end to it all soon. A lot of people have had enough and upped sticks to escape the blasted rockets.'

'Family I know did that,' Popeye volunteered. 'My old pal John Gardiner's gone to the country and taken his wife Doris and their grandkid with him.'

Trudy stopped removing the dressing and glanced at Popeye. She remembered the family, of course, although she didn't know Mr Gardiner had finally married his fiancée. Neither did she know that they'd left Shoreditch. She'd never forget how close she'd come to adopting Rosemary Gardiner's beautiful little girl. Then Rosemary had changed her mind and broken her heart. Even now

Trudy felt a twinge of pain in her chest at the thought of what she'd lost. It seemed daft to imagine she could have loved the child from the short contact she'd had with her. She'd delivered many infants since, but none had stuck in her memory in the way that blonde angel had.

'I know John Gardiner's family. I delivered his grand-daughter. Do you know what they named her?'

Frank racked his brain, screwing up his grizzled features. 'Hope! Sure that's what John said. Bet she's pretty if she's like her mum. Good looker, that Rosemary Gardiner, as she was, of course. Don't know what name she goes by now.' He paused, perhaps hoping that Trudy might supply it but the nurse continued dabbing his scab with antiseptic.

'Rosemary and my Lenny went to the same school. I know he liked her,' Frank continued. 'I reckon he'd've taken things further with the gel, given a chance, but . . .' Popeye shook his head, a grimace on his face describing Lenny's rejection better than words could've. 'Old John never speaks about his son-in-law – never speaks about his daughter neither – but you can tell he's proud as punch of the nipper,' Popeye chuckled.

'She was a beauty,' Trudy said, blinking back a prick-ling heat in her eyes.

'I'd've liked grandkids,' Popeye reflected. 'Too late now, though.'

'You just told me you've got a lady friend,' Trudy ribbed him. 'Make an honest woman of her and never say never.'

Frank roared a laugh. 'You're right, Nurse. There's life in this old dog yet, but I reckon Shirley's childbearing days are behind her. When I said she was younger'n me didn't mean she was no spring chicken. She's forty-nine

179

next birthday and I'm sixty-four.' He winked his good eye.

'And you're looking very good on it, too, if I may say so,' Trudy said stoutly. Having finished patching him up, she collected her things together. 'Best be off; take care of that hand and your ticker.' She nodded at his chest. 'When I'm back this way I'll call in and see you, if you're about.'

Frank walked Trudy to the door, feeling he should offer the woman something for her trouble. 'Need anything, love?'

'No, not at all. I was passing this way anyhow,' she said, guessing he was offering to pay her for her time.

'How about a few clothing coupons? Got a few going spare.'

Trudy hesitated. She did need some summer blouses now it'd turned very warm and she'd no coupons left. 'Well . . . I . . .'

Frank tapped his nose to indicate it was a secret. 'You just ask me for whatever you want in the way of rations and I'll get it for yer.' He trundled into his front parlour and pulled open a drawer. 'Keep a little stash at home for me good friends, y'see.' He returned with some clothing coupons.

Trudy stared at them, realisation dawning over what the man had been printing on his press when he injured his hand. But they were good; she'd never have spotted anything amiss in their colour or design.

'Take 'em up town . . . Oxford Street . . . get yerself a nice frock.' Popeye closed her hand on the coupons on her palm. 'If you want more just ask.'

'Thanks,' Trudy said faintly and pocketed them.

'Take care of yourself, love,' Popeye called out as the

nurse wheeled her bike out of his front gate. He watched her go, thinking that for a woman of her age – which he put at coming up fifty, same as Shirley – she wasn't a bad looker. And unlike his girlfriend, who was hard to please, Trudy seemed easy-going and kind with it.

CHAPTER SIXTEEN

'I told you not to come back here.'

'Yeah, I remember.'

'So are you too thick-skinned or too thick-headed to do as you're told?' Rosie demanded.

She was pleased she'd covered her shock and managed to sound confident. As days had passed with no sign of Conor Flint she'd relaxed, believing he'd accepted that her dad had told him the truth. Yet niggling at the back of her mind had been an idea he would return, if only to see her. The tension between them that day had been as much to do with attraction as aggression. For the first time in many years she'd talked with a man while her wandering mind wondered how his mouth felt. There was no point in denying that she found him handsome, or that she knew he was exercising self-control for her sake rather than her father's. The grievance he had was real, even if John Gardiner had been wrongly implicated in it because of past misdemeanours.

'I told you I'd be back, Mrs Deane; and I reckon you've

been expecting me so don't bother with the outraged-innocent act. It doesn't suit you, does it?'

His smile seemed rather sinister to Rosie and her face grew hot as his eyes drifted to her bare fingers. He was letting her know that he'd understood Peg Price's hint about her absent wedding ring.

'If you've got something to say, don't be shy, spit it out,' Rosie snapped. Good-looking he may be, but she didn't care what a common criminal thought of her. But then her father had been one too so she curbed an urge to throw that barb at him.

'I've been trying to work out where I've seen you before.' Conor flexed the bruised knuckles on his right hand. 'Last night I got into a scrap and suddenly it came to me.'

'If we'd had a fight I'm sure I'd remember it,' Rosie returned flippantly,

'Oh, I'd remember that tussle, too,' he said silkily. 'I fought *over* you, not *with* you.'

Rosie looked startled; he wasn't joking, or even smiling any more.

'It happened when you were working at the Windmill Theatre. You did work at that place a few years back, didn't you?'

A silent intake of breath abraded Rosie's throat. If he'd recognised her from that time then he must have watched her posing on stage. The idea that he'd seen her nude was mortifying, flaming her cheeks again.

'What if I did?' she finally blurted.

'Just thought you might like to apologise as I once took a punch in the mouth on your account.'

Rosie darted a searching glance at him. She couldn't recall him from those days but that wasn't surprising.

During her time as a nude statue in the theatre's living tableaux she'd been pestered by hundreds of servicemen lying in wait at the stage door. And there had been occasions when men had fought to get her attention. Winning permission to take a fêted Windmill Girl for a drink was quite something to a fellow, and probably still was, Rosie realised.

'You don't remember me, do you?'

'Sorry. It was a long time ago.'

'February 1941,' he said.

'Did you write it in your diary?' Rosie mocked. 'I must have made quite an impression.'

'Oh, you did . . . on every man who watched you up there, but that's something else you know, isn't it?'

Rosie did remember him then. A corporal and a sergeant had come to blows over her and although the younger man had won the fight, she'd chosen to go for a drink with the senior of the two. The incident had sparked a bitter argument with some of the Windmill's chorus girls. They'd called her a show-off and a tease, dragging the theatre's name through the mud.

Rosie knew that at eighteen she'd been silly and vain, but she wasn't owning up to it to Conor Flint. The fracas was brought further into focus the more she dwelled on it. The sergeant had been stocky and fair-haired, and she'd gladly escaped his company after a single drink at the Starlight Rooms when he started taking disgusting liberties.

Rosie knew that had been her trouble: as the theatre's new recruit she'd loved rivalling the experienced girls for compliments, but she'd been too trusting and naïve with men to know how to handle the attention when she got it. Flaunting herself had always been different from giving herself, but her admirers had never seen it that way. Her rapist certainly hadn't . . .

'Remember me now?' Conor watched the play of emotion on her face. He'd embarrassed her by bringing up her racy past more than he'd intended. The ebullient little flirt he remembered was nowhere in sight. If he pushed her further she might either slap him or burst into tears.

'I . . . I met lots of people then,' Rosie stammered. 'All the men were the same to me . . . just drooling punters.'

'Yeah . . . that was me.' Conor grunted a sour laugh, stuffing his hands in his pockets. 'But I'm different now,' he said coolly.

'Me, too,' Rosie avowed with the bleakest of humour.

Three and a bit years had passed since that night yet there was no hint of the fresh-faced soldier she'd rejected in favour of his older colleague. Conor Flint's features had hardened and seemed permanently set in lines of cynicism that slanted his narrow mouth and creased the edges of his deep-blue eyes. Only his hair, thick and very dark, looked the same.

'If you're here to reminisce, I'm too busy. But I will say sorry you got in a fight over me and that I went out with your pal instead of you. Satisfied?'

'What do you think?' He was pinning her gaze down while he produced a pack of cigarettes from his pocket and offered her one.

Rosie shook her head, closing the door until just a few inches remained between it and the jamb. 'I'm expecting somebody at any minute. It's not a good time for you to be hanging around.'

'It is for me.' Conor's lazy gaze travelled over the silky

pink wrap she was wearing and trying to shield from his view. 'You could apologise properly and agree to a night out with me. Perhaps at the end of it I might be satisfied.'

'I wouldn't go out with you if you were the last—' Rosie bit her lip, knowing insults weren't wise. 'I'm getting ready to go to a dance with some friends.'

Rosie still had a lipstick clutched in her hand. She'd only outlined her top lip when she'd heard the ratatat on the door. A party of people from Station 97 was going to a shindig at the town hall. Tom lived in Hackney and had said he'd give her a lift as he had to pass her door. She'd whizzed downstairs to invite her colleague to wait in the parlour for her while she put on her dress and shoes. Now she was regretting not having peered out of her bedroom window before opening the door so readily.

'Is your dad coming back on a visit? I'd like a chat with him.' Conor shifted off the step as though preparing to go away.

'No,' Rosie retorted.

'Doesn't matter; I'll go to Gravesend and have a word with him.' He sauntered off down the garden path, feeling a bastard for resorting to that.

'You bloody won't!' Spontaneously Rosie nipped after him, before glancing towards Peg Price's house, hoping the woman hadn't spotted her cavorting in her dressing gown with Mr Flint, 'the gentleman'.

A wail from an air-raid siren made Rosie automatically turn her face up and mutter a curse beneath her breath.

'You'd best get to a shelter.' Conor's tone had turned serious and he began scouring the murky twilight. The whole day had been overcast with rumbles of thunder threatening a storm. There was no sight yet of approaching aircraft but the terrifying throb of engines was growing louder with every passing second.

'I've a cellar; I stay in that.'

'Well, get down there quickly.' He pointed as the first black shape broke through the cloud at high speed.

'What about you?' Rosie was back-stepping towards her front door, her glance veering between the doodlebug and him.

'Is that an invitation?'

'Oh, come inside!' Rosie ordered, her conscience getting the better of her good sense. She speeded into the hallway as a deafening roar drowned out further conversation. 'I hope Tom's safe. He might be close by and hammering to be let in soon.' Quickly she led the way to the cellar, flicking the light switch on the wall at the top of the stairs before descending them. A single bare bulb on the limewashed cellar ceiling gave little light but threw large eerie shadows onto the rough masonry walls.

'It's always cold down here, even in summer,' she said to break the ice.

Conor sat down on the hard-backed dining chair her father sometimes used when his bad leg ached from lying down for too long. Rosie paced to and fro, then perched on the mattress and draped the blanket around her shoulders, as much to hide her state of undress as for warmth.

'Usually, if there's time, I make us a flask of tea,' Rosie chattered on to cover her uneasiness. 'That helps.'

'D'you want my jacket?'

'No, I'm fine, thanks . . .' A moment later she nearly jumped out of her skin as the first rocket exploded and showered them with brick dust loosened from the ceiling. 'That sounded close.'

'Where were you going?'

'Going?'

'You said you were going out with Tom to a dance.'

'Oh . . . the town hall. The local Church arranged it for convalescing servicemen.'

'Tom's your boyfriend?'

'Tom's an ambulance driver who's on the same shift as me. We're on again bright and early in the morning.'

'So he's not your boyfriend?'

'No, he's not. Are you on leave from the army?'

'Sort of. I'm convalescing . . . Perhaps I'll invite myself along to your dance,' he suggested drily.

'You've been injured?' She raked him over with her eyes. He looked healthy enough to her.

Conor waggled his left shoulder. 'It's on the mend now.'

'When are you going back?'

Conor grunted a laugh. 'Not as soon as you'd like me to, Rosemary Deane, of that I'm sure.'

Rosie shuffled backwards on the mattress till her spine was pressed against the gritty wall. She drew her knees up to her chin and hugged them. He had a rough yet quiet voice, and she found the tone oddly soothing.

'I couldn't have timed it better to get injured,' he added when she continued staring wide-eyed at him. 'If I'd not taken a bullet, I'd've probably asked for a bit of compassionate leave.' He paused. 'My elder brother was killed in a blast and my mum took it bad.'

'Sorry about that,' Rosie said with genuine sympathy. 'Did his house get destroyed?'

'He was miles away from home when it happened.'

'I see . . . Did he leave children?' Rosie had been nine when her mum had died. She still missed her and

188

thought about her every day. She knew it must be much worse for little ones to cope with losing a parent in an air raid. It was so sudden . . . so brutal a loss. People went about their daily lives knowing the worst might happen yet expecting to survive. She'd gone to the Café de Paris with her friends with no thought that they might not all return to work the next day. One moment they'd all been dancing and drinking; the next, one of them was dead.

'Saul didn't have children, just a wife. He looked after business and family matters so things are a mess at the moment.'

'I can imagine . . .' Rosie was aware of his eyes burning her profile and burrowed further into the blanket, pulling it closer about her shoulders. Eighteen-year-old Rosie would have thrown it off, let him have a good look at her figure, then run a mile when he acted on the temptation. She hated the person she'd once been.

'Why did you get into that fight?' Her clasped hands were on her knees and she rested her chin on them.

'I wanted to take you out for a drink.'

'No, not *that* fight.' Rosie tutted. 'You said you'd been in a scrap last night.' She nodded at his bruised knuckles.

'It was nothing much.'

'It was either money or a girl,' Rosie guessed, trying to lighten an atmosphere that seemed to be filling with sultry heat despite the cold cellar walls.

'It always is.'

'So which was it?'

'Both, and neither worth the effort.'

'Very gallant,' Rosie muttered. 'I'm sure she'd be pleased to know it.'

'She does know it; I told her. Doesn't make a blind

bit of difference, though; she'll carry on giving strangers the come-on to spend money on her then slap the bloke down when he expects payment in kind.'

Rosie flinched beneath the brutal truth. He could be talking about her, and he knew it. But he didn't know that she now despised that type of girl as much as he seemed to.

'Were you protecting your sister from somebody?' she asked after a long pause.

Conor lit a cigarette, brooding that he regretted flooring the docker for Patricia's sake in the Red Lion last night. At one point his past girlfriend had perched on the fellow's lap, no doubt to make him jealous. 'She's not my sister, she's just somebody I know,' he said. He knew he'd have no regrets fighting again for the blonde he was with now.

'It was good of you to step in and help her then.' Rosie guessed he was talking about his sweetheart although he seemed reluctant to call her such. And it was hypocritical of him to run the woman down. Conor Flint was no model of fidelity; he'd need no more than a certain smile to join her on the mattress. Oddly, she trusted he would wait for a signal before making his move.

'D'you miss your daughter?'

Rosie threw back her head, frowning at the vibrating ceiling. 'Of course I miss her; I speak to her on the telephone sometimes and feel like my heart's breaking.' Vaguely she was aware of a bell clattering. It sounded like an ambulance and there was a rumbling in the distance as a building collapsed.

'And what about her father?' Conor asked quietly.

'What about him?' Rosie got up and paced to and

fro, the blanket trailing on the floor in her wake. His suspicions about her marital status had been made clear in the way he'd asked about the child's father rather than her husband. Suddenly she went to the bottom of the cellar steps, listening. 'I thought I heard a knock on the door.'

'I'll go.' Conor got up and disappeared up the cellar steps two at a time.

A few minutes later Tom descended into the cellar with Conor following behind.

The newcomer collapsed on the vacant chair, fanning his grimy face and breathing heavily. 'I thought I was a goner. I couldn't drive through so I left the car and dashed here on foot. I had to clamber over a mountain of rubble.' He brushed down his dusty trousers. 'Hope we don't miss the dance.' Pulling a handkerchief from his pocket Tom started scrubbing dirt from his face.

Rosie was glad to see that her colleague looked bright as a lark despite his ordeal. She quickly made introductions, noticing Tom glancing curiously at her visitor as the men shook hands. 'Mr Flint came to see my dad.'

A moment later, she realised that Conor might resume their conversation about her daughter and her heart jumped to her throat. None of her colleagues – not even her friend Hazel – knew that Miss Gardiner masqueraded under a different name. And that was the way it had to stay.

She darted a frantic look at Conor and gave a subtle shake of the head, hoping he understood her signal. His calculating smile told her he understood very well. But there was no reassurance in his eyes that he'd comply with her wordless plea.

'So you didn't know that Rosie's dad's had the good

sense to skedaddle to Kent then?' Tom glanced at Conor, who'd propped an elbow on the cellar wall rather than perch on the mattress beside Rosie.

'Thought he might be back here on a visit. When *is* he coming back on a visit?' he asked Rosie, laughter in his voice. He dragged on his cigarette stub.

Tom swung a glance between them, sensing the electricity. He gave Rosie a wink, which she realised meant that he thought Conor attractive too.

'He won't be back for ages; he's got too much sense to return here.' Rosie's sniping made Conor smile as he looked down, grinding out the cigarette butt beneath his foot.

The all clear sounded and Tom started brushing himself down with renewed vigour. 'If we get going we'll not be too late. Everybody else has probably been delayed, in any case.'

'I'll get dressed. It won't take me long.' Rosie noticed her colleague's startled glance; Tom had obviously thought her fully clothed under the enveloping blanket. 'I was getting ready when the siren went off,' she blurted in explanation and started for the steps.

It took Rosie less than five minutes to put on her dress and shoes and drag a comb through her hair. Having finished colouring her mouth with crimson lipstick she stood back, surveying her reflection in the dressing-table mirror. Her silvery hair seemed waywardly wavy, but she'd no time to sleek it. Her complexion was still rosy from constant blushing; opening her compact, she toned it down with a few pats of powder, giving her nose a final dab. Picking up her handbag, she went downstairs to find Conor and Tom chatting in the hallway.

'Suppose we'll have to walk. Won't get back to my

192

car and the buses'll be overflowing, if they're running at all,' Tom said.

Rosie was aware of Conor's appreciative glance but he didn't compliment her on her appearance as she collected her jacket from the hall cupboard.

'I'll give you a lift if you like. My car's outside.'

'Would you? You're a dear.' Tom put a hand on Conor's arm.

If Conor hadn't realised straight off that Tom had no romantic interest in women, Rosie reckoned he must've guessed by now.

'Enjoy yourselves,' Conor said as Rosie and Tom alighted from his car a few minutes later. He got out and stood on the pavement with them.

'You can be my chauffeur any time.' Tom pumped Conor's hand in thanks for the ride. He crooked an elbow at Rosie to escort her into the dance.

'Go on in. I'll join you in a mo,' she told him. When Tom was out of earshot she turned rather bashfully to Conor. 'Thanks for the lift, and for not saying anything.'

'Saying anything about what?'

'You know what.'

'Yeah, but I want you to tell me.'

'Well, you'll wait for ever then.' Rosie didn't sound shy now.

He caught her arm as she would have walked away, tightening his fingers when she stiffened. For a moment Rosie held her breath, thinking he was either going to kiss her or coerce an answer out of her. He did neither.

'You look beautiful,' was all he said, and let her go.

'That colour suits you very well, Gardiner.'

'Oh . . . thanks.' Rosie smiled at Stella, glancing down

at her turquoise summer dress. It was a shade of blue she favoured as it matched her eyes. They were standing together on the edge of the function room watching some of their colleagues Jitterbugging.

Rosie became aware of Stella giving her another appreciative look and she blushed.

'It's all right, I'm not going to ask you to dance, dear,' Stella said in her wry, weary way.

'I know . . .' Rosie couldn't help but give a nervous giggle at the unspoken message that she could relax because Stella didn't fancy her. The woman the DSO did fancy was attempting to waltz with Tom while being jostled by couples capering energetically to the jazz band.

'Norris should let her partner teach her a few steps of the Jitterbug,' Stella said, watching her girlfriend's sedate progress round the dance floor. 'He offered to but she said a waltz was more her mark. I wouldn't mind learning how to do it.' Stella attempted to copy a few of the frantic steps, hands waving at her side and stout knees jerking up and down.

Rosie had never seen her boss acting so carefree and she wondered if Stella had had more to drink than the two gins she'd seen her down. On impulse Rosie said, 'I'll teach you . . .' and grabbed at Stella's fingers. 'I learned how to dance when I worked at the Windmill Theatre.' She pulled her Senior Officer forward then began, with little pushes and shoves, to get Stella to spin about on the fringe of the Jitterbuggers.

'I didn't know you were a Windmill Girl, Gardiner,' Stella said as, laughing, they came face to face.

'I was a nude in the living tableaux, but don't broadcast it; I was just a kid in those days.' That she'd been immature in more than just years back then ran through

194

Rosie's mind as she whipped Stella to arm's length while demonstrating how to jiggle the hips. She felt quite joyous and uninhibited without knowing why. She'd had two brandy and sodas but had certainly not sunk enough to be sozzled. She and Stella met quite often on the same shifts but they'd never been so informal with one another before, although Rosie had liked her DSO since the day of her interview.

'A nude, were you indeed?' Stella puffed breathlessly and gave a wink. 'I won't tell a soul; we've all got our racy little secrets.' She glanced at Thora.

The music stopped and laughing people started strolling from the dance floor. Suddenly Stella pressed Rosie's fingers. 'I'm here if you want to have a chat at any time, you know.'

Rosie darted her a glance. 'A chat?' she asked brightly but felt a pang of apprehension in case Stella was hinting at something specific.

'You haven't danced as much as the others this evening, and not from a lack of willing partners.'

Rosie smiled. 'I haven't said no to them all!' she protested mildly. 'I did the Foxtrot with that poor chap over there.' She nodded at a private with an arm in a sling. 'And I danced with him too,' she indicated a corporal who had a walking stick. 'I trod on his foot,' Rosie ruefully related, although the mishap hadn't been her fault. When Corporal Smith had asked her to dance she'd immediately agreed, thinking of the time she'd rebuffed another Corporal, called Flint, and she'd come to the surprising conclusion that she regretted it. Having discarded his stick Smith had tried to keep his balance by hanging on to her but had almost pulled them both over, much to his embarrassment.

'You're a very pretty girl and bound to attract the chaps.' Stella paused, pondering on something. 'Despite the crowds and hubbub everywhere in London there are a lot of lonely people wanting to snatch a little happiness, perhaps for the last time. And who can blame them?'

Stella raised Rosie's hands in her own. 'Thank you for that dancing lesson, Gardiner. I very much enjoyed it.' She sighed, glancing about at the happy faces of their colleagues. 'It's good to have a break every so often.' Stella nodded at somebody over Rosie's shoulder just as the band struck up again. 'Your corporal is on his way back. You can't have bruised his toes too badly, dear.'

After a waltz in which they both stayed upright Rosie let the soldier return her to her friends but refused the drink he offered to buy her. After he'd left to rejoin his pals Hazel slipped onto the seat next to Rosie.

'He's quite a dish. Seeing him again?'

'No . . .' Rosie tutted. 'He's got a sweetheart. She's serving with the NAAFI in Scotland.'

'Never mind; plenty more fish in the sea,' Hazel said. 'I've still got Dr Clark in reserve for you anyway.'

'Wonder how they're coping over at Station 97? They must've got a call out after that awful raid this evening.' Rosie frowned. A good many of her colleagues who weren't on shift had struggled through the debris to attend the dance at the Town Hall. A core of defiance still existed in those determined not to let the Germans batter their morale as well as their city.

Rosie was aware of Hazel chattering about the billet-doux she'd received from Chuck but she was only half-listening. She finished her drink while watching Stella and Thora dancing together. Stella was attempting to teach her partner the few steps of Jitterbug Rosie had demonstrated.

From what Stella had said to her Rosie guessed her boss suspected she was lonely. Did she also suspect she lived a double life? If her DSO had found out something about her, Rosie trusted Stella would keep the knowledge to herself. The woman had hinted that she could be told something in confidence, but still Rosie was determined to guard her privacy carefully. They all worked together . . . ate together . . . some had died together, according to Stella's account of two crew members who'd perished on a call-out back in the Winter of 1940. But what did any of them really know about each other? Hazel happily volunteered personal information about herself. But Rosie had only sketchy details about others' backgrounds, just as they knew little about her. Since her attendance at her first major incident, when Jim Warwick had told her about his wife and son to calm her down, he'd not mentioned his family again. Really, they were all just strangers drawn together in a common aim to help save the lives of people caught up in a hateful conflict.

'Raffle!'

Hazel nudged Rosie to gain her attention. 'Got your tickets ready? They're drawing the numbers.'

Rosie drew some small pink papers from her dress pocket. 'I never win these things.'

'Me neither,' Hazel moaned. 'Could murder those peaches 'n' all. If I win I'll end up with the boot polish.'

'Very useful too.' Rosie couldn't remember the last time she'd tasted tinned fruit. A few minutes later there was just the tin of peaches left on the raffle table.

The number was called and Rosie and Hazel groaned, simultaneously screwing their tickets up.

'Fix!' Hazel called good-naturedly as Stella waved the winning ticket then collected her prize.

'We could do with that tin of fruit in the canteen to liven up the rice pudding,' Tom called out, making the others laugh.

'No fear!' Stella said. 'These are being put away for Christmas.'

Corporal Smith caught Rosie's eye, raising his beer glass in salute and farewell now the evening was coming to an end. She smiled back, gave him a wave on standing up, but thoughts of another man were niggling at her mind again as she collected her handbag and jacket, ready to leave. Conor Flint hadn't been the only fellow to compliment her that evening though it was the memory of *his* words and voice that was now stuck in her head.

CHAPTER SEVENTEEN

'Ah, nice to see you,' Popeye lied. 'Come on in.'

As Conor Flint crossed his threshold, Popeye caught a glimpse of the two fellows lounging against the Humber parked outside. His heart plummeted to his boots; he'd hoped the man would turn up alone, as last time.

Flint had telephoned him and told him plainly of his intention to take his stock of petrol coupons in compensation for John Gardiner's booze. Popeye's protestation that he'd no idea what coupons the other man was talking about had been quickly silenced. Conor had also admitted breaking into his warehouse and could list everything inside it that Popeye had hoarded over decades. As most of it had been stolen or counterfeited Popeye knew Flint had him over a barrel. He'd need to tread carefully or the bastard might grass him up to the coppers . . . anonymously, of course.

Popeye had considered attempting a swindle but that'd gone out of the window now. Conor was nobody's fool, unlike his brothers, and if the scam went wrong the two gorillas loitering outside would enter the fray and maul him.

He'd recognised Steven Flint from the day he'd turned up with his brother Saul to collect an order of pornography. Popeye hadn't liked him from the off; the youngest Flint boy reminded him of his Lenny, all gob and swagger.

As for Mickey Rook, he was a well-known thug who'd hired out his fists to several East End outfits. But it seemed his loyalty was now reserved for the Flints because his sister had married into the clan.

Shuffling down the hallway after the younger man, Popeye realised his own back-up was far too weak to be of any bloody use whatsoever if things turned nasty.

'This them, here?' Conor lifted the lid of a cardboard box on the table.

'That's it,' Popeye said in a defeated sigh. As a last resort he was willing to give plan B a go. 'Can hire you out a couple of blokes to shift that lot round the streets, if you like. Cheap rates and they've even got the use of me motor.' Popeye jokily elbowed Conor in the ribs. 'Ain't as if you'll be short of petrol for me Citroën, is it?'

'Got my own people for deliveries, thanks.' Conor cast a look at Frank Purves' sidekicks. If he'd been in a better mood he'd have had a chuckle at being offered their services.

As it was he simply braced a hand on Popeye's table and began examining the counterfeits. They were top quality but still he wondered whether his brother Saul had lost his marbles, getting himself involved with the likes of Popeye. Judging by the clowns the printer used as henchmen, Purves was fit for retirement. Yet Conor was glad Saul had come over to Shoreditch on business or he wouldn't have crossed paths again with Rosemary.

He knew the unlikely lads were watching him; the short, grizzled one had lost a hand but definitely looked to be the fitter and more able of the two. The fat fellow with the limp was unhealthily sallow and unattractively surly.

'I know they don't look up to much but they've been doing the business fer me and even pulled in a few new customers out on the rounds.' Popeye inclined closer, pouring his visitor a whisky. 'Thing is . . . we go way back, and I like to see 'em all right. They need the wages and they're honest as the day's long.' Frank added that straight-faced despite knowing that Midge Williams and Rufus Grimes were as bent as nine-bob notes. 'See . . . now you've taken all me stock of coupons, Mr Flint, it'll be some while before I can get up and running again and give me crippled lads a day's work.'

'I'm gonna hear violins in a minute, am I?' Conor said sourly, still counting coupons.

In fact Popeye couldn't give a toss about Midge and Rufus, but he did want Conor to employ them. It was the only way he was likely to get some of his coupons back. Midge was a dab hand at playing both sides to the middle. Popeye was confident the little man could work his magic on a fair amount of the coupons just till things started rolling again. As it was, Popeye was out of paper and ink to run off more, and almost out of money too, what with Shirley always wanting this and that. The idea of having to break into his investment savings was almost choking him.

Midge and Rufus were fiddling off him, Popeye knew, but he was prepared to turn a blind eye because his old cronies were cute enough to make sure the customers rather than their boss suffered.

'So now you've taken all me petrol rations off me,' Popeye repeated forlornly, hoping for a more sympathetic response this time.

'I've not taken them off you,' Conor corrected, straightening from his lounging position. 'I've purchased them with my five hundred quid plus all the interest you owe me. This is business and, all things considered, I reckon I've been generous and patient.'

'Without a doubt you have,' Popeye grovelled, nodding gravely. He realised Conor's civility didn't make him a pushover. And he didn't reckon the bloke's generosity and patience were on his account either, but he'd racked his brains over why he'd not been back sooner with his demands and couldn't come up with an answer.

Conor knocked back his whisky and Popeye was disappointed to see him already preparing to leave. In a matter of seconds his visitor had loaded the coupons back into the cardboard box and handed him the empty glass.

'Tell you what, you can have Midge 'n' Rufus on a trial, if you like,' Popeye blurted. 'Then if they do all right you can settle up with me later. I wouldn't let 'em out in me car, would I, if they was no good?'

'Ain't interested in them or your sob stories.' Conor lifted the box and within a few minutes Popeye was wrathfully watching the Humber pulling away from outside his house.

'What did he say?' Midge and Rufus chorused as soon as Popeye came back into the room.

'You heard what he bloody said,' Popeye snarled. 'You ain't deaf as well as the rest, are yer?' He began pacing to and fro in his back parlour. 'Fucking bastard! Took the lot! That was worth much more'n five hundred quid!'

'You should have kept some hid,' Rufus muttered.

Popeye turned on him. 'That's what I should've done, should I?' he mimicked sarcastically. 'Flint knew exactly what I'd got in Houndsditch down to the last packet of fags. Surprised he didn't ask fer them 'n' all.'

Popeye hadn't mentioned the break-in at the warehouse to his cohorts until now, fearing he'd be thought a fool for allowing it to happen. He'd known for some time that the padlocks on his warehouse wouldn't keep out a skilful picklock but he'd been too tight-fisted to shell out for new ones. Conor Flint had had the decency just to take a look around and close up on his way out, Popeye had to give the man that.

'Bleedin' hell! You can get out of shtoock by printing off some more coupons, can't yer?' Midge sounded outraged by his boss's carelessness.

'What with? No paper, no ink, no nothing.'

Rufus's shoulders sagged. He'd got to go home and break it to Gertie that the work had dried up. Since he'd been bringing in a nice few bob and handing over his knocked-off coupons, she'd been cosying up in bed again instead of turning her back every night. 'No point hanging about here, is there? I'm getting off now.' Rufus stomped to the door. 'If things straighten out and you need me you know where to find me.'

Once Rufus had gone Midge slumped down uninvited into Popeye's armchair and helped himself to the whisky. 'Can't you get nothing on credit at the wholesaler?'

'What, and lose me discount for cash? That'll eat into profits.' The idea of being overcharged was something else that stuck in Popeye's craw.

Midge slanted his boss an old-fashioned look but knew better than to criticise. Popeye was still his port in a storm. 'I blame that John Gardiner fer this.' Midge downed a shot of Scotch and wiped his mouth with the back of his hand. 'He's loused it up for all of us and brought them Flints down on our backs.' Midge peered at Popeye for his reaction. He knew he'd have to stir his guvnor into some sort of action or his income would dry up and he'd be back rummaging in dustbins. For years Midge had had to lay low and earn what he could, when he could. If he showed his face at the Labour Exchange for a handout he'd be done for as soon as they asked for his name and checked his background. Even the people at a couple of the soup kitchens he'd frequented had started asking awkward questions so he'd stopped going.

'Them Flints'll be back. Now they know what you've got stashed they'll clean you out, Pop, mark my words.'

Popeye was already brooding on the possibility that his new padlocks might not keep Flint out any better than the old ones. It took a thief to catch a thief, so they said, and he reckoned he might be finished because Conor Flint, and not the Old Bill, pulled the rug on him.

'Can't you get Gardiner to change his mind?' Midge burst out in desperation. 'If he sets up his still again me 'n' Roof can deliver bottles instead of coupons.' Midge jumped to his feet, flailing his good arm, annoyed at Popeye's inertia. 'There's gotta be a way of persuading the fucker to play along! You'll be done for, else.' He jabbed a cautioning finger.

'Shut up! I'm thinking!' Popeye roared.

There was nothing likely to change John Gardiner's mind, in Frank's opinion. He'd got no scandal to blackmail the man with. Gardiner lived a pretty clean life now, and Doris wouldn't be that bothered to learn her old man had dabbled on the wrong side of the law before they'd got together. That avenue would lead nowhere and just give John the hump that his missus had been dragged into things. Grassing the distiller up to the police was also pointless as John would return the favour and Popeye had far more to lose than he.

Gardiner's weak points were his womenfolk. Him and Doris were no great romance, that was plain to see. But Rosie and his little granddaughter were another kettle of fish; he adored them both. John had let on once that Rosie had gone berserk when she'd found out Lenny was delivering to him labels for counterfeit booze brewed up in the cellar. From what Popeye knew of John Gardiner's daughter, she was an independent and opinionated sort who'd holler blue murder if she thought she was under threat.

So that left only the nipper as a bargaining tool. Popeye reckoned that if he managed to do John Gardiner a good turn on account of his little Hope, then tit for tat was on the cards and Popeye could name his own price.

'Not seen you in a while, Gertie. How've you been?' Rosie called out.

Grabbing her change from the stallholder, Gertie elbowed her way towards Rosie, who was also dodging marketgoers to meet her.

'Well, this is a nice surprise,' Gertie said when they were face to face. 'I wondered if I'd ever again run into you out shopping now you're up to your armpits in bandages.' She grinned, giving Rosie a spontaneous hug.

'I've wanted to see you, too,' Rosie said, returning the embrace. 'I'd've called round on my day off but I lost your address. Let's find a spot over there.' Rosie indicated a break between the stalls in Petticoat Lane where they might chat without being jostled.

'I'll write me address down for you again before I forget.' Gertie delved into her bag to tear off a scrap of envelope, then scribbled on it with a pencil got from the same place. Having handed it over she shook the paper bag she was holding. 'Just bought some thread to sew up me husband's shirts. He's bust the buttons off on a couple, the podgy sod.'

'I've bought Hope some hair ribbon. I couldn't resist it; it's such a lovely colour and matches her eyes.' Rosie pulled out of her bag a twist of tissue paper containing a small coil of turquoise silk.

'Matches your eyes too,' Gertie said. 'Lucky thing, you are, having such lovely looks.'

Rosie smiled her thanks for the compliment but was thinking that for all Gertie's chirpiness the woman looked tired and worried.

'No Victoria today?' She'd been surprised to see Gertie without her daughter.

'Rufus is minding Vicky for me. She's getting too big for the pram and the little madam plays up if she's on her reins for too long.' Gertie shielded her eyes from the late August sun, feeling hot and bothered. She gave Rosie an envious glance; the younger woman looked as poised and pretty as ever despite the sultry heat. 'Life seems to be treating you well as an ambulance auxiliary. Enjoying it, are you, if that's the right word?'

'I'm glad I joined,' Rosie replied. 'But I'll admit there've been times when I've felt overwhelmed by it all.'

'I know you must see some terrible sights.' Gertie sounded solemn and there was a deep sadness lurking at the backs of her eyes.

'The others have been taking the worst of it for me up till now.' Rosie didn't elaborate; this woman of all people needed no description of the carnage facing an ambulance crew following a bombardment. 'I've got my driving test soon.' Rosie was both buoyed and terrified by the forthcoming event.

Tom had told her to expect the examiner to be rigorous. On his test he'd been required to drive with a full pail of water on the floor of a makeshift ambulance. Tom had sloshed some water over the sides of the bucket due to the double declutching needed in the boneshaker, but the RAC official had passed him anyway saying that on the whole his gear changes had been acceptable.

'You'll pass with flying colours,' Gertie encouraged.

'My colleagues are nice,' Rosie volunteered. 'I've found a good friend in a girl called Hazel Scott. We all go out sometimes to a dance or the pictures on days off.'

'Must be nice . . .' Gertie sounded rather wistful. 'Your dad's looking after Hope, is he, when you're working? Don't forget I can lend a hand if you're stuck at any time.'

'Thanks for the offer, but Hope's gone to Gravesend with her granddad,' Rosie explained. 'They're staying with my stepmother's family. It was agony waving Hope off but . . .' Rosie didn't want to sound pious and say that she'd bear any heartache to keep her daughter safe. Back in the days when they worked at the Windmill Theatre Gertie used to boast she'd never let strangers care for her kids. How the poor woman must regret that decision now. 'I speak to Hope on the telephone most days. I race home from work for that treat and it keeps my spirits up.'

'Sensible of you to send her away like that,' Gertie said quietly. 'If I'd done the same with my boys instead of being selfish . . .'

'I doubt I'd've let Hope out of my sight if she wasn't with somebody who loves her.' Rosie squeezed Gertie's hands.

'Joey and Vicky and me spend more time down the bloody air-raid shelter than ever we did during the Blitz. First peep from the siren and we're off like greyhounds from a trap. Rufus comes too when he's about. And he's home most of the time since he lost his job.'

'So he got some employment?' Rosie was glad to change the subject; Gertie's eyes were glistening from speaking about her lost boys.

'He had a delivery job, but the work's dried up now.' Gertie left it at that. She didn't want a nice person like Rosie Gardiner to know her husband – or she, for that matter – handled fake ration books. Ashamed or not, Gertie missed having the independence her earnings from the coupons had given her. She also missed having Rufus out from under her feet for the best part of the day. Her husband was again sitting scowling in his chair for hours on end.

'Any nice fellows been chatting you up in the Ambulance Service?' Gertie asked, determined to stop brooding and enjoy this chance meeting with Rosie.

'No such luck!' Rosie matched Gertie's bantering tone but at the back of her mind she wished that Conor Flint hadn't immediately entered her head at Gertie's mention of nice men. From what she knew of him, he was anything but nice, and whether he'd chatted her up or intimidated her was debatable too. But she couldn't forget the look he'd given her when he'd told her she looked beautiful. He wanted her, that was plain, but there'd been gentleness as well as desire in his eyes.

'I'm at work this evening so'd better get cracking.' Rosie pocketed Gertie's scrap of paper. 'If we don't bump into each other I'll pop round and see you as soon as I get a mo.'

The two friends said their farewells then wove paths through the crowds, heading in different directions.

On getting back from her shopping trip Rosie quickly undressed and started putting on her uniform. She'd made herself late by idling with Gertie in the market. She was buttoning up her crisp white blouse when she heard the ratatat. Past experience had taught her to have a scout out of the window before answering the door. With a frown she went downstairs to open up, shrugging on her uniform jacket.

'Hello, locked yourself out, have you, Irene?' A year or so ago Peg's daughter had accidentally left her key at home and Rosie had invited the girl in for a cup of tea while Irene waited for her mum to return. At the time Hope had been toddling and Irene had made quite a fuss of her, treating her like an amusing little toy.

'Not locked out, Mrs Deane,' Irene mumbled, shifting uneasily. 'Just wanted to talk to you, if that's all right?'

'Oh . . . d'you want to come in then?' Rosie issued the invitation when the girl didn't immediately say what was on her mind.

Rosie was curious to know what might have brought Peg's daughter calling; usually if they spotted one another in the street they'd exchange a hello or a wave but that was about it. Peg had no doubt warned her daughter to steer clear of the brazen hussy up the road. But whatever Irene wanted to say Rosie hoped she'd be quick about it so she could get on.

'I'm sorry about me mum being such a cow to you,' Irene blurted before Rosie had got the door properly closed behind her.

'That's all right, don't worry about it.' Rosie smiled neutrally, wondering why on earth the girl had felt it necessary to come and tell her that. 'I'd make a pot of tea, Irene, but haven't the time as I'm off to work.'

'Sorry . . . didn't realise . . . I'll go . . .' Irene turned back to the door, shoulders slumped and greasy head bowed.

Poor Irene seemed even spottier and fatter than Rosie remembered her. She felt guilty for having insulted the girl to her mother months ago. Irene took after her dad, both in build and in character. Rosie reckoned that inheriting Peg's sour moods would've been far more of a handicap than Irene's stolid homeliness.

'I've got a few minutes yet before I set off,' Rosie said, trying to make amends with kindness. 'Come and take a seat in the parlour.'

Irene suddenly snorted back a sob. Then, unable to control herself, began weeping noisily, her forearms raised over her face to hide her distress.

'What's wrong?' Rosie demanded in alarm, prising Irene's arms off her face to hear what the girl was mumbling. She got a handkerchief from her pocket when Irene started scrubbing her wet face with her cardigan sleeves.

'Don't know what to do, Mrs Deane,' Irene gasped.

'About what?' Rosie guided her hiccuping visitor towards a chair in the parlour.

210

'I've been seeing a boy,' Irene choked out. 'Mum's gonna kill me when she finds out.'

Some months ago Doris had told her about Peg's daughter and Bobby West getting friendly behind the park shed. But Rosie hadn't a clue why Irene would choose to confide in her about romance problems.

'Bobby West's your sweetheart, isn't he?' Rosie wanted to get to the heart of the matter, conscious of the clock ticking on the wall. She was due on shift in five minutes.

Irene nodded. 'How d'you know about us? Is everybody yakking about me already?' She scrubbed her eyes again, sniffing loudly.

'My stepmother heard that you'd been seen together, that's all.' Rosie patted the girl's arm in reassurance. 'Why don't you tell your mum you like Bobby? If he's polite she might let you walk out together, y'know. Sometimes parents get funny if they think you're going behind their backs.' Rosie hoped that was sound advice. It struck her that she'd need to practise what she preached when Hope got to be Irene's age. Her beautiful little daughter would attract a lot of admirers. At present the idea of any randy fellow laying a finger on Hope filled Rosie with fury and dread. 'Have a sit down and a breather, then you'll feel better about going home and facing your mum.' Rosie pulled out a chair at the parlour table. As Irene perched on the edge of it Rosie noticed a bump beneath her dress that hadn't been obvious when the girl had been standing up. It didn't look like puppy fat.

Irene blushed, pulling her cardigan's edges over her belly. 'Mum won't let me 'n' Bobby walk out . . . and she'll never let me have me baby neither,' she blurted.

Rosie bit her lip, wishing she were still in blissful

211

ignorance of that explosive news. Irene was expecting her to come out with something helpful but whatever she said Peg would be livid with her for interfering, and mortified to know her daughter had spread such a private matter before the family could hush it up.

'Your mum's not guessed yet?' Rosie asked, surprised to see Peg's daughter shake her head. The woman seemed to be an expert at spotting a scandal yet had missed one right under her nose.

'Me mum's always saying I'm too fat . . . never looks no further than that,' Irene said resentfully. 'She's always going on about you being an unmarried mother, too.' Irene peeped at Rosie from behind a curtain of lank, mousy hair. 'Me dad gives you credit for the way you conduct yourself and bring up your little gel.' Irene picked at her ragged fingernails. 'I think me mum don't like you just 'cos me dad does. Anyhow, I think me dad's right about you, Mrs Deane.' She slid an admiring glance at Rosie. 'I've always wanted to be like you, even when you used to work at the Windmill Theatre. You was so glamorous and pretty.' Irene hung her head again. 'I've come to see you 'cos I want to conduct meself properly, and I want to keep the baby. If me mum gets her way she'll make me give it up, or get rid of it before anybody knows and starts gossiping. What shall I do?'

Rosie speared agitated fingers through her hair. Again she glanced at the clock on the wall as it gained fifteen minutes past the hour. She knew it would be callous to usher Irene out of the house at such a critical time. 'Does Bobby know he's got you pregnant?'

'He's told me to get rid of it, 'cos he's too young to be tied down. Don't know how to get rid of it and neither does he.' Irene's expression turned angry. 'He's only sixteen but he reckons he'll join up if me dad finds out and sets about him.' Irene raised her bloodshot eyes, pleading wordlessly for assistance. 'Don't want you to think I'm being rude or nosy, but there's nobody to talk to who understands how I feel. You kept your little gel . . . and your dad's been nice about it . . . so I might be lucky, eh?'

'Hush . . .' Rosie crouched down at the side of Irene's chair as she started weeping again. Rosie knew she could act indignant but Irene had come to see her from desperation, not malice, and she'd not the heart to have a go at her.

'Did the fellow run out on you?' Irene's watery eyes were fixed on Rosie's face. 'My dad says he must've been mad if he did.'

'It was different for me,' Rosie said quietly. 'I . . . didn't want him to stay.'

'But you always wanted your little girl?'

Rosie nodded although she remembered how determined she'd been to have her precious daughter adopted in those weeks after the birth. Nurse Johnson had nearly been Hope's mother.

'You need to tell your mum or your dad,' Rosie gently persuaded. 'I won't let on that you've said a word to me, promise.' She sighed, as Irene's crying got louder and she began shaking her head. 'You must, Irene, because they'll know eventually, and then it'll be worse for you.'

Irene nodded dejectedly.

'Come on, off you go now.' Rosie helped the girl to her feet. At the front door she said softly, 'My dad did go mad, and I did think that things would never come right for me just after Hope was born. But they did. I'm happy now. And you will be, too.'

Rosie watched Irene close the gate, wishing she'd managed to come up with a better solution for the girl's predicament. But what was there? Irene, young as she was, had already worked out for herself the options that were open to her: an abortion, or a scandal. Most parents wanted to avoid the disgrace and shove the baby out of sight. Her own father had, but from the moment he'd seen the small angelic face peeping from swaddling he'd changed his mind. Rosie hoped with all her heart that the Prices would feel the same way, because judging by Irene's waistline she might already be too far gone to take the dangerous backstreet route.

CHAPTER EIGHTEEN

'You look just the ticket: short and skinny.'

Rosie had been bandaging a gashed forehead when she received that backhanded compliment. She was jerked away from her patient and marched off, leaving the poor woman collapsed on the pavement next to her dead husband and robustly cursing all Germans to perdition.

'There's a little chap trapped down there. That hole isn't big enough for any of us men to clamber through, but you might measure up.'

Rosie pushed back her tin helmet to stare at the stocky chap, grinning amiably at her. He still had hold of her elbow and was studying her figure with scientific approval as though inspecting a thoroughbred racehorse. His meaning suddenly became clear and made Rosie's insides lurch. Confined spaces terrified her.

'Rosie Gardiner, meet Dr Richard Clark.' Hazel Scott had trotted over to them, and made a quick introduction. She even managed a knowing wink for Rosie to indicate he was the heart-throb from the first-aid post.

Hazel's gas mask was hanging about her neck and she shoved it aside, looking over her shoulder. 'We've got a girl with a broken arm on a stretcher over there. She's told us her younger brother's in the basement; bad news is that his leg's wedged beneath some fallen concrete. He was howling, she said. But it's gone quiet in there now.' Hazel nodded at the jagged opening that led into the murky bowels of the ruined house. 'The lad's sister managed to crawl out through here.' Hazel gave Rosie's slender frame the once-over in much the same way Dr Clark had. 'She's fourteen but not that much different in size from you.'

'Would you have a go at rescuing the poor little blighter?' Richard Clark hunkered down, pulling away debris to widen the entrance and show Rosie what she was up against. The rocky passage seemed to dip down at a perilous angle before disappearing from view. He leaned in, shouting, then they all kept quiet, straining to hear any sound that might indicate human life endured beneath the tons of rubble. 'I'd go in myself and investigate,' he said, frowning at Rosie, 'but I'd not manage more than a yard or two before getting stuck and being a bloody hindrance to everyone.'

Hazel eyed her own buxom figure with a grimace that made words superfluous.

Rosie licked her lips. Two pairs of eyes were on her, demanding an answer. She knew there was no time for dithering. A yes or a no was all that was required.

''Course I'll give it a go,' she croaked.

Hazel gave her shoulder a hearty pat. 'Well done. Knew you would, Rosie.'

'If the lad's got any broken bones, you'll have to use your own judgement about whether to manhandle him.

If he seems willing to move he's probably fit enough to do so,' the doctor quickly instructed. 'Guide him back so we can see to his injuries out here. Don't hang about patching him up.' His voice became harsh. 'If you can't help him and things look hopeless, report back at once, Miss Gardiner . . . no unnecessary heroics.' He looked up at some groaning joists that had collapsed to form a charred apex. Roof tiles were being shivered downwards to pile up in what remained of the guttering.

'Dr Clark means no use you croaking in there too,' Hazel interpreted bluntly.

'You can give him a jab of this if he's in distress.' Richard snatched a syringe from his medical case. 'It should stop the worst of it for the poor little chap.'

Rosie stretched out shaking fingers for the capped needle and put it in a pocket. With an intake of breath that seemed interminable she dropped to her knees. Immediately she drove herself forward on her elbows, allowing nothing into her mind other than the thought that she was relieved she was wearing her twill trousers rather than her regulation skirt. But she'd not got far into the blackness before the demons attacked. The choking dust mingling with the fear-induced nausea at the back of her throat made her chest heave and her cheeks billow. Lowering her face to her forearms she dug in for a moment, taking a breather, counting out ten seconds slowly. Again she pulled herself onwards, covering ground, inch by inch. She looked up at the uneven stones above her head, blinking grit from her lashes. By touch she made out the iron legs of a bedstead to her left, realising that it had probably crashed down through ceilings and floors to land in the basement. She wriggled under it and gave silent thanks as the access widened into a low cave; she still couldn't stand but at least she no longer had entombing brick scratching her sides.

Rosie heard a faint cough, then another. She took the torch from her breast pocket, bouncing the light this way and that until she saw the little boy up ahead, about thirty feet away.

'Try and keep still, there's a good lad, till I can take a look at you.' She had forced cheerfulness into her hoarse voice.

'It hurts . . . my head hurts . . .'

'I know; but you're doing well, aren't you? I reckon the soldiers out fighting Jerry would like to be as brave as you.' Rosie scuttled on as carefully as she could. She was terrified of dislodging masonry that might fall and block her path. She halted to adjust the chinstrap on her tin helmet. The perspiration on her forehead was running into her eyes and she flicked her head to dislodge it before dropping to knees and elbows, crawling onwards as the tunnel tightened. Broken glass was beneath her gloved palms and she tried to swipe it aside, knowing she'd meet it again on the way back.

'What's your name?' Rosie called out. The boy had gone quiet and that was more unnerving to her than hearing any yelps of pain. 'Mine's Rosie and I know where you are, y'know.' She came to a halt, flopping down to rest her chin on a filthy fist. Taking the pencil torch out of her breast pocket again she waved the beam to and fro to soothe him with the light. Then she steadied it on his face, making him flinch from the glare. Her heart leaped to her mouth as she realised he was probably only six or seven. She turned the beam on her own face so he could see her. 'I'm very close by and about to get you out of here. Will you tell me your name?' she asked again.

'Herbert . . . Herbie, me mum calls me,' came a faint response followed by a dry cough.

'Right then, Herbie,' Rosie was enormously relieved that he'd not lost consciousness. 'Bet you're ready for a nice hot cup of char, aren't you? I know I am.'

She just caught his murmured yes and realised he'd started crying. 'The ladies from the WVS have set up their canteen outside. The kettles are singing away . . . can you hear them? So, we'd best get you on your feet and in the queue in case they run out of Bourbons.' With a final frantic effort Rosie hauled herself to his side, panting heavily by the time she reached him. She allowed her pumping chest to relax against her hands for a few seconds. Then she shoved the helmet back on her head and assessed him. But it was hard to tell the dirt from the caked blood on Herbie's small face.

She gave him a grin. 'Well done. Is it just your head that aches?'

'And my leg.' He pointed solemnly at the leg trapped under rock.

Putting the torch between her teeth, Rosie examined him by running her hands over his arms and shoulders while trying to keep the torch steady. He had a deep cut on his cheek and another on his scalp but he kept turning his head to protect his eyes from the torchlight, preventing a proper examination. Rosie studied the large slab of concrete imprisoning the boy. It looked far too heavy for her to lift on her own. She felt cold sweat dripping down her spine because she knew she couldn't go away and leave him. Not now.

'If I have a go at shifting this big boulder d'you reckon you could scoot backwards, Herbie?'

He nodded, tears of pain and fright beading his lashes in the torchlight. 'Will my leg ache more if you move it?' he gulped.

'Don't think so . . .' Rosie said honestly. She had no idea what sort of mess his shin might be in. With any luck the bone could be intact.

'Want to get out . . . I'm hungry . . . missed me tea 'cos I was playing football.'

'Can't have that, can we?' Rosie said. 'Bet you play in a team with your pals, don't you?'

'I play at the back.'

'Crikey, your pals'll need you up and running again then, won't they? Who's going to stop the other teams shooting at goal if you're laid up?' While talking Rosie had been using the torch to try to find something nearby to use as a lever. There was a length of timber just within reach but she knew if it was wormy it might splinter and break. If the slab were to crash back on little Herbie's legs it would shatter them.

She leaned sideways, her fingers spread wide, stretching until she felt she'd rip her arm from its socket. Eventually her nails made contact with splintery wood and slowly she worked her hand along its length till she could grip it. By hauling back on one elbow she managed to drag it towards her, then slowly manoeuvre it into position underneath the slab. With a foot she guided the plank into place, slowly shifting it to and fro until she was satisfied with her engineering. Then she rammed it home with two savage stamps until it was stuck fast.

'We ready then, Herbie?' Rosie panted, a wedge of fearful emotion thickening her throat. 'Can you move backwards for me now as fast as you would if the other team were on a run for goal?'

She watched for his nod, accompanied by a faint smile, the first she'd seen him give.

'Righto . . . when I say "Now!", you scoot. The opposition's coming and off you go . . . Now! After them, they're past you, you can't let them win, Herbie,' Rosie panted in desperation, feeling that her arms and neck muscles would explode from the load they were bearing.

The timber cracked and the rock fell with a thud that lifted Rosie inches off the floor and filled her mouth with dust.

Rosie's head dropped to her crossed forearms. 'Can you hear me, Herbie?' she called. 'Please say you can . . .'

'Have they really got Bourbons?'

Rosie gasped a sob of utter relief into the grimy material of her sleeves. 'Oh, yes, . . . and I'll get you two, I promise, Herbie.'

Rosie emerged into the humid night, Herbie clinging on to her left foot with two determined hands. Obliquely she heard applause and cheering. Exhaustion hit her like a physical blow and much as she wanted to help Herbie out into the air she couldn't. But there were strong hands lifting the boy onto a stretcher and raising her to stand on unsteady feet.

'Bloody marvellous job!' Hazel thumped Rosie's back then took the cigarette from between her lips and stuck it in Rosie's mouth. 'No arguments! Have a good drag; you need it.'

Though she hadn't smoked in years, Rosie did as she was told, finishing off the cigarette with relish. She drew the smoke deep into her dusty lungs, coughing all the while.

'Cup of tea?' Hazel suggested, opening a new pack of cigarettes.

'She deserves a double Scotch . . .'

'And a medal . . .'

Rosie heard the disembodied praise and was aware of a succession of uniformed people – firemen, policemen, the women from the WVS canteen – snatching a moment to trot over and pat her on the back. But she was too concerned about keeping her promise to Herbie to acknowledge them properly.

'Get two teas, Hazel, one for Herbie. And make sure you get him a couple of Bourbons to go with it, won't you?'

'Anybody home?'

'Come in, love. Got time for a drink today?'

'Oh, thanks, Mr Purves. Don't mind if I do have a brew. I'm parched.'

'Can open a bottle of brown ale, if you prefer.' Popeye emerged from the back parlour and gave Nurse Johnson a wink.

'I'm on duty! You trying to get me sacked, Mr Purves?' she complained, parking her bike then stepping over the threshold. Trudy had been pedalling past and seen his front door open. A lot of the houses also had their windows flung wide to let in a breath of air on what was a sticky Indian summer afternoon.

'I will rat on you, love, if you don't stop calling me Mr Purves. Me name's Frank to me friends.' Popeye pulled out a chair at the table. 'Now sit down and I'll put the kettle on.'

Frank had kept the dressing on his thumb although the wound had healed up. He'd liked the idea of Trudy popping in to see him and laying her soothing hands on him. Since his counterfeiting business had hit the buffers, affecting his cash flow, Shirley had become a constant nag and was driving him up the wall.

'You look smart, Frank,' Trudy said, cocking her head to assess his appearance. He had on a pristine shirt and a tie, despite the heat.

'In your honour, love.' He did a little jig. 'Thought you might pop by, seeing as it's a Wednesday,' he added jokily, making his visitor tut at him. In fact what he'd said was the truth. For the past two Wednesdays Frank had spruced himself up and left his door open, hoping to tempt the nurse to come in if she was on her rounds in the district.

'Let's have a gander at that hand, then, while the tea's brewing,' Trudy said as Frank emerged from the kitchen and put the milk and sugar bowl on the table.

Frank sat opposite her and stretched his fingers out on the tablecloth.

'Almost good as new, it is. Just let the air get to it,' Trudy gave her verdict, having examined the pink flesh. 'Can't do any more for you.'

'You can . . .' Before the nurse could drop his hand to the cloth Frank turned his fingers, clasping hers. He coughed and loosened his tight collar from his flushing neck. 'If you want to say no, just say no . . . but I wondered if you'd like to come to the pictures Saturday night?' The surprise on the woman's face made him quickly set her free. 'Sorry, love . . . Forget about it. I'm just a silly old sod.'

'What about your friend Shirley?'

Popeye glanced at her. So Trudy must have been thinking about their conversations or she wouldn't have remembered his girlfriend's name. He shook his head regretfully. 'Me 'n' Shirley ain't been getting on. I reckon it's time to call a halt to that.'

'When?' Trudy asked pointedly, sitting back and crossing her arms over her chest. She didn't fancy Frank but he did make her laugh, and she had precious little fun in her life. Besides, she was lonely and a casual companion would be nice to have. But she wasn't getting involved in any rivalry with another woman who might have deeper feelings for him.

'When?' Frank pretended to be mystified while he mulled that one over.

'When are you telling Shirley you're not seeing her again?'

'Whenever you say, love.' Frank had made his decision and suddenly felt quite light-hearted.

'And how will Shirley feel about it all?'

Popeye shrugged. 'Reckon she'll soon realise it's for the best, if she don't already. Ain't seen her in more'n a week.'

That was good enough for Trudy. She gave him a smile. 'I wouldn't mind seeing the picture on at the Odeon, if that's all right with you, Frank?'

'Even treat you to a penn'orth of chips on the way home, if yer good.'

He winked his good eye, making Trudy guffaw.

CHAPTER NINETEEN

'There's a man over there staring at you.' Hazel nodded at the bar then took another sip of her gin and orange. 'Wouldn't mind having that dreamboat's attention myself. Only joking . . . my Chuck's the man for me.' She sunk her chin into a cupped palm, gazing whimsically into space. 'He's taking me to meet his folks soon.' Hazel waggled her ring finger. 'Sparkler'll be on that in a few weeks. Can't wait to get married and have kids. Don't care if it's a poor do. My cousin had registry office, in her work costume and laddered nylons, then a cheese sandwich in a pub afterwards.' Hazel blew a sigh through her pouting lips. 'Got to grab at it, I reckon, 'cos we might be blown to kingdom come tomorrow.'

Rosie understood her friend's philosophy on life, sad though it was. She often wondered if her father had married Doris with the same depressing attitude. The couple argued so much that it seemed weird they'd bothered tying the knot when they could have jogged along as they were. But Rosie was surprised to hear that

Hazel hadn't met Chuck's parents when her friend considered herself practically engaged.

'I thought Chuck had been your boyfriend for ages.'

''Bout seven months now. Chuck told me his parents are miserable sods who've frightened off his past girlfriends. That's why he's still single at twenty-nine. But he's determined they won't send me packing, so he wants to pick the right time.' Hazel thumped the table with a fist, causing Tom and Jim, sitting opposite, to stop talking about football and start listening to the girls' conversation. 'They won't shift me so easily! Chuck's getting the ring first, then taking me along to make the announcement. I'm twenty-six soon and want my man, so if they don't like me . . . tough!'

'Does your mum like him?' Rosie knew that her friend's parents were estranged; Hazel never saw her father or the older sister he'd taken with him when he set up home with another woman.

'Oh, she thinks Chuck's nice enough. They've only met the once but Mum don't care what I get up to, anyhow. She's got religion since the new vicar moved into the village. Reckon she's got her eye on him.' Hazel snorted amusement. 'Speaking of people having an eye on someone, I reckon that fellow might come over and speak to you.' Hazel craned her neck to look past Rosie at the people at the bar. 'Go on, give him a smile, he's gorgeous. Oh, hang on, he's with a girl, though.' Hazel had spied the blonde seated on a barstool.

'What man?' Rosie glanced casually over a shoulder. She was used to her friend's matchmaking. Hazel couldn't understand why any single girl wouldn't want to chase a romance and an engagement ring.

'D'you know him?' Hazel had noticed her friend's expression change.

'Sort of . . . through my dad,' Rosie said, gulping her drink. The idea that Conor Flint might come over and greet her as Mrs Deane had made her mouth dry. The pub's smoky atmosphere hadn't concealed the mocking intensity in his eyes as they'd met hers over the rim of his glass.

Rosie reminded herself that they'd got over their initial hostility. Last time they'd met they'd parted on reasonable terms. He'd given her and Tom a lift to the dance and told her she looked beautiful. He'd been perfectly charming. But he was an unpredictable man . . . unfathomable . . . and she knew she'd be wise to err on the side of caution with him.

'That's your dad's friend Mr Flint, isn't it?' Tom grinned. 'He did us a good turn, didn't he, Rosie, getting us to the ball on time.' He struck a theatrical pose. 'I felt like Cinderella even though Prince Charming was driving a Humber rather than a pumpkin,' he quipped. 'Shall we go over to say hello?'

'I'll just have a quick word with him on my way out,' Rosie said, knocking back what remained of her brandy and soda and standing up. 'It's time I got going anyway; I promised Dad a phone call before bedtime.'

Quickly Rosie said goodbye to her friends, wishing she'd gone straight home when she'd clocked off instead of having one for the road with her colleagues in their local. Then it struck her that, in her absence, Tom might have had the opportunity for a good chinwag with Conor; he seemed keen to get reacquainted.

Rosie edged a path through some rowdy workmen, avoiding their coarse compliments and sour smell as best she could. Glancing at the bar, she noted that Conor was on his way to meet her.

'Nice surprise, bumping into you, Mrs Deane.' Conor drew her away from the press of oily-overalled men.

'Don't call me that!' Rosie hissed quietly.

'Why not?'

'You know why not,' she muttered, flicking a glance up at him.

'True, but I'm still waiting for you to confirm some details.'

Rosie glanced past him, sensing that they were under observation. An attractive woman with bright blonde hair and crimson lips was watching them while talking to a younger man.

'Never seen you in here before,' Rosie said, hoping to find some neutral ground.

'I'm over this way on business. Come in here often, do you?'

'We sometimes have a quick drink before heading home. I'm with colleagues.'

'Yeah . . . the uniform sort of gave it away.'

'You don't live round here then?'

'Live Wapping way. Been to the solicitor's this afternoon to tie up some matters about my late brother's estate.'

'Is that your brother? He looks like you.'

'Yep.'

'What's his name?'

'Steven.'

'Is that the woman you had a fight over?'

'Nope.'

'Oh . . . who is she then?'

'My sister-in-law.'

'Man of few words, aren't you?' Rosie muttered. She was reluctant to give him the upper hand but before she set off home she had to ask him not to betray her. 'I'm catching my bus; would you step outside with me so I can say something?' Rosie set off without waiting for a reply, trusting he'd follow.

As soon as the pub door swung shut on them she blurted, 'The people at work know me as Miss Gardiner, so if we meet by chance when I'm in their company—'

'Fine by me,' he smoothly interrupted.

'And they don't know about my daughter.'

'Didn't think so.'

'Glad you understand.'

'Not sure I do . . . Like I said, I'm waiting for you to explain a few things.'

'I don't have to explain a damned thing to you!' Rosie exploded, feeling cornered. 'And I think you've got a fucking nerve expecting me to.'

He grunted a laugh, moving past her as though going back inside.

Quickly Rosie yanked on his sleeve, halting him. 'Where are you going? I'm not finished yet. D'you promise to keep quiet, then?'

'What's it worth?'

Rosie let go of him and furiously dug in her handbag. Whipping a pound note from her purse she thrust it at him in deliberate insult. She knew very well the reward he was after wasn't money. 'That's all you understand, isn't it? Oh, not enough for you?' she taunted when he didn't even look at the cash. His eyes were holding hers easily, unpleasant amusement in their depths. Rosie turned her head, feeling ashamed of her behaviour.

'Sorry,' she eventually said. 'Shouldn't have sworn at you . . . don't know why I let you rile me.'

'Know what I think?' Conor said quietly. 'I think there's more to your temper than you having an illegitimate daughter to hide away.'

'I don't hide her away!' Rosie cried, then bit her lip. 'I don't! She's gone away with her granddad so he can keep her safe from all this.' Rosie gestured at broken buildings on the opposite side of the road.

'You could have gone with her.'

Rosie shook her head. 'No, I want this war over with so she'll be free. There are enough people shirking doing their bit and making grubby money out of the chaos.'

'You mean me?'

'If the cap fits . . .' Rosie muttered.

'I'm going back to my regiment as soon as I'm signed off fit. And the "grubby money" your father got out of his still . . . spend any of it for him, did you?'

'No, I did not!' Rosie burst out before remembering that Hope's layette, together with the cot and pram, had been paid for out of her father's savings. John had also been prepared to meet the cost of her abortion out of his nest egg. She knew very well that counterfeit booze had built his bank balance.

'You're no different from me, Rosie. We're caught up in a mess other people made, and now we have to do things we don't like, and associate with people we don't like, because of it.'

Rosie gazed at him; it was as if he knew that her father was partly to blame for her having a secret to keep.

'I certainly don't like you, or what you do. And you don't have to explain yourself to me, 'cos I'm not about to return the favour.' Rosie snapped her face away from his.

'I want to explain things to you, 'cos I've gone beyond pretence now, even if you haven't.'

Rosie felt indignant at the inference she was play-acting. 'I'm not pretending anything!'

'You're doing it now: pretending you don't like me and that you don't know I want you.'

Rosie swallowed, avoiding his eyes and hating him for being so blatant about it. She'd prefer it to remain as it was between them . . . just hint and innuendo that would allow her to think about him in private, lying in bed in her empty house with nothing else to do through sleepless nights but reflect on the people occupying her mind.

'D'you promise to be careful what you say when my colleagues are around?' she asked stiltedly.

'Yes.'

'Thanks,' Rosie said. 'Your brother and sister-in-law are probably wondering where you've gone.'

On cue the door swung open and the blonde sauntered out. Conor blasphemed beneath his breath.

'Oh, there you are, Conor. Thought you'd gone off and left us.' Angie linked arms with him. 'Gonna introduce us, then?' She tilted her head to one side, assessing Rosie's appearance. 'What's that get-up?' Angie crinkled her nose at Rosie's uniform as though it gave off a bad smell. 'Auxiliary Fire Service, are you?'

'Ambulance Auxiliary,' Rosie returned, taking an instant dislike to the older woman. But she held out a hand. 'I'm Rosie Gardiner.'

'Angie Flint.' Having limply shaken hands, Angie asked, 'How d'you two know each other then?'

'Through my dad.' Rosie was tempted to tell the woman to mind her own business but she didn't want

231

it to seem that she'd been having more than a casual chat with Conor.

'Go back inside.' Conor disentangled himself from Angie's possessive clutch, battling his irritation.

'It's all right, I'm off now . . . got a bus to catch.' Rosie turned away and started walking briskly towards the corner.

'Toodle-oo,' Angie called mockingly.

'Want a lift?'

'No, thanks all the same, I'll wait.'

Conor wound up the car window then got out and came to stand next to Rosie in the bus queue.

'Go away. You're making people stare at us.' She darted a look to and fro.

'Get in the car then.' He took out his cigarettes and offered her the pack.

Rosie took one and drew on it before his match had extinguished. She'd taken up smoking again after the night she'd rescued little Herbie.

The bus pulled up and people surged forward to get on board, Rosie included, but when it set off, she wasn't on it. She turned to Conor, a look of confusion on her face. He put out a hand, beckoning, and she went to him.

He straightened her lapels, his eyes travelling over her drab uniform. 'Pink suits you better,' he said, cigarette wagging between his lips.

Rosie ignored the reference to her dressing gown. When he'd pulled up moments ago she'd been reflecting on the identity of Angie Flint's husband. Steven looked too young to be married to a woman in her thirties. 'Was your sister-in-law married to your late brother?'

'Yeah, she was Saul's wife. Angie's taking it hard . . . as you can see,' he said with biting irony.

Rosie didn't protest when he took her arm and steered her towards the car.

'Pick a subject, shall I?' Conor said after they'd driven about half a mile in silence.

'I think I'd sooner start a conversation.' Rosie avoided his challenge.

'Off you go then.'

'Your sister-in-law fancies you.'

'I'll pick a subject,' Conor said drily.

Rosie turned her head and stared at him. She'd spoken half in jest, but it seemed it was no joke. 'It's true, isn't it?'

Conor shrugged.

'She's your brother's widow yet she's already chasing after you?' Rosie sounded disgusted.

'She gets no encouragement from me, whatever she might say.'

'What does she say?'

'Nothing worth listening to these days.'

'Did your brother know about . . . things?' Rosie gestured the rest of her meaning.

'Yeah, Saul knew. He knew it was over, too.'

'Over?' Rosie shot him a blameful glance. So any affair was partly his fault, she guessed.

'Me and Angie knocked about together before Saul was daft enough to marry her. After that it was finished between us. Now he's gone she thinks she can pick up where we left off. I'm not interested.'

'But she is?'

'That's about it.'

'It's as well they didn't have children then.'

'Amen to that,' Conor drawled solemnly.

Rosie was intrigued – and oddly piqued – by his romantic entanglement with his brother's wife. But she didn't want him to think his affair with his sister-in-law interested her so she changed the subject.

'Your brother Steven looks young.'

'He's eighteen in the autumn but says he's joining up before then. I want him to stay and take care of things at home. He reckons it's my turn to do that. Perhaps he's expecting me to desert.' Conor gave a half-smile. 'My little brother wants a taste of adventure. I think he's under the impression we've been having a bit of a lark in France.'

Rosie understood the bitterness in his voice. 'Were you there for the D-Day landings? Is that when you got injured?'

'Yeah, I took a bullet in the shoulder on Sword Beach.'

'You look to be recovering well. I imagine it was dreadful over there.'

'Dunkirk was worse.' He turned his head. 'Let's talk about something cheerful.'

'Did you get your money back off Frank Purves?'

'I took payment in lieu.'

'You needed some printing done?'

Conor turned towards her, laughing. 'He's good at what he does. So, yeah, I had some printing off him.' He pulled up outside Rosie's house and turned off the engine. 'Nightcap would be nice.'

'Haven't got any booze.'

'Doesn't have to be kosher. I trust your old man's skilled enough not to poison me.'

'Haven't got any of that either,' Rosie said hoarsely.

'Cup of tea, then.'

'All out of tea . . . used up the rations.'

'I might be able to help you there,' Conor said drolly, thinking of the coupons he'd seen in Popeye's warehouse. 'Glass of water?' he suggested sardonically. 'Or is the tap out of action?'

Rosie glanced at him. 'Got work in the morning . . . up bright and early.'

'Me, too. Have you got a boyfriend?'

Rosie looked startled. 'Me? No!'

'Why d'you say it like that?'

'Like what?'

'As though having a man in your life's out of the question. You're a beautiful girl, as you know; you must get asked out.'

'I'm a mother now.'

'You're a woman, too.'

'That's all finished with.'

'What's all finished with?'

'Look, I worked at the Windmill Theatre when I was eighteen, and didn't have a clue about things,' Rosie stormed, feeling again that he'd cornered her. 'I don't want constant reminders of what my life used to be rammed down my throat.'

'Wasn't thinking of ramming that down your throat,' Conor said.

'Oh, well, if we're being clever, what were you going to ram down my throat?' Rosie demanded, through gritted teeth. 'Come on, why don't you say it? You think I'm a tart. I've got an illegitimate child because I've no morals and I used to strip off and flirt so it serves me right I got in trouble. Especially as I turned you down.' She swiped spontaneous tears off her lashes. 'That's it, isn't it? You can't get over that I rejected you. Well, if it makes you feel any better, Corporal Flint, your sergeant made me feel sick. Most of them did . . . all of them . . .'

Rosie jumped out of the car and flung off his hand when he stopped her by her door.

'Was it a serviceman got you pregnant?'

Rosie shook her head. 'No . . .' she said hoarsely, remembering the coward who'd raped her. 'He'd no stomach for that sort of fighting.'

Conor dropped her hand and stepped back, staring at her with dark unsettling intensity. 'I see . . .' His voice was barely audible. He rubbed a hand across his mouth, fingers travelling on to pinch the bridge of his nose. He prowled along the pavement for some yards before returning to her side. Slowly he dipped his head and kissed her cheek.

''Night, Rosie,' he murmured.

Without another word he turned and got in his car, pulling away immediately.

Rosie shrunk back against the front gate. From wanting him gone, she suddenly wanted him with her. But he wouldn't be back. Men like Conor Flint, who were attractive to the opposite sex, were repulsed by women like her, who couldn't respond to them.

But she wanted to be able to.

Rosie watched the car turn the corner with tears soaking her cheeks. She didn't want to flinch from a man's touch but she did. Lenny Purves might be dead but she couldn't escape him. He'd left her his legacy: an adorable child and a frigid body.

Rosie went indoors and found her dad's rotgut whisky in the sideboard. She poured herself a drink and took it with her upstairs to bed. It wasn't until after midnight that she remembered she should have phoned her dad and spoken to Hope.

CHAPTER TWENTY

'Thought it was high time I came to introduce myself; I bet you don't remember me, do you?'

Rosie had been cutting the dead heads off roses in the front garden when the sailor appeared, leaning on the gate and startling her.

She shielded her eyes from the evening sun with her fingers to get a better view of him.

'I'm Charles Bellamy . . . Doris's son. Charlie to me family.' He extended a hand. 'And I reckon we are family now, ain't we, Rosie?'

Quickly Rosie wiped her fingers, sticky with sap, on her skirt and shook his hand. 'Oh . . . right . . . nice to meet you.' She felt awkward, unsure what to say. She vaguely remembered Charlie Bellamy from when she was a youngster. Doris and her only child had lived a few roads away. In one of their rare friendly chats Doris had told her that within the space of one month her husband had got her pregnant and got himself shot in Flanders.

'Shall I put the kettle on, or are you pushed for time? Rosie felt uncharitable for hoping that he would go away but she sensed she wouldn't like her new stepbrother. There was a mite too much familiarity in his eyes, despite the way he'd courteously tucked his naval cap under an arm when speaking to her.

'I'd love a cuppa. Got a forty-eight-hour pass.'

Rosie led the way indoors, noting that Peg Price was making a show of sweeping her front path while keeping a beady eye on her. She gave the woman an ironic salute, letting her neighbour know she was well aware of being spied on.

Fleetingly, Rosie wondered how young Irene was coping. She'd not heard any commotion coming from the Prices' house, and Peg's daughter still ambled up and down the road, looking fat and miserable. There'd been no opportunity for Rosie to have a chat with Irene and ask how things were going. Probably, unable to face her mother, the poor girl had decided to let things ride.

'So . . . you still a Windmill girl then, are you, Rosemary?' Charlie studied Rosie from beneath his eyebrows as he sat down in the parlour.

'No, not been working there for years,' Rosie called, disappearing into the kitchen. Her instinct to get rid of him quickly heightened at his remark and the look that had accompanied it. She filled the kettle and set the cups, aware that he'd come up behind her.

'Your wife'll be pleased you're back on leave,' Rosie said over a shoulder, feeling suffocated because he was standing too close to her. 'You'll be catching the train to Gravesend soon, won't you?'

Charlie shrugged. 'Now me mum and your dad have set up camp in our house with your kiddie it's got too crowded for my liking.' He gave Rosie a direct stare. 'Bet you've got plenty of room here, ain't yer?' He raised his eyes to the ceiling. 'Any chance of kipping here while I'm staying over in London?'

'Sorry . . . my boyfriend wouldn't like that arrangement,' Rosie lied fluently.

'Who's that, then? Yer dad said you weren't settled with anyone new.' Charlie sounded rather indignant.

'Don't tell my dad everything, do I?' Rosie snapped, fed up with his personal questions.

'Your little gel's a beauty, just like her mum, ain't she?' Charlie's gaze wandered over Rosie's rear view.

'I'm very proud of her.' Rosie stirred the teapot. She felt her insides tighten, resenting his breath on her neck. She wished she knew what this man had been told about her past. Doris tended to stick to the story of her stepdaughter being Mrs Deane, a widow, but Rosie suspected the woman's close family might know better.

'Pity about yer husband, Rosemary. Where did he cop it? Artillery, wasn't he, so I heard?'

His sly tone of voice confirmed Rosie's suspicions. When she felt a heavy hand massaging her shoulder in a show of comfort, she immediately shrugged him off but kept up the sham. 'His body wasn't recovered . . . sorry, I don't like to talk about it. Sit in the parlour and drink this, shall we?' She carried two cups of tea into the room, placing them on the table.

'Your Toby's a fine lad. Saw him and your wife at the wedding . . . shame you missed it. Only a small quiet affair but nice all the same.' Rosie was determined to change the subject and to remain civil, despite a growing urge to show him the door.

'Yeah . . . couldn't make it being as I was sailing past Gibraltar at the time.' Charlie gulped his tea. 'Wasn't

239

expecting 'em to up and get leg-shackled. Don't know why they did at their age, if I'm honest.'

Rosie knew her view matched his but she said, 'Wartime, isn't it? People do funny things.'

''Spose . . .'

He sat back in his chair and stared boldly, making Rosie feel uneasy again.

'Remember seeing you on stage at the Windmill; used to say to me pals: that blonde up there, I know her . . . used to be neighbours, we did, when she was just a flat-chested kid. Ain't a kid now, though, are yer, Rosie?'

'Don't hardly remember you at all. 'Course, you're a lot older than me, aren't you? You were married when I was in junior school.' Rosie got up and opened the sash window, feeling hot.

'Bet you miss the work . . . all that glitz 'n' glamour,' Charlie purred.

Rosie darted a glance at him. She could see he'd finished his tea and she wished he'd get going. 'Prefer what I'm doing now.' She picked up his empty cup and her own and took them to the kitchen, hoping he'd take the hint.

'So . . . what *are* you doing now, Rosie? Must still be in showbiz. Crying shame else, with that figure . . .' Charlie had stationed himself in the kitchen doorway, a shoulder propped on the jamb with his arms crossed over his chest. 'Built for attention, you are, gel.'

Rosie knew he'd got her trapped and she'd either have to ask him to move or push past him to get out.

'Better get that; I'm expecting somebody.' The knock on the door had greatly relieved Rosie. She'd spoken the truth, too; she was certain she'd open up and find Peg on her step, ready to cross-examine her about her gentleman caller.

Charlie sauntered away into the parlour and Rosie went to open the door, cursing below her breath because he'd made himself comfortable again.

She went pale as she looked up at Conor.

He glanced past her as Charlie gave a loud cough, on purpose Rosie reckoned, so her visitor would know she already had company.

'Bad time?'

'No . . .' Rosie breathed, feeling strangely euphoric once the shock of seeing him had worn off. 'Not at all. Come in.'

When they entered the back parlour Charlie was on his feet and immediately swinging a glance between the couple.

'This is my stepbrother, Charlie Bellamy. And this is Conor Flint, friend of my – friend of mine.' Rosie had previously introduced Conor as her father's acquaintance, but just now she knew she'd far sooner be stranded in his company than Charlie's. 'My stepbrother's off to visit his wife in Gravesend. My dad's been staying with Charlie's family . . . as you know.'

Conor shook hands with the sailor. 'Won't hold you up as you've got a journey in front of you.' The words seemed inoffensive but at odds with the expression in his deep-blue eyes.

'Say hello to them all for me, won't you?' Rosie said as she walked into the hall with her stepbrother.

He gave a terse nod. 'So that's yer boyfriend, is it?'

Rosie gave an almost imperceptible nod, hoping Conor hadn't heard what Charlie had said.

'So what d'you do now you're not a Windmill girl?' Again an unpleasant glint was in his eyes.

'I'm an ambulance auxiliary.'

241

Charlie looked as though she'd shocked him. He licked his lips. 'Stationed round here, are yer?'

'Mmm . . . Robley Road. Station 97.'

'Best be off. Thanks for the tea.'

Rosie waved to Charlie as he closed the gate, then she shut the door and with a deep breath went back to the parlour.

'How are you?'

They spoke the question simultaneously. Rosie gestured for Conor to continue and thought he would say something but instead he frowned through the open sash window. The net curtain billowed gently in the summer breeze but he seemed oblivious to the lacy veil brushing his face.

Rosie felt a poignant sadness as she watched him battling to find the right words to speak to her. Previously his confidence had been unstoppable, his arrogance overwhelming. But he was different now.

'I know you want to apologise for having got me wrong, but there's no need,' she said softly. 'There you were, thinking I was up for a good time, and I don't blame you. It's what most men think when they recognise me.' She could have added that even her married stepbrother classed her as a slag. But she kept her thoughts about Charlie to herself. 'When men discover I've got a daughter and no husband . . . well, it just confirms their suspicions about me and my past.'

'Are you hoping I'll deny it, Rosie?' Conor grimaced wryly. ''Course I thought I was in with a chance of getting you into bed. It's why I've kept coming back. It's why I've not bothered seeing the girl I used to knock around with. Pat's her name. She was the one I got into a fight for.' He plunged his hands into his pockets. 'No great romance, but she was all right till I saw you.'

Rosie nodded, blinking heat from her eyes, angry at herself for feeling like weeping when she'd nothing to cry about.

'Well . . . perhaps she'll take you back, or you'll find someone else . . .'

He grunted a mirthless laugh. 'Won't help. Can't stop thinking about you, that's the problem.'

Rosie examined her hands, picking at the thorn nicks from the pruning she'd done. 'Been cutting back in the garden. Better go and tidy up . . . left the shears and the secateurs out there. The kids round here'll pinch anything, soon as your back's turned.' She glanced at Conor; he was watching her with a look in his eyes she'd never seen before. She hoped it wasn't pity. The idea that it might be straightened her shoulders and strengthened her voice. 'Anyhow, I know my dad was an idiot ever getting involved with Frank Purves again. I know you could have made life miserable for him, so thanks.' Rosie abruptly went into the kitchen and started washing up the teacups, straining to hear the telltale sound of her front door closing. He'd salved his conscience and her pride by coming to see her and she thought it fair to give him a chance to slip away.

She upended the washing-up bowl into the butler sink, then turned about to see him stationed in the doorway, just like her stocky, sandy-haired stepbrother had been earlier. But Conor Flint, with his lean frame and dangerous dark looks, didn't intimidate her; quite the reverse. She was tempted to rush at him and hug him for comfort. But of course she wouldn't because he'd get the wrong idea.

'Who was it?'

243

'It doesn't matter now.'

'Tell me.'

'He's dead, so it doesn't matter now.'

'Who killed him?'

Rosie stopped drying the saucers and looked at him. 'What makes you think somebody killed him?'

He grimaced. 'I would've.'

Rosie knew he meant it.

'Did your dad go after him?'

Rosie resumed drying the crockery. 'Dad didn't need to. He died in a nightclub. Drank some moonshine and passed out, then set fire to the mattress with a cigarette.' A darting glance caught him frowning so she explained, 'The club was a brothel, too. He was in bed with a prostitute. They both died.' Suddenly she flung down the cloth and gripped the edge of the sink until her knuckles showed bone. 'Can we not talk about this?' She spun about. 'Is your mum feeling better?'

'Want to come and see her?'

Rosie gazed at him, wondering if he was joking. 'Why? I don't think I can help.' She gave a smile. 'My forte is crawling about in bombed-out buildings tending to small boys trapped in the rubble.'

'Really?'

Briefly Rosie told him about Herbie, glad to lighten the atmosphere between them, even if it was at poor Herbie's expense.

When they'd got him to hospital they'd discovered that the lad had a fractured skull, whereas his trapped shin had suffered just cuts and bruises. Rosie had heard her patient was making a slow recovery and she was planning on visiting him when the doctors said he was ready. At present only his family were allowed in.

'Quite the heroine, aren't you?'

He sounded genuinely impressed rather than patronising; nevertheless Rosie's smile faded. 'Just doing what anybody would do. If it was my child in there, hurt and frightened, I'd want somebody to do that for her.' She paused. 'Herbie's mum had gone to the shelter with her other kids. Herbie's only six but she had three younger than that; he was out playing football with his pals and naturally rushed home to find his mum when the sirens sounded. Do-gooders say she should have waited for him to return rather than leave her eldest daughter behind to wait for him. But who do you save? All of them? One of them? Just a wrong decision . . . that's all it takes to lose them. A friend of mine lost three of her little sons because she and her husband weren't home when the bombs dropped.' Rosie knew she'd never fully comprehend Gertie's pain and suffering. 'But Herbie's doing all right – that's the main thing – and nobody to blame if he wasn't, 'cos we're all careless at times.' The thought of the day her baby daughter had only by luck escaped injury in the bombing haunted her mind and she knew it would continue to do so till the day she died. Hope might have suffocated in her pram because she'd forgotten the infant existed.

'You're a good girl, Rosie, know that?'

'Sorry . . . went on a bit, didn't I?' Rosie replied bashfully. 'Wasn't angling for praise.'

'I know,' he said softly. 'Fancy going to the flicks later?'

Rosie shrugged, avoiding his eyes. 'I should get on with the ironing.'

'See the film . . . have a bite to eat . . . bring you back . . . won't even try to kiss you . . . Scout's honour.'

The gentle humour in his voice made her smile and raise an eyebrow at him. 'You have to make the sign or it's not a proper promise.'

Solemnly he raised his fingers to his forehead.

'Do I know you? What've you done with that scoundrel Conor Flint?' she teased.

He laughed, throwing back his head and Rosie joined in, laughing till she cried.

'Come here.' He held out his arms.

Without hesitation Rosie went to him, nestling into his shoulder and letting him hold her and stroke her hair because the good tears had turned to bad before subsiding.

'Pick you up at seven?'

Rosie sniffed. 'Thanks.'

'What for?'

Rosie shrugged, again feeling shy. 'Understanding,' she said, and went back to the kitchen, smiling to herself when she heard her front door quietly being closed.

CHAPTER TWENTY-ONE

'Don't think I took to your stepbrother,' Conor said.

'Join the club!' Rosie replied with feeling.

'D'you know him well?'

'No, I hardly know him at all; he turned up to introduce himself this afternoon. My stepmother has always lived round our way but I was a school-kid when her Charlie got married and moved off.' Rosie paused. 'Don't remember ever having had a conversation with him before today. He's a lot older than me.'

'I'd say he's about my age,' Conor said ruefully.

'Really? You seem younger. Perhaps you're immature,' Rosie teased, earning herself a heavy hand planted on the scruff of her neck.

She hunched her shoulders to her ears. 'Only joking,' she squeaked, laughing. His fingers stroked tenderly on her nape before sliding away to plunge back into his trouser pocket.

'Did Charlie say or do something to make you dislike him?'

Rosie shook her head. 'Just found his manner a bit

unpleasant.' With hindsight she was prepared to give her stepbrother's crafty remarks the benefit of the doubt. It might have been Charlie's clumsy way of being complimentary.

They were strolling side by side, having just emerged from the Odeon. There had been vivid sunshine when they'd gone in but they'd exited into twilight an hour and three-quarters later. Rosie glanced up at the starry heavens, arms crossed over her middle.

Softly, she murmured a prayer that there wouldn't be an air raid. 'Please don't come tonight.'

'Think you're hoping in vain, Rosie,' Conor said flatly. 'They'll be over before dawn.' He casually ruffled her blonde hair. 'If there can be a good side to these doodle-bugs it's that they're a sign Adolf's been badly rattled by the D-Day landings. He'll run out of rockets and launching sites along the French coast if we can keep pushing the Krauts back inland. Sooner or later those damned V1s won't make it past the Channel.'

'Please God you're right.' Rosie suddenly squeezed Conor's arm. 'Oh, no, look who's coming! Crikey! That's a turn-up!' she gasped. 'Never imagined I'd see those two walking arm in arm!'

From the expressions on the faces of the approaching couple they were also surprised at this unexpected meeting.

'Is it too late to cross over the road?' Rosie whispered.

''Fraid so. Who's the woman with Frank Purves?' Conor asked.

'She's a midwife. Nurse Johnson delivered Hope, and . . .' Rosie tailed off. She'd almost blurted out that after Hope was born she'd nearly let the woman adopt her daughter.

'Frank . . .' Conor said in terse greeting.

'Taking a stroll then, are yer, Mr Flint?' Frank's wonky vision settled on Rosie. 'Didn't know you and John's daughter were acquainted.'

'No reason why you should,' Conor returned coolly.

'How've you been keeping, young Rosie? A mum now, ain't yer, so I heard?' Popeye sounded amiable. 'Seen your dad recently, or is he still out of town?' he asked, sliding a subtle look at Conor.

'Dad's still away,' Rosie answered quickly.

'Got a bit of unfinished business, have me 'n' John, so when you speak to him, love, remember me to him, won't yer now?' Popeye was boiling up, and feeling a worse mug than before for letting Flint take his petrol coupons. The randy sod hadn't pursued John Gardiner for his booze or his money because he was knocking off the man's daughter! The lucky bastard had got a leg over with a Windmill Girl for no extra charge.

Popeye knew that John's daughter had been on the stage, posing starkers. His Lenny had told him all about that, not that it had been any secret. Most of the folk roundabouts had known that the good-looking Gardiner girl had got a part in the theatre's famous performances. John would never be drawn on discussing his Rosie's job, and anybody who brought it up, hoping for a bit of smut, was disappointed.

Popeye was bent on getting his revenge on John. There had always been an amount of rivalry between them but Popeye liked to think he was top dog. Popeye hadn't intended taking John for a ride on the distilling deal; he'd have paid him up fair and square once the profits started rolling in. But Gardiner had done him up like a kipper, when he was least expecting it. John might only have got away with fifty quid out of five hundred but to Popeye the humiliation and betrayal was as strong as it would have been had he been cheated out of the lot.

'Nice to bump into you,' Rosie lied, desperate to get going in case Popeye mentioned his late son. She could feel the nurse's eyes on her and she gave Trudy a brief nod, stepping away.

'And how's your daughter?' Trudy asked. 'Must be two now; Hope's her name, isn't it?'

Rosie had never told the nurse her daughter's name and it annoyed her that Trudy had made it her business to find it out. 'She's very well, thanks. She's staying with her granddad.'

'Lost yer husband, didn't you, dear?' Popeye sounded sympathetic but if the girl was knocking about with Flint he reckoned he knew what sort she was. He wondered if her kid was her husband's or a punter's, or whether she'd ever even had a trip down the aisle.

Rosie nodded, making brief eye contact with Trudy. The midwife hadn't forgotten their conversation about her using an alias because the neighbours were gossiping.

'Be seeing you . . .' Conor put an arm about Rosie's shoulders to lead her on.

'Reckon you will be,' Popeye replied through his teeth.

'You've gone very quiet since we bumped into those two.' Conor tickled Rosie's cheek with a knuckle to gain her attention. 'Not worried about Popeye, are you? He won't bother your dad. He knows he got what he deserved. I was never going to go after John for any cash. I used that as an excuse to come round and get to know you.'

They were parked outside Rosie's house and she

glanced through the dim interior of the car at Conor. 'You make it sound as though you're still at loggerheads with Frank Purves. I thought you had some printing off him to square things up.'

Conor stretched out his legs under the steering wheel, easing back in the car seat and pillowing his head on his clasped hands. 'I did get some printing off him. Didn't say he wanted to give it to me, though.'

'You didn't hit him, did you? He's just an old man.'

Rosie hadn't been able to escape an unpalatable truth this evening. Frank Purves was Hope's grandfather. In the past she'd banished that fact from her mind. Popeye had been just somebody who used to know her dad years ago. But things had changed. Purves had turned up like a bad penny, worming his way into John's life again. And this evening she'd come face to face with him, and he'd mentioned her daughter. Nurse Johnson's presence had only served to heighten Rosie's uneasiness.

Just after Hope's birth she'd been at a low ebb and had confided in her midwife, something she now bitterly regretted. She had a niggling fear that the sheltered little world she'd built for herself and her daughter could be under threat. Trudy might tell Purves that she'd never had a husband, and that Rosie had once almost let her adopt the child.

The thought of Popeye discovering Hope had his blood running in her veins terrified Rosie. She glanced at Conor. She didn't want him to know either. She liked him, and was starting to trust him. He'd guessed she'd been raped, but he'd had the decency not to ask her to confirm what had happened. But she couldn't predict how he'd react to knowing that Popeye's son had been her attacker.

251

'Did you hear what I said?'

Rosie started to attention, shaking her head, and looking apologetic.

'I said of course I didn't hit him, what d'you take me for?' Conor smiled at the memory of Popeye offering him the services of his two crippled henchmen. 'Frank's just an over-the-hill racketeer. He's got a couple of youngish blokes as his back-up. First glance you'd take 'em for middle-aged but they're likely to be no more than early thirties. Both of 'em seen better days. Felt sorry for them 'cos they're probably war cripples.'

'I'd better go in. I'm on early shift.' Rosie had just noticed Peg's blackout curtain twitching. The woman was a tireless nosy parker.

'Right . . .' Conor nodded slowly, without looking at her.

'Neighbours are spying on us,' Rosie explained.

'Right . . .' he said again.

Rosie anticipated him saying, 'Well, let's go inside then.' He didn't, but the words filled the space between them. She sat tensely, wondering if he'd give her a peck on the cheek as he had before. She'd liked the feel of his mouth on her skin. When he sat unmoving she leaned in quickly and kissed him on the cheek instead, uncaring if Peg Price had seen her. 'Thanks for taking me out.'

'Do it again?'

'Mmm, I'd like to.'

'Forget about Frank Purves.'

'Yes . . . I will,' Rosie said stoutly. But it was a lie. She couldn't forget about Hope's other grandfather now or in the future. She felt as though the Sword of Damocles was hanging over her. The meeting between the four of them had been an omen of bad things to come.

Rufus twiddled the knobs on the wireless to tune in a news broadcast as it was coming up to one o'clock.

'I need some wages. The tight-fist should pay us a retainer while he's sorting things out.' Midge was pacing restlessly to and fro in front of his seated brother-in-law.

The idea of Popeye shelling out so freely made Rufus guffaw in disbelief. 'We talking about the same person?' he asked. 'You got more chance of one of us passing a medical and enlisting than him doing that.'

'Don't fuckin' want to enlist,' Midge snorted. 'Just want to get back earning. We was doing all right, you 'n' me, driving Pop's motor and delivering counterfeits.'

'Yeah, we was,' Rufus agreed nostalgically. Once he'd got the hang of driving the Citroën, he'd enjoyed those trips out with Midge, haring along narrow country lanes close to Edgware, whooping like a couple of kids on a seaside outing. And the cash had been good to have, too.

Midge flopped down on the couch in Rufus's parlour, restlessly tapping his feet on the bare wooden boards. He'd just been round to Popeye's place to try to persuade his boss to give him a sub against future work. Popeye wasn't having any of it, and had been like a bear with a sore head still moaning about Flint getting his petrol coupons and John Gardiner stitching him up. But he'd boasted about his new lady friend and how he liked taking her out for a ride in his flash motor. Midge had slunk out without even getting a tot of Scotch out of the miser.

A few moments after sitting down Midge was again

on his feet, peering out of the window for a sign of his sister returning home. He knew he'd have to shift a bit lively if Gertie showed up. She'd not softened towards him. He still had to creep in and have a cuppa and a chinwag with Rufus when the coast was clear.

'Stick the kettle on, Midge, will yer?' Rufus leaned his ear close to the gramophone, listening to the lunchtime bulletin through crackling interference.

Midge cast a jaundiced eye on his brother-in-law. 'I'm not yer servant; you've got me sister to fetch 'n' carry for you.' But he got up and stomped into the kitchen, rattling crockery about and missing the moment when Gertie let herself in.

'Can yer lend us a few bob, Roof, before I go?' Midge called plaintively, pouring boiling water on tea. 'I ain't had a hot meal in an age and as fer getting me end away . . .'

'Shame about that . . . and no, he bleedin' can't,' Gertie snapped, standing in the open kitchen doorway with her hands on her hips. She knew her brother had been coming round in her absence and she'd turned a blind eye to it because, much as she detested Michael, Rufus was content to have his company. And Gertie had come to the conclusion that no price was too great to pay to shut her husband's moaning up.

Today she couldn't pretend ignorance of her brother's clandestine visits. Joey was due in soon, too, and she didn't want the two of them clashing. Joey despised his uncle, and Gertie knew her son was starting to dislike his father for allowing Midge houseroom.

'Where's me little Vicky?' Rufus asked genially, trying to lighten the atmosphere.

'Becky's playing with her out the front.' Gertie turned

her attention back to Michael. 'You can drink that, then get going.' She nodded at the cup of tea in Midge's hand. 'Get it down yer.'

'He's been round Pop's and only come here to let me know there might be some work coming up soon.' Rufus stuck up for his brother-in-law with a white lie.

Gertie pretended to be unimpressed when in fact the idea of Rufus getting back out earning was music to her ears. 'When's that then? This week?'

'Not sure yet . . . Pop's gonna let us know,' Midge said, gulping at his tea.

'In other words, sometime never,' Gertie said sourly.

'Ain't our fault this all come about.' Rufus felt affronted. He knew his wife was itching to get him out from under her feet.

'Gardiner deserves a right spanking for putting a spoke in the works,' Midge snarled. 'I remember a few years back him 'n' Pop and Lenny was doing a roaring trade with bottling up and labelling the rotgut. Then all of a sudden, right about the time that Lenny croaked, Gardiner packed up his still.' Midge took another slurp of tea. 'I thought it was Popeye wanted out as he was cut up over Lenny, but he reckons no. John called a halt and never would say why.'

'Probably about the time his grandkid was born.'

'According to Pop, it were long before that.' Midge smirked. 'Pop reckons John's daughter's a part-time tart who used to be on the stage and got herself in the family way. Pop's theory is that Gardiner withdrew into his shell because he didn't want questions asked about his grand-kid's father. Seems they made up some tale about the girl's husband dying in action when they'd only been married a few months.'

Gertie had been half listening to their conversation from the kitchen while pulling some shopping out of her bag. She'd been thinking about finding work now Rufus was back at home and able to babysit. But the groceries and the jobs were abruptly forgotten as the bits and pieces she'd heard lined up in her brain. She went back into the parlour and asked, 'What's this girl's name?'

Midge and Rufus turned to stare at Gertie.

'Dunno . . . why d'you ask?' Rufus said.

Gertie shrugged. 'Used to char up in the West End theatres, didn't I? Thought I might know her.'

'Rosie . . . that's it,' Midge burst out, pleased at having brought the name to mind.

'Sound familiar, does she?' Rufus asked his wife, pleased she'd joined in the conversation and seemed to have calmed down.

Gertie shook her head. Turning away she went back to the kitchen. 'Finished that bleedin' tea, have yer?' she called over a shoulder. 'Come on, get going before Joey gets home.'

The moment she heard the back door closing Gertie locked it, then went in to the back parlour. She sat down on the couch, picking over in her mind what she'd heard and finding it did make shocking sense to her.

'If I tell you something, d'you promise to keep it to yourself?' she asked her husband.

Rufus was trying to tune the wireless to a variety programme now the news had finished. The ear-splitting whining noise filled the room, making Gertie shout at him to turn the bloody thing off.

'Was that *him* in here again?' Joey bawled over the tuneless racket. He'd just passed Midge out in the street and had spat in the gutter as he did so. He'd let himself in and now stood glowering at Rufus. 'Don't want him in here. I hate him and you!'

'Who d'you think you're talking to?' Rufus roared, struggling up out of his chair again, puce in the face. 'You bleedin' cheeky little git. You'll feel the back of my hand . . . telling me what to do in me own home.'

Joey turned and stamped up the stairs.

'What was you saying, love?' Rufus asked his stony-faced wife. He got out his handkerchief and patted his red face.

Gertie had jumped up when Joey stormed in, ready to lunge between father and son if necessary. Joey seemed to be finding his feet now that he was out at work. He was finding his voice, too, and Gertie didn't like kids back-chatting their parents any more than Rufus did. But she knew her son had a point.

'Weren't saying nothing at all. Will say this, though, and you'd better listen: Joey's right about Midge. Tell him to stay away.'

CHAPTER TWENTY-TWO

'Ssh . . . here she comes! We'd better pick the right time to tell her.'

Rosie guessed she'd been the subject of the men's cautious whispering. 'Tell me what?' she asked.

Tom and Jim were standing in the common room, uniformed and ready to go on shift. Rosie glanced around.

'Hazel not turned up yet?' The wall clock showed just after nine o'clock; it was unusual for her friend to be late.

'Probably on her way,' Tom said, prowling to and fro and feeling awkward that Rosie had overheard his comment.

'Come on, out with it!' Rosie's smile transformed to a frown. 'Has my driving test been rebooked after all?'

Rosie had almost failed her driving test for braking too sharply and filling the examiner's turn-ups with water from the bucket on the floor. The fellow hadn't taken the soaking too well but had given her a pass as he'd said he believed her nerves had got the better of her. She was now a relief driver and still doing a bit of night-time practice with Jim by her side giving sound advice. The blackouts could be cripplingly hazardous, what with the broken glass, and the civilians popping out of the dark when least expected.

'Crikey! Hazel looks upset.' Tom stopped pacing, having spotted his partner. 'Something must've happened and that's why she's late.'

Rosie noticed her friend had halted by the door. Hazel was puffing furiously on her cigarette as though building up her courage to come and join them.

'What's the matter?' Rosie kept her voice soft as she approached Hazel and noticed her eyes were bloodshot.

Hazel burst into fresh tears so Rosie ushered her along the corridor and out into the fresh air of the courtyard to talk privately. Hazel was a stoic character who usually took upsets in her stride.

Hazel dropped her cigarette butt and stamped on it, indicating her distress held an edge of temper. 'He's thrown me over. The rat! He's thrown me over when we were supposed to be getting engaged.' Hazel pulled a note from her pocket, glancing at a paragraph of pencilled scrawl before crumpling it in a fist. 'Didn't even have the decency to tell me to my face. Just sent this!'

Rosie hugged her friend. 'He's a bloody fool, then, and you were far too good for him,' she declared.

A sob burst from Hazel. 'He reckons his folks have found out about us and we'd best cool things in case they cut up rough. I know he means it's finished. He didn't have the guts to say so, though.'

'D'you want him back, if he's scared of his parents at his age?' Rosie enquired.

Hazel yanked a packet of Capstan from her pocket.

Clumsily she tried to light up but dropped the Vestas on the concrete. Rosie scooped up the box and a couple of matches then lit two cigarettes. For a few minutes the two young women smoked silently.

'I've already written back to him and told him he's a pathetic specimen, tied to his mummy's apron strings,' Hazel spat, snorting smoke from her nostrils.

'Hear, hear!' Rosie exclaimed. 'That's the spirit!'

Hazel scrubbed at her face with a handkerchief. 'Bloody mascara's run all over the place, I suppose,' she sniffed, looking at the sooty stains on the hanky.

Rosie took the sodden cloth and wiped the make-up off her friend's cheeks. 'There . . . scrub up well, don't you?'

'Might just as well look a fright now I've no man to call me own.' Hazel gave a wan smile.

Rosie was pleased to see that Hazel seemed to have calmed down. 'If Dr Clark finds out you're fancy-free, he might ask you out.' Rosie had noticed the doctor watching Hazel when they bumped into one another out on calls. Rosie was full of admiration for the way her friend capably strode about attending to vomit or gore without a hint of squeamishness. Richard Clark often watched Hazel too, smiling in a special way that went beyond admiration of her professional competence.

'I'm off men after this,' Hazel muttered, but managed a wry grimace. She dug in her handbag for her purse and pulled out a photograph, which she thrust at Rosie. 'Tear that up for me; can't bring myself to do it.'

Hazel had shown her the small square snap before. Chuck looked clean cut in his naval uniform with his cap and sunglasses warding off the Mediterranean glare. Rosie tore the photo into four pieces.

'Thanks. And this one.' Hazel pulled another picture from her bag's inner pocket and handed it over.

Rosie's fingers were gripping the top, ready to rip, when she glanced at it. She brought the image closer to examine it, then burst out, 'What's Chuck's full name?'

'Why d'you want to know?' Hazel said, rummaging in her bag.

'Tell me his name,' Rosie demanded quite brusquely.

'Charles Bellamy, but all his navy pals call him Chuck,' Hazel answered with a frown. 'He doesn't like being called Charlie. Says that's what his folks call him.'

'They do,' Rosie confirmed, shocked. There was no doubt: she was staring at the photograph of her step-brother in civvies. Then she remembered how Charlie had seemed odd when she'd told him that she worked at Ambulance Station 97. And no wonder! Hazel had believed him her fiancé, but the swine had dropped her like a hot potato now he realised his adultery might be uncovered.

'You know him, don't you?' Hazel took the photo back, gawping at it.

Rosie was reluctant to make her friend cry again, yet Charlie Bellamy deserved to be exposed as a liar and a cheat, as much for his wife's benefit as for Hazel's.

'He's married, isn't he?' Hazel burst out in sudden enlightenment. 'His "folks" are a wife and kids!'

Rosie was relieved that she'd only to confirm her friend's suspicions rather than grass Charlie up, though he deserved it. 'I'm so sorry, Hazel. My dad married Doris Bellamy, Charlie's mother.' Rosie frowned. 'We're sort of related although I've only spoken to him once. He's got a wife and son, and if I'd realised Chuck and Charlie were one and the same, I'd've told you sooner.'

'What a *bastard*! No wonder he said his family wouldn't like me! Well, the poor cow's welcome to him!'

Jim and Tom approached cautiously, giving warning coughs as they stepped outside.

'Everything all right?' they chorused.

'Everything's just fine,' Hazel said, sniffing fiercely. She tilted up her chin. 'Cleaning out the jalopy, I suppose, are we, first thing? Might as well get started.' She and Tom set off in the direction of the parked ambulances, Tom throwing a bewildered look over a shoulder as Hazel marched ahead.

'Her boyfriend's thrown her over and, believe me, she's better off without him,' Rosie briefly answered Jim's unspoken question.

He raised his eyebrows and shook his head, about to follow their friends when Rosie caught his sleeve and looked into his kindly eyes.

'Why were you talking about me earlier, Jim? What don't you want me to know?'

Jim looked sad, and sheepish. 'We thought it best not to say anything just yet . . .' he sighed. 'I don't know why because it'll be just as upsetting to know later as it is right now.'

'It's not about my driving test, is it?' Rosie asked.

Jim wearily shook his grey head. At that moment Rosie thought he looked more than his fifty-seven years.

'Young Herbie didn't make it, after all, Rosie.'

'What d'you mean?' Rosie demanded, feeling ice enclose her heart. 'I'm going to visit him on Friday when he's not so sleepy,' she announced. 'I phoned the hospital and they said his family didn't mind me going in to see him . . .'

'His concussion proved to be worse than they thought.

He had a brain haemorrhage. He died in the early hours of this morning. Stella Phipps got a call from Richard Clark. He knew our two crews would want to know the little lad's fate. Stella passed on the news before she went off duty this morning.'

Rosie felt her lower lip starting to tremble and her eyes swim with tears. She tipped back her head blinking at the blurry blue sky, screaming inside at the injustice of it.

Jim put a comforting hand on her shoulder, then let it fall to his side. Quietly he stood with her, listening to her sobs before he said huskily, 'Don't ever think it wasn't worth it, and you'll quit and knit socks instead. If the service loses the likes of girls like you, Rosie Gardiner, we're all buggered.'

'What did you say your name was?'

'I'm Rosie – Rosie Gardiner – and I'm pleased to meet you, Mrs Flint.' Rosie peered through the gloom at a small wizened face with a coil of plaited hair pinned either side of it.

'Likewise.' The elderly woman cocked her head, studying Rosie as though still making up her mind about her, whatever she'd said.

Conor slanted Rosie a private smile while showing her to an armchair by the hearth.

'Open the curtains, shall I, Mum? Let some light and fresh air in for a while before it gets proper dark.'

'No, you don't!' Hilda Flint's tiny figure was struggling up from the chair. 'Y'know Saul don't like people spying in on 'im. Keep 'em drawn.'

'Saul's gone, Mum.' Conor left the curtains as they were and sat down in the armchair opposite his mother, planting his elbows on his knees.

'He's off doing deals, ain't he? Him 'n' yer father's always out earning.' Hilda rubbed together arthritic fingers. 'Bringing in this, ain't they, so I can have me fags 'n' milk stouts in the evening?' Slyly she added, 'Look after me, those two do . . .'

'Dad's gone 'n' all, Mum . . . long time ago. They're both dead.'

'Dead! That's a fuckin' wicked thing to say about yer own.' Hilda sent a poisonous look at her son while he continued to regard her with mild interest.

Conor had brought a few milk stouts and a pack of cigarettes in with him. He rose and put a bottle by his mother's chair and a packet of Capstan on her lap, to no response.

'It's too warm in here, Mum; open the door, shall I?' Conor took off his jacket and loosened his tie.

There was a fire burning in the grate and the small room felt stifling and reeked of stale beer and tobacco smoke.

'Leave the door alone. I'm cold . . . could do with a bit more coal on that,' Hilda snapped.

Rosie exchanged a glance with Conor, biting her lip to stop a slightly outraged chuckle. The fug was almost unbearable, but she kept her cardigan on although perspiration beaded her top lip.

'Get the girl a cup of tea then.' Hilda smiled at Rosie. 'What's yer name, dear?' She opened a bottle of stout and poured it into the dirty glass wedged by her hip on a cushion.

'Her name's Rosie; she's told you that already.'

Rosie had listened, fascinated, to the exchange between mother and son. She admired Conor for not humouring her, as she obviously wanted him to, but Mrs Flint seemed cantankerous rather than upset, and that made Rosie wonder how much of her confusion was put on for effect.

'Want tea, Rosie?' Conor asked.

''Course she wants a cup of Rosie Lee, don't you, Rosie?' Hilda slapped her thigh and chortled at her little joke.

Conor shook his head in a resigned way. He got up and went through to the kitchen.

As soon as he'd disappeared, the woman shot her frail figure forward on her seat, craning her neck. The rainbow-hued crocheted shawl draping her shoulders dropped onto the chair back. 'Only fair to warn you, love, he's a sod around the women. Worse'n me other two boys put together. Saul's got a wife, and Steven – he's me other lad – he's only ever had one girl at a time.' She jerked her head at the kitchen door. 'Him!' she spat. 'Too randy by 'alf. Come a cropper, he will, and get a dose of the clap.' Hilda sat back in her chair and folded her hands, assessing the effect she'd had.

Rosie was stunned but she was determined not to show it because she knew that's what the woman wanted. In an odd way she was glad to have this glimpse into Conor's upbringing. She didn't like his mum and she guessed the woman didn't like her. More tellingly, Hilda Flint didn't seem to like Conor either, and that saddened Rosie, making her want to champion him. Perhaps he *was* a womaniser but so far he'd been good to her, and that was enough.

'Don't say much, do you?' Hilda sounded irritated as she dragged the shawl back up about her bony shoulders.

'Sorry, had a tiring day at work.'

265

'Doing what?' Another impolite question.

'I'm an ambulance auxiliary.'

'Are yer now?' Hilda harrumphed. 'Could've done with one of your lot showing up when my Saul got bombed. Bled to death, he did. Now me life's ruined without him. Best son in the world, he was.'

'I'm very sorry about that,' Rosie said, and she was. She knew from distressing experience that casualties who might have survived didn't when crews were unable to get through because of fires and debris blocking the roads.

'Left behind a wife, did my Saul . . . she's no good.' Hilda grimaced disgust. 'Weren't never right for him. Angie's *his* cast off.' Again Hilda jerked her head at the kitchen where the kettle had started to sing.

By now Rosie was wishing Conor hadn't left the room. She felt increasingly awkward, and convinced that he was aware of the horrible way his mother was talking about him. Yet he was a loyal son and had not bad-mouthed his mother to Rosie.

'You're pretty but Pat's his girlfriend now, so I've been told, not that he brings her in. Perhaps he'll swap yer if you're better in bed.'

Rosie fidgeted, wondering whether to try to distract the old woman by offering condolences about Saul's death. She decided to avoid mentioning the subject. 'I'm only just getting to know Conor, Mrs Flint—'

Hilda snorted. 'You watch him then 'cos he'll be inside yer knickers 'fore yer know it, then leave yer high 'n' dry with yer belly swole.'

'Want another milk stout, Mum?'

Conor was in the doorway holding two cups of tea. He put them on the table.

'Ain't started on this one yet,' Hilda said, making a show of taking a swig from her glass.

'Talking too much, were you?' Conor said.

He beckoned Rosie and she immediately stood up and went to him.

'Right . . . we're off down the road for a drink.'

'Well, put them bottles where I can reach 'em, if yer going already,' Hilda ordered testily. 'Waste of me tea 'n' milk, that was,' she tutted, pointing at the untouched cups on the table. 'If the girl didn't want none, she should've said.'

''Bye, Mrs Flint.' Rosie gave a small wave as Conor took her hand and pulled her out of the door.

''Bye, Pat . . . nice to see yer. Pop in again . . . I get lonely, y'know . . .'

'You can see why Steven wants to escape abroad, can't you?'

'I can see why *you'd* want to,' Rosie replied, aware Conor was still holding her hand though they were outside on the pavement.

'I did warn you.'

'Not quite enough, though.' Rosie's amusement held a hint of reprimand. In the car on the way to his mother's he'd said the woman could be difficult. Rosie classed her father as *difficult*; Mrs Flint was something else entirely.

Conor let go of Rosie's hand to shrug into his jacket, then they began strolling along the street towards the Red Lion.

'Why d'you bring me to see her?' Rosie shot him a glance. 'You know what she said about you, don't you?'

'Yep.'

'So why?'

'Has she scared you off?'

'No, but I don't have to live with her.'

'Neither do I.'

Rosie accepted the cigarette he was offering, glancing at him. 'Oh . . . where d'you live then?'

'Round the corner. Got my own place. Steven wants to move in with me.'

'But you won't let him,' Rosie guessed, dipping her head to the flame cupped in his palm.

Conor smiled an affirmative. 'Somebody has to keep an eye on her. She'll drop a fag down the side of her chair when she's drunk and set light to herself. Wouldn't be the first time.' He suddenly threw back his head. 'Sorry . . . stupid thing to say. Didn't mean to remind you of—'

'You didn't. I never think about him,' Rosie quickly interrupted.

'Who? Tell me who you never think about.'

Rosie avoided his eyes. 'Why? You don't know him.'

'You did.'

'Not from choice,' Rosie blurted. 'Never liked him even when . . .' She suddenly clammed up. He had a knack of making her say more than she wanted to.

'Even when you were kids?' he guessed.

'That's enough!' Rosie pulled away from him, cigarette clenched between two quivering fingers. She dropped it, ground it out with a toe. 'I'd better go home. Work in the morning . . .'

'Yeah, work in the morning,' he mimicked, softly sarcastic, but he caught her by the elbows, jerking her forward when she tried to walk off.

Rosie kept her head lowered, knowing he was staring down at her, brooding.

'D'you believe any of what she told you about me?'

'Some of it,' Rosie answered. 'Well, you told me about your sister-in-law and girlfriend so that didn't come as a surprise.'

'She wanted it to.'

'I guessed as much,' Rosie said. 'That's why I kept quiet and didn't encourage her.'

'What about the rest?'

'You've been fair to me up till now,' Rosie said with a shrug.

'In other words, you're not sure about the rest.'

'Does Pat get on with her?'

'Pat hardly knows her. My sister-in-law told Mum I was seeing Pat. I never take girls in there.'

'I'm not surprised,' Rosie said wryly.

'It's not that. I've never bothered before showing anybody what I'm made of.'

Rosie raised her face to meet his eyes. 'And your father?'

'He was worse. A bully and a womaniser. He turned her into what she is.'

'Are you like him?'

'No. I look like him . . . so people say. Handsome, he was, obviously.' He smiled as he took her hand, pulling her on. 'That's why Mum's set against me. I remind her of him.'

'Thought she missed him. She spoke as though she did.'

'Just keeping up appearances; every old girl round here has nursed her black eye and pretended her husband's a diamond. Didn't see her shed a tear when he was put in the ground. Since then it's been rose-tinted spectacles all the way.'

He pushed open the door to the pub and with an arm about Rosie's shoulders, ushered her in.

Rosie hadn't expected the whole saloon bar to go quiet while everybody turned and stared at them and then greeted Conor with coarse shouts.

''S'all right,' Conor murmured, gently urging her forward. 'Come on. I want Steven to meet you.'

CHAPTER TWENTY-THREE

'What you drinking then, Rosie?' Steven asked after Conor had introduced them. 'Reckon you're a gin 'n' orange type of gel.'

'Yes, thanks . . . that'd be fine,' Rosie said, feeling so overwhelmed by unwanted attention that she'd have agreed to a pint of hemlock.

Angie Flint was perched on a barstool. As soon as she made eye contact with Rosie she hopped down and sauntered over.

'I remember you: Rosie from the ambulance service.' Angie had wedged herself between Conor and Rosie, separating them. She combed her coral-tipped fingers through her hair, and a glimpse of chunky gold pinned to an earlobe flashed through the silver strands. 'Don't know how you can bear to deck yerself out in that horrible dark suit.' Rosie's stylish summer dress and cardigan got a thorough appraisal, but there was no compliment.

'No choice in the matter,' Rosie said. 'Comes with the job.'

Conor seemed occupied talking to his brother but Angie knew he was keeping tabs on everything they were saying. And she knew why. He'd found a girl he really liked this time.

'Conor might be your dad's pal; but I reckon you're keen to know him better yourself, aren't you?'

'Perhaps I am.' Rosie was determined not to feel intimidated. She sipped her drink and glanced about. A sulky brunette with large red lips straightened in her chair, a challenge in her eyes as they met Rosie's.

'Better warn you about him then, 'cos I reckon you're out of your depth,' Angie purred.

'Don't bother,' Rosie replied. 'His mother's already given me a talking-to.'

'So he's taken you to see the old girl,' Angie snickered in surprise. 'That's a first.'

Rosie gazed at Conor's profile, wondering why he'd abandoned her to his old flame's jealousy. But she wasn't about to seek his protection. She should be able to look after herself and give as good as she got. She'd been a Windmill Girl and back in those days rivalry and catfights had been par for the course.

'Told you about *her*, has he?' Angie jerked her head at the brunette watching them. 'That's Pat Ford and the old dragon with her is her mum, Ethel; he's finished with Pat . . . so he says.' Angie clucked her tongue. 'Bloody typical of him to try and rub her nose in it by bringing you in here. He's a bastard like that, playing one of us off against the other.'

'She's got nothing to worry about from me,' Rosie returned, draining her glass. 'And neither have you.' She realised she preferred the company of Conor's obnoxious mother to this crowd of raucous men and gaudy women. Steven Flint seemed nice, but as for the rest of them . . .

Rosie's gaze flitted over labourers standing cheek by jowl with men in flash suits, pulling luxuries from their pockets and hawking them around. She watched money change hands for a watch and a silver lighter. A group of soldiers was stationed at the far end of the bar, buying cigarettes and vodka from another spiv. And they all knew Conor. He'd received bawled greetings from every corner of the pub.

It was easy to believe there wasn't a war on in this part of town. Mrs Flint squandered fuel on a warm evening when most people struggled to keep their bunkers stocked in wintertime. Rosie knew she wouldn't bother asking him why he indulged his mother, buying her black-market coal to keep her house ridiculously hot. He'd put a ten-shilling note in Peg Price's collecting bowl, exactly the sum she couldn't afford to pay for a week's rent on a small furnished room for her and Hope. At the time she'd thought him acting flash. Now she realised he'd done it because he could . . . in the same way he could afford to sound mildly put out at being owed five hundred pounds.

The Flints and people like them were different from the working-class East Enders she'd been bred amongst. In this pub the atmosphere was seedy yet sweetly perfumed by women in heavy jewellery, and bank notes littered the slop-covered bar. Her father used to count out coins to take when he treated himself to a trip to the local. And John Gardiner had always had the decency to be ashamed rather than brash about his criminal activities.

Rosie guessed that for Conor ducking and diving

wasn't a necessary evil but a way of having everything he wanted.

And he'd told her he wanted her.

'Ladies' convenience in here somewhere?' Rosie asked, sliding her empty glass onto the bar.

'Show you if yer like,' Angie said, nodding to a corner.

'I'll find it, thanks.' Rosie didn't want Angie Flint dripping any more poison in her ear. Besides, she didn't need the ladies' room.

'That door leads to the street . . . just in case you want to use that as well,' Angie informed her mockingly. 'Don't fit in round here, do you, Ambulance Rosie?'

'But you do,' Rosie returned before slipping into the crowd. She was annoyed that Angie had guessed she'd no intention of powdering her nose. Neither did she want Conor's sister-in-law thinking she'd gained a victory in sending her packing. But primitive intuition was telling Rosie to leave, and gratefully she let the pub door swing shut behind her.

She knew he'd come after her as soon as he realised she'd fled. And she wanted to be somewhere out of sight when he did.

An alleyway or a tube station she could dash into would serve as shelter and as she hurried along, peering over a shoulder, it seemed as though she'd been sucked into a dark sinister place and she was trying to outrun Lenny through Soho. She'd bumped into him outside a nightclub and been unable to make him take no for an answer. Then a pal of his had side-tracked him, allowing her some precious minutes to make her escape. But he'd caught up with her, grabbed her by the throat and forced her to the ground with him . . .

'Whoa . . . where you off to?'

Rosie lashed out blindly, till Conor let her go and backed off, hands slightly elevated in surrender. She stumbled back against the wall, her chest heaving with gasped inhalations.

'Sorry . . . didn't know it was you.' She could see she'd scratched his cheek.

'Who d'you think it was?'

'You don't have to see me home.' Rosie composed herself and thrust her shaking hands into her pockets. 'You can stay and have a drink with your friends.'

'I thought *we* were friends.'

'I don't like them.'

'D'you like me?'

Rosie glanced at him, standing in front of her, blocking her in.

'Do you like me, Rosie?'

'I . . . I don't know,' she said. 'Will you move so I can get past?'

'I'll take you home.'

'No . . .' She pulled a hand from a pocket to gesture. 'You don't have to babysit me. I can find my own way home.'

'Yeah, but you don't have to 'cos I'll take you.'

'I don't want you to!' Rosie cried. 'Just go away. I can find my own way home.' Still he didn't move and Rosie lacked the courage to shove him aside.

'I know you can; you found your way underground through a bombed-out building so getting to Shoreditch should be a piece of cake.' He came closer, hands moving to hold her, but they dropped back and he rested against the wall by her side. 'Have a cigarette. Take one!' he insisted, pulling a cigarette out of the pack for her, and lighting it before turning it and placing it between her lips.

Rosie dragged on it deeply. 'Sorry I scratched you. You startled me, that's all.'

'Don't be frightened of me, Rosie.'

'I'm not.'

He smiled sideways at her, cigarette drooping in his lips. 'Perhaps you should be. Scare myself sometimes, stupid way I act.'

'Why did you take me in there, with those people?'

'Because I'm an idiot.' He took her hand and eased her away from the wall.

'Take you home.'

'No . . . it's all right . . .'

'Don't say it's all right, Rosie, 'cos it fucking ain't.' The words emerged in slow staccato bursts.

Rosie knew then his mild manner was a sham but she let him lead her back to his car, parked outside his mother's house, rather than carry on resisting.

'Did you visit that lad in hospital?' Conor asked as he pulled away from the kerb.

A look of intense sadness had flitted over Rosie's features at that reminder. She hadn't told him about little Herbie's death.

'No . . . no, I didn't.' Rosie clammed up, knowing if she started to explain she'd end up crying, she felt so jittery. She could already sense her nose stinging and sniffed.

Rosie kept her eyes on the skies as they sped through London. The streets seemed unusually quiet, as though others knew what they did not and an attack was imminent. But no siren sounded and they pulled up outside her house in what seemed like just a few minutes.

'I want you to know who I am, that's why I took you there,' Conor said. 'Those are the people I grew up with, work down the docks with, sleep with.'

Rosie moistened her lips. 'I didn't know you were a docker.'

'That's why I took you there. I want you to know. That's who I am. Nothing to hide.' He turned fierce eyes on her. 'Thing is, Rosie, I'm still not sure who you are 'cos you're still hiding . . . and that's the way you want it to stay, isn't it?'

Rosie nodded, looking quickly away.

He stretched out a hand to turn her face back to his but instinctively Rosie shrank from his strong masculine fingers.

He grunted a hoarse, fatalistic laugh. 'Yeah . . . and then there's that.' He punched his fist against the steering wheel, then immediately got out of the car and came round to open her door.

'I'm sorry about the kid dying. I know it must be a choker after what you went through to save him.'

'How did you know?' Rosie gasped.

'I can work most things out for myself. But I shouldn't have to, and there's a lot you should just tell me.'

Rosie knew he'd left his car door open because he was going to drive off straight away. And, oddly, she didn't want him to. Now she'd calmed down she wanted them to finish the evening on good terms.

'Go in, it's late. Take care of yourself.'

She suddenly realised he was saying goodbye, not good night, and her stomach lurched. She wanted to know for sure so blurted out, 'Are we going out again?'

'Have you decided if you like me?' His gaze was boring into her profile.

Rosie nodded.

'You like me?'

She nodded.

'And trust me?'

Rosie moistened her lips, then nodded.

'Enough to let me touch you?'

'I don't know . . .' she murmured.

'Well, when you do, come and find me. I've showed you where.'

Rosie watched the car's dim rear lights till they were just faint needle pricks before she went inside.

She went to the sideboard and poured herself a large glass of moonshine. She sat in bed smoking and drinking and staring out into the darkness. A vivid trail of fire was arcing the heavens, and she sat and watched it. The siren sounded late yet still she stayed where she was, wondering if he'd gone back to the pub to find brassy Angie or sullen Pat, and sleep with them. If what his mother said about him was true, perhaps he'd bedded them both . . . at the same time . . .

Rosie drew shakily on the cigarette and thumbed tears off her lashes. She might think herself a cut above those women but at least they were women, not empty shells. The ground shook, jolting her out of her stupor and into thoughts of her daughter. Jumping out of bed she raced down two sets of stairs into the relative safety of the cellar.

'You've seemed a bit browned off lately, gel.' Popeye glanced at Trudy as they strolled along the path in the park. 'Fancy a trip down Kent way to buck you up? I'll show you where me and Lenny used to go hopping, if yer like. Yalding, it was. Nice place. Took him fer a week in August most years when he was at school. Us grown-ups had some larks after dark when the work was done and kids were akip.' In fact, Popeye's intention in heading in that direction was to find John Gardiner rather than have a holiday. Frank wanted his fifty pounds back off the man, with interest, or John would get the treatment.

Popeye was confident that Midge and Rufus, between them, should manage to swing a bit of lead pipe at a man to teach him a lesson. In their heydays, both his henchmen had been a force to be reckoned with. Rufus had had the brawn and Midge the sly speed to make an impact.

'What I'd like's a trip down Memory Lane, and take a different turning this time,' Trudy sighed. 'Been looking back on my life just lately and wishing . . .'

'You wish you'd got married, you mean?' Frank had guessed before from things his girlfriend had said that she regretted devoting her youth to other people's children rather than her own.

'I do,' Trudy owned up. 'I might not have loved any man the way I loved my childhood sweetheart, but I might have rubbed along all right with somebody else. A family's what I miss. Would've liked kids . . . nearly had one a few years back.'

Frank cast a startled eye on his girlfriend. She looked a bit too long in the tooth to be producing sprogs. 'What, you had a miscarriage you mean?' he asked carefully.

Trudy burst out laughing. Pulling Frank by the hand she led him to a bench so they could sit and talk. 'No, I did not have a miscarriage. I've never even got engaged. What d'you take me for?' But she sounded amused rather than angry as she watched a trio of boys playing cricket. 'I had a chance to adopt an unmarried mother's child but then the girl went and changed her mind on me.'

279

Frank tutted. 'Weren't bloody fair after you'd set your heart on it. I suppose she was a bit of a good-time gel, was she?'

'She was a showgirl in the West End but she seemed nice enough. Never found out who the father was but got the impression he was a wrong 'un and she didn't want reminders of him. Then she went back on her word and kept the baby.'

Trudy wondered if she'd disclosed too much and he might guess who it was she'd been talking about. Frank knew the Gardiners and she didn't want to cause the family any trouble. But since they'd bumped into Rosie out walking with her boyfriend, Trudy couldn't put little Hope Gardiner from her mind. She wanted to unburden herself and then, with Frank's blunt perspective on things, banish the longing for a family from her head because at forty-nine it was too late to get pregnant but not too late to rear children.

Frank had an agile mind and almost immediately he'd pounced on the probable identity of the unmarried mother. Ever since the day they'd bumped into Conor Flint and Rosie, Trudy had been a bit melancholy. But Frank remained sitting, arms crossed over his chest and face screwed up thoughtfully as though chewing things over.

'Reckon I've hit on who you mean, Trudy. Only know one showgirl round these parts and I've always had me doubts about her kid's father copping it before anybody had met him.'

'I was just telling you something in confidence; it wasn't a problem to solve, Frank,' Trudy said quickly.

'You were going to adopt Rosie Gardiner's baby, were you?' Frank patted at Trudy's hand in comfort.

'I never said that, Frank! Don't you go saying I did.' Trudy jumped to her feet. Something in his expression made her wish she'd not confided in him.

'Don't fret, love; soul of discretion, me,' Frank soothed. He gave a sprightly little leap to his feet and, pulling Trudy's arm through his, he led her back towards the path.

The smile on Popeye's face stretched from ear to ear as they strolled. So, now he'd no need to get rough with John Gardiner to get even. He had a much better way of persuading the man to see sense, hand over his fifty quid and set up his still.

The apple of John's eye was a bastard and the man wouldn't want that bandied about. And not only that, his daughter was likely to get knocked up again if she carried on seeing Conor Flint.

'Stop off for a few bevies on the way back, shall we, Trudy?' Popeye suggested jovially. He felt he had something to celebrate.

CHAPTER TWENTY-FOUR

'I feel rough . . . think I'm going to throw up again.' Hazel clapped a hand to her ballooning mouth.

'I ordered you home, Scott.' Stella Phipps had emerged from her office in time to see Hazel making a dash for the ladies' convenience. 'How are you Gardiner? Any symptoms to worry about?'

'Not so far, Ma'am,' Rosie replied with a sigh of grim relief.

A bout of food poisoning had spread like wildfire through Station 97, depleting numbers. Bluebottles were thought to have spread the infection from the pigswill out in the yard to the canteen and both shift leaders had blamed each other for failing to impose rigorous cleaning regimes.

The senior staff members that hadn't been affected were now out on active duty with the rank and file volunteers. Janet Lawson, Rosie's shift leader, had got such a bad dose of sickness and diarrhoea that she'd ended up in hospital for a few days and hadn't yet returned to work.

Those who had escaped the infection were doing double hours and sleeping on mattresses on the floor to keep the station open for business.

Hazel reappeared, groaning and clutching her tender belly.

'Home! Now!' Stella pointed at the exit.

'But the all clear's not sounded yet. We might get a call out,' Hazel protested. 'We're already short staffed.'

'You ought to go and get some rest, Hazel,' Rosie said kindly. Her friend's complexion was ashen and although Rosie admired Hazel's conscientiousness she anticipated the young woman being more of a hindrance than a help if they were sent out on an emergency.

'God, you look terrible,' Tom announced bluntly as he came up beside the trio of women in the corridor.

'Thanks,' Hazel said, suppressing a burp.

'Where's Warwick? Has he clocked in yet?'

'He's just 'phoned in to say he's got the runs.' Tom pulled a face.

'There's enough of us here to make up a couple of crews. That'll have to do,' Stella said. 'I can drive, Norris can be my assistant, and Gardiner can pair up with you,' she told Tom.

'I'll man the 'phones then if we get a call out,' Hazel insisted. 'I can nip to the toilet when I need to. Clarice can't do all the dockets and 'phones by herself.'

Stella jerked a nod of acceptance.

'I'll see you in my office, Gardiner.' Stella turned away and opened the door just behind her.

Rosie's heart increased tempo. She'd not forgotten the talk she'd had with Stella at the dance and wondered if the woman had something more specific to say this time rather than dropping hints about secrets. Rosie's apprehension increased when Hazel gave her a mystified look before walking off along the corridor with Tom.

When Rosie entered Stella's office the older woman was rummaging in a cupboard where stationery was kept. Stella produced her raffle prize of a tin of peaches and held it out.

'I wanted to give you this in private. Not enough for us all to have a taste so I thought you might like to take it home.'

Rosie blinked in surprise but didn't immediately take the gift. 'Well . . . It's awfully kind of you . . . Are you sure you'd rather not save it for Christmas?'

'Christmas is a long way off. Anyway, I expect I'll be on my own. Shame not to share it with someone.'

Rosie could think of nothing to say other than, 'Oh . . . sorry to hear that . . .'

'Norris's husband will be back home, she expects. He's top brass in the army.' Stella cleared her throat then thrust the peaches at Rosie. 'Do take it; children love fruit . . . My nephews do anyway . . . Nice treat . . .' She put the tin on the edge of the desk. 'Now, off you go, I've got to get these timetables sorted out; never know if that damned telephone might ring and scramble us any second.'

'Thank you.' Rosie picked up the peaches and turned for the door, feeling in a daze. She'd no idea that Thora Norris was married, or that Stella Phipps had nephews. But she no longer wondered if Stella knew her secret; it seemed she did, and the gift for Hope was Stella's way of saying it made no difference to her that her newest recruit was an unmarried mother.

Tom took far greater risks driving in the blackout than Jim did, Rosie thought while hanging onto the door handle for support as they swerved around a corner in the Studebaker. By the time they reached the address of the incident in Stepney Rosie's heart was in her mouth. Twice they'd almost collided with other vehicles as Tom raced through the dark streets with just infernos lighting the way as he careered around obstructions.

She breathed a sigh of relief as the vehicle braked sharply some distance from a burning building. She jumped from the ambulance carrying her gas mask and her medical bag then hared, stumbling, over bomb wreckage towards what looked to have been a church hall about a hundred yards away.

'Harvest Festival was taking place in there. Quite a few kids and their parents trapped inside,' Stella shouted.

Stella and Thora had set off first when the call came through and had arrived a few minutes before Rosie and Tom turned up. Tom sprinted up with an armful of blankets ready to be used to wrap the casualties.

The roar of the fire was drowned out by the chug of another rocket overhead. But they knew they were safe from that one, even if some other poor souls were not; the murderous weapon would glide on for a distance once the engine cut out before diving on a target.

'There's kids down here, you fucking bastards,' a fireman shouted, tears dripping from his sooty eyes, as the screaming in the church hall reached a crescendo. He shook a furious fist at the sky while the other held the hose steady on the burning building.

'It's the ones you can't bloody hear that's the problem,' Tom said, giving the fellow a sympathetic pat on the back.

Rosie bit her trembling lip against the howl of anguish pulsing in her throat. The feeling of uselessness was hard to endure. But until the fire was contained there was nothing much they could do.

'Let's get the stretchers ready,' Tom bawled at Rosie, grabbing her elbow and shaking her.

Like an automaton Rosie darted after him, blocking the horrible mental images that were torturing her mind. She knew the sight of burned and broken bodies would soon be a filthy reality . . . but not yet. She widened her eyes on the debris-strewn ground she was covering, scouring it for anything likely to trip her up as she bounded towards the ambulance. Once there, they worked together with ferocious efficiency, wordlessly yanking the stretchers from their runners and stacking them ready to be carried back.

And then the darkness exploded in white light. Rosie was lifted off her feet and against the open door of the ambulance, banging her back and scalp with some force. Instinctively she twisted sideways, gripping an edge of metal as a blast of violently hot air hit her, threatening to suck her from her life support and carry her away. She screwed up her face, trying to fight against the pain in her ears and the incandescence in her skull. As the vortex of blast pressure decreased, Rosie let go of the door and fell to her knees on the ground, her arms cradling her head.

She panted, fighting to keep the blackness at bay. She wanted to yell out to Tom but though her mouth opened and closed no sound could be forced from her throat. Finally she struggled to her feet, swaying against the ambulance door that had saved her, as Tom lifted himself upright beside her, batting at his ears.

'Are you all right?' Rosie gasped out, staring at Tom's dirt-streaked features. He was grimacing at her and she realised he'd not heard what she'd said. She shouted her question again, shaking his arm.

He nodded. 'Gone deaf,' he mouthed, poking at his ears again.

Rosie gasped in a breath, then another, her body heaving with the effort. She turned to gaze back to the spot where minutes ago she and Tom had been waiting with Thora and Stella for an opportunity to tend to the blaze victims.

An inferno now marked where their colleagues and the church hall had once stood. In shock she stared for almost a minute then looked at Tom to see he was crying, his shoulders quaking; nothing could have survived that.

'Ready to go?' Rosie croaked out after a couple of false starts, her face running with a mixture of brine and blood from the cut on her scalp.

Tom nodded. In unison they stooped to pick up the stretchers and set off back the way they'd come.

CHAPTER TWENTY-FIVE

'Dad! What are you doing here?'

Rosie had been pegging out washing in the back garden when she'd thought she'd heard a noise in the house. She'd hurtled inside, scared somebody had broken in, and got the best surprise of her life.

'Oh, my darling!' Rosie swooped on her daughter, cuddling her in her arms so tightly that Hope squealed. But the feel of her little girl's arms about her neck was heavenly. Rosie kissed a hot pink cheek. 'Miss your mummy, did you?'

Hope nodded solemnly, tightening her grip on Rosie's neck.

'Why've you come home, Dad? Why didn't you write and warn me? Where's Doris?' Having rattled off her breathless questions Rosie spun round with her daughter. 'Oh, I'm so pleased to see you,' she murmured into Hope's silky fair hair.

'Get that kettle on, Rosie. I'm parched.' John sounded weary, in body and in mind.

Rosie put her daughter on her feet and gave him a

searching look. Already her euphoria was fading; her father had yet to explain his sudden return and she sensed it wasn't going to be good news. But she'd draw her happiness out for a while and delve deeper after the new arrivals had had something to eat and drink.

'She's fasto . . . the journey must have exhausted the poor love,' Rosie said as she came back into the parlour. She'd tucked Hope up in bed as soon as the child had finished her milky tea and jam sandwich. Halfway through 'Baa Baa Black Sheep', Hope had curled on her side, thumb in mouth, and fallen deeply asleep.

'Put the kettle on again, Rosie. I'll have another brew before unpacking. I left the case in the hallway.'

'Why d'you come back, Dad?' Rosie sat opposite John at the table once the kettle was filled and on the gas stove. She took his hands in hers. 'Have you and Doris had a bust-up?'

'Sort of,' he said, withdrawing his bent leathery fingers from his daughter's smooth palms. 'Weren't really her fault; it's that bloody son of hers. Charlie's back home on convalescence.' John grimaced disgust. 'Not much wrong with him, if you ask me. Just scratches on his legs from shrapnel, but he's managed to swing it. Anyhow, he made it clear we'd outstayed our welcome. I ain't stopping where I'm not wanted, and I told 'em so.' John's lips tightened. 'Doris tried to make light of it . . . you know . . . saying her boy was just having a snap 'n' snarl 'cos he's in pain.' John shook his head. 'Didn't fall fer that 'cos it ain't the first time Charlie's come out with snide remarks about us being in the way. So I got our stuff together. Doris said she was staying and weren't ever coming back here to get blown up. So I told her, do what you like.' John clasped his hands together on the table. 'She said Hope could stay. But I weren't leaving my princess there with them. Doris don't love her like we do, and she makes no bones about showing it. So here we are, back home again.'

'I wouldn't have wanted you to leave her, Dad. But it's wonderful to have you home. I've been lonely here on my own.'

John gave his daughter a penetrating stare. 'That's another reason I had to come back. In the middle of our barney Charlie come out with something else made me want to knock his teeth down his throat. He said you was entertaining Conor Flint in my house. True is it?' John's lower lip started to tremble as he read his daughter's embarrassed reaction. 'Have you . . . has he made you do things, Rosie, 'cos he says I owe him money and you've been trying to protect me from him?'

Rosie jumped to her feet. 'No! He's not like that. He's nice.'

'*Nice!*' John was also on his feet. 'He ain't *nice*, and if you think he is it's 'cos he's better at handling women than Lenny was! Have you been to bed with him, Rosie? Tell me! He's after his fifty quid's worth off you, 'cos I got away with it. I'll kill him, I will!'

'Hush . . .' Rosie had turned white with strain, but she embraced her distressed father. 'Nothing like that's gone on, Dad, honestly.' She hadn't seen Conor for some weeks and the more time went on the more she wanted to. She'd not contacted him because they both knew what that would signal. She wasn't ready for intimacy; she didn't know if she ever would be. So her father had nothing to fear.

John pulled himself from his daughter's arms and flopped down in the chair. 'I did have some of Flint's money, Rosie: fifty pounds I took off Popeye and didn't give it back when I should've.' He blew his nose. 'Charlie said that you called Flint your boyfriend.' John shook his head. 'He ain't your boyfriend, love, whatever sweet talk he comes out with. Him and his brothers are all spivs 'n' pimps, Pop told me that. Reckon it's one of the few truths to come out of that bastard's mouth.'

Rosie swallowed a painful lump in her throat. 'Perhaps he is those things, but he's treated me well. Anyway, he won't be back now so no need to worry. And I only told Charlie that Conor was my boyfriend to get rid of him.'

John was up on his feet again. 'Charlie done something, has he?'

'No!' Rosie could tell her father's guilt was making him panicky. 'He called to say hello and asked if he could stop here instead of travelling to Gravesend. I said my boyfriend wouldn't like it, but really I was worried Mrs Price would spot him coming out of the house in the morning. Luckily, Conor turned up and Charlie put two and two together and I just went along with it to hurry him on his way.'

'You think it was lucky Flint turned up here?' John gave a sorrowful sigh. 'You do like him, don't you? Oh, Rosie . . . I wish I'd never gone to Gravesend. You've not fallen for him, dear, have you?'

''Course not!' Rosie blurted but her heart had leaped to her throat in the way it always did when she lied to her father. 'I can understand why you wanted to avoid Charlie. I don't like him either.' She decided to keep quiet about Charlie being an adulterous rat. Heaven only knew how Doris would react if she discovered that her son had been romancing an ambulance auxiliary as though he were a carefree bachelor.

'Have you still got that fifty pounds, Dad?' she asked, inwardly praying her father hadn't spent it and was intending to return it.

John nodded. 'Don't worry, love, it's going straight back to Popeye tomorrow, then my hands are clean.' He sat down again with a faint smile. 'Another cup of tea'd be nice.'

Rosie filled the kettle and lit the gas stove, glad her father seemed to have calmed down and that he had promised to return the money to Popeye. She trusted he would.

'So . . . how's it all been going at work?' John called out.

Rosie set the cups and sniffed back spontaneous tears at the memory of the colleagues who'd been blown to smithereens in Stepney. So had the fireman, and the people trapped inside the building. But Rosie couldn't tell her dad about any of it; he would again be on his feet, frantic with worry that she might be next to cop it. And terrified as Rosie was, as her remaining colleagues were, about the risks they were running, they were all determined to carry on.

'I'm being kept busy, as you can imagine,' Rosie said, sounding quite jolly. 'I've made some friends and been out dancing with them.'

John came up behind his daughter and laid a hand on her shoulder. 'I'm proud of you, y'know; should have told you that sooner.'

Rosie turned about and gave him a watery smile. 'I know you are,' she croaked.

'What is it, love?' John crooned, taking his daughter in his arms and stroking her soft silver hair.

'So pleased to see you and Hope . . . Such a lovely

surprise,' Rosie mumbled, the words muffled by his shoulder as the tears flowed.

'Come on, buck up,' John said gently. 'We're back for good.' He gave Rosie's back a rub. 'What's this?' John had turned his attention on the tin of peaches in the cupboard and picked it up.

'A friend gave it to me.' Rosie wiped her eyes with her hanky. 'She won it in a raffle but gave it to me. She said children love fruit.'

'You told somebody about Hope then?'

'She guessed,' Rosie said. 'But she'll keep it to herself and . . . She's gone away now anyhow.'

'Well, that's mighty nice of her.' John turned the peaches in his hand. 'Good sort was she? You'll miss her, I'll bet.'

'One of the best, she was,' Rosie said, handing her dad his cup of tea. 'And yes, I'll miss her dreadfully.'

'Fancy going greyhound racing on Saturday?' Patricia was sitting on the edge of Conor's bed in her petticoat, reapplying her smeared lipstick. 'Mickey's going with some pals; we could get a big party of us up.'

'You go. I'll be busy this weekend.'

Pat put down the hand mirror she'd been using and pouted, watching him shrug into his shirt. She'd been dressed already this morning then she'd teased Conor into taking her back to bed for a quick romp.

'Go for a drive today, shall we? How about Southend? I'm bored.'

'Get a job then.'

'What . . . ambulance auxiliary?' Pat taunted, and got a hard glance before Conor quit the bedroom, buttoning up his cuffs. She flung herself back on the mattress. He might have responded to her seduction and started sleeping with her again, but she knew his heart wasn't in it, and never would be. When they'd first got together, months ago, she'd made the running and eventually caught him. She'd been optimistic that she could make Conor buy her an engagement ring, despite Angie hanging around like a bad smell. Now Pat knew she was just being used, and if she told him she wasn't having it and he could show her some respect and affection, he'd shrug and show her the door.

And it was all the fault of that prissy bitch he'd brought to the pub. Angie had told her the girl's name was Rosie and she worked for the LAAS. And it seemed she'd given Conor the elbow. Pat knew that must have surprised him when he was so popular with women. She was hoping it was his pride that was hurting but something told her it wasn't. He seemed different . . . frustrated . . . even when he was on top of her.

Conor found a pint of milk in the kitchen and took a swig from the bottle. He sat down at the table and started to read the paper, then folded it with a curse when he spotted a report of an ambulance bursting into flames in Hammersmith.

The phone started to ring and he answered it to hear his mother's screeching voice on the other end of the line.

'The little bleeder's gawn down the recruiting office, I know he has,' Hilda whined. 'I'm gonna lose another one of me sons, and if I do I'll blame you.'

'He's down at the docks, Mum.' Conor looked at the clock on the wall and knew if his brother had been on late shift he would have been home by now.

'No, he ain't; he didn't come home last night. Ain't seen him in nearly two days.'

'I'll come round in a bit.' Conor put the receiver down.

'Who's that?' Patricia had got dressed and entered the kitchen. 'Angie, is it, checking up on you?'

'Seen anything of Steven lately?' Conor asked.

Pat shook her head, but she avoided his eye. She knew Steven had enlisted because Mickey Rook had told her. Her and Mickey went way back. They'd been sweethearts at school, then Pat had outgrown him and found herself more sophisticated lovers. But she'd had a fling with Mickey recently while Conor had remained unresponsive to her.

'Mickey know where Steve is?' Conor asked sardonically.

Pat flushed, knowing he was on to her, on both counts. 'Can't be a surprise to you to find out your brother's gone and joined up; he's been saying he would fer months. And I'm glad.' She coiled her arms about Conor's neck, rubbing together their groins. 'If you stop around here a while longer . . . I'll make sure and thank you,' she purred.

Taking Pat by the elbow, Conor led her to the door.

''Ere, what you doing?' she said indignantly. 'Ain't even had a cup of tea for me breakfast yet 'cos you took me back to bed. You can't just throw me out when you've had what you wanted, you know.'

'It was what you wanted. If you don't like it, don't turn up on me doorstep every fucking evening.'

'You're a right bastard, aren't you!' Pat stormed.

'Yeah . . . I am.' Conor closed the door behind her, then went back to pick up the receiver that had been ringing ever since he'd put it down.

*   *   *

295

'Ain't stopping; just come to give you this.' John thrust an envelope at Popeye; the man was looking at him as though he'd seen a ghost.

'Well, this is a bleedin' surprise, I must say!' Popeye recovered quickly. 'Thought you was miles away in Kent, mate, and I was gonna fetch up down there and say hello. Looks like you've saved me the trip.'

'Make sure that gets back to Flint. I'll find out if it don't.' John jerked the envelope containing fifty pounds, wanting Popeye to take it off him.

'Come in . . . let's have a chat and a cuppa. Tell you what, I'll find us summat a bit stronger.'

Popeye flung the door wide and after a moment's hesitation John stepped over the threshold. He didn't want anything more to do with Popeye but he did want to find out what had gone on in his absence.

His daughter might think the docker was all right but John knew differently. Conor Flint was a businessman with a reputation to preserve and he wouldn't have walked away from a sour deal smiling. There would've been a price to pay . . . there always was.

Popeye poured two whiskies and then opened the envelope, taking a cursory peer inside. He lobbed it on the table and took a sip of his drink. The last thing he wanted off John Gardiner now was five tenners and a handshake. He wanted John to resurrect his still and make them all some *real* money. He'd suffered because of the man, and he was after compensation.

'Sorry about going off with that; needed it to settle us in Kent,' John explained gruffly. 'But sorted things out now.'

'Back home then, are yer?'

'I am. Doris ain't.'

'How about the nipper?'

'She's back with her mum, where she should be,' John snapped at the impertinence.

'Yeah . . . need their mums, don't they?'

John thought Popeye sounded sarcastic but he let it ride. He wanted to ask his question and get going. 'Flint's off your back then, is he?'

'Oh, yeah; I got him off me back . . . at a cost.'

John licked his lips, knowing he was about to hear something bad.

'Took all me stock of petrol coupons, didn't he? Worth thousands, they were. Left me and Midge 'n' Rufus high 'n' dry. Been scratching around fer cash, and me with a lovely new girlfriend to impress. How does that look?' Popeye narrowed his good eye on John. 'You ain't been popular, pal, causing all that trouble when all you had to do was set up yer still and give the man what he wanted.' Popeye laid a heavy hand on John's shoulder. ''Course, now Doris ain't about you'll be able to get to work again, won't yer?'

John shrugged him off. 'Already told you I ain't ever getting back into that.'

'Reckon you are, mate, 'cos if you don't you'll cause yourself and your lovely little family a mighty lot of trouble.'

'I ain't frightened of you and yer threats. As fer Flint, him and Rosie are on good terms.'

'Yeah . . . saw that, John, with me own eyes.' Popeye leered. 'That girl of your'n knows how to put it about, don't she?'

'What did you say?' John snarled, fists tightening at his sides. 'You insulting my daughter?'

'I wouldn't do that, John. But other people would

when they find out that kid of hers is a bastard and she's lying about having been married.'

John turned the colour of parchment and his mouth worked like a beached fish.

'I know what it is to have bad blood in the family, mate,' Popeye crooned, all sympathy. 'Be the first to admit my Lenny was no good, so I ain't calling your gel a slag 'cos she got herself in trouble . . .'

John lunged at him, pummelling at Popeye's face and body with his fists. 'She didn't get herself in trouble!' He roared through foam-flecked lips. 'Your fucking Lenny did! He was a monster and if the bastard was still here I'd kill him all over again. He raped my daughter . . . he *raped* her, left her covered in blood 'n' bruises in some stinking alley . . .'

The red mist in John's eyes faded and he suddenly realised what he'd done. He tottered back from Popeye as though he'd accidentally touched something venomous. But the horror shaping his features wasn't the result of recalling his daughter's dreadful ordeal; fear for the future was churning his guts now the terrible secret was out.

Popeye had been about to swing a right hook at his assailant's head when snippets of John's ranting had started penetrating his brain and he'd been stunned into paralysis.

Now he stood massaging his battered chin, blinking at John. His hand became still as he finished slotting the pieces of puzzle in place.

'You stay away from me and mine,' John spat, darting for the door.

Popeye leaped into action, dragging John back by the collar. 'Sounds to me like you've a bit more explaining to do 'fore you get off.' Popeye's lips flattened on his stumpy brown teeth. 'You telling me we share an interest in that little kid?'

With a sob of anguish John tried to nut him and break free but Popeye was ready for him. Neither man was fit but Frank was heftier and he knocked John to his knees with a crafty blow to his windpipe.

Popeye crouched down so his face was level with John's purple complexion. 'My Lenny was poisoned to death with a bottle of bad rotgut. Know anything about it, do you?'

'Fuck off,' John croaked. 'He set fire to hisself . . .'

'Yeah . . . 'cos he dropped his fag after he passed out drinking rotgut. Yours, weren't it? You fuckin' murdered my son!'

'You can't prove a thing,' John wheezed through his damaged throat.

Popeye stood up, gazing at the wall with his jaw dropped open. Then he looked down at the man gasping for air and he gave him a savage kick in the head. He bent down again. 'That kid's Lenny's, ain't it?'

John tried to anchor himself on Popeye's shoulder to drag himself to his feet. His only focus now was to get out of the house before Popeye beat all the truth out of him, or killed him trying.

Popeye shoved John off so he sprawled on the floor again. He started to pace to and fro, gurning in disbelief at the mad thoughts circulating in his brain.

With a monumental effort John forced himself to get up, swaying unsteadily, and stumbling towards the door. His vision was blurred with the blood trickling from the wound on his scalp. Even so, he could see enough of Popeye's expression to know the man wasn't finished with him yet. John changed direction, stumbling to the table as though for support, but he grabbed the whisky bottle, smashing it against the wooden edge then lunging towards Popeye's face with the jagged glass.

John staggered to the front gate, whimpering with the excruciating pain in his skull. He'd managed to take his enemy by surprise, slashing at him then kicking him in the balls. The tactic had given him just enough time to haul himself out of the house. But, looking back, he could see Popeye moving behind the door, his hand cupped over his gaping cheek.

'You're done for now, mate!' Popeye bellowed as John limped away into the dusk.

'It's nothing . . . don't fuss, Rosie.'

John had collapsed in the hall. He'd dragged himself home, swaying like a drunk, glad of the darkness and of the air-raid siren that had sent people scuttling for shelter, allowing him to pad through the empty streets unobserved.

Rosie fell to her knees by her father. 'What on earth . . . oh, Dad!' She clapped a hand to her mouth, her eyes filling with tears. 'Where have you been? Who did this to you?' She sank back, recalling what her father had said about Conor being owed fifty pounds and that he'd take his money's worth out of her. He hadn't got any more out of her than holding hands and a peck on the cheek.

'Did Conor do this to you?' Rosie whispered, dreading hearing the answer.

John carefully shook his aching head. 'Popeye. The bastard still wants me to make moonshine. Told him no, and he didn't like it.' John couldn't bring himself to tell

300

his daughter the whole truth. Not yet. His eyes smarted with tears of guilt and remorse as he realised the extent of what he'd done. He'd gone to see his old associate with the best of intentions and had been hijacked by his own stupidity. On the interminable trek home he'd tried to work out how Popeye had found out about Rosie's secret; the man hadn't been pissing in the wind. Popeye had known Hope was illegitimate.

With Rosie's help John managed to get into the back parlour. As soon as she'd got him lolling in an armchair she scooted to get him a glass of water.

'Get us a Beecham's Powder, love. Me head's thumping fit to burst,' John panted.

Again Rosie disappeared into the kitchen and came back with the medicine, stirring the milky water briskly with a spoon. She handed it over and John threw it back as though it were Scotch.

Rosie thrust her fingers into her hair. 'Will he leave us alone now you've had a fight over it?' Her little daughter was asleep downstairs in the cellar, and she thanked God that Hope hadn't been up and about to see her granddad in such an awful state.

John nodded, keeping his face low so his daughter wouldn't see the despair in his face. He knew it wasn't over with Popeye; it was just beginning. 'Soon as I'm well enough we'll take Hope away again. We'll get out of London, and you'll come too this time.'

'But my job—'

'Never mind your fucking job!' John's fingers, supporting his bowed head, crabbed into talons. 'We go away . . . fresh start for all of us. Please, Rosie, do as I say.' He began to weep softly into his palms.

'It's all right, Dad . . . hush . . .' Rosie soothed him

301

by stroking his hand, her fingers staining with his blood. 'I'll get hot water and a flannel and clean you up . . .' They both instinctively ducked as a loud explosion sounded close by, rattling every door and window in the house.

Rosie had been fretting down in the cellar about her father still being out during an air raid. She'd loitered at the top of the stairs with the cellar door ajar, straining to hear his key striking the lock. The moment it had she'd burst out to help him down the stairs. The sight that had met her eyes had winded her like a punch in the guts, making her nauseated.

'You'll have to try and get into the cellar, Dad. Quickly! They're dropping very close.'

The slow descent to their musky shelter was marked by John's gasps of agony. Rosie tried to soothe him with murmured encouragement but by then she was crying too as his blood dripped down over her arms and clothes onto the cellar steps. She was finding it hard to block out the memories of that other time when her father had been dreadfully injured during a raid. But no Luftwaffe bomb had inflicted his wounds this time. Rosie knew she now feared the enemy close to home far more than she did the Germans.

She listened to her father's laboured breathing. He lay on the mattress, eyes closed, twitching in pain, and Rosie prayed that he wasn't concussed because he might lose consciousness. She'd cleaned him up as best she could with a towel found on the mattress and had been relieved to find that the wound on his scalp had started to form a sticky crust beneath matted hair. Rosie wiped her hands on a less sodden edge of linen, then threw the stained cloth aside. She settled down next to Hope, gently smoothing her daughter's hair as she lay sleeping. She sensed there was more to her father's distress than having taken a bad beating. He'd started to cry and insisted they get away, and she knew that's what they must do because there was evil lurking; she could feel it.

'Rosie! You there, Rosie? We've got to go now.'

Rosie stretched across to reassure her father with a touch on his arm. He sounded delirious, as though he'd started from a terrifying dream. 'I'm here. Go back to sleep. I will come with you. Soon as you're well enough we'll go away somewhere safe. I'll give my station boss a week's notice, promise.'

CHAPTER TWENTY-SIX

Gertie was still being a miserable cow to him so Midge
hadn't visited Rufus this morning, knowing it was
washday and his sister would be around. Instead he'd
headed in Popeye's direction in the hope of a handout.
Just as he'd turned the corner Midge had seen Frank's
lady friend go into the house, so he was loitering, waiting
for her to leave. Bored of peering from behind the hedge,
he'd decided to mosey off to the British Legion to cadge
a fag when the door opened and out she came. The
nurse set off up the road at quite a speed with her
face on her boots. As Midge nipped through Popeye's
front gate he was praying the couple hadn't had a row
or he'd have more chance of getting blood out of a
stone than a cup of char out of his boss.

'How you doing, Pop?' Midge rattled off, squeezing
himself into the hallway before Frank could shut him
out. It was a dingy passage, painted sepia brown, and it
took Midge a moment to notice that Popeye had a large
dressing on his cheek. 'Bleedin' hell! What you done to
yerself?'

Popeye didn't answer; he shuffled back down the passage, Midge following dejectedly behind him.

'What's gone on then?' Midge asked cautiously. He sensed that Popeye was festering on something seriously bad. 'Saw the nurse leaving a moment ago; been in to patch you up, has she?'

Popeye fingered the lint. He refilled the whisky glass on the table and poured another shot for Midge. 'Glad you come by; got something for you to do.'

Midge brightened up. 'Yeah? Back swinging on the deliveries, are we?'

'You and Rufus can use me car to collect the stuff I need to get going. Me account's open again at the wholesaler's.'

Midge knocked back his drink, feeling happy as Larry. 'How d'you come a cropper?'

'John Gardiner did it just after he give me back the fifty quid he nicked.' Popeye loosened the dressing and winced as he peeled it off, showing Midge the deep damage to his cheek. Trudy had agreed to stitch him up but apart from that she'd made it clear it was over between them. She'd been disgusted when he'd told her what had happened. She'd blamed him for betraying her trust and using private information, told in confidence, against the Gardiners. Much as he was fond of Trudy, Popeye was prepared to sacrifice her for the chance of getting to know his grandchild. Besides, he reckoned once he was in touch with the little girl, Trudy would come round. She'd told him she would've loved to have mothered Rosie's kid. At the time Popeye hadn't taken a lot of notice of what she'd said, but he knew things now that he hadn't known then. As far as he was concerned, Trudy was still his girlfriend and he'd

305

no objection to her spending time with his little granddaughter.

Having taken a good look at the puckered flesh on his boss's cheek Midge whistled through his teeth. 'Gardiner deserved a right good kickin' fer doing that to yer.'

'He got a kicking, all right. But weren't about the money; was personal. So there's another job I've got for you, if you're up for it.'

Midge put his empty glass back down on the table. 'Go on,' he said. 'I'm listening.'

'Keep this just between you 'n' me. Don't tell Rufus 'cos if he blabs to his missus the world'll know.'

Midge sensed big money was in the offing now, and he didn't mind what he did to get it. As far as Midge was concerned he was a dead man, and had been for some time, it was just a question of when his luck would run out. Before it did, he'd do anything in a bid to outrun the grim reaper.

'You still got a blade and prepared to use it?'

Midge jerked a nod, fingering the weight in his coat pocket. He never went anywhere without a knife. Owing to his size Midge had been vulnerable to bullies; from an early age he'd been vigilant about having help at hand. At one time he'd had a gun too, but he'd lost that along the way.

'Right, sit down then and I'll tell you all about it,' Popeye said, pouring them both another drink.

'Hello, stranger! This is a lovely surprise. Come in, I'll make us a pot of tea.'

Having put the brake on the pram Rosie unbuckled Hope, lifted her out, then followed Gertie inside her home.

'Excuse the mess,' Gertie said, stepping over a pile of

newspapers that Rufus had left scattered round the base of his armchair. 'He's an untidy sod, me 'usband. He's out delivering, thank heavens, so we can have a natter in peace.'

With a clap of her small hands Vicky jumped off the couch and trotted to greet her friend.

'Look at that,' Gertie said. 'Not seen each other in ages yet they remember one another.' She led Rosie through to the kitchen and filled the kettle. 'So your dad's home on a visit from Kent, I take it?'

'He is back,' Rosie said, putting Hope down so the children could play chase. 'But he's not at all well at the moment.'

'Lot of it about. My Rufus had bellyache fer days last week. Probably down to the amount of ale he sinks, though.' Gertie clucked her tongue.

'I've no time for tea actually, Gertie. I've come to ask a favour, and I'm sorry it's such short notice,' Rosie said awkwardly. 'I wouldn't burden you but Dad's too ill to look after Hope just now and I was wondering if you'd have her while I go to work.'

Her father was brighter than he'd been a few days ago following his beating, but Rosie knew that her lively little daughter was beyond his control. And he'd realised it too; John hadn't protested when she'd said she'd ask a friend to have Hope while he recovered.

'You want me to babysit?' Gertie sounded delighted.

Rosie nodded. 'Just for this afternoon, if you would. I tried to get leave so I could nurse Dad but we're short-staffed and I'm the only relief driver available today. I feel I should turn in as I stayed home with him yesterday. And what with these bloody rockets coming thick and fast, we're getting calls day and night.'

'You passed your test, then?'

Rosie nodded.

Gertie bent down to talk to her daughter. 'Lucky girl. You've got a little friend to play with this afternoon.'

'Are you sure you don't mind? I'll be back and pick her up before seven o'clock.' Rosie delved into her bag and brought forth some milk and fish-paste sandwiches.

'Didn't need to do that!' Gertie protested. 'I'd've given her her tea.'

'No, I must; rations are tight and it's only fair.' Rosie looked again at Gertie. She liked the woman, and their daughters got on well, but she felt uneasy about leaving Hope with anybody other than her dad. But she also felt a fierce loyalty to the LAAS and the colleagues and friends she had there, and soon would lose. She'd given in her notice and felt terribly sad and empty to be leaving Robley Road. 'Are you sure you don't mind?' she again asked.

'Don't mind one bit!' Gertie exclaimed. 'Be a pleasure – and you drive carefully.'

Once Rosie had left, Gertie found all of Vicky's toys and put them on the couch, then she picked up the children and placed one either side of the few rag dolls and wooden bricks. She made her cup of tea, then settled down opposite the little girls with a contented smile on her face, watching them play.

'In here,' Gertie called when she heard the front door being opened.

'Who's that?' Joey had come into the parlour and grinned at Hope.

'She's me friend's little gel; Hope's her name. Little blonde angel, ain't she, Joey? Vicky loves to see her. Me and Hope's mum used to work together at the Windmill, way back.'

Joey liked little 'uns, and he sank to his knees in front of the couch and started building bricks with the children, using the cushion as a base. 'Can I show her to Becky? She's a dope fer kids.' Joey sounded gruff. He and Becky often took Vicky for walks, one either side of her, holding her hands, swinging her between them.

He was getting to like Becky more and more; all through the summer they'd been sitting on her front step, talking for hours about getting better jobs and better money, then saving enough to run off to live in a cottage in the countryside. Joey knew it'd never happen, even if Becky didn't, but pipe dream or not, it put a smile on his face while he rode the butcher's bike and took round the orders to the big houses.

Gertie peered out of the window. 'Where is Becky? Bring her in, can't you?'

'She won't come in here 'case *he* turns up,' Joey said bluntly.

His father teased him and Becky non-stop when he was about, calling them lovebirds and making twittering noises. Now Becky refused to enter the house just in case he rolled up unexpectedly and embarrassed her.

Joey picked up the rag dolls and danced them together in front of the little girls' laughing faces. Hope made to snatch one of them and Joey jigged it out of reach, making her chuckle and try again.

'Well, all right, you can show her to Becky for a few minutes then bring her back in,' Gertie said, smiling at Joey.

She felt for him. Although her remaining son was growing up, working and walking out with a girl, in his heart he'd always be a grieving boy yearning for his little brothers to play with.

*   *   *

'Well, this has been a bloody uneventful four hours so far.' Hazel was speaking while furiously polishing the common-room windows with her screwed-up newspaper. 'Not even an expectant mum to deal with.'

Rosie, beside her, wrung out her cloth in the bucket of water, then continued washing. 'Wonder if poor Jim's feeling better?' she said. Jim had taken a tumble off the kerb in the blackout and sprained his ankle. He'd hobbled in on crutches to show them he wasn't malingering. He'd moaned that it was typical he'd done himself a damage while off duty rather than on.

While Rosie worked alongside her friend, she was only half contributing to their conversation. Hazel's chatter had flowed over her because serious worries were cramming Rosie's head. She was fretting about Hope and whether her daughter was behaving herself. Worse, the poor little thing might be crying because she was missing her mum and granddad. Her daughter didn't know Gertie well, and didn't know the woman's husband at all. Rosie hoped that the fellow wouldn't be angry to discover a stranger's child beneath his roof.

Then Rosie had the anxiety of her father maybe taking a turn for the worse, or being in need of anything while she was out. He'd promised not to answer the door to a soul and to stay in the basement in case a siren sounded. He'd never be able to descend to the cellar under his own steam, so had agreed to remain down there all day. Before she'd left that morning Rosie had made him comfortable with extra blankets and put sandwiches and a flask of tea next to his bed.

Her greatest fear had been that Popeye would come round after her vulnerable father, but John had reassured her on that score. Frank Purves hadn't got away scot-free during their fight; her father reckoned his opponent would also be licking his wounds for a while yet.

Rosie dropped her cloth into the bucket and buffed the smears from the glass with newspaper. She stood back staring at the gleaming pane. 'Right, that'll do,' she announced. 'Let's start up the ambulance.'

Following the tragic deaths of Stella and Thora at Stepney, Janet Lawson had been promoted to DSO. Tom had taken on the additional role of Shift Leader as well as being an ambulance driver until some new people were taken on. In the immediate aftermath of the tragedy the atmosphere at Station 97 had veered between shock and disbelief. But a defiant war cry had gone up in the common room the following day led by a battle-weary Tom and Rosie. Amidst the tears, everybody had vowed to defy the Germans to their last breath and increase their efforts to save as many lives as possible. But it was inevitable that volunteers would be slow in applying once they were aware of the reason for Station 97 being depleted in numbers.

Jim had taught Rosie to check the vehicle's engine from time to time during the day. It was no good sprinting out on an emergency to find at the last moment that the blighter was playing up, he'd told her. Rosie glanced at the clock; she'd be relieved when her shift was over and she could collect Hope.

'I shall miss you when you leave, you know,' Hazel said as they walked outside. 'Jim reckons he'll never get another assistant as good as you.'

'I shall miss you lot, too,' Rosie returned stoutly. 'Never know, perhaps I'll be back at some time when Dad's feeling more the ticket.' Rosie had told her colleagues she'd got to quit and care for her crippled father for a while. She was glad she'd not lied and had got away with being merely economical with the truth.

'I'll pair up with you today if we get an incident.' Hazel winked. 'I've already had a word with Tom. He doesn't mind me abandoning him 'cos his friend's swapped shifts and can jump in my seat if need be.'

'Nights are drawing in already.' Rosie glanced up at the sky where a low autumn sun was streaking orange into blue. She realised it would be getting dark by the time she got to Gertie's to pick up Hope.

'Spoke too soon.' Hazel stared upwards as the air-raid siren wailed.

Rosie searched the skies too, but nothing was yet visible. She trotted on across the yard to the ambulance and turned the ignition. The engine jumped into life and throbbed noisily. But she was hoping Station 97 wouldn't get a call and she wouldn't be driving it later. She'd reassured herself that Hope would be safe during a raid: Gertie had told her she hared to the shelter with her kids every single time an alarm sounded. But Rosie just wanted to bring Hope home to reassure herself she was safe.

Joey and Becky were swinging the little girls between them, making them giggle, when they heard the warning. Joey let his sister's feet touch the ground. Hope, thinking it was her turn, put out her arms to him.

Becky picked her up, balancing her on her jutting hip like a seasoned mum. 'You're so pretty,' she said, kissing Hope's forehead. 'Wish you was mine.'

'Come on, better get home. Mum'll be worrying.' Joey glanced back and saw Gertie by their gate, waving frantically at him.

They had moved towards the end of the street in their game of lifting the little girls off their feet and swishing them to and fro, higher and higher till they whooped with delight. Gertie had come out several times to check that everything was all right with the children, bringing them some biscuits and a flask of tea so they could all carry on enjoying being outside on such a glorious afternoon.

Joey picked up Vicky, and with an arm about Becky he hurried her along with him.

When they were almost halfway home a car pulled up, crawling at the kerb beside them.

'Get back home, son, and help yer mum to get all of yous down the shelter,' Rufus had bawled through the Citroën's open window.

He frowned at Becky carrying a little girl. He knew the Pugh family didn't have any youngsters and he didn't recognise the toddler as belonging to any of the neighbours.

'Who's that?' He smiled at the beautiful child and she shyly averted her face.

Joey could see his uncle in the car beside his father, steering one-handed and looking pleased with himself with his homburg pulled down low over his eyes like a gangster.

'Her name's Hope. Mum's babysitting for a friend who used to work at the Windmill with her.' Joey put on a sprint as the siren continued to wail but he could tell that Becky was struggling to keep up.

The car stopped and Midge hopped out. 'Here y'are, love, let's take her for you. Bit of a weight, ain't she? Chubby little thing . . .'

Midge relieved Becky of the child and Rufus also took

Vicky and put her on the back seat of the car. 'You two big 'uns run on. We'll bring these two. Go on, get going,' Rufus bawled at his son.

The bigger kids did as they were told, and Rufus was soon scouring the skies for a sight of the threat. 'There it is, the Kraut bugger.' He pointed towards the sunset. 'Too bleedin' close fer comfort. Shoreditch, that'll land, I reckon.'

Midge didn't answer. He was laughing silently, but he wasn't sharing the joke with Rufus. Popeye had told him not to.

The Citroën pulled up outside Gertie's home at the same time as Joey and Becky did. Gertie pushed Joey towards the house.

'Get yer coat, Joey; it'll turn cold overnight. Bet yer life we'll be stuck down there for hours.'

Joey did as he was told, waving to Becky as she pelted on up to her own gate.

'Bring those two little 'uns in,' Gertie yelled at Rufus, before turning and going to find the belongings she always took with her to the shelter.

Rufus entered the house, carrying his daughter. 'I'll come with you. Finished fer the day now, love.'

'Where's little Hope?'

'Midge is just bringing her in, then he's off down the British Legion, he said.'

After a few seconds Gertie felt a twinge of panic. She dropped her bag and raced to the front door. The car had gone and there was no sign of Midge or Hope.

CHAPTER TWENTY-SEVEN

Rosie felt as though she might explode with anxiety as she swerved the ambulance around obstacles. The clatter of the bell sang in her skull but she hardly registered it. Every time she'd speeded up in her race through the streets she'd had to brake, then coax the vehicle over debris strewn in the road. She'd backed up, gears screaming, and taken a run at an impassable hillock and was now fretting that the front tyres had punctured. But as they'd bounced back to earth and jolted onwards she'd again stamped on the accelerator.

'Doing great . . .' Hazel encouraged her. 'Chin up, Rosie! The explosion is right up the other end of your street. I can feel it in me bones. We can do this, we always do!'

'I know,' Rosie croaked. 'Please God,' she whispered, 'let my dad be all right . . .'

The vile images of the Stepney disaster wouldn't stop circulating in her mind. Nothing had remained of Stella and Thora, or of the fireman who'd cursed the Hun. The rocket had landed just a yard or two from them

315

and in a way Rosie had been glad of small mercies. The prospect of having to gather up and identify bits of those two particular victims had made her feel bilious. She'd never really come to know Thora as their shifts had rarely coincided and she had been a reserved woman. But Stella, Rosie had liked and admired . . . and taught to dance . . .

They'd done what they could for the people in the Church Hall. None had survived but nevertheless Rosie and Tom had worked on alongside the firemen throughout the night, recovering remains out of a sense of respect for the deceased and their families.

Tom had suffered days of deafness, and a deep cut to his left arm, but he'd refused to stay away from Robley Road to recover. Similarly, Rosie's gashed scalp and the painful bruises that had covered her back had not kept her at home. Now the scars were fading from her body, if not her mind. Rosie knew she'd been luckier than Tom who might suffer a permanent loss of hearing in one ear. She'd gained better protection than he from the ambulance doors and she nightly whispered a prayer of thanks, sure her mum had been her guardian angel, just as she was sure Prudence Gardiner had watched over her when the Café de Paris was hit years ago.

Tom and Rosie had returned to the station, speechless with shock. Hazel had then patched them up and, unusually, left them alone once she understood the enormity of what had happened. The following day, having snatched less than four hours' rest on mattresses at the station, Rosie and Tom were both back at their posts, hollow-eyed from grief and exhaustion. Thankfully, the food poisoning that had been responsible for Stella and Thora being on active duty was now forgotten and nobody had the energy, or the will, to say any more about where the blame might lie for that episode.

'Move, damn you!' Rosie shouted at a motorist having an animated discussion with a policeman. He was hanging out of his car window and gesturing at the flames that Rosie knew were from fires in her neighbourhood. It had been about twenty minutes after they'd heard the siren that afternoon that they'd got a call-out to an incident in Shoreditch. Rosie had nearly swooned on hearing the name of the street they were being sent to, but she'd raced outside to start the engine while Hazel collected the docket from Clarice.

The policeman waved the motorist aside, and Rosie on, and she rammed her foot on the accelerator.

'It's the Prices' house that's taken the worst of it, and those to the left,' Rosie gasped, bringing the ambulance to a shuddering stop. 'And it looks like May Reed's lost part of her roof.'

Her father's house, many yards away in the opposite direction, appeared untouched, and momentarily Rosie was rooted to her seat in relief.

'Your place safe, is it?' Hazel demanded briskly. She'd had her door open before the ambulance came to a halt and had already jumped down.

'Thank God . . . yes, it is,' Rosie gasped. Feeling guilty and selfish at her reaction, she pulled her mind back to the job in hand and scrambled out of the vehicle. Her training kicked in and she sprinted to open the back of the ambulance and get the equipment ready.

'You're needed over here!' A fireman beckoned to them and pointed to a huddled figure with a hand clapped over her eye.

'Let's have a look at you then, Mrs Reed,' Rosie said,

recognising her neighbour at once as she gently removed the woman's fingers from her head. The eye was dreadfully mangled but Rosie managed to say cheerily, 'Right . . . let's get a dressing on that, then get you into the ambulance, and you'll be right as ninepence.'

'Rosie Deane, ain't it?' May panted, trying to blink at the young woman through sticky hair.

'Just Rosie'll do,' Rosie said, glad that Hazel was out of earshot dealing with another casualty.

'Lost me eye, ain't I?' May snorted a sob.

'You'll be winking again next week. Hold still, almost finished.' Rosie continued winding the bandage as gently as she could about the woman's head.

'Peg all right, is she?' May asked, wincing with the effort of speaking. 'Lucky mine are all out at work. Just me home. Peg's husband, Dick, was out, but I think her 'n' Irene were indoors.'

Rosie was squinting through the wavering heat mist at the firemen directing hoses at the top windows of the Prices' house. The ground floor seemed to have escaped the blaze so far.

'They could've made it down to the cellar.' Rosie adopted an optimistic tone but she'd seen enough as an ambulance auxiliary to know that people were often just moments too late seeking shelter.

'God help us! What's happened to my gel?'

Rosie had just settled May in the back of the ambulance when she saw Peg Price had barged through firemen to the front of a group of neighbours; some were assisting the walking wounded who'd been peppered by flying glass.

'I was visiting me sister in Hackney.' Peg gaped in horror at her house. 'Where's my Irene?' she screamed.

318

As a fireman made to restrain her rushing towards the blazing house, Rosie hurried over.

'Where's me daughter?' Peg begged Rosie. 'Seen her, have you? She's been in all day, not feeling well with dreadful bellyache; she was up in her bedroom.' The woman's appalled eyes widened on the shattered top-floor windows.

'Not seen her yet, Mrs Price.' Rosie glanced at the fireman, who was shaking his head, dashing her hopes that a survivor had been pulled from the wreckage.

'Someone's in there!' A shout went up from the front and Peg beat the fireman off with her fists, surging forward to clamber over jagged timbers towards what remained of her home.

The fireman grabbed Peg again just as Hazel trotted over, calling, 'Young woman name of Irene's in there; she says she can't come out. She sounded hysterical.'

'Fire ain't properly out.' The fireman sucked his teeth. 'Wait a bit, if I was you, before attending to her.'

'What, wait till it's too late, you mean?' Hazel returned drily. 'I'll go in this time,' she firmly told Rosie. 'You've done more'n enough just lately.'

Rosie knew that Hazel felt guilty for having been off sick on the evening of the Stepney incident. All the staff who'd been too ill to work now knew fate had smiled on them even if they hadn't seen it that way at the time.

'I'll talk to Irene: I might be able to calm her down, as I know her,' Rosie said, as the·two young women climbed over wreckage towards the house.

'Let it cool down a bit; you might set fire to your clothes,' a younger firemen advised as Hazel tested the uneven ground that led into the fumy hall.

'Put the hose on me,' Hazel said bluntly, hoisting her medical bag. 'Ain't had a bath this week.'

'Daft cow,' the fireman said, but his crinkle-cornered eyes were full of admiration. 'I'll come with you then; summat might need lifting. Can't do that on yer own, young lady like you.'

'You'd be surprised what we can do on our own, chum,' Hazel challenged.

'Can you hear me, Irene? It's Rosie from down the road; you'll soon be out.'

'Mrs Deane? Is it you?' A note of utter relief shrilled in Irene's voice. 'Come and help me. Don't want nobody else. Is me mum there?'

'She's here, Irene, and don't worry, she's fine. Are you trapped? Are you in pain?'

'Who's she talking to?' Hazel asked, looking around. 'Who's Mrs Deane?'

'I am,' Rosie admitted.

'Right . . .' Hazel said, masking her surprise. This was no time for personal questions.

'Someone's coming to help you. Her name's Hazel. Where are you, Irene?'

'Only want you!' Irene screeched. 'Tell 'em to leave me alone. I ain't coming out.'

The fireman shoved back his helmet and gawped at Hazel, who in turn stared at Rosie.

'She's gone into bad hysterics. Ain't that unusual. Better give her a shot of something,' the fireman said. 'Last one like that fought like a demon to stay under the stairs.'

A terrible thought had occurred to Rosie. In all the commotion she'd forgotten that Peg's daughter was pregnant, and probably nearing her time. A shock such as this might have induced a miscarriage. Peg obviously had no idea her daughter was pregnant or in her panic she'd have blurted it out. But she had said that Irene had been laid up with bellyache . . . and Rosie remembered such cramps.

She couldn't broadcast her fears; if she were wrong, and Peg *had* found out and had made her daughter have an abortion weeks ago, Rosie knew she'd do Irene untold damage by mentioning the matter in front of the neighbours. The girl's reputation would be ruined for no reason.

'I'm coming in to see you, Irene,' Rosie yelled. She felt Hazel's strong grip on her shoulder, squeezing in a show of support and admiration.

'Give us a shout if you need assistance, Mrs Deane,' the fireman said.

'She's crawled underground through rubble; walking in there's a doddle for her,' Rosie heard her friend proudly tell him.

As Rosie squirmed her way under and over wreckage, water dripped on her from the hoses directed at the top floor, soaking her head and shoulders. She knew she should be worried about her false identity having got out, but it seemed a triviality at a time like this. Stella would never have probed for details about her other life; Hazel was bound to. And Rosie would offer up answers because she no longer cared who knew that she had a beautiful little girl and was raising her on her own. 'Where are you, Irene? Guide me,' she shouted, shaking the water from her head and keeping her medical bag secured beneath an arm.

'Back parlour . . .' Irene started to cough.

Inside, the room was a maze of mangled timbers and the unbearably humid atmosphere made Rosie gasp.

321

She caught sight of Irene crouching in the furthest corner and scrambled towards her.

'Can you move? Where are you hurt?'

Irene stared at her lap and Rosie saw the pool of blood soaking her skirt.

'Have you miscarried?' she croaked.

'Don't know. Don't tell Mum. She still don't know,' Irene whimpered, grabbing at Rosie's leg as though to prevent her leaving. 'Don't tell my mum . . . please, don't.'

Rosie hunkered down and pinched Irene's fleshy chin in her slender fingers. 'Hush! It'll be all right. Let's have a look at you.'

'Don't tell . . .' Irene keened.

'Shush now!' Rosie ordered harshly, feeling her heart drumming beneath her ribs. Rosie lifted back Irene's filthy skirt and saw the gore. Her shaking hand plunged forward to investigate then almost recoiled on encountering a small smooth head, but it raced on over a tiny sleek body, with a beating heart.

'You'll have to help me, Irene, 'cos I'm no great shakes at this. Hold back your clothes so I can see what's what.'

Irene did as she was told and gently Rosie drew the tiny infant towards her into view, staring at its minuscule limbs in wonder. It was far smaller than she recalled her daughter had been at birth and Hope had been just five pounds. Cradling it in the crook of an arm, she opened her bag and cleaned mucus from the baby's face with lint.

'What is it?' Irene whispered, aghast at the sight of the purple creature. 'Is it a baby? It hurt something awful. I was in bed with bellyache but managed to get downstairs when the siren went off.'

Rosie cleaned the tot's nether regions of blood and vernix. 'You've a little boy. I think he's weeks early, though. We need to get going and get you both to hospital.'

'I'm staying here. You take him. Mum'll kill me. She don't know.' Irene shuffled back on her posterior towards the wall, jerking the umbilical cord.

'Keep still!' Rosie commanded. 'I'll have to cut this and separate you.'

Suddenly the baby gave a wail and so did Irene.

'Make it be quiet! They'll all hear,' Irene choked. She lunged forward as though to silence the infant.

'I said keep still!' Rosie found herself snarling. She knew that Irene was frightened, but so was she and it was making her impatient.

'Can't we just leave it here?' Irene garbled in a whisper. 'Please . . . hide it over there where nobody'll see it. I don't want it. I can say I fell and cut meself badly but I'm all right now. Then nobody'll know . . .'

Rosie forced up the girl's chin with her hand. 'Now you listen to me, Irene, you'll do nothing of the sort. Your mum'll be upset at first but she'll get over it. She'll have to . . . like my dad had to.' Rosie waggled the girl's face as Irene started to snivel. 'And you'll cope . . . like I had to. And you'll be a good mum . . . like I'm a good mum. And in a year's time you'll wonder how you came to feel such love for something you didn't want and wanted to hide because she's beautiful and your heart wants to burst with pride every time she wakes up in the morning . . .'

Rosie blinked the mist from her eyes, realising she'd been talking about her daughter, and saw that Irene was silently howling. Quickly Rosie fumbled scissors from her bag and cut the cord, then clumsily knotted it after a few tries with her nervous fingers. She took off her jacket and carefully wrapped the baby, then stood up, cradling him against her shoulder. She held out a hand to Irene but the girl screwed her face up, shaking her head.

'You said you wanted to be like me, didn't you?'

Irene nodded, snuffling and smearing mess from her face.

'Well, bloody well be like me then. Get up! Let's go!'

Irene extended her trembling fingers and Rosie grasped them, jerking her to her feet. She put an arm about Irene's shoulders, hugging her fiercely in praise and encouragement. 'Well done,' she said then began guiding the new mother back over the rubble.

'Christ Almighty! You'll need a stiff drink after that, then, love.'

Rosie had just recounted to her father what had happened out in the street and shocked him to the core. He'd heard the blast close by, but it was the news about Peg's daughter that had made him offer his own girl a livener.

'Can't have a drink, Dad, I'm still on duty.' Rosie gave a tired smile. 'We've dropped the patients off at the hospital and I only popped in to see how you are. Hazel's waiting for me outside; I've got to get the ambulance back to the station, then I'm going to fetch Hope home.'

'Your friend Gertie'll keep her till morning, won't she, love? 'Spect she's guessed you've been held up with the raid.' John shifted on the mattress. He was still in considerable pain but the tale he'd just heard had taken his mind off his own problems. 'Gertie won't expect you to

324

turn up at this time of the night. Must be almost nine o'clock by now.'

'I want Hope home with me,' Rosie said quietly. She'd been kneeling by the side of the mattress to talk to her dad, and now she stood up wearily. Her uniform felt stiff with muck and blood from the newborn, and her hair, though dried, had plastered to her scalp. But she knew she'd not rest till she was wheeling Hope home in her pram through the black and damaged streets of Shoreditch.

CHAPTER TWENTY-EIGHT

'Me husband's out looking for me brother now,' Gertie sobbed. 'He's been searching for hours. He's been back once. He went first to the British Legion to find out if they'd seen him. That's where Michael reckoned he was heading when the siren went off. Rufus is in a terrible rage; he'll kill Midge if he finds him, and good riddance, I say.' She shook her head into her hands. 'I'm so sorry, Rosie; don't know what to do . . . Please don't hate me, or Joey; it 'specially ain't his fault.'

Joey was sitting on the couch with his little sister; he bowed his head on hearing his name mentioned. Vicky, too, was unusually quiet; young as she was, she'd sensed the sad atmosphere.

'Where's your husband gone now?' Rosie's shock on learning Hope was missing had robbed her of the will to cast blame on anybody. Something inside was screaming but she felt too numb to cry.

'Don't know; he's been gone ages. Might've gone to his boss to find out if he knows where Midge is. Frank Purves is his name and he lives—'

'Frank Purves?' Rosie echoed in a hoarse whisper.

'Popeye, they call him, and he lives—'

'I know where he lives.' Rosie rushed past Hope's empty pram by Gertie's front door, bursting out into the night.

She charged in the direction of Popeye's house, stumbling and pulling herself along in the blackout against walls and hedges to find junctions and crossroads. Her breath was burning her throat and her chest heaving so badly that when she finally dragged herself to his gate she stood leaning on it, panting and retching.

She banged on the door, calling out Purves' name but the house remained silent and dark.

'You're making a bleedin' racket, love. You after Frank?' A man next door had opened up to make his complaint through a narrow crack.

Rosie nodded.

'Saw him go out in his car earlier. With another fellow, he was.'

'Did you see a little girl with them?' Rosie demanded.

'In his car, he was,' the man repeated, shaking his head, then closed his door.

Rosie collapsed to sit on the front step, her head in her hands. Her forearms slid up to cover her scalp and she rocked to and fro, sobbing till her eyes were arid and reason edged back into her brain. She wiped her nose with her knuckles and got up.

'I'm going to the police. I don't care if you get locked up – it's your fault!' Rosie shouted.

'I know it's my fault, Rosie,' John choked, using his sodden hanky on his face. 'But please don't involve the police. Let me try and reason with Popeye. I'll give him every penny of me savings . . . I'll do anything he wants to get her back. Just wish I'd known who your friend Gertie was earlier.'

Rosie turned white. 'What do you mean?'

'Your Gertie's husband's a petty criminal and her brother is a navy deserter who stabbed his mate. Oh, Rosie, you stupid gel! You should never have left Hope with such wrong 'uns.'

'I've never met those men . . . I like Gertie . . .' Rosie whispered. She sat down on the edge of the chair in the cellar, wrapping her arms about herself. 'I'm going to the police!'

'Popeye knows that he's Hope's grandfather. He guessed too that . . .' John wiped a hand over his mouth, unable to finish the confession.

'He can't know Hope's Lenny's! How could he?' Rosie dismissed angrily. Her eyes widened as she read her father's expression. 'You told him?' She pushed to her feet, her heart vaulting to her mouth.

'I didn't mean to!' John whined. 'He was calling you vile names, saying people would think you a slag when they found out you was an unmarried mother. He said he saw you putting it about with Conor Flint. I just exploded and it all come out. I told him Lenny was a monster, and he was!' John raged.

As if in a trance, Rosie sank back to the chair. 'He'll think he has a right to Hope. He'll say to the police he's Hope's family.' She gazed in horror at her distressed father. 'What have you done, Dad?'

'Well, *I* didn't tell him you weren't a widow! How'd he know that?' John burst out. 'That's why it all come about: him finding out that was a lie! And you never told me he'd seen you 'n' Flint out together.'

'It wasn't important; Popeye was out walking with Nurse Johnson . . .' Awful enlightenment made Rosie screw up her eyes in anguish. 'He found out from her! Trudy must have told him she was going to adopt Hope.'

'That midwife believed you was a widow. I remember telling her myself your husband had died in action,' John argued.

'I . . . I told her the truth, when we were discussing the adoption.' Rosie owned up in a whisper. 'We'll have to go to the police, Dad.' Rosie's shoulders started to quake. 'Oh, please . . . I can't stand it . . . I want her back.'

John limped to his daughter and enclosed her in an unsteady embrace. 'I'll go and see Frank . . . talk sense into him . . .'

Rosie shook her head, unable to speak at all because of sobs racking her. She calmed herself to hiccup, 'We'll get the police.'

'There's something else Rosie . . .' John sniffed, and a long pause followed. 'Popeye's guessed I gave Lenny the rotgut that killed him. He can't prove it, but he might turn me in, and if they investigate and things go bad for me . . . it's a murder charge.'

Rosie was staring at her father through gritty, uncomprehending eyes, as though he'd spoken in a foreign language. 'What d'you mean, you killed him? He died in a fire in a nightclub.'

'After I found out what he'd done to you, I pretended to him I didn't know 'cos you'd kept it a secret. I pretended to him we was still mates. I gave him a bad bottle of moonshine, made it 'specially for him, I said . . . like it was a present instead of poison. He took it, pleased as punch, and a few days later he was dead.'

Rosie was so shocked she couldn't blink. 'He got the bad drink in a nightclub . . . that's where he got it.'

John shook his head. 'Don't reckon he did. He was always too tight to pay bar prices.' He stared defiantly at Rosie. 'Not sorry fer what I did. I'd do it again, for you. That animal left you there on the ground, bleeding . . .' He paused. 'The police might still have the bottle as evidence. What if they get prints off it after Popeye grasses me up? We'll get her back, Rosie. Just me 'n' you'll do it on our own, I swear we will.'

Rosie sat motionless for several seconds, then she said hoarsely, 'No we won't, Dad. We haven't got a chance.'

Rosie stood by the pub and listened to the clamour inside. Somebody was playing a piano and a woman was belting out 'Roll Out the Barrel'. She looked down at her crumpled uniform, realising she looked dirty and unattractive. She'd not wasted time in changing her clothes before hailing a taxi to take her to Wapping. She slipped off her jacket and straightened her blouse over her breasts although the white cotton was stained with Irene's baby's blood. Her shaking fingers raked through her fair hair, trying to press some style into it. With a deep breath she tilted up her face and walked in.

This time her appearance didn't cause a break in the hubbub; it was almost closing time and the patrons of the Red Lion had better things to do than bother eyeing a bedraggled ambulance auxiliary. Only one person immediately noticed her, as though he'd been watching the door for her arrival, just as her frantic gaze had searched for and located him.

Conor put down his glass and Rosie whimpered with relief as he weaved through the crowd towards her.

She'd wondered what to say . . . how to plead with him to help and how she'd offer him anything he wanted just as long as he brought Hope back. But when he was so close that she could feel his warmth and smell his scent, all she could do was stand before him, quaking, not hearing a word he was saying because her grief was shrieking again in her head, deafening her. And then they were outside and she was clinging to him, grinding her forehead against his shoulder and howling soundlessly.

She wasn't sure how she got to his home – whether she fainted and he carried her there, or she walked – but she surfaced again, shivering on his chair, just as he came out of the kitchen carrying a glass of brandy. Rosie took it with an unsteady snatch and gulped it immediately in case she dropped it.

'My daughter's gone,' she whispered, hearing his question this time.

Conor came down beside her, his face level with her own and she could see the hunger in his eyes.

'What d'you mean, she's gone?' he demanded in a strangely calm and quiet voice.

'A man called Midge kidnapped her.' Rosie pressed her fingers to her mouth to try to contain the nausea fomented by the hideous fact.

'Popeye's sidekick? Do you know why he's taken her?'

Rosie nodded and started to recount what had happened, jerkily at first, but as Conor remained still and silent her concentration strengthened. She told him about her father going to return the fifty pounds to Purves; about them ending up fighting, and John being too badly beaten to babysit; and the dreadful conclusion when she'd found out that her father had probably deliberately killed Lenny for raping her. Then she stumbled, and retraced her way over every vile fact. As she finished Conor was shrugging into his jacket and holding out a hand to her.

She shook her head. 'I'll stay.'

He turned and looked at her.

'I'll stay where I am,' she whispered. 'Bring her back here.'

'I don't need to; I know where you live.'

Rosie shook her head. 'I can't go back there. I blame him, you see. I've always blamed him for what happened to me. If he hadn't started making moonshine and getting into business with the Purveses . . .' She swallowed, blinked at the ceiling. 'What will you do?'

'Whatever I need to.'

'So will I,' Rosie said, and she went out into the hallway and climbed the stairs.

'I had the fucking locks changed so you wouldn't break in again. Ain't come at a good time, though, have yer, son, being as I'm in here?'

'Time's all right for me, Frank. Been in the wars, have you?' Conor nodded at the wound on the older man's cheek.

Frank ignored the taunt. 'You must've seen the Citroën outside.' He narrowed suspicious eyes on Conor.

'Quick on the uptake . . . I like that.' Conor nodded at Midge. 'He gonna use that knife or play with it?'

Midge had sprung up from his chair and had pulled the blade from his pocket on seeing Flint emerge from the shadows in Popeye's warehouse. Midge had also thought the chump had broken in to burgle and picked the wrong time, but he was starting to feel uneasy. He noticed that Frank was edging a hand towards his desk drawer, as though he might jerk it open. Midge knew his boss kept an old army revolver in there because he'd seen it and a few stray bullets rattling around.

'Well . . . Midge might stab yer, and I might say he had to in self-defence when you come in here to rob me tonight.'

'Could've robbed you months ago.'

'So what you here for then?' Frank asked genially, although his busy mind had already pounced on the answer.

Flint was sleeping with Rosie Gardiner and she'd persuaded him to help bring her daughter back. But Frank wasn't having that; the man was an outsider and could mind his own business.

Popeye had accepted he'd no family left, and previously it hadn't bothered him that much. His wife had died so long ago that sometimes he couldn't recall her face; his son had been a nasty piece of work, and Popeye believed John Gardiner about Lenny raping Rosie. But Lenny had done something right after all in leaving him a grandkid who looked like she could've been a model for those china dolls lined up in Gamages. As far as Frank was concerned the Gardiners didn't deserve to keep little Hope. Her mother hadn't even wanted her and had tried to give her away, whereas he'd cherish the gift of her every day of his life.

Midge kept pace with Conor as he strolled to and fro in the aisle between stacked boxes, his knife pointing at the man's guts.

'Looking for someone, are yer?' Frank taunted. 'She ain't here; *my* grandkid's somewhere safe. I've just come along to me warehouse to pay Midge his wages.'

'Well, you'd better tell me where my daughter is, 'cos

if you don't I'll use that knife on your throat before I remove his other arm.'

Popeye slowly got to his feet. 'What you fucking talking about? What shit's that whore got you talking?' Popeye snarled. 'She's *my* granddaughter . . . my Lenny's kid . . .'

Conor laughed. 'Who told you that? Gardiner? Not saying he's lying 'cos that is what he believes. Seemed easier at the time to let him think a dead man'd knocked up his daughter than a live one had run out on her. But I'm back now and I want what's mine.'

'You're fucking lying!' Popeye dragged the gun out of the drawer and aimed at Conor's chest. 'You didn't even know Rosie back then.'

'Yes I did. I knew her when she worked at the Windmill; I got into a fight for her with my old sergeant and a lot of people remember it, especially him, being as I beat the shit out of him. Spring 1941, it was . . . I remember it well. I remember her well. You never asked yourself why I'd bother sending my brother over here to get involved in a two-bob outfit who knows a distiller name of Gardiner? Weren't you I was interested in, you prat, it was them. Soon as I found out about my daughter I was after getting me foot in the door.'

Midge glanced at Popeye, wondering where this was going. It seemed to him that there was more sense in what Flint was saying than what Popeye had told him. Lenny raping John Gardiner's daughter and getting her pregnant, then getting poisoned for it, seemed too far-fetched. Midge had worked with Lenny for years back in the old days, and got to know him. He remembered that Lenny had always used prostitutes. He didn't recall Popeye's son bothering women out of his league, and

Rosie Gardiner was definitely that. Midge had seen her a few times and had been very impressed by the stylish blonde showgirl.

'Get going and make sure Hope's all right; she might have woken up. I'll take care of this.' Popeye lobbed a key at his cohort. He'd left Hope at a hotel, fast asleep. She'd been crying for her mum so Frank had given her a dose of laudanum to knock her out for a few hours while he paid Midge off and decided what to do. But he reckoned she might be waking about now and start hollering. He was planning on taking the child round to Trudy's in the hope of winning his girlfriend over with the news that he was going to fight for custody of the little angel. He was sure that once he told the courts John Gardiner was a murderer and the child's mother was a whore who'd tried to give away her baby, he'd have a real chance of success.

Once Frank had got over the shock of meeting his only surviving flesh and blood, and the little darling had given him a smile, he'd been smitten. Frank had told Midge the kid was staying with him, and Midge had shrugged because he knew he could add a nought to the sum he was expecting in payment. Midge was easy to control; if the price was right he'd do whatever he was told.

Frank had known that Gardiner would be after him, although he was confident that John wouldn't involve the police. He hadn't reckoned on Flint being so involved with Rosie, but he was lying about the kid being his, Popeye knew it.

Once Midge had gone Frank cocked the pistol at Conor's head. 'Nice try, son, but you'll have to go back and tell her it won't wash. Tell the Gardiners 'n' all that we can work things out between us. Ain't saying they can't see the kid – we're all family – but I can give her more than they can. I can certainly afford a better lawyer if it turns nasty. I know that John Gardiner murdered my son . . . don't forget that . . .'

'Yeah, and don't you forget that if I'd got to the bastard first, you'd have been burying him in bits.' Conor seemed as though he was ready to start strolling again but he suddenly launched himself across the desk, punching the gun upwards with one hand, while his other smashed open the wound on Frank's cheek. As Popeye fought to control the pistol his finger tightened on the trigger, sending a bullet thudding into the ceiling. Connor grabbed the older man by the nape, ramming his face down into the desk with a sickening crunch. He jammed his knee on Popeye's back, pinning him there while wrenching the gun from Frank's rigid fingers.

'Hope ain't yours, is she?' Popeye gasped through the blood bubbling off his split lips. 'Admit it! You're fucking lying!'

Conor dragged him by the collar towards the exit, gritting his teeth as pain shot through his damaged shoulder. 'Don't even want to hear you say her name again. Where's Midge gone?'

Once by the doorway Popeye tried to break free but he was savagely punched down close to a tall stack of cartons filled with printing paper. Conor lit a cigarette and held it over an open box. He knew that sticking it on the man's good eye would have less effect than threatening his money. 'Where's he off to?'

'You ain't gonna do that.' Popeye struggled to a sitting position, blinking in horror at red-hot ash dropping onto the paper. 'There's ten grand's worth of merchandise in here. You could have half of it if you piss off and leave me in peace with me granddaughter.'

Conor dropped the cigarette, then deliberately felt in an inside pocket and took out a pewter flask. He upended the lot on top of the paper; even when the flames soared up to the warehouse ceiling he kept shaking whisky out of the metal flask.

Popeye tried to scramble up as the heat from the fire became unbearable but Conor ground his heel harder into his chest.

'The Mermaid Hotel,' Popeye shrieked. 'That's where Midge has gone to get her. Now help me put this out 'fore everything goes up.'

Conor removed his foot. 'Put it out? I was thinking of locking you in and letting you burn.'

Midge drove along glancing every so often over his shoulder at the child on the back seat. He knew that Popeye was expecting him to take the girl to the warehouse. But Midge had a bad feeling about things. He was sure he didn't have a conscience to be bothering him, and he knew he didn't like kids, but the little 'un was an innocent in all of this. Besides, he didn't want Flint after him, and Midge reckoned the man had more claim on the kid than Popeye did. So unless Popeye killed Flint the Wapping boy would be a thorn in everybody's side. Midge didn't reckon Popeye had that sort of bottle. When he got back to the warehouse, he reckoned his boss would probably hand him the gun and expect him to pull the trigger after he'd scarpered with the kid. Midge had been provoked into stabbing Jack Chivers; he wasn't sure he could kill in cold blood.

In Midge's opinion the feud with John Gardiner over

the distilling business had made Popeye lose his marbles. On impulse, Midge did a U-turn in the middle of the quiet street; he'd picked up the kid at his sister's place and that's where he was dropping her off. After that they could fight it out amongst themselves. He'd got his wages in his pocket and he knew Popeye wouldn't shell out any more now things had turned sour. So Midge was ready to disappear.

Midge took his hand off the steering wheel to change gear and saw the black Humber speeding towards him. Though he ducked his head he knew Flint would recognise Popeye's flash Citroën. Midge stamped on the accelerator, roaring along the dark streets, but he had his eyes in the rear-view mirror and saw the Humber wheeling around to start a pursuit.

Midge made the top of Gertie's road and knew if he went into it he'd have to reverse out. By that time Flint would be on him. Midge braked, shooting the child off the seat and making her cry in alarm. He nipped to the back door, dragging the little girl out by an arm. 'Go on, clear off,' he snarled, giving Hope a push. Seconds later he was crashing the gears and the cabriolet leaped forward.

Conor saw the Citroën's tail-lights and he knew he'd not been that close earlier; the vehicle had stopped for some reason. He slowed down, wondering if his eyes were playing tricks on him or if he'd actually seen a flash of fair hair in the blackness. He swerved and braked, then jumped out. He sprang round to the nearside of the car, crouching and searching but finding nothing. He got a torch from the glove box.

'Hope?' he called, sensing she might be close but too terrified to answer.

He walked slowly along the street, swinging the torch on and off the doorsteps and found nothing but empty milk bottles. Then he saw her crouching down by a low brick wall as though she'd made an effort to hide.

Conor closed his eyes and offered up a prayer as he walked over and sat down on the kerb close to her. He was at a loss to know what to say so he didn't frighten her any more than she was already. Her huge eyes were dry but the expression in them was heartbreaking. He kept the torch low, shining it between them on the pavement.

'Wanna go and see your mum? She's waiting for you,' he said gruffly, feeling choked with emotion. He lifted the torch slightly to illuminate her reaction.

Hope pulled a trunk with her tiny lips, darting glances at him.

'Know who I am?'

She slowly moved her head from side to side.

'I'm your mum's friend, called Conor. You got friends?'

She nodded.

'Yeah? What's their names, then?'

'Vicky 'n' Joey 'n' Becky.'

'You got more friends than me.'

Hope nodded, almost smiled but pouted instead.

'Mummy know your friends, does she?'

'No . . . she's at work . . .'

'She's home now. Go and tell her about them, shall we?'

'All right.'

Conor held out his hand and shone the torch on it so she could see it.

As soon as she touched him he lifted her up in his arms and carried her to the car.

CHAPTER TWENTY-NINE

Midge saw flames shooting into the night sky and wondered if he'd missed a lightning German raid. He'd not heard the siren again. He'd intended to park up Popeye's Citroën outside his house, then get going to the train station. He knew his boss would be gunning for him – properly gunning for him with his pistol – once he discovered he'd let the child go. Midge knew he'd no option but to get away till things calmed down. He'd turn up again at some time – perhaps when the war was won or lost – and he understood what he needed to do to survive. But for now he had enough cash in his pocket to keep him on the move.

Midge had seen the Humber stop in Gertie's road and reckoned Flint had found the kid wandering about. Midge hoped he had. She was the prettiest little thing he'd seen in a while and it was right she go back home to her mum.

Popeye was no good for a child like that. He'd never been any good for anybody, even his own kid. Lenny had turned out to be a useless tosser. If Frank kept

Gardiner's granddaughter he'd just ruin the girl's life, not improve it.

Midge started slowing down as he realised the fire in the distance was coming from the area where Popeye's warehouse was. An omen of what he might find if he turned in that direction got the better of his instinct to flee and he spun the wheel.

'Where the fuck have you been?' Popeye roared through his puffy bleeding lips the moment Midge jumped from the motor outside his warehouse.

Midge gawped at the inferno, slowly digesting all that it signified.

'Been waiting for you to turn up,' Popeye snarled. 'Where's me granddaughter?'

Midge slowly approached his boss, half collapsed against the wall on the opposite pavement to the blaze.

'Flint do this to yer?' Midge shouted over the roar of the fire. 'Phoned the brigade, have yer, Pop?'

'Too bleedin' late for that!' Popeye cried, tears in his eyes. 'That's a lifetime's collar in there.' He pointed a shaking finger at the burning doors. 'Everything I own gone up in smoke. I'm gonna have him for this! I swear on me granddaughter's life I'll have him or die trying.' Popeye staggered over to the Citroën and peered inside. 'Where is she?' He swung about. 'What you done with her?'

'He took her,' Midge said evasively. He was wishing now he'd not come round to take a look at what was going on but had kept going.

With difficulty Popeye yanked open the passenger seat door and fell in. 'You drive, mate,' he told Midge. 'Get going over Wapping way.' With an effort he pulled the gun from his inside pocket and started to push bullets into the revolver.

On hearing a bell getting louder, Midge reversed the car at speed out of the hot alley.

'Get going before the bleedin' fire brigade turn up,' Popeye yelled. 'Ain't answering no questions.'

'Got insurance?' Midge asked brightly.

'Fuckin' insurance!' Popeye spat. 'Ain't worth the paper it's written on.'

Midge reckoned no further answer was needed then. Popeye was skint. But as he fought with the gears, he bucked up, interested to know what Popeye thought he was going to do to Flint to get even. Whatever it was, Midge had already decided to watch from afar. There was nothing in it for him.

'Me friend'll never forgive me fer this. Only time she asks me to mind her little Hope and I mess it up. Rosie hates me now, I know she does.'

Rufus patted his wife's quaking shoulder. 'Calm down, love. She must have found the little girl. That's why she ain't been back. Bet yer life her family's got the police involved and serve Midge right if that's his number up at last. Ain't before time.'

'You'll have to go out looking again, Rufus. Go back and try Popeye's place again. Someone might be in now.' Gertie glared at her husband as he remained seated.

'Me feet are killing me, love; you know I can't get about like I used to with this damned injury.' Rufus waggled his trouser leg. 'Anyhow, the old bloke next door said they'd driven off and no sign of a kid. Midge wouldn't take her there. What would old Pop want with a kid? If it ain't gonna turn him a profit, he ain't interested.'

'He wouldn't stoop to . . .' Gertie swallowed. She

knew she should have spoken up sooner about her suspicions that Rosie Gardiner was John Gardiner's daughter, the fellow Popeye had a feud with about distilling. She'd wanted to keep the confidence that Rosie had placed in her when she'd told her she was an unmarried mother who hated being gossiped about. Rosie had naturally wanted to protect Hope from spiteful people, and Gertie could understand that. She knew her neighbours would have a field day if they knew that her Vicky wasn't Rufus's.

'What was you going to say, love?'

'Popeye wouldn't stoop so low as to kidnap John Gardiner's granddaughter to make him start up his still, would he?'

Rufus looked gormless for a moment while that sunk in. 'You ain't saying yer friend's related to the distiller?'

'I think she is,' Gertie owned up.

'But Midge don't know that.' Rufus struggled to his feet. 'Well, reckon Midge might know that, actually. There's been something making that brother of your'n smirk lately.' Rufus's mouth tightened into a hard line. For days Rufus had suspected that his brother-in-law thought he had one over on him. 'I'll go back round Popeye's place. Might try the warehouse too, just in case . . .' he said grimly as he shrugged into his jacket.

'It could've been Vicky as well. That scumbag could've driven off with 'em both,' Joey said, his narrowed eyes fixed on his lap. He had been sitting on the settee listening to his parents arguing for hours. His father had come back several times to report he'd had no luck turning up hide or hair of Midge or the child. Now Rufus had gone back out and Joey and his mother had been sitting in silence, lost in their own troubled thoughts.

Gertie shook her head, although she knew her son had spoken the truth. 'He wouldn't harm his niece. He knows I'd kill him if he did.'

Joey had earlier put his little sister to bed while his parents were going at it hammer and tongs. As he'd kissed her on the forehead he'd thanked God Vicky was safe. But he was crying inside for the little girl who was missing. Hope was sweet and Becky had loved playing mum to her.

'Going up the road to see Becky,' Joey said, getting up.

'It's too late to be paying visits,' Gertie protested. 'Must be close to midnight.'

'Don't care; Becky'll be waiting for news. Said I'd tell her if we had no luck finding out anything.'

'Come straight back if the siren goes,' Gertie called after her son.

Joey hurried past Becky's house and straight to the telephone box on the corner. He ferreted in his pocket for change, looking over his shoulder as he dialled the number. Round these parts nobody grassed family up, however evil they were. But as far as Joey was concerned, Michael Williams wasn't his family. And he wanted him dead.

'Take another route,' Popeye shouted when Midge slowed down, then stopped to allow an oncoming army truck and several cars to file around the pile of bomb damage blocking the road.

'Ain't doing a three-point turn 'less I have to,' Midge snapped back. 'Ain't exactly the world's best driver, am I?' He ruefully displayed what remained of his right arm.

'Well, let me drive,' Popeye barked, blinking blood from his good eye.

'You can't see nuthin' at the best of times,' Midge

chortled. 'Look, we're moving again. Shut up and sit back.' Midge shoved the gear stick forward and pulled off with a lurch.

He motored on, putting his foot down as the road became deserted.

'Slow down!' Popeye hissed.

'You just told me to get going,' Midge protested.

'Old Bill . . .' Popeye had glimpsed through his blurry vision a police car parked up.

Midge immediately braked, then when the vehicle pulled out after him, he jammed his foot down on the accelerator. He licked his lips. 'They was bleedin' waiting for us.' He glanced agitatedly at Popeye. 'The law's on us; Flint or Gardiner have grassed you up. Kidnapping a kid's a serious offence.'

'You don't know that; could be they clocked you speeding.' Popeye glanced over a shoulder. He knew if they were stopped he'd have some explaining to do, not least about why a man with one arm was driving his car, and he was looking badly beaten.

'Pull round a corner and we'll swap places on the quick so I can say I was driving.' Popeye started scrubbing at his bloodied face with his hanky in an attempt to look more presentable.

'Ain't stopping fer nobody,' Midge growled. He knew as soon as the police started asking questions he'd be arrested, and after that he'd face a hangman's noose for Jack Chivers' murder.

'Slow down!' Popeye bawled as the Citroën's engine roared.

The bell on the police car started to clatter and he turned to gawp through the back window at the police gaining on them.

'Go down by the docks; lose 'em easy down there,' Popeye panted. 'Lots of alleys 'n' sheds. Might find one open we can pull into and hide.'

Popeye's heart was thudding, making him feel faint. If the police stopped them and searched them he'd be arrested as well as Midge. He had a gun and bullets on him. And he knew Midge had his blade in a pocket. Midge was a goner if he was caught – they both knew that – but Popeye reckoned he might still be able to talk himself out of things . . .

'They're gaining on us,' Midge said quite calmly, eyes in the rear-view mirror. 'Apart from that, Pop, we're almost out of juice.' He glanced at the dial, the needle pointing at empty.

'Find somewhere quick then . . . here . . . down here!' Popeye pointed desperately at a long narrow lane leading off into blackness.

Midge took it, tyres screaming and shoved his foot to the floor. If Popeye had been able to see, Midge inwardly laughed, he'd've known that this road didn't lead anywhere other than the water.

But it was good enough for him. He'd sooner drown than swing, in any case. As for Pop . . . well, he'd got nothing left so he'd probably thank him in the long run . . . if he could . . .

CHAPTER THIRTY

Rosie had sat watching the closed door, her hands locked on her opposite shoulders, for what seemed like hours. She had been sure she'd spring from the seat the moment she heard the sound of a key in the lock. Instead when it opened she remained statue-like, gazing at her daughter. Slowly she wobbled to her feet, holding onto the arm of the chair. Her hands fluttered to her face, up over her hair, then the sob broke and she rushed forward and took Hope from him, smearing her tears against the child's neck. 'Thank you,' she whispered over and over again.

Conor went into the kitchen and filled the kettle, then put it on the gas stove even though he didn't want tea. He guessed she didn't either. But he reckoned it was probably what people did at such a time. He turned and stood in the doorway, hands braced on either jamb and watched as Rosie sat her daughter on the chair then removed the tot's shoes, talking to and touching Hope in a way he remembered his mother had done with Steven as a kid. But he couldn't remember her ever fussing over him.

Rosie looked up, smiling shyly, but he went back into the kitchen. She joined him in there with Hope in her arms. 'She told me she's got more friends than you,' Rosie said with a sweet attempt at a normal conversation.

Conor raised an eyebrow at Hope and set two cups. 'Does she want a biscuit?' He smiled as Hope nodded before her mother could answer.

'You'll spoil her,' Rosie said as he handed her daughter an open packet of custard creams. She took one out and gave it to Hope, then put the rest back in the cupboard.

'Can I have a drop of hot from that kettle and give her a wash?'

''Course . . .' He poured steaming water into the tin bowl and mixed it with some from the tap till it was lukewarm.

Rosie sat Hope on the kitchen table and started taking off her clothes. 'Have you got something to dry her with?'

'Somewhere . . .'

He went out and she heard him on the stairs, then he came in with a bar of soap and a flannel and towel.

'Lucky girl . . . nice soap . . . Pears. We have the cheap stuff.'

Conor poured the tea, then left them both cups and went to sit down on an armchair with a newspaper open on his knees.

'Can I put her to bed in the spare room?' Rosie asked. Her daughter was pink and fragrant from a thorough washing, dressed in just her vest and knickers and ready to be tucked up.

Conor closed the paper and sat back in the chair regarding her steadily. 'Gonna tell me why you're doing this?' He made an exasperated gesture and stood up. 'It doesn't matter . . . I already know. It's time for you both to go home.'

'I don't want to go home.'

He gave a soft bitter laugh. 'Oh, yes you do.' He pulled his car keys from a trouser pocket. 'What's more, I want you to go home.'

Rosie hugged her daughter to her, rocking the child who was already drifting off. 'D'you want to get rid of me because you're expecting someone?'

'Why d'you ask?'

'The phone went. I answered it because I thought it might be you.'

'Who was it?'

'She said her name was Patricia. She was rude so I put the phone down on her.'

'Right . . . definitely time for you to go home, then. She'll be on her way round.'

Rosie knew he was being deliberately cruel to keep her at arm's length. 'Let her come; if you won't tell her to go away I will. She can have you tomorrow. This is my night,' Rosie said with a poise she was far from feeling. 'You told me to come and find you when I trusted you enough. Here I am.'

'Why tonight?' He turned, deep-blue eyes boring into her profile. 'What am I, a mercenary to be paid off? A dog to be rewarded for good behaviour? Or did you think I'd let that maniac have her unless you agreed to stay with me? Which is it? All of it? What about last night . . . and the night before that . . . when I wanted you? You didn't come over then and tell me you trusted me enough.'

Rosie flinched, wondering if he was hurt more than angry. She hadn't expected more than a token rejection

349

from him, to preserve his pride, before he took her to bed. 'I thought you'd be pleased. What d'you want me to do, beg you to take me upstairs? All right I will . . .'

Conor laughed, swung narrowed eyes her way. 'Don't push me too far, Rosie. Take her home. You've got what you want.'

'I want you to have what you want, too.'

'You don't know what I want.' He looked at her. 'Do you?'

'And Patricia does, is that what you mean?' Rosie said. 'You think I'm not up to the job?'

She thought he'd laugh and drawl an answer but he walked away and struck a fist on the wall, leaning into it.

Rosie went into the hallway with Hope hugged tight to her chest and climbed the stairs to the smaller room. She'd gone into the big bedroom earlier. Just after he'd left she'd curled on her side on his mattress, staring sightlessly at the wall, with the tobacco musk of him beneath her cheek. But the sweeter smell of Jicky perfume on the other pillow had driven her back to the living room to continue her vigil in the armchair.

She tucked Hope in, smoothing her soft hair back from her brow in long slow strokes till her daughter's eyes fluttered closed. Still she sat with her, watching her sleep until she was drowsing herself and her chin was sagging towards her chest. She jerked awake and went back downstairs. Conor was lounging in the armchair, legs stretched in front of him, in the way her father would do on a Sunday afternoon after a roast dinner, in those old, glorious days when such things had existed for her family.

'Are you angry with me?' Rosie asked softly, unsure if he'd dozed off.

'No.'

So he wasn't asleep. 'I . . . I didn't mean to insult you, if that's what you think I did. It's just . . . I don't think you appreciate how much it meant to me, what you did. I'd've done anything to get her back.'

'What if I'd not managed to bring her back? What if I couldn't find her?'

'I knew you would. It never crossed my mind otherwise,' Rosie said simply and truthfully.

'Would you have done anything for Midge to barter for her?'

Rosie licked her lips. 'Yes . . . I'd do anything for anyone – even Lenny, if he was still alive – to have Hope safe at home.' She jerked up her face. 'I suppose that disgusts you.'

'No, it's as it should be between a mother and her kids. But you don't need to get into that with me.'

'Why not? I thought you liked me.'

'Yeah?' he said, sounding sarcastic. 'What makes you think that?'

'I'm not frightened of you now. I might've been once but not now.' Rosie tilted her head to read his lowered expression. 'I know you'll be kind and gentle . . .'

He jerked forward, sank his head into his hands, spearing fingers through his long dark hair. 'D'you know how French women feed their kids when they've been bombed out or their husbands have been carted off by the Gestapo?' He looked up, his eyes fierce and narrowed.

Rosie shook her head, although she knew the answer, and she hadn't fooled him by pretending otherwise.

'They say they're not frightened and they like you. The week before it might have been a Nazi they'd stripped off for . . . the uniform doesn't matter, so long as food or francs or cigarettes change hands at some point.' He sat back, but his eyes never left her face. 'They're lying too; they detest all of us. But they keep on coming.'

Rosie swallowed, feeling chastened and anxious. 'Are you talking about somebody in particular . . . a woman you really liked?'

'Never met any woman I *really* liked over there or over here. Then I came home with a bullet in the shoulder and everything changed.'

'I don't blame those women . . . I don't blame you; you must get lonely . . .' Rosie blurted, feeling relieved that he hadn't fallen in love with a French girl. 'Why're you telling me what you do over there? I don't want to know.' She spun away from him, feeling suddenly angry.

'I don't do anything, that's the point, but there are lots who do, and brag about it afterwards, especially if they've copped off without paying.'

'I told my dad I was coming here to ask you to help, and the only thing that frightened me – frightened me to death – on the journey was that I'd turn up and find you'd gone back to your regiment.'

'Next week you would've.'

'You're going back?' Rosie asked forlornly, turning back to face him.

He nodded.

'I'll miss you. I have missed you . . . that's the truth.'

'I've missed you, too.'

'Good, that's a good start, isn't it?'

Rosie saw him smile to himself, shake his head in mock despair. She heard the low fluid swearing beneath his breath. Aloud he said, 'She's nodded off?'

'Mmm . . .'

Rosie sank down by the side of his chair, curling her feet under her, feeling nervous. She wanted to get closer to him, yet knew he'd move away if she said or did something wrong.

'I don't want to talk about how you got her back for me. I don't care what it took anyway,' Rosie said. Her hand slid over his, idle on the chair arm. She thought for a moment he was going to slip free but he didn't.

'You asked me if I liked you . . . and trusted you. I do. I like you and trust you a lot and I know you think I'm just saying that because . . .' She glanced up at him to gauge his reaction to her amateur seduction, but he had his eyes on the opposite wall. 'You think I'm saying it because of what you've done for me tonight, but it's not that. It's honestly not that.'

'How many others were there?'

'What?'

'Before he raped you, how many men had you slept with?'

Rosie knew her blush had betrayed her. 'It doesn't matter now.'

'How many men had you kissed then?'

'Lots,' she said defiantly. 'Lots of them. I kissed that sergeant of yours, for a start.'

'You said he made you feel sick.'

'He did. But it was my own fault; he got the wrong idea. They all got the wrong idea. They thought I was a sophisticated vamp. I expect you did too. I was stupid and naïve.' She sank her teeth into her lower lip; she'd not told anybody other than her father how bitterly she regretted her behaviour. She moved her hand on Conor's, almost a caress. 'It should've been you; it would all have been different then. I wish it had been you,' Rosie told

353

him with quiet vehemence, realising she'd never meant anything more. *If only . . .* whispered through her mind. If she'd spent the evening with him she'd have been a Windmill Girl with a boyfriend to write to overseas. She would have welcomed him home, waiting in a fever of anticipation, as Hazel used to when she knew Chuck was due back on leave. But for her and Conor it would have been no half-hearted affair, it would have been real. She believed that as much as she understood he was waiting for a sign from her that he could trust. He wanted to be sure that gratitude and debt played no part in what might happen between them tonight. But such honesty required some answers.

'My dad said you Flints are pimps and spivs.'

'Remind me to thank him,' Conor said drily.

'Are you?'

'A spiv, perhaps; a pimp, no. Nor was Saul. By all accounts, my father ran a few brasses down by the docks for the sailors during the war. Last war, that is. He's been dead about eighteen years.' He tilted his head against the chair back, gazing at the ceiling. 'I'm no saint but I don't reckon I'm a proper villain either. I've always had regular work. Other than that, I do what I have to when I want more.'

'What more do you want?'

'It's in my blood . . . who I am. I showed you that,' he said tonelessly.

'What more is there to want?' she persevered. 'A house, a job and a family to love – that's all there is, really.'

'Is that why you worked at the Windmill Theatre? For just a job and a family to love?'

Rosie felt heat flood her cheeks at his cool irony. She'd

wanted the glamour and the excitement, and the adulation. She couldn't deny it.

'There's always a price to pay for thrills,' Rosie said stiffly. 'I paid it and it wasn't worth it.' She withdrew her hand from his, folded it into the other on her lap. 'He thought me a whore. He saw me come out of the Palm House with a bruise on my face and my dress torn and said I must've short-changed a punter. He said I wouldn't short-change him.' Rosie paused. 'It was the second time that night a man wanted to rip my clothes off. First time was inside the place. An army major, he was. He went off in a rage when I told him no. But first he whacked me and tore off some buttons.'

Conor sat forward with a jerk and sank his forehead into a hand. 'What were you doing at that dive, for God's sake?'

'A workmate from the Windmill and her boyfriend took me along. I was paying rent on a room in their house. They told me it was just a nightclub; I found out later it was a brothel. Turned out he was a pimp and she was working for him as well as at the theatre. They'd set me up with a client . . . oh, it doesn't matter.' Rosie frowned at her fingers. 'I just ran out when I realised what was expected, and straight into . . .' She couldn't utter Lenny's name. She glanced at him, wondering if she'd repelled him with her pathetic conduct. She changed position, kneeling then sinking back more comfortably on her heels. 'Would you have still wanted to take me for that drink if you'd known I was just a silly little girl?'

'I was counting on it.' Conor smiled crookedly.

'No, you just told me you're different. You didn't need to though. I *know* you're different . . . not like them.'

Rosie cocked her head, realising he was making a joke of it because she'd moved him with that story. 'You're not like your family either,' she said. 'You're certainly not like your mum.'

'That'll please her.'

After a pause Rosie asked gently, 'Why doesn't she like you?'

'Because I'm not like the others. I never needed her in the way they did. She never needed me either . . . till now.' He shrugged. 'I was always the kid in the middle, stuck between the baby and the big boy taking over from his dad.'

'I was stuck in the middle,' Rosie said.

'Thought you were an only child.'

'I was. I got stuck in the middle of my mum and dad. She left him, you see, when I was little. Went off with another man. Then she came back for a while, before she passed away. I wanted them to get on and be happy, but it seemed it was only me that did.' Rosie shook her head. 'Think it was a relief for Mum to die and get away from all the long, cold silences.'

'Got anything cheerful to talk about?' Conor asked in that dry way he had.

Rosie looked thoughtful. 'Persuaded a girl to come out from a bombed-out house today, if that counts.'

Conor tenderly traced a finger down her cheek, touched the dirty collar of her shirt with a finger flick. 'You look as though you've been coal mining again.'

'My road got bombed. Oh, our house is standing and Dad's all right,' she reassured him, seeing his concerned frown. 'It was further up,' she chattered on, glad of a neutral subject. 'Do you remember Mrs Price? You gave her ten shillings. Her house was hit and her daughter went into labour. Well, Irene might already have been in labour before the explosion. But the shock must have brought the baby shooting out. Poor girl. She's only fifteen. Baby's premature . . . I pray he survives.' Rosie raised her eyes, finding Conor watching her steadily. 'Mrs Price won't be able to have a go at me any more, not now her daughter's an unmarried mother, too.'

'Had a rough time of it, haven't you?' he said gruffly.

'Didn't bother me,' Rosie said, immediately defiant.

'You wanted to give Hope away.'

'She wasn't Hope then . . . just *his* baby,' Rosie retorted hoarsely. 'Popeye told you?'

Conor nodded.

'It's true,' Rosie admitted huskily. 'I didn't want any reminder of him. I thought I'd never be able to look at her and not hate her because of him.'

'I told Frank she's mine and the rest's a pack of lies. I'll keep telling him that, and anybody else for that matter, for as long as you want me to.'

Rosie was momentarily speechless with astonishment. 'Why did you do that?'

'Why not? Could've been true, if you'd come for that drink with me. Dates almost work out.'

'Yes . . .' Rosie murmured, her eyes engulfed by his. 'If it gets out . . . what you've said . . . will it cause trouble for you with people like . . .'

'Like?'

'Like Patricia,' Rosie blurted, suddenly feeling possessive. 'Your girlfriend'll be hopping mad if she finds out you've done that, and I can't say I'd blame her.'

Conor smiled; an old smile, the sort he used to give her when he knew he had the upper hand and was pleased about it. 'You're jealous.'

'No, I'm not,' Rosie said, bristling. 'I've always known about your women. You told me, remember, about her and Angie.' She scrambled up at the same time as he got to his feet.

They stood facing one another and Rosie felt suddenly awkward and annoyed without knowing why. 'Sorry . . . it's none of my business what you tell any of them, especially your girlfriend.'

'You know she's not my girlfriend. That's why she's not come round. She knows I'll throw her out. I told you I'd finished with her.'

'So you did,' Rosie said brittly. 'But she phones you up and your bed smells of perfume.'

'The sheets need changing.'

'You don't have to explain to me!'

'Yeah, you really believe that, don't you, Rosie?' he taunted. ''Course I have to explain to you. Whatever you want I do, because you're what I want. All right, I'll admit I slept with her last week. She phones me up, comes round and sometimes I'm tempted to let her stay.' He closed his eyes. 'I thought there was no chance you'd ever feel for me what I felt for you, so I drink too much and sleep with other women.' He shoved a hand through his hair. 'I'm signed off fit and getting shipped out to France next week and fuck the lot of them here.' He drew her closer. 'Trouble is, now you're here with me and I don't want to leave you . . . don't want to leave my daughter either.'

'Oh, Conor,' Rosie choked, and flung her arms up about his neck, pressing herself against him and fiercely kissing his cheek.

He crushed her to him, his hands gently caressing. 'Kiss me properly . . . please, Rosie.'

Rosie hadn't kissed a man for years and even then she'd received rather than given, and hadn't liked much of it at all. She placed her mouth on his, moving it softly to and fro till she felt his lips tilt into a smile.

'You even kiss like a virgin,' he said, drawing her head back to his when she would have indignantly reared away. 'It's not a complaint, Rosie,' he said gently. 'God knows, it's a compliment, knowing what you've been through. How did you manage to stay so sweet and decent after what he did to you?'

'I wouldn't let somebody like him ruin my life,' Rosie said. 'Not when I had you waiting for me.'

He swung her up in his arms, nuzzling her cheek with soft wooing kisses. 'You know I love you, don't you?'

'I do now . . . and . . . I . . .'

He put a finger on her lips. 'Tell me tomorrow, if you still want to.'

'I will,' she said. 'Over and over again.'

'I don't reckon I've ever made love either . . . not really . . . not like I want to now with you. My first time, you might have to show me how.'

Rosie cupped his unshaven chin in a hand. 'I might enjoy that, Corporal Flint.'

'Sergeant. I got promoted.'

'Must be a quick learner, then. Are you?'

'Nope . . . could take all night . . .' he said, and closed the door with his foot on the way up the stairs.

CHAPTER THIRTY-ONE

'Come back to bed.'

Rosie was standing by the window in her petticoat, peering out. 'Somebody's knocking on the door,' she said.

'Forget it . . . it's probably the milkman. Come back to bed.'

Rosie dropped the curtain on the morning sun peeping over the rooftops. She kneeled on the mattress, leaning over Conor to kiss him. His fingers immediately slid to the back of her head, holding her close while she tasted his lips, like a hungry child about to devour an exciting new treat.

'You all right?' he asked, smoothing a curtain of silky fair hair back from her face.

'I will be after we've done it all again so I can make up my mind if I like it,' she said provocatively then squealed when he rolled her onto her back. She wriggled in delight as his sweetly seductive mouth slipped over her lips then travelled on to her throat and earlobes.

'Like that?' he teased.

She nodded, coiling her arms about his neck. A moment later, attuned to the sound, she slipped free and sat up, clutching the eiderdown to her chest.

'Come here, sweetheart . . . you're up early,' Rosie said breathlessly. Her daughter was hovering just inside the door, rubbing her eyes. Hope had never seen her undressed with a man before. In fact the only man the child really knew was her granddad.

Conor slid to the opposite side of the mattress and came upright, buttoning up his trousers before turning to the little girl, slipping a vest over his head. 'Have a nice kip in my house, did you?' he asked Hope and came round the bed to pick her up.

She nodded her fair head, giving him a shy half-smile.

'D'you remember my name?'

'Conor.'

'Clever girl,' he praised and ruffled her hair. 'Hungry are you? Find some bread and jam, shall we, and a nice cup of tea?'

Hope's reply to an offer of breakfast was drowned out by some hollering from outside.

Rosie's eyes widened on Conor. 'That's your mum's voice,' she hissed in a horrified whisper.

Conor elevated his eyebrows but seemed no more than mildly surprised, or put out, by his mother visiting him at the crack of dawn. He went to the sash window and shoved it up, one-handed, still holding Hope.

'What in Gawd's name's that you've got there?' Hilda yelled up at her son, jerking her wizened face at the child.

'Her name's Hope,' Rosie said, coming to stand at

361

Conor's side, annoyed at the way the woman had referred to her precious daughter. Apart from that she felt she should support him against the harridan.

Hilda planted her hands on her bony hips, mouth pursed. 'Hah . . . so it's you then is it?' she spat. 'Turned out to be better in bed than the other one, did yer, or is she up there 'n' all?' Hilda barked a nasty laugh. 'Just getting to know him, Mrs Flint . . . ' she mimicked what Rosie had told her. 'Didn't take yer long to know him pretty damned well, did it? Well you can take yerself and yer kid off now he's done with yer. I've got important things to talk about with me son . . .'

'What d'you want Mum?' Conor cut across Hilda's rant.

'I want my Steven back, that's what I want. You go 'n' fetch him from Surrey 'fore he finishes his training and gets shipped out.' She pointed at the child. 'And don't want no bastards in the family. The kid's father can have the cost of shelling out on that one.'

'Yeah, he can and I'll give my daughter whatever she wants.' Conor started pulling down the sash. 'Now go home. I'm not getting Steven, he's made his choice.'

'Just you wait a fuckin' minute!' Hilda roared. 'I ain't finished . . .'

'I'm busy.'

'Yeah, can see that,' Hilda snorted, but the rest of her coarse observation was cut off as the sash was rammed home and the curtain fell in place.

'You meant what you said then?' Rosie was gazing up at him, eyes glowing. She'd not really believed until now that he'd announce to his kith and kin that he was Hope's father.

'I meant it.' He glanced at the beautiful child in his

362

arms with a rueful smile. 'She'll need her dad when the boys start coming round after her.'

Rosie nodded, waiting, hoping he'd ask her immediately before a proposal burst from her instead. She knew now how Hazel had felt being in love and yearning to be married.

A stone hit the window, making Conor curse beneath his breath. Putting Hope down, he used both hands on the sash this time to shove it up.

'Me mum's just seen Hilda in the corner shop; she told her you've got a girl in there and a kid. What the fuck's going on?' Ethel Ford had nipped out to get a paper and a pint of milk a few minutes ago and met Hilda in Wainwrights. As soon as she'd got the gist of what the woman was saying Ethel had hurried back home to drag her daughter out of bed and recount that Conor had knocked a girl up years back and had now moved her and her kid into his house. Pat had needed no second telling and had raced round to confront them in her dressing gown.

'Nothing's going on that you need to know about,' Conor said. 'Clear off.'

'You had *me* in that bed not so long ago,' Pat screeched. 'And what's this about a kid? Your old girl gone senile, or something?'

'No . . . she's not,' Rosie said, whipping into view next to Conor. 'She's a pain in the backside, without a doubt, but his mum's not mad.'

'Might've known it was you answering his 'phone last night,' Pat stormed. 'Ain't he turfed you out yet? Come down 'ere, then, you cow; I'll soon send you packing.'

Conor tried to pull Rosie away as though to shield her from any more unpleasantness. But she whipped free of him and leaned on the windowsill staring down into the sulky brunette's face. Without make-up Pat looked washed out. 'We're getting married, so it's you slinging your hook. Don't come back here, or you'll be sorry.' She pulled the sash down and turned, pink-cheeked, to Conor.

'Sorry . . . overdid it, didn't I? D'you think she'll take any notice of me?'

'I wouldn't mess with you . . .' he said, laughing.

Rosie went to sit on the edge of the bed, feeling silly for having jumped the gun when he'd not asked her to be his wife.

Conor put Hope on the mattress beside Rosie then crouched down in front of her.

'So . . . did *you* mean it?'

'What?'

'Are we getting married?'

'You haven't asked me,' Rosie replied, the colour in her cheeks deepening.

'Only 'cos I haven't got you a ring yet, or asked your father for his permission.' He sat down beside her. 'You deserve everything done properly, Rosie,' he said, cupping her blushing face in a hand.

'Just say it,' Rosie pleaded, drawing her daughter to her side with an arm about her. Barely had the age-old question passed his lips when Rosie breathed, 'Yes . . . oh, yes, please.' She pulled him down on to the bed, giggling, and Hope, wanting to join in the game, jumped on top of them.

'Rosie. Hold up!'

The raucous shout stopped Rosie in her tracks. She swung about and saw Peg Price waving and hurrying in her direction. Rosie handed her door key to her new fiancé, saying, 'I'd better have a word with her. I want to find out how Irene and the baby are, in any case. Would you take Hope inside? Dad'll be frantic with worry about us.' She gave Conor a grateful smile as he led her daughter towards her front door.

Rosie had just lifted Hope off the back seat of the Humber when Peg, who'd been salvaging in the wreckage of her home, called to her. Rosie squared her shoulders wondering whether she was about to get a mouthful, or a pat on the back.

'I'm so sorry about you getting bombed out, Mrs Price.' Rosie hoped the less explosive subject of her neighbour's property being blown to bits might be a good place to start this conversation. She could see the woman had been crying: her eyes were bloodshot and her lashes wet.

'Least of me troubles . . . just glad we're all still breathing,' Peg croaked. She wiped her sooty palms on her pinafore. 'Poor May has lost her eye. Popped in to see her in the hospital last night. She won't be out for a good while, the poor cow. Not that she's got a home to go to now.'

Rosie gave a sorrowful sigh, although she'd guessed that May Reed had been badly injured when she'd patched her up. 'Have you been re-housed yet?' Rosie asked, glancing past at the Prices' obliterated home.

'Moved in with Dick's sister round the corner. She said we can stop with her till the council find us something.' Peg pushed straggly wisps of hair into the scarf knotted on top of her head, giving Rosie humble peeps all the while. Suddenly she lunged at the younger woman's hands, clasping them to her bony chest. 'Gotta thank you for saving my Irene. You was terribly brave going in there when it could've all collapsed around yer ears.' Peg fiddled again with her headscarf. 'Irene said that she confided in you about the baby and you told her months ago to speak up about it.' Peg shook her head. 'Silly gel! Wish she had told us so me 'n' Dick could have . . .' Peg sniffed, blinked in consideration. 'Don't know what we would have done; anyhow too late to worry over it, just got to make the best of things. Better to be angry than grievin'.'

Rosie smiled agreement to Peg's philosophy, glad the woman seemed to have mellowed. 'The baby's doing all right?' she asked, hoping to hear that he was. 'And Irene too?'

'Irene's right as rain, as for the baby . . . tiny little scrap, he is, but the doctor said he's a fighter. Ain't quite four pounds in weight but they're planning on letting him and Irene come home in a couple of weeks. Dunno how we'll all cope, or what we're gonna say to people . . .' Her voice wobbled.

Rosie gave Peg's hands a comforting squeeze before gently removing herself from the woman's grip. 'You'll all just get on with it. And you'll tell the gossips to mind their own business, same as we had to,' Rosie said simply.

'I know I deserved that,' Peg mumbled. She blew her nose and bucked herself up. 'Dick won't leave the little lad alone. The matron had to throw him out of the maternity ward last night for outstaying his welcome.' She almost smiled then cleared her throat instead. 'Sorry for being a spiteful cow to you. Even if you hadn't done so much for my Irene I should still be ashamed of meself, and I am.' On impulse, Peg shook Rosie by the hand. 'I know yer dad's proud of you and I ain't surprised. Lucky man, he is; so's that nice Mr Flint I just seen go in yer house with little Hope.' Peg sounded more like her old self. She managed a wink before her shoulders slumped and she returned to rummage with her husband in the charred wreckage of their home.

'Don't cry, Dad, it's all turned out right in the end.'

'I know . . .' John blubbed, mopping his face with his hanky. 'But I've caused you more problems than I ever should've and me little granddaughter too. I'm so ashamed of meself. And I'm so sorry, Rosie, for everything. Don't hate me . . .'

'Of course I don't hate you, Dad.' Rosie put her arms around her father. 'Can't say I've not felt like throttling you at times . . . but I know I've done my fair share of stupid things in my time to make you mad. Forgive and forget now, eh?'

John looked bleakly at the man standing a diplomatic distance away so father and daughter could have a private reunion.

'Come on, cheer up, it's a day for celebrations,' Rosie patted her father's back. 'Hope's safe and . . .' Rosie's words tailed off. She glanced at Conor as he squatted down to stack bricks with Hope on the parlour floor. She'd let him bring up the subject of their wedding, as he'd said he wanted to formally approach her father.

When she'd entered the house following her talk with Peg, Conor had been in the process of helping her father up the cellar steps so they could make themselves comfortable in the parlour. It seemed that Conor had only briefly answered John's questions about Hope's ordeal and Rosie was thankful for that. Her father seemed too emotional to be told more than the bare bones at the moment.

367

'You'd better make an honest woman of my daughter after keeping her out all night,' John suddenly burst out, only half-joking. He stuffed his hanky in his pocket and puffed out his chest as he limped to confront Conor in his role as protective father.

Conor came slowly upright, his amusement subdued. 'Take it you'll not object then if I ask her to marry me, Mr Gardiner?'

'Well . . . had high hopes for her, of course. Accountant . . . solicitor . . . with her looks she could have her pick of eligible fellows.'

'Dad!' Rosie exclaimed, shaking her head at Conor in apology.

'I'll do my best to be worthy of her, Mr Gardiner,' Conor solemnly promised.

'Make sure you do,' was all John said but he gave his daughter a subtle smile as he limped to the settee and sank down. 'Come and tell granddad what you've been up to.' He held out his hands to his granddaughter.

'Don't question her, Dad,' Rosie said quickly. 'I want her to forget about it.'

'I know,' John answered gruffly. 'Just gonna talk about her little friend, that's all.'

Rosie pulled Conor by the hand into the kitchen, then rested back against the sink.

'Sorry about him, he can be so rude.'

Conor smiled. 'I reckon my mum can trump him,' was all he said before putting a hand either side of her and leaning close. 'I want us to get married before I go back overseas. Then you can call yourself Mrs Flint, can't you, Mrs Deane.'

'That'll be nice . . .' Rosie murmured against his mouth.

'Is that Peg come knocking, d'you think?' John called

out following a bang on the door. 'Conor said you was talking to her outside. That old cow better not turn up here with a begging bowl, the trouble she's tried to stir us up.'

'She's got bad luck of her own to keep her occupied now, Dad, so a little sympathy wouldn't go amiss,' Rosie called over Conor's shoulder.

'I'll get the door,' Conor offered.

The sound of children's chatter brought Rosie out of the kitchen just as Hope trotted to greet Vicky who'd arrived with her mum.

'Please let me stay just long enough to say what I have to. That's all I want,' Gertie burst out. She put a hand to her chest, breathing heavily. Her eyes were fixed on Hope, devouring the child. 'I'm so glad she's all right. I've been beside meself with worry. Not had a wink of sleep; nor's Rufus . . .' She started to cry, wiping her eyes with a hanky.

'You 'n' me both,' John snapped belligerently. He'd guessed he was talking to Midge's sister and struggled to his feet to have a dingdong.

Rosie put a restraining hand on her father's shoulder. 'Gertie's not to blame for any of this trouble. She was doing me a favour babysitting because you were laid up after that run-in you had.'

The pointed remark reminded John that he'd started the ball rolling on this particular calamity many years back when he'd got involved with his own, and Frank Purves', illegal enterprises. Chastened, he sat down.

'We got Hope back yesterday and she's fine, Gertie.' When her comforting words seemed to have no calming effect on her friend Rosie added, 'I know you and your husband had nothing to do with it, Gertie. It's just a case of bad luck and bad company. '

'Does your husband know where Midge is?' Conor asked bluntly.

Gertie nodded, looking apprehensive as the handsome stranger moved closer as though to interrogate her.

'It's all right, Gertie, this is Conor . . . we're getting married.' Rosie slipped her hand through her fiancé's arm while making proper introductions between the two. 'Conor found Hope and brought her back last night. He's dealt with Frank Purves before so knows what sort of devil he is.'

Gertie's moist eyes darted back to Conor. 'I expect you already know what happened to my brother then, if you were there.'

'He drove off in Frank's Citroen; that's the last I saw of Midge.'

'You don't know he's dead then?' Gertie whispered so the laughing children wouldn't hear what was being said.

'Dead?' John chirruped, looking joyfully shocked. 'Well, that's a turn up.'

Conor frowned, wondering if Midge's sister was lying to throw him off the scent. From the moment he'd set fire to the warehouse he had known that before he returned overseas he'd need to take steps to protect Rosie and her family from Popeye's malice. But he didn't regret what he'd done. Frank Purves wasn't simply a racketeer, he was an evil monster who would have taken a little girl from the people who loved her while claiming the moral high ground. But without his little empire, housed in that warehouse, Popeye was impotent. Eventually though he'd rebuild his stock. Conor knew the man would have cash stashed somewhere to start him off ducking and diving again.

'Rufus went out looking for Popeye and Midge again

this morning,' Gertie explained, shoving her hanky up her sleeve. 'He banged on Frank's door and a neighbour came out and told him Popeye wouldn't ever be coming back. The police had been round, the fellow said, and asked questions because Frank Purves' car had gone into the river by Wapping with two men inside.'

Rosie and Conor exchanged a look as they guessed the identity of those in the car, and why they'd been in the vicinity. Popeye and Midge had driven to Wapping because they'd been on their way to get even and snatch Hope back.

'Me 'n' Rufus was worried that little Hope might have been in the car as well but the police didn't know about it.' Gertie started to weep again. 'That's why I had to come round and find out if she was all right. Been torturing us, it has.' Gertie pulled her hanky back out to scrub at her eyes. 'They've just recovered one body so far . . . it was a man of about sixty, so it wasn't Midge, must've been Popeye.'

'Good riddance to bad rubbish,' John piped up, still sounding cheery.

'Sorry to come 'n' bother you like this, but needed to put my mind at rest.' Gertie took a deep breath and with a final wipe of her eyes, picked up her daughter. Vicky began to wriggle and squeal to get down so she could continue playing.

Gertie knew guilt played a part in her distress. She couldn't blame it all on Rufus, and earlier he'd told her so in no uncertain terms. Her husband might have got embroiled again with Midge and Popeye, but once she'd got her hands on the fake ration books, and the extra money they brought in for her, she hadn't wanted Rufus to give up working for a counterfeiter.

'Let's meet up again in a few weeks, when this has blown over and we feel calmer.' Rosie followed Gertie into the hallway, wanting to let her friend know that she bore no grudges. 'I'll be a married woman by then,' she added, feeling quite excited.

Gertie gave Rosie a spontaneous hug that was fully returned. 'I'm pleased for you, Rosie. He's a good looker and I can tell he makes you happy. 'S'pect you're wondering where I got your address from. Rufus knew where John Gardiner lived. He knows of your dad in a roundabout way . . . through Popeye.'

Rosie grimaced understanding; Gertie had discovered her father had been a criminal too, in his time.

'Men!' Gertie snorted. 'They're a pain in the backside.'

'I can't say that I'm sorry about what's happened to Frank Purves or your brother without being a hypocrite. I expect Popeye knew that Conor lives in Wapping and he and Midge were coming after him for Hope.'

'I'm not sorry they're gone either,' Gertie returned hoarsely. 'But for me mum 'n' dad's sake I expect I'll put up a pretence when we come to bury Michael. He was never no good and I'm relieved he went like this rather than breaking me parents' hearts by swinging on a gib.'

Back in the parlour, John was gazing at his future son-in-law's broad back as Conor stared out of the window into the autumn afternoon. 'If that were any of your doing, you've got my eternal thanks, son.' John kept his voice low and his eye on the door for his daughter's return.

'Nothing to do with me.' Conor pivoted about, hands in pockets and assessed his future father-in-law. 'Popeye and Midge were alive last time I saw 'em.'

John shrugged. 'Nevertheless you brought back me granddaughter and for that alone you've got me deepest respect.'

'I'd like to be able to return you that sentiment, at some time John,' Conor said.

CHAPTER THIRTY-TWO

'I'm going to carry on working at the LAAS. I've put my notice in but I don't need to quit now so I'll withdraw it. As soon as Dad's fit to mind Hope, I'll start my shifts again.'

'Keep you out of trouble, I suppose, won't it,' Conor said. 'But you stay safe and no more tunnelling underground.'

'Just want this damned war over with,' Rosie sighed, laying her head on his shoulder. 'When you're posted, you'd better write to me every day, you know.'

'I will.'

Rosie's head was crammed with ideas about what life together might bring them but first a victory was needed to allow her to realise her dreams. The delay was frustrating yet she still felt happier than she could ever recall being in her twenty-two years. They'd left Hope with her granddad for half an hour and gone out for a short drive to get some privacy before Conor returned home to Wapping. He had parked in a quiet turning so they could chat about the future while blackbirds welcomed the twilight with a haunting evensong.

'I know I said last night that I didn't want to know how you got Hope back from Midge and Frank Purves, but please tell me you didn't . . .'

'I didn't . . .' Conor answered. 'Not to say I wouldn't have, if I'd needed to.'

Rosie snuggled against him. 'I'm glad, for your sake, not theirs. Wouldn't want you in court over those two wrong 'uns. Perhaps it was just an accident. Anyhow, they deserved what was coming to them. Poor Gertie; disaster seems to follow her around.'

The air-raid siren made Rosie jerk upright, wailing, 'No, not now!'

Conor had already turned the ignition and put the car in gear. The darkening horizon was streaked with orange fire from the tails of a dozen or more V1 rockets speeding in their direction.

They were home in a few minutes and Conor helped John safely into the cellar while Rosie hurried behind with a sleepy Hope in her arms. A moment later an explosion made them duck.

'That was close,' Conor muttered.

'Lightning don't strike twice in two days. Jerry hit here yesterday. Give us a break will yer?' John shouted at the ceiling then gave a nervous laugh.

Within a short while of them making themselves comfortable on the chairs and mattresses, ambulance and fire-engine bells were audible. Suddenly Rosie groaned as the noise reminded her where she should be. With all the recent drama she'd completely overlooked the fact that she was an ambulance auxiliary who should have been on shift at Station 97. 'I forgot to go to work. And I didn't ring in either with an excuse. I hope they managed to cover for me.'

'Well, you had a bleedin' good excuse to miss yer shift, didn't you, seeing as your daughter was kidnapped,' John retorted a second before the wall exploded.

Rosie instinctively grabbed her daughter and spun away from the flying shrapnel, curving her body protectively about Hope. She felt her back being peppered with debris and cowered close to the ground. The impact of the rocks stung but she knew she'd sustained no more than cuts and bruises. Hope was screaming but a quick examination reassured Rosie that her daughter was unharmed, just terrified. She put the child down by the cellar steps away from the worst of it then scrambled back through the choking dust filling the cellar, feeling her way. Her father was groaning on the mattress.

'That's not done me legs no good,' he moaned, sounding dazed, while heaving plaster off his shins.

'Conor?' Rosie tried to rub the grit from her eyes but made the smarting worse. She saw where he was then. A huge slab of bricks and mortar had detached in one chunk, locking him, crouching, in a corner. She weaved her hand through a gap till she could touch him, her fingers racing to and fro till they found one of his hands to squeeze. 'Can you hear me? Are you all right?'

'Think so.' His warm fingers stroked her palm. 'Get yourself and Hope out of here, Rosie. Get help for me and John.'

'I'm not leaving you 'n' Dad . . .' she choked.

'You are! Get out now!' He coughed. 'We might take another hit. Get out of here, damn you! You rescue other people's kids . . . now save your own.'

Rosie knew he wanted to antagonise her to spur her

into action because his concern was for her rather than himself. But his spirit and the strength of his voice gave Rosie hope that he wasn't too badly hurt. Filtering through her shock was the knowledge that Conor was right. Hope was her first priority and always would be. And he'd applaud her view. *It's as it should be between a mother and her kids*, he'd said when she'd admitted she'd prostitute herself to keep her daughter safe.

Rosie became aware of Hope tugging on her skirt and glanced down at a small dirty face smudged with tears. 'Come on, poppet,' Rosie croaked, scooping her up.

'I'll be back soon, Dad,' she reassured her father before quickly making for the cellar steps.

Outside Rosie could see that at least three houses were ablaze on their side of the road. The bomb that had wrecked their cellar seemed to have exploded in the house next door. It had been partially obliterated during the Blitz and had stood empty ever since.

Further along the street Rosie spotted the fireman who'd attended the scene yesterday during Irene's rescue, unwinding a fire hose. She jogged clumsily towards him, panting in anguish because she couldn't move faster, weighted down with Hope. Her daughter was still howling, frightened by the commotion. Rosie murmured soothingly to her, sensing her own distress was upsetting the child.

'Mrs Deane, isn't it?' The fireman tipped up the brim of his helmet and looked at Rosie as she came to a breathless halt by his side. The flames he was dousing were putting an orange sheen on his perspiring profile. 'Off duty then? What's up?' He'd blinked sweat from his eyes and read her agitation.

'My family are trapped just along the road.' Rosie

retreated from the searing heat of the inferno, pointing back the way she'd come

'What happened to you?' Hazel had just jumped from the Studebaker that had screeched to a halt at the kerb and was racing across the pavement. 'Knew something was up when you didn't turn up for work. Then a call for Shoreditch came in.'

'We've been hit, this time, Hazel.' Rosie tasted the tears, salty in her mouth, although she'd not realised she was crying. 'Our cellar wall's been blown in and my dad and my fiancé are still down there. Please help me get them out.'

'Badly injured?' Tom barked. He'd sprinted after Hazel and heard what had been said.

'Don't think so, hope not,' Rosie rattled off. 'But Conor's trapped behind a block of masonry. Please hurry . . . if the fires spread that way . . .' Rosie was unable to voice her horrific fears, or block from her mind the people in the church hall at Stepney who'd burned to death.

'Let's go then,' the fireman commanded and immediately handed his hose to a colleague. He pelted after Rosie who, trusting them to follow, had set off.

Hazel put on a sprint and caught up with Rosie. She eyed Hope while trotting at Rosie's side. 'Dead ringer for you, she is,' she puffed.

'My daughter,' Rosie said and even her distracted state couldn't erase the pride from her voice.

Lou Rawlings was outside her house gawping at the devastation all around. 'First Peg and May. Now you. Be my place next, know it will,' the woman said morosely.

'Mind Hope for me, will you, Mrs Rawlings?' Rosie gasped, handing her daughter over.

Lou willingly obliged. It was already going round the neighbourhood that the Gardiner girl was a heroine in the LAAS. She'd saved Peg's daughter's life, and Irene's baby, that nobody had known a thing about. And if people asked about it in the wrong way Peg gave them a choice mouthful.

Rosie raced to her door, blocking the tormenting thoughts of little Herbie from her mind. He'd been trapped and had seemed to have minor injuries . . . but they'd killed him all the same.

She vaulted over debris in the hallway and led the team down into the cellar. Obliquely she was aware of the all clear sounding and swore aloud at the irony of it.

'I reckon you must be Mr Gardiner. I'm Hazel come to fix you up,' Hazel said, sitting beside the grizzled man on the mattress. 'Let's have a gander then. Blimey! Couple of stitches needed in that.' Hazel opened her medical bag and drew out lint to dab at John's torn shin.

'Same bleedin' leg as last time,' he grumbled.

'Best way; at least you've got one good 'un then,' Hazel ribbed him.

Rosie yanked the fireman by the elbow over to where Conor was trapped in the corner and Tom followed.

'All right mate?' the fireman said genially, bending and assessing the boulder from all angles.

'I will be once you move this fucking thing,' Conor replied succinctly.

Tom turned to Rosie, grinning. 'He's all right then . . .'

Between them the three men manoeuvred and shoved with much groaning and growling till the huge slab of masonry was tipped over. It fell back with an almighty thud that sent a cloud of particles into the dusty air. The moment Conor was free Rosie rushed at him, hugging him so violently and tenaciously that he had to lift her with him to stand up. He kissed her gently on the forehead and sat down on the filthy mattress with her beside John.

Conor delved inside his crumpled jacket for a packet of cigarettes while Rosie ran her hands over him checking for injuries. She dabbed dirt off the bloody cut on his cheek with her hanky. 'That might leave a scar,' she said but with relief in her voice that the damage didn't seem to be any worse than that.

'Got a fag mate?' Conor asked Tom, throwing the badly mangled pack of Weights onto the bed.

Tom handed his cigarettes round and they all took one, cleaning him out.

'I remember you from the other night. Hazel, isn't it? Remember me, do you, Hazel?' The fireman asked, puffing away on his cigarette.

Hazel cocked her head eyeing him through the smoke drifting between them while continuing to patch John up. 'Yeah, I remember you. And who might you be? Gonna introduce yourself then?'

'Phil Redwood, and pleased to meet you again, Hazel.'

Rosie and Conor exchanged a humorous look.

'Well, I feel like a gooseberry,' Tom said in a highly camp voice.

Everyone guffawed, even John, and Rosie felt tears of relief on her lashes. She turned to Conor, kissing him on the cheek, tasting the copper of his blood. 'You should go to hospital for a check-over,' she said as he winced when she cuddled him.

He shook his head. 'No need.'

'Right, done here, but not out there.' Phil pointed to the street sucking deeply on his cigarette. He ground out the stub and strode towards the stairs.

'Same goes for me . . .' Tom followed the fireman.

Hazel stood up. 'You'll be up 'n' running again in no time, Mr Gardiner.'

'Many casualties?' Rosie asked.

'Not sure yet . . . won't know till the fires are under control.' Hazel gazed at her colleague enquiringly then set off after the men with a parting wave.

'Another pair of hands would be useful, I expect,' Rosie called. She looked at Conor and he took the cigarette from his mouth and stroked her face. It was all the approval she needed; she knew he'd care for her father and get him to safety.

'Lou Rawlings is minding Hope. Will you come and fetch her and look after her till I come home?'

He nodded, standing up and for a moment Rosie's throat closed with the love she felt for him. She briefly touched together their lips, conscious of her father watching them, but she murmured the words, closing her eyes as another fingertip caress rewarded her.

Then she was running up the cellar stairs calling, 'Wait for me Hazel . . . I'm coming too.'

EPILOGUE

8th May 1945

'Stella and Thora . . .' Rosie shouted a toast, lifting her gin and orange.

Glasses were raised and swigged from as the ambulance auxiliaries in the pub remembered their colleagues who'd perished on duty.

'Won't ever forget those two,' Rosie said.

'Won't ever forget anybody I met here, even if I reach a hundred,' Hazel slurred, leaning an elbow on the bar and looking dreamy. 'But . . . new life opening up at last, and won't be sorry about that.' She proudly polished her engagement ring with a thumb. 'Meeting Phil later in Trafalgar Square and we're gonna dance till dawn then set off to Essex to see Mum about the wedding arrangements.'

'Conor's home today,' Rosie said, a gleam of excitement in her eyes. 'Hope he gets back early so we can go out and celebrate for a couple of hours.'

'You grabbed yourself a hunk there, Mrs Flint. So

why did you call yourself Mrs Deane?' she sounded mystified.

'Deane's my mum's maiden name,' Rosie answered quite truthfully.

'I'd've called myself Mrs Flint from the off,' Hazel said. 'You'd have cornered him sooner that way.' Her heavy black lashes drooped in a tipsy wink. 'Can tell he thinks the sun rises in you.'

All of Rosie's colleagues now knew about Hope, believing her daughter to be Conor's. They also thought that following a rocky start they had fallen in love all over again and got married. Apart from the few people who were aware that Lenny Purves had raped her, nobody was any the wiser. Rosie realised that at some time there would be the dilemma of whether Hope should know who'd fathered her but time enough when her daughter was older to cross that bridge . . .

Jim was standing with his wife and as he saluted her Rosie raised her glass, remembering his kindness on her first ever call-out when the row of corpses had nauseated her. Then her gaze travelled on over her boisterous colleagues: Tom, Clarice and Janet . . . just a few of the ambulance auxiliaries who today, on the glorious 8th May, were finally getting the sack as were she and Hazel and Jim.

Peace had come, at a terrible price for some families, but nobody wanted to reflect on that just yet. In a week or two when the euphoria had died down Rosie knew that her family, in common with everybody else, must turn their thoughts to the new problems that faced them as they pieced their lives back together. But nothing would fit as it had, or ever be the same.

'Top up anybody?' Tom called, weaving drunkenly

through the revellers with a bottle of gin he'd purloined from behind the bar. The landlord simply grinned, and wagged a finger on realising what he'd done.

'Not for me; off home now. Got to get my husband's tea,' Rosie joked, to much cat-calling.

'That's what it's called now, is it?' Tom chuckled. 'Mind you . . . I'd do anything for him. Conor's a sweetheart.'

Rosie hugged all her colleagues, giving Hazel a kiss as well as an embrace. Amidst the good lucks and good wishes were promises to write and telephone, and Rosie stuffed into her pockets all the slips of paper with addresses on that were thrust at her. And she knew she would keep in touch. Like Hazel she'd keep close to her heart until the day she died the memories of the colleagues that she'd laughed and cried with and toiled beside, sometimes until her eyes were dry and her bones ached.

Out in the sunshine she dodged, laughing, past a group of rowdy sailors who tried to make her dance a jig with them. Further on up the road she bumped into Mrs Price and Irene.

'I recognise that pram,' Rosie said chirpily, feeling quite merry now the fresh air had hit her, even though she'd only had a couple of gins.

'Reckon you do know it 'n' all, love,' Peg said with a grin. 'Holding up all right though, ain't it?' She gave the handle a tap. 'Made to last these were. Quality.'

Rosie had donated Hope's old Silver Cross to the Prices as her daughter had grown out of it. 'And how's my godson doing?' Rosie had been invited to be the baby's godmother and Irene had also chosen the name Ross as a tribute to the young woman who, in her mind, had saved her life and her son's.

'He's screaming blue murder all night long,' Irene raised her eyebrows in exasperation. But she gave Ross a fond maternal smile.

'Colic . . . or teeth,' Rosie said knowledgeably. 'You'd never believe he weighed in at under four pounds.' Rosie stroked the cheek of the chubby child sitting up in his pram.

'Gonna eat me out of house 'n' home in a few years, know he is,' Peg complained with a proud look at the little chap. 'You off home then?'

Rosie nodded. The Gardiners and the Prices were again neighbours. Following the blast that had destroyed their cellar they'd been rehoused round the corner, next door to Dick's sister where the Price family had decided to all live together.

'Best be off,' Peg said. 'Dick wants a party in our house later. I said I'd get some sandwiches made if I can lay me hands on some bread somewhere. You lot coming round? More 'n' welcome, y'know that.'

'Conor's back this evening . . .' Rosie started to make an excuse before a dig in the ribs stopped her.

'You'll be busy then, but send John 'n' Doris in,' Peg said lewdly, making her daughter tut disapprovingly. 'Come on, bread'll all be sold out.' Irene pulled her mother on, giving Rosie a smile before they continued up the road.

As she set off Rosie spotted somebody else she recognised, on the opposite pavement. She waved and trotted across and for a moment the two women simply gazed at one another. Although they'd said months ago they'd meet up, they never had until now.

'Well, here we are at last . . .' Rosie said. 'The day we've been waiting for, Gertie.'

'Been a long time coming . . . too long . . .' the older woman sighed, hoisting Vicky onto her hip as the child started to whine.

'Going out to celebrate with your husband tonight?' Rosie asked amiably.

'Yeah . . . going to Piccadilly Circus and taking Vicky with us,' Gertie wiped her daughter's nose with a hanky. 'Joey'll probably bring his sweetheart. Talking of getting engaged the two of 'em, and only just turned fifteen.'

'Grow up quickly, don't they?' Rosie said then wished she'd not. The air was thick with the memory of three little boys who'd never age or talk of getting engaged.

'How about you? Your husband back yet?' Gertie asked brightly.

'Due at the station about seven o'clock. Going home to get myself out of this . . .' Rosie pulled at her uniform jacket. 'And put on something pretty. Hope he's not delayed, then we'll all be off out, even Dad with his gammy leg.' Rosie chuckled. Her father had recovered well after the explosion in the cellar, but he did like to play on it, especially since Doris had returned from Gravesend, moaning about what it had cost to stay at her daughter-in-law's.

'Wonder what's in store for us now?' Gertie said, gazing at the blue sky and shaking her head. 'One thing's for sure: there's not going to be much work about for a man with a limp and a damaged hand. Popeye was a nasty sort but he provided for Rufus. So did me brother in his rotten way. Odd, but I miss Michael, and I never thought I'd ever say that.'

Rosie put a comforting hand on Gertie's arm, hearing the tears in her suffocated voice. 'Did the funeral upset your parents?'

'Never buried him . . . never found him. Just Popeye got recovered and laid to rest. Me husband went to pay his last respects. Rufus said he owed it to him for the work, if nothing else. Only Rufus and Frank's next-door neighbour was there. Never really found out what happened that night other than the police were chasing the car and it turned sharp and disappeared off the jetty into the water.' Gertie gave a sigh. 'Anyhow, you enjoy yourselves later, Rosie. Take care of yourself.'

'And you do the same.' Rosie gave Gertie's arm a pat and set off, feeling a peculiar certainty that she'd not see Gertie again.

She'd lost touch with much of her past, she mused as she walked on, and more of what was familiar would slip away to be replaced with new. Her childhood home, the very street where she'd been raised, was gone. Only a few of the houses remained occupied by resolute sorts like Lou Rawlings who'd cling on until the bitter end when the demolition men moved in.

Rosie threw back her head, letting the sun warm her face. She was ready for a new start with the man who'd taught her to love and trust and desire him in a way she'd never have believed possible. She opened her eyes and blinked. She stopped, her heart drumming beneath her ribs.

He'd stopped too and had dropped the kitbag he was carrying to the pavement.

She realised he'd been watching her walking towards him, and had waited to savour the expression on her face when she spotted him. Rosie smiled joyfully, allowing him his victory then she drew in a breath and ran, one hand on her heavy skirt holding it away from her flying legs. She launched herself at him and was spun round and round in strong arms, her cheek pressed into his rough uniform.

'You're early!' Rosie wailed. 'I was just on my way home to change into something nice and come and meet you at the station.'

'Couldn't wait. Swapped places with another bloke to get home sooner.'

'Bet it cost you,' Rosie said, stroking his unshaven chin.

'Worth it . . . just for this.' Conor gave her a slow thorough kiss. 'How's Hope?'

'Excited. She knows Daddy's coming home today.'

'And John?'

'Yeah . . . he's just the same.' Rosie smiled, adoring him with her eyes and caressing fingertips. 'You look tired. We don't have to go out and celebrate this evening.'

'I'd sooner stay home but I'm not tired, promise . . .' Conor smiled his villain's smile, the one that once would have made Rosie blush and feel nervous. Now it quickened her pulse for a very different reason.

'Dad and Doris have been invited next door to a party later so once our daughter's asleep I want you to keep that promise, and lots more besides . . .'

If you enjoyed

Rosie's WAR

discover these other fantastic
reads from Kay Brellend.

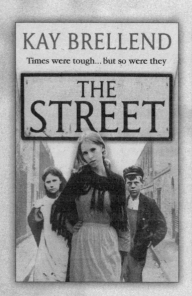

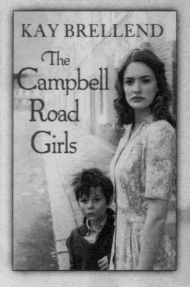

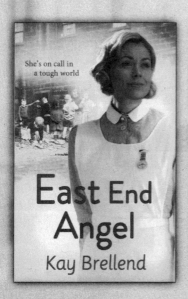

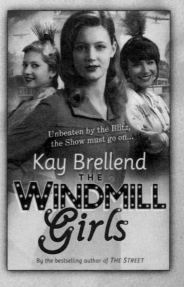

All available to buy now.